THE STAFF OF
FIRE AND BONE

Talitha,
Thank you for
bringing joy into our
home. I hope you like it!

BY

MIKKO AZUL

DEDICATION

to all heroes still learning to discover their own unique gifts

THE
STAFF OF
FIRE AND
BONE

TABLE OF CONTENTS

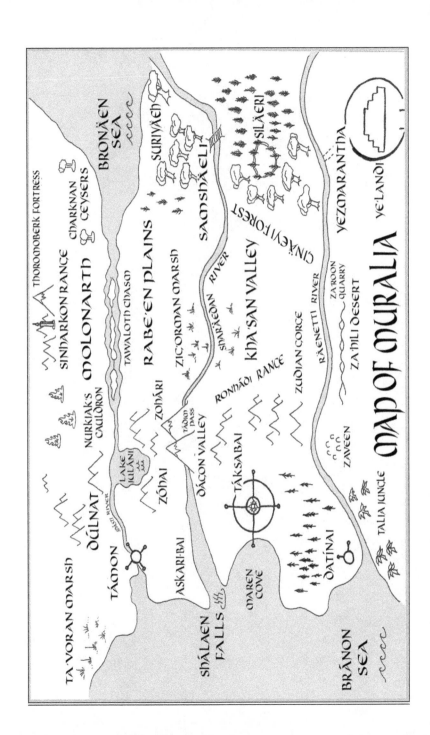

ChAPTER 1 - OUTCAST

Cédron's heart pounded in his chest as he slammed his back against the tunnel wall. The ground tremor was the longest he'd ever experienced. Dust and dirt trickled into his eyes as he glanced at the cracking ceiling.

"This was a bad idea," Cédron muttered under his breath as more debris poured from the widening striations, causing him to lose sight of his friend Zariun, who had flung himself against the opposite wall.

"My idea wasn't bad." Zariun followed Cédron's gaze to the ceiling, his eyes wide and white against his dark skin. "It's all about timing."

Cédron snorted, shaking the dust out of his golden hair. "Yes, and just like the crashing wave formation you taught your acrobatic troupe, your timing is awful."

The dark-skinned young man crossed his arms over his chest and rolled his eyes. "It's not *my* fault the ground shake started – that's your department! Besides," he shrugged, "all we need is a little more practice after the tournament, and the acrobatic troupe will have my crashing wave formation down."

Zariun was the third generation leader of the Yezman acrobatic troupe that traveled with the Varkaras Caravan, entertaining and thrilling people from all the lands. The young leader was always coming up with difficult and often dangerous formations for the troupe to perform as he attempted to fill the very large void his father left when he died. Some were more successful than others, and the crashing wave formation was the most intricate and challenging routine Zariun had created, and not without injury.

Cédron frowned. *The ground shakes have gotten more frequent lately, but that's not my fault either. They have nothing to do with my 'abilities.' These ground shakes are scaring people. When people are frightened, they look for someone to blame. Why is it that being different always makes me guilty?* The ground ceased its rumbling, but the torch continued to sputter as motes of dirt sprinkled in the flame. Cédron willed his heart to slow its pace, swallowing the fear of being crushed beneath the weight of the castle above him.

"Come on, let's go before something else happens." Zariun grinned, springing down the tunnel with Cédron following closely behind him. "We'll be out from under the castle and hitting the open city in another couple of turns."

"Are you sure you know where we're going?" Cédron asked, glancing back to get his bearings as they turned another corner.

"Would you quit worrying?" Zariun hissed. "I told you, I'll bring you out right behind the competitors' tents. Nobody will even notice you. Now be quiet, and let's go!"

The two boys crept silently further down the secret passages that led from the castle's interior walled gardens into the labyrinthine tunnels beneath the city of Dúlnat's streets. The young heir's dislike of dark spaces and their many-legged inhabitants had kept him away from the underground city. Instead, Cédron had spent most of his childhood exploring the deep forests of the Ronhádi Mountains, away from the city and the hostile eyes of his father's people, who hated him. Being born the only son and heir of Regent Kásuin Varkáras was enough to set any boy apart, but having a Shäeli demon for a mother did nothing to warm the Askári people to their future leader.

2

Cédron's father had taken over the family's merchant caravan when he was a young man. Traveling throughout Muralia, he and his caravanners had learned to embrace the uniqueness of the various lands, including their peoples. The caravan was wealthy from trade and respected across the land. Kásuin built the city of Dúlnat as a refuge for those artisans and immigrants from other places who wanted a place to live free of the prejudices so rampant throughout the lands. The Askári who settled there learned to embrace the foreigners, especially those very talented glass workers from Yezmarantha. However, bringing a Shäeli wife home pushed the threshold of tolerance beyond reasonable expectations. Cédron had never been popular among his people, but even those few friends he had made shunned him now. Zariun had been the only boy to remain friends with Cédron, their mutual love of acrobatics and daring stunts forming a bond that couldn't be severed by something as trivial as superstitious prejudice.

Cédron ran his fingers through his hair, removing the spinner's webs that had tangled in it. He tried to hide the shudder the insects gave him from Zariun's sharp black eyes. He hated the tiny crawlers, but he hated showing weakness even more. Zariun wouldn't easily pass up an opportunity to tease him.

"Don't worry Cédron." Zariun chuckled, waving his torch high above their heads to ignite the sticky filaments. "The crawlers don't eat much. You're tall, but there isn't enough meat on your bones to make you worth their while."

Cédron grimaced. "That's comforting."

Zariun grinned in reply and continued on, holding the torch high enough to burn anything that might hang down. Their journey would end near the tournament fields where Cédron's adopted brother Tóran was preparing to compete for the first time. Cédron's thoughts drifted to what his brother must be feeling right this moment. He wondered if the stout warrior was as apprehensive as Cédron knew he would feel if he was in the same position. He was so preoccupied that he wasn't paying attention to where he was placing his feet. Cédron stumbled over the large piece of brick flooring that had shifted in one of the recent tremors and stuck up from the ground.

Crying out as he toppled forward, Cédron threw his hands up in front of him to brace his fall. The wild magic of his untrained Árk'äezhi poured out from his outstretched fingers and raised the floor to meet his falling body. The entire tunnel began to quake from the structural compromise. Cédron's heart leapt into his throat, choking the air from his lungs. Ahead of him, Zariun picked himself up off the ground where he'd been thrown and reached for the sputtering torch.

"Are you trying to get us caught?" Zariun hissed as he grasped the torch and blew gently on it to increase the flame.

Cédron swallowed a lump in his throat and took deep breaths to try and still the pounding of his heart and soothe the magic still prickling his skin. "Of course not, I tripped. All this," he waved his fingers at the shelf of bricks that had cushioned his fall, "just happened. I didn't do it on purpose." He looked at Zariun's wide eyes gleaming in the torchlight and felt a pang of guilt. "I'm sorry. Are you ok?"

Zariun looked down, brushed dirt off his scarlet shirt and re-tied the laces at his neck. "As long as nobody comes to investigate, we should..." Zariun's mouth snapped shut. His head cocked to one side.

Further down the corridor, they heard muffled voices and footsteps coming their way. Both boys froze. Cédron's stomach knotted as the implications of discovery reached his conscious thought. If he was found outside the castle, his father's ire would be the least of his problems.

Motioning silently, Zariun tiptoed down the tunnel as quickly as he could without making any noise. Cédron followed, holding his breath. *I wonder if my absence has been discovered... or maybe they're just investigating the*

ground shake. Please let them turn down a different tunnel...
Cédron sent this silent prayer to Hamra, the goddess who presided over births and deaths. He wasn't ready to leave this life and hoped the deity would spare him the horrible demise he would surely suffer if he was discovered by the wrong people.

The boys crept silently down the tunnel, their ears straining for sounds of pursuit. Several silent minutes passed before Cédron relaxed enough to allow full breath. Their journey took them further beneath the city. Cédron could hear the thundering of the falls below the castle just off to his left as they continued towards the tournament grounds. They walked in silence until they reached a split in the tunnels. The path to the left angled upwards and seemed in good repair, but Zariun waved the torch down the tunnel to their right. Cédron had never explored this section of the tunnels, as the ever-increasing ground shakes had caused the older ones to collapse. Zariun was suggesting that they head straight into the compromised section that was filled with debris from earlier damage.

"Do you think it's safe?" The fair-haired boy whispered, eying the tunnel and wiping his sweaty hands on his trousers.

Zariun stuck the torch into a crevice in the wall and rounded on his friend. "Look, do you want to see your brother before he's annihilated in the tournament or not? This is the only way to smuggle you out safely with everyone in Dúlnat here for the festival."

Cédron shuffled his feet and stared at the floor. "Fine, let's keep going."

The boys continued their march down the passageway, dodging large chunks of rubble and stones that had fallen. The air was musty and stifling, increasing Cédron's discomfort with their ill-advised plan. He hadn't seen much of his adopted brother since Tóran had pledged himself to the Hármolin Legion the year before. Though not related by blood, the two had grown fond of each other in their youth together in the castle. *If only things could have stayed as they were, I wouldn't have to sneak around like this.*

Cédron's stomach clenched. He'd been sequestered in the castle since Dormantide when the first signs of his powers had manifested. Instead of earning his father's pride like Tóran had when he'd joined the legion, Cédron had become a source of fear and stress for his parents. Although the Regent had tried to keep the knowledge of his son's abilities secret, rumors had cropped up over the past two seasons that he'd been absent from view. The tense relationship Regent Varkáras had with his legion after taking a Shäeli bride had blossomed into blatant hostilities once their son came of age.

"I just don't want to cause any trouble... not for Tóran or for my father."

Zariun cuffed Cédron on the shoulder. "Come on, would I lead you astray?"

Zariun's dimples disappeared into his cheeks as he winked and switched the torch to his left hand. Turning it upside down, he ground the flames into the powdery rubble at their feet, eliminating their main source of light. Cédron pulled out a couple of glow stones from his pouch and squeezed them, charging them with his energy. A faint red light emanated from the stones. He gave one to Zariun.

"Is it much further?"

In the dim light, Zariun's teeth gleamed eerily within his tawny cheeks. Cédron's knees weakened when Zariun brought them to a halt and pointed up at the ceiling. A faint circular ring of light was outlined within a narrow crawlspace.

"You'll have to spring me up there so I can open the top and make sure the coast is clear for you, ok?" Zariun handed the glow stone back to his friend.

Cédron put the stones back into his pouch and surveyed the narrow crawlspace with his hands on his hips. The circular space was a good man's length above them and the walls didn't look terribly solid. He could use a windstone to lift himself and Zariun, but Cédron quickly discarded the idea. The force of wind he'd need to lift the both of them could cause the tunnel to collapse. He had a bloodstone with him and considered using it to make himself invisible, but realized that the Árk'äezhi required to do so wouldn't allow him to also help Zariun out of the tunnel, so he discarded the idea almost as soon as it occurred to him. *I'm so glad Uncle Rováen taught me that trick; it may come in handy if I get into trouble out there!* Sighing at the obvious risks with their impromptu plan, Cédron surveyed the distance up towards the hole again and nodded to Zariun.

"Ok, I'll spring you up just like we practiced in the three-on-three formation." Cédron rubbed his sweaty hands in the dirt, brushing them off on his thighs.

Zariun nodded. "Perfect. You'll need to launch me higher than you did last time, though. I need to be able to catch the sides of that opening."

Cédron centered himself beneath the circular opening, crouched down, and laced his fingers together. Nodding to Zariun, the boy tensed for the brief impact of his friend's full weight. Zariun took several paces back down the dark tunnel before charging forward on light feet. He sprang into the air just before reaching Cédron and landed with one foot in Cédron's hands. Heaving with all his might, Cédron lifted his legs and arms, tossing Zariun straight up towards the crawlspace. The dark-haired boy shot up and punched out with his hands and feet, just catching the sides of the circular space. Cédron held his breath as Zariun's feet slipped a couple of inches before gaining purchase on the dirt. Exhaling slowly, he watched as his friend inched his way toward the circle of light by pressing his back and legs against the walls and sliding his body upwards.

When he reached the top, Zariun slowly raised the round wooden door that lay above his head. The late morning rays of the daytime deity Lord Shamar shone down into the murky tunnel. Cédron realized that Zariun was climbing out of a hollowed tree trunk. *Ingenious! I never would have suspected that.* After peeking around, the dark boy lifted the top completely over on its hinges and pulled himself through the opening. Moments later, a thick rope fell down next to Cédron.

"Come on!" Zariun's head poked over the side. "Everybody is watching the Master of the Lists put up the challengers' names and crests. If we hurry, we can get to Tóran's tent with nobody the wiser."

Cédron nodded and clenched his teeth. Grasping the rope, he gripped with his feet as he pulled himself up hand over hand. He was suddenly grateful for his lithe frame. If he'd had Tóran's muscular bulk, it would take him too long to shimmy up through the opening. In seconds, Cédron was over the lip of the trunk, and Zariun was closing the lid camouflaged with bushes and berries. The two boys scurried toward the back side of the brilliantly-colored pavilion with the Varkáras crest flying above it. Zariun lifted the flap and nodded to Cédron to edge himself inside behind the large tapestry that hung against the back of the canvas before sliding in next to him.

"Let me go first so that his manservant doesn't report you, ok?" Zariun winked, his grin deepening the dimples on his cheeks.

Cédron's mouth had gone dry. He nodded mutely at his friend, taking a moment to still his pounding heart and force a pleasant expression. He desperately wanted to show his support for his brother and hoped that Tóran would appreciate the risk rather than scold him for taking it.

"Hail the conquering hero!" Zariun sang out, poking his head out from behind the tapestry.

Cédron watched from their hiding place, grinning as Tóran whirled around, causing the manservant fastening his leggings to lose his balance and fall over. The young legionnaire quickly apologized and pulled the man to his feet while looking around his semi-private space for the owner of the song. A slow grin played along the warrior's mouth as he spied Zariun's dark curly head.

"Give me a few moments to gather my wits." Tóran excused his manservant, waiting until he'd left the tent before turning back to his visitor.

Zariun clasped arms with the younger Varkaras brother. "I brought you a visitor." He grinned and winked at Tóran. "It's all clear. Come on out."

Behind the tapestry, Cédron took another steadying breath before making his appearance.

"Cédron, what are you doing here?" Tóran whispered, looking around to see if anyone else had noticed his unauthorized guest. "Are you insane? What if someone sees you?"

"I couldn't miss your special day," Cédron replied as the two clasped arms in greeting. "It's rare indeed for a legionnaire to qualify for the Warrior's Challenge his first year eligible. Just try not to embarrass us."

Tóran snorted. Though one year Cedron's junior, Tóran appeared several years older than Cédron with his muscular frame and the dusting of dark hairs along his jawline. Tóran pulled his long dark hair back and braided it before tying it off with a leather thong.

"At least I'm getting the chance to prove my worth." Tóran rolled his eyes. "I'm so tired of people thinking that I've been given my rank because of our father. Once and for all, I have to show them my skills."

Zariun grinned and punched Tóran on the shoulder, ignoring the wince the soldier tried to hide. "Well, I can vouch for your skills now, can't I? Remember that time when I taught you to run up that wall, flip over and land behind your opponent. I thought the Weapon's Master was going to faint!"

Tóran sighed, grinning at the fond memory. "Of course I remember. There aren't any walls in the tournament square, but I have incorporated lots of acrobatic tricks you've taught me. It's the main reason for my success – nobody knows how to anticipate my next move."

Zariun slapped his own chest. "Yep, and I'm the one who made you who you are today!" He grinned, his dark eyes glinting. "Woe to the poor fools who have the misfortune of facing Dúlnat's finest warrior!" The dark lad grabbed the edge of the tent flap and peeked outside. "The coast is clear. I'm off to get some seats. Fight well, my friend!"

Tóran grinned ruefully, shaking his head as Zariun scampered off. "Well, we'll see if I can at least keep my head today. I was a little too slow earlier and got myself into a little trouble."

Cédron cocked his head to one side. "How's that?"

Tóran exhaled gustily. "I nearly lost my head in the qualifying rounds yesterday." Tóran pulled off the sliced gorget from around his neck to show his brother the seeping bandage.

"Laylur's beast! Father's still letting you compete?" Cédron asked, his tone slightly off from the jovial pitch he'd tried to cultivate.

Tóran's smile faltered just a little. "Yes, I think he's become quite excited about it actually. The Weapon's Master told him that I could make it into the final rounds if I can keep from getting hurt. Áreon Kíris is the favorite to win, but I should make a good showing."

"I will send a prayer to Orwena that you don't have to face him on the field. He's half again your size and twice as mean!" Cédron said, scratching the back of his head.

Orwena was the goddess of war, sister to Hamra and Azria. The moon daughters, as the three deities are called, were represented in Muralia's three moons and worshipped for their various specialties. Cédron hoped that the warrior goddess would watch over his younger brother. Áreon Kíris was a brawler, an unscrupulous fighter inside the ring and out of it.

Tóran grimaced. "Your confidence is overwhelming."

"But you're barely eligible for the tournament," Cédron said, the hairs on the back of his neck prickling. "You know that Áreon has a reputation for being a vicious fighter."

"I can handle that oaf, should I face him," Tóran replied coolly. He fidgeted slightly with his hauberk, dropping his eyes. "You...will you support me in the stands?"

Cédron was silent for a moment as he looked down at his brother. Cédron met Tóran 's eyes, their sepia ink irises locking with his own moss green ones. Although he'd only seen fifteen full Autumntides, Tóran's love of the martial arts gave him added bulk and strength that his tall, slender brother would never develop. They were so different, never more obviously so than this very moment.

"You know that wouldn't be wise." Cédron sighed and walked over to the open front of the pavilion, admiring the view of both the castle and the tournament grounds from this hidden vantage point. "I don't know why I let Zariun talk me into coming down here. If any of the Askári see me outside of the protection of the castle, I could be in real trouble."

Cédron watched the young apprentices racing back and forth across the competition area, bringing water and food to the legionnaires they attended. He smelled the pastries and breads that the vendors had been working on since before dawn and smiled in anticipation, hoping that his Uncle Roväen would bring him some of the festival fare as promised. He sighed. Cédron hated being cooped up in the castle, though he knew that his parents did it for his own protection.

From the first moment his demonic powers had revealed themselves, he'd been barely able to leave his chambers unaccompanied. The hushed conversations and awkward glances had only become more frequent over the past few months. His guts twisted like a flock of twillings circling inside him with their rapid, tiny wings. At that moment, he realized it would be impossible for him to even consider eating the festival pastries.

Looking upward, he saw blue skies populated by the wispy tendrils of clouds that whispered of the morning's long-gone mist. The Ronhádi Mountains ringed the white city of Dúlnat with a blanket of evergreen trees, making the city glow like a pearl nestled among emeralds. Gazing toward the castle, the Regent's outcast son reveled in the riot of flowers that assailed his senses from the lush gardens just outside the castle walls.

"I miss walking in the gardens," he sighed wistfully, absentmindedly combing his fingers through his golden hair. "There really is no comparison to them in all of Askáribai."

Tóran joined his brother in gazing out the front of the pavilion, his face tense as he knotted the end of his sword belt. "You'll not be watching me then?"

Cédron's gaze hardened and his jaw clenched as he turned away from the beautiful view to face his brother. "Uncle Roväen has worked hard with me, and I've made some progress with the wild magic, but I doubt that father has convinced the Askári people that I'm not a demon. I don't know if keeping me holed up in the castle has helped by keeping me out of sight or simply added fuel to the rumors that have sprung up lately."

Tóran nodded; his fellow legionnaires had intimated as much. There was speculation that Regent Kásuin planned to formally name Cédron as his successor despite the public outcry against such a move. Some soldiers were already muttering about revolting as a response to such an offensive decision.

"Father may be able to place guards around you to keep you safe so you can watch the competitions," Tóran suggested. "I'd try to steer clear of any legionnaires, though. There are many who don't support father's recent decisions..."

Cédron snorted, his lip curled slightly. "The last thing he's going to want to do is call attention to my presence."

Tóran avoided his brother's eyes as he slid his sword into the scabbard and tucked his braid beneath his helmet. Cédron noticed his hesitation and pressed the issue.

"What about you? Will you support father if he names me successor?"

"Look, Cédron," Tóran began defensively. "you've always been different, but having uncontrollable magic really frightens people."

Cédron blanched. "Who does it frighten? Nobody is supposed to know about my powers."

Tóran shifted uncomfortably, his eyes cast downward.

"How did that get out?"

Tóran scowled. "It doesn't matter now. People have been watching and waiting for an excuse to hate you since that Shäeli woman bore you."

"But…but you love Maräera. She's been like a mother to you." Cédron stuttered.

Tóran shifted on his feet and fidgeted with his belt. "It's complicated. I have new allegiances that I have to honor. As much as I'd like to support your claim to the Regency, the best I can do is to try and stay out of the fray. It's the best any of us can do."

"Even Jorrél and Pánar?" Cédron asked, shuffling his feet in the dirt floor of the pavilion.

"Blast it! Especially Jorrél and Pánar!" Tóran swore. "We're legionnaires now, and you *know* what that means."

"But we've been friends since childhood," Cédron protested. "I'm still the same person I've always been. Does that count for nothing?"

Tóran pursed his lips. "I told you, it's different now!" He seethed, slamming the palm of his hand on the top of his sword pommel. The young legionnaire's face flushed with the heat of his hauberk and the ire rising from his chest. "You've shown the magic of your demon mother…and sealed your fate."

Cédron opened his mouth to deliver his own angry retort when his Uncle Rováen entered, whistling. The elderly Shäeli surveyed the tense situation with his shrewd blue eyes. His shaggy silver brows knit together when he saw Cédron shrinking behind the tapestry.

"Humph, I thought you might have tried something imprudent like this. We will discuss your foolishness later," he growled.

Cédron opened his mouth to protest, then snapped it shut when he saw his uncle's glare. With one hand subtly held up to Cédron in warning, the old man strode over to Tóran and clasped his arm.

"Good to see you, Tóran!" Rováen grinned, all traces of his ire erased. "Best of luck in the rounds. I understand you're a favorite...and not only with the young ladies!" He winked, reaching into the large pouch hanging at his side. "Your father asked me to give you these."

Rováen pulled out two heavy chains made of golden medallions embedded with the Varkáras family crest. A golden ray of Lord Shamar's light stole through a gap in the tent, striking the Shäeli's silver hair, creating a brief halo. For a moment, Rováen shone with the power and authority of his youth. A cloud drifted across the light and the moment was gone. He placed one chain around Tóran's shoulders, securing it with the clasps on the surcoat so it wouldn't be dislodged during the competition. He pulled Cédron away from the tapestry and placed the second one on the fair boy's shoulders.

"Two proud sons of our tiny realm." Rováen smiled at his work, then he turned to Cédron. "You are not to leave my side, do you understand? Let's get ourselves settled before the rounds begin."

Tóran stood stiffly as his manservant returned, casting a dark look at the two Shäeli outcasts. Tóran stepped in between his servant and his family, blocking the man's hostility. The manservant double-checked Tóran's fittings and secured the new, thick, leather gorget about his neck. Cédron could still see irritation in Tóran's eyes, but it seemed to be tempered with something else. *Indecision? Guilt?* Cédron didn't want Tóran focused on their argument, so he extended his arms in peace. Tóran's countenance softened as he embraced his brother.

"Rovaën can keep an eye on me, so I'll be able to support you from the stands. Zariun is holding our seats. Make us proud today!" Cédron smiled at Tóran and punched his shoulder as he released his embrace.

"Of course. My best moves are those Zariun taught me. Tell him I'll run circles around Áreon and anybody else I face!" Tóran grinned as he waved them away.

Rovaën handed Cédron a light wool cloak. "Throw this on and we'll sneak out of here before anyone suspects you've escaped your cage."

The Regent's son smiled gratefully as he clasped the compass rose-shaped buckle and pulled the hood over his pale hair. Nodding to his uncle, the two ducked out of the tent and into the full brilliance of Lord Shamar's rays. The daytime deity's light shone with the intensity reserved for high elevations. In addition to the light, the onslaught of smells, sounds and colors from the throngs of people preparing for the tournament and festival hit them like a furnace blast. Swirls of fabric danced before their eyes as the people jostled each other for position into the tournament grounds. Folks had come from every major and minor settlement for miles around to sell their wares or simply to partake in the largest festival in Askáribai.

"Stay close," Rovaën muttered under his breath to Cédron as they entered the crowd.

Cédron clung to Rovaën's arm as the two jockeyed amidst the crush of bodies surging towards the entrance. Both Shäeli kept their cloaks on with cowls thrown over their heads as loose disguises.

"What if we get separated?" Cédron grunted after taking an elbow in the ribs from an eager father pushing his sons forward.

Rováen turned his head and looked at Cédron from deep within his hood. "We won't. Just link your arm with mine; it will be harder for anyone to break us apart."

Cédron wrapped his arm around his uncle's and linked their elbows. They huddled together like two old crones, shuffling through the gate and into the enormous tournament grounds, which were lined on both sides with vendors and artisans hawking their wares from food to footwear. Sizzling and popping reached their ears about the same time as the scent of grilled vegetables and fried bread reached their noses. Cédron's stomach growled in anticipation of the grilled shad rolled in sativa bread with sorrel and the tart atoca berries.

His mouth watered. "We don't have to take our seats immediately, do we?" he asked Rováen. Now that he had Rováen to guard him, his fear of being caught was replaced by hunger.

A smile played beneath Rováen's long silvery beard. "You don't want to wait to get back to the castle for the festival fare I promised, right?"

Cédron grinned. "I would never presume…"

"Ha!" the old man barked, wagging his finger at Cédron. "I know better than that, young man. Now, where would you like to start?"

Cédron stuck his nose into the air and inhaled deeply, sampling the scents on the air. He turned sharply to the fishmonger's stall.

"Fresh shad! My favorite!" He exhaled and pulled his uncle toward the vendor's crackling fryer.

Cédron stood unobtrusively behind Rováen as the older man ordered the rolls and paid the fishmonger with two flecksun coins. The blue-hued currency glinted as Lord Shamar's rays caught the crystal flecks embedded in the stone. Rováen handed the wrapped roll to Cédron and they stepped out of the milling crowd to find a quiet place to enjoy their tiny feast.

"Mind you don't drip any of that shad roll on your shirt, Cédron." Rováen eyed the bright red berries and dripping fat from the grilled whitefish that was escaping the edges of the flatbread.

"Don't worry," Cédron mumbled, his mouth full of the steaming fish. "Nothing escapes me when I'm this hungry!" He sucked in air, as his food was still very hot, and used his fingers to catch the dripping fat from the corners of his mouth.

Rováen chuckled, shaking his head. "Ready? " He lifted his chin towards the placard posted above the grounds showing the various contestants and their progressions. "I see Tóran made it through the first round."

Cédron followed his uncle's gaze and spotted the Varkáras flag near the top. "Right, but that's no big surprise. Do you think he could actually win this thing?"

Rováen shrugged beneath his cowl and motioned Cédron forward. "It wouldn't surprise me. He's got acrobatic training from Zariun that gives him speed and agility that the other legionnaires don't have. That and his natural talent…come on, let's find our seats."

Cédron nodded. He knew all about Tóran's natural talent. He was proud of his brother's accomplishments; he just wished that his own abilities were valued as well. Their father had ordered a great feast to celebrate Tóran's coming of age and decision to join the Hármolin Legion. Cédron's own coming of age had forced his father to hide him away in disgrace. Following his uncle along the winding road through the vendors, Cédron felt the atoca berries sour in his mouth. *What if I'm more of a liability to my father by remaining here? Maybe it would be better if I applied to study at the Mage's Guild in Taksábai. The capital city is*

*much larger, and I would be less conspicuous there. I'll have
to ask him about that after the festival.*

A crowd of people blocked his way, and he lifted himself
up onto his toes to see what was impeding their forward
progress. After a few attempts to skirt around the side of the
blockage, Cédron turned to Rováen. "I feel like a shadfish
trying to swim upstream in this crowd."

The man next to him turned at the sound of his voice and
gave him a strange look before moving on. Cédron realized
with a pang of ice-cold fear that his uncle was no longer
walking next to him. Cédron stopped on the side of the
trampled walkway and craned his neck up and down the area
to find the tell-tale hood that masked his uncle's silver hair.
Hundreds, perhaps thousands of people milled around the
vendors' stalls and the tournament fields. Nowhere could
Cédron find anyone wearing a hooded cloak or spot the
glittering silver of Rováen's long hair. *Perhaps he stepped
into one of the brewers' stalls.* He angled toward the large
pavilion and peered into the gloom of the shaded area that
housed the various ale masters and brewers, but he saw no
sign of his uncle.

The midday heat and hooded cloak were beginning to
make him uncomfortably warm, but his skin prickled from
cold panic. People were already beginning to glance
curiously at him: a lone traveler appearing to be lost and
wrapped in a traveling cloak on a warm Suntide afternoon. If
he wasn't careful, he would attract too much attention to
himself. Cédron bit his lower lip and scanned the streets
again. A few yards away, he spotted two young legionnaires
heading his direction. He wasn't sure if they'd seen him or
not, but he didn't want to stick around to find out. The
Hármolin Legion had been decimated by the Shäeli during
the War of Betrayal, and Cédron's unpopularity was a result
of the deep-seated hatred between the two races. He realized
that he'd better find a place to lie low until they passed and
he could locate his uncle.

Cédron quickly slipped between two leatherworkers' stalls and snuck around to the back. There was a small sitting area with an empty barrel and a small table that the merchant had obviously used earlier. Cédron sat on the barrel and leaned back into the alcove between the stalls. In the distance, a roar of cheering went up from the tournament field, signaling the arrival of the next combatants. *I hope I'm not missing Tóran's fight; I promised him I'd show my support.* Cédron reached into his pocket and grasped the flat piece of polished beryl that Rováen had given him as a scrying stone. Maybe he could scry for his uncle and alert him to his location. Cédron looked around to see if anyone was watching him. It wouldn't bode well for him to be caught using magic by the Askári merchant. Cédron leaned back, shrinking further behind the stall as he pulled out the flat stone and set it in the palm of his hand. He closed his eyes and concentrated on Rováen's image.

"Well, well. What have we here?" A nasally voice startled Cédron from his task, causing him to jump to his feet. He quickly shoved the polished beryl into his pocket.

The two legionnaires had spotted Cédron and separated, coming around the back side of the merchants' stalls from either direction to prevent his escape.

"A gift from Lord Shamar and Lady Muralia to honor the festival of Narsham-Vu," said the second legionnaire, an unpleasant smile twisting his lips.

Icy tendrils of fear trickled down Cédron's spine as he realized his danger. He looked around for anyone who could, or would, assist him. His guts twisted as he realized he was very much alone with these two soldiers. He could use magic to set their uniforms on fire or whip up a wind storm to blind them while he ran away, but that would only prove that he was a danger. *That sort of incident would not sit well with father.*

Reaching into his pouch, Cédron grasped the large bloodstone that would make him invisible. He tried to slow his breathing and clear his mind, but the advancing legionnaires terrified him. He couldn't concentrate on the stone's properties. *I knew this was a bad idea.* The sweat on his hands caused the stone to slip, taking with it any chance of escape. Slowly, Cédron pulled back his hood and faced the two legionnaires. They were both shorter than he was, but much heavier and well-muscled, in addition to being armed with short swords at their waist. Cédron pulled the curved knife he had in his sash and held it defensively in front of him.

"I don't want any trouble," he said, sizing up his opponents and seeking any avenue of escape.

The two legionnaires chuckled and closed in, preventing him from running. "Perhaps you don't, but we're not going to let you get away from us so easily, you Shäeli freak." The legionnaire with the nasal tones cracked his knuckles.

Cédron looked closer at the two advancing young men. The shock of recognition rooted him to the ground. Pánar and Jorrél! They'd grown in the year since they'd pledged to the legion. Both had sparse beards and deeper voices, but their menacing posture and words were unmistakable. They had been completely immersed in the Hármolin Legion, where the old hatreds against the Shäeli had been ingrained in their training. Cédron faced his childhood friends and clenched his fists. *I don't want to hurt them, but they look like they want to kill me. If I defend myself and pit the legion against me before the festival, all father's plans will be ruined.* Cédron desperately wanted his father's approval, but he couldn't just let these two kill him.

Jorrél and Pánar stepped in closer, drawing their swords. Cédron brandished his knife, passing it from one hand to the other in an attempt to distract them. It wasn't working. As if taking a cue from someone behind the legionnaires, Cédron looked out past them and nodded. He dropped to his knees, pretending that he was ducking an attack from behind his opponents. Jorrél and Pánar instinctively ducked and turned to see what was coming at them. Cédron launched to his feet, punching the backs of his opponents' knees as he jumped forward. Jorrél and Pánar fell forward from the unexpected blows, but reacted quickly as their training had taught them, rolling and flipping back to their feet, then springing toward Cédron just as he started to run. They each caught a shoulder and pulled Cédron back into the alcove. They shoved him to the ground, Jorrél kicking his knife from his hand. Cédron's heart sank as his only weapon spun out of reach.

"Is that the best you've got?" Pánar grinned, standing over Cédron who now lay in the dirt on his back.

"Let's just kill him and be done with it," Jorrél growled. He kicked Cédron in the side and knelt down with his short sword pointed at his face.

Pánar stomped on Cédron's stomach, causing his victim to double up in pain. Then, walking slowly around to his head, the legionnaire stomped on his face. Pain exploded in Cédron's head as Pánar's foot broke his nose. Blood gushed into Cédron's eyes and down his throat. He choked.

"No, I want to have a little fun first." Pánar's voice echoed in Cédron's head.

The blows came steadily, whether from fists, feet or sword pommels Cédron couldn't be sure. His eyes had swollen nearly shut and he couldn't tell whether it was Jorrél or Pánar who picked him up and threw him against a barrel laying on it's side in the back of the alley. The air in his lungs exploded from his body as his shoulders and back struck the barrel and broke through the wood. He could feel splinters entering his side and back as he fought to remain conscious.

"What's going on back here?" a deep voice from the stall called out. Cédron heard Pánar and Jorrél step around in front of him.

"We're just having a bit of fun," Jorrél whined. "I'm afraid my friend here has broken your barrel. Let me pay you for the trouble."

Cédron heard the jingle of coins being dug from a pouch, tossed through the air and captured by the merchant.

"Take your revelry to the brewer's pavilion. I have a business to run here," scolded the merchant.

The two legionnaires laughed. "Certainly, sir. Perhaps you could let our friend here sleep off his ale...he's had a little too much celebration already."

"Pah, off with the two of you then," the merchant replied gruffly, and he stood there to make sure they left before returning to his patrons at the front of the stall.

Cédron felt Jorrél's breath on his face as the soldier bent down. The stench of day-old garlic and onions from the previous night's dinner filled Cédron's raw and swollen nostrils as Jorrél promised him that they would see each other again. Cédron allowed himself to relax only slightly as he heard their footsteps retreating in the dirt. When the merchant was satisfied that they would cause no more trouble and only their drunken friend remained, he too went back to his business.

Cédron lay on the ground stunned, his whole body throbbing. He struggled with the knowledge that Jorrél and Pánar would probably kill him if given the chance, even though they'd once been friends. *They pounded my Shäeli flesh and my Shäeli blood, as if making me disappear from Dúlnat could erase Laräeith's Betrayal and keep the world safe from demon magic. It's been a thousand years since the war, and still nothing has changed. The Askári will never accept me. Father's plans will fail, and I'm going to die.* Cédron opened his eyes and tried to raise his head. Stars throbbed behind his swollen eyelids. He shook his head slowly, grateful that his neck hadn't been broken. He tried to get a breath. *I wonder who the greater fool is; Zariun for tempting me to escape the castle, or me for following him?* His mind slipped into darkness.

CHAPTER 2 - RÄESHAS DILEMMA

The wind blew Räesha's long silver hair back behind her like a streaming banner, and her eyes blurred with tears. She blinked to clear them and ducked her head down closer to her mount's thick, feathered neck as he soared high over the Ginäeyi Forest, the green canopy a deceptively peaceful blur beneath them. Räesha's blood thundered through her veins with the thrill of riding the magnificent beast, especially as it hunted.

The läenier folded his broad wings and dove faster as he neared the flock of kessäeri flying low above the trees of the forest. The golden raptor's wingspan exceeded 40 feet, one of the largest läeniers in her wing. His dive caused Räesha's eyes to water from the biting air. Screeching his hunting cry, the enormous raptor extended his talons and grasped a juicy young fowl from the flock as it scattered in panic. Räesha felt the exultation of the successful hunt and steered him down near the valley floor where she could dismount, allowing the beast to eat his prey in peace while she sought her own meal.

"Well done, Yongäen," she said softly and stroked the beast's powerful shoulder once she'd slid down. She quickly braided her long silver hair and shoved it under her green cap for camouflage.

The läenier regarded his rider with amber eyes, and then bent his head to his prey. *Broken neck. Very efficient.* Räesha smiled. The raptor stood over the fat indigo bird, cocking his head sideways to hear if anything other than his rider approached. Satisfied that they were alone, the enormous beast tore through the downy blue feathers of the kessäeri's belly and ripped into the steaming flesh with his curved beak.

The Sumäeri warrior watched the noble animal with pride. Her heart raced at the fierceness with which he rent flesh from bone. *How he keeps his beak and golden feathers clean despite his macabre feast is always a wonder*. To be partnered with this regal animal was the culmination of many years of hard training and had been the crowning achievement in her family's long line of Sumäeri warriors. No Angäersol had ever been accepted into the elite läenier wings, which made Räesha uniquely qualified for her current mission. This quick foray for food was the only delay she would allow herself and her mount.

Räesha ran smoothly into the trees, her lithe body accustomed to long hours of hunting and tracking. She disappeared from sight, the foliage tattoos covering her body blending perfectly with the underbrush of the forest. Räesha moved silently, her aquamarine eyes scanning the ground for the movement of grubs or for any plants that she could eat.

She readily found the climbing jicama vine and cut off a tuber slightly bigger than her hand. Slicing off the fibrous rind with her long hunting knife, she bit into the crisp white flesh, wiping its sweet juices from her chin. Closing her eyes, Räesha began the ritual of gratitude that had been taught to the Shäeli by Lady Muralia and her daughters when the Shäeli were first created; a ritual carried on by the Sumäeri, despite the abandonment of the deities.

Räesha pricked her finger with the tip of her blade and let a drop of blood fall onto the vine where she'd cut off the jicama, finishing the prayer. The ruby drop sparkled like a jewel as it absorbed into the vine. This offering would speed the healing of the severed plant and allow it the nourishment it would need to bear more fruit.

Sitting on a fallen log to enjoy her feast, Räesha mulled over her father's warning. Although she was a Sumäeri warrior and a läenier rider, she would be heading into the Wushäen's domain, fraught with its own challenges. The rivalry between the Sumäeri warriors and the Wushäen of Siläeria had evolved over the centuries from playful competition to outright hostilities, particularly in recent years.

The Angäersol family had historically served Samshäeli for generations as Sumäeri and Räesha, the eldest of the five Angäersol daughters, carried on the family heritage with pride. The only spot marring their perfect service as Sumäeri was her youngest sister Lanäe, who'd chosen to be a Wushäen, one of the keepers of the gigantic tree Auräevya, the source of all magical energy.

Räesha had harbored misgivings over her sister's choice, particularly since Lanäe had always been so spoiled and demanding. *I knew she'd never adjust to the austere life of service to the tree when she had always been catered to by doting parents.* Lanäe's theatrics about having visions in order to get her way had always been so annoying, particularly as it usually worked. Now her unseemly behavior had landed her in serious trouble. If their father hadn't specifically requested that she investigate, Räesha would have been happy to let her sister wallow in the consequences of her own behavior.

Rinsing her mouth in the narrow stream that gurgled near her resting spot, Räesha cupped the water in her hands and called her father's name. Clear sapphire eyes enveloped by wrinkles peered out at her from the liquid in her palms as her father answered the scry.

"I'm just outside of Siläeri." Räesha spoke to the image. "Did you want me to try and negotiate for Lanäe's freedom or just attend the tribunal as an observer?"

Her father's eyes darkened. "Please do whatever you can for Lanäe. We would certainly welcome her home with no shame if they want to dismiss her from her duties."

Räesha looked away, rolling her eyes. *Typical. Four daughters all passed the Sumäeri trials, but the one who seems to give everyone the greatest amount of grief is coddled.*

"I will, father," Räesha sighed.

"Contact me as soon as you hear anything," the image in her hand said. "You might try speaking to the Doyäenne first to see if the Wushäen would be open to any mitigation."

Not likely. "I'll do what I can and get back to you as soon as possible." Räesha smiled slightly at the image before letting the water seep through her fingers, breaking the connection.

* * *

Clouds darkened the midday sky, obscuring the enormous shadow of the läenier that would have blanketed the ground as it approached the center of the Siläeri settlement. The gust of air produced by the läenier's powerful wings heralded its arrival, stirring up dust and pine needles from the open commons that was oddly devoid of laborers.

A sense of foreboding tugged at the back of Räesha's mind, heightening her senses as she dismounted from the orange-gold raptor. She looked around, noting the location of the many tree houses connected by a complicated network of ladders and bridges made of wood and vines. The structures formed concentric rings around the commons, extending as far as she could see in every direction from the center of each tree to a height that must have exceeded eighty feet. Everything was still. Although she saw nobody, she could tell by the prickling of the tiny hairs on the back of her neck that she'd been seen and was being observed. Unsure of where to go, Räesha pretended to fuss over her beast, tightening the riding straps and inspecting the orange downy feathers on his powerful legs.

She straightened as a boy raced down the path from the largest of the tree houses. Breathless, the youth stopped several paces back from the fierce raptor's gaze and extended his hand to Räesha, palm up in the formal greeting.

"Welcome, Sumäeri," he panted, keeping his eyes on the raptor. "The Doyäenne extends her apologies for not welcoming you herself... Um, we were unaware you would be coming." The boy glanced at the läenier, his hands fidgeting nervously at his sides.

Räesha smiled slightly. Extending her palm, she replied, "Seek peace, little brother. I thank you for your message. May I see the prisoner?"

The runner glanced back at the building he'd just exited and shook his head. "She is not allowed visitors." He swallowed, shrinking away from the raptor who craned his neck towards the boy for a closer look.

Räesha frowned. *How am I supposed to run interference for her if I can't get her version of the story?*

"I've been authorized by the Näenji Council to interrogate her. I wouldn't recommend hampering my mission," she lied calmly, hoping the youth wouldn't call her bluff.

Sensing his rider's inner turmoil, the raptor stepped closer to Räesha. The boy yelped, taking several quick steps backward. Räesha placed a hand on the beast's golden shoulder and murmured gently. The läenier turned his head sideways to see the runner better, and then nudged his rider with his head. Räesha clicked a few times, reassuring the beast. She released him to perch high in the trees where he would be able to keep watch for her. Turning back to the boy, whose eyes were as wide as kessäeri eggs watching the läenier's flight, she asked to see the Doyäenne instead.

"Sh...she's getting ready for the tribunal," the boy stammered. "I'm to offer you refreshments and..." The boy

27

glanced around, then smiled up at Räesha whispering, "And then I'll take you to the prisoner."

The tension in Räesha's shoulders and stomach relaxed as the boy led her into the trees to the open-air kitchen and eating area for guests. The wind whipped through the branches, showering the two of them with needles and small leaves, so the youth motioned for her to sit at a small table beneath the protective inner boughs of the tree while he ran to get food and drink.

Räesha scanned the surrounding area and buildings and noted the presence of a few people in the kitchens and some women who were watching young children a couple huts away, but otherwise the city of Siläeria sat silent. The air was heavy and still, like the pressure before a thunderstorm. She sensed the acrid tang of fear in the air. Its sourness coated her tongue and nostrils, turning her stomach. *What could be causing such widespread anxiety? Certainly Lanäe could be annoying, but there must be something else contributing to the general sense of unease.*

Presently the young boy returned, laden with a heavy tray of cochäera meat and roasted vegetables. Räesha smiled and assisted him as he labored to lower the platter to her table. The cooks had left the small swine's head attached to the body, its round tusks and bristling topknot reminding the Sumäeri of her one brief encounter with a Meq'qan shaman in her early training days.

"This is certainly too much for me alone." She winked at the boy. "You must join me...I insist."

Räesha could see the internal battle raging behind his eyes. Boys his age were always hungry, but he was on duty and knew the repercussions for abandoning his post.

"I'm sure the Doyäenne would consider it proper hospitality," Räesha cajoled, pulling out a chair for the boy. "You wouldn't want to be guilty of abandoning her guest, would you?"

Indecision clouded his face for another second, and then he brightened. "No, I suppose I wouldn't."

Waving the boy into the seat, Räesha sat across from him and began carving the succulent cochäera meat, then heaped a pile of the steaming roots onto the boy's plate. Räesha watched his nostrils widen and lip curl in distaste. She chuckled.

"If you're going to grow up strong, you have to eat more than just meat," she admonished.

The youngster pouted, then pierced a tuber with his knife and crunched it between his teeth, grinding away at the bitter purple root. Räesha smiled, putting the boy further at ease. She'd need him comfortable to get the necessary information out of him.

Räesha learned that his name was Jäeden and that he'd been a Wushäen for two years. She asked him about life in Siläeri and how he liked being a Wushäen, protecting the gigantic tree Auräevya. After his initial hesitation, and her removing the requirement that he finish his vegetables, the boy talked freely as he chewed the smoky meat of the cochäera.

"...but I've always pulled kitchen duty, *never* latrine." The boy leaned closer to Räesha and whispered conspiratorially. "I learned early not to cross the seniors; just act like they know everything and they leave you alone."

"Very astute of you." Räesha nodded. "Is that what got the prisoner in trouble?"

Jäeden nodded slowly. He looked around instinctively, even though the area was deserted. "Yeah, it was. She came in here all high-and-mighty, telling the seniors how to treat the blight that developed on Auräevya..." He clapped his hands over his mouth, eyes wide.

Räesha's stomach tightened. Her blood ran cold in her veins. *Auräevya has developed blight? How could such a thing happen? If Auräevya sickens or dies, we will lose our*

29

connection to the Árk'äezhi energy of the world and all the Shäeli will die.

Even when Laräeith had destroyed or warped the other lands' sources of Árk'äezhi, causing the imbalance that still troubled their world, it hadn't caused any damage to Auräevya. The tree was the only barrier left holding the betrayer's demon mentor Laylur in his subterranean prison deep within Lady Muralia's depths. If the demon were freed, he would ravage the land, wiping out all life in his anger and retribution.

"Laylur's beast! How could this happen?" Räesha breathed, shock registering on her face.

Jäeden shook his head. "Nobody knows. It just sort of spread slowly and went unnoticed for a while. Now everybody is working on a cure."

"That explains why nobody is around...they're all trying to heal the tree?" she asked.

"Yes, all the time." Jäeden nodded. "We've been working all day and all night in shifts, but nobody can figure out what's wrong or how to heal it."

Räesha drummed her fingers on the table, thinking furiously. "So, what did this prisoner do to land herself in such a predicament?"

Jäeden shrugged. "I guess she thought she was some great healer or something. She tried to tell the seniors they were going about it in the wrong way, and they threw her in the cesspool."

Räesha barked a laugh. The image of her fussy and spoiled sister being tossed into the muck of the cesspool would have been amusing if not for the seriousness of her impending tribunal. *Still, insubordination shouldn't have been such a significant offense. There must be more going on than this Jäeden really knows.*

"That doesn't seem too bad," Räesha mused. "Did something else happen to get her in trouble with the Doyäenne?"

Jäeden grinned and leaned in again. "They say that she started wailing about seeing spirits or having visions or something. The Doyäenne gave her a chance to admit she was making it up, but she wouldn't. She started to get hysterical, and that's when they locked her up."

Räesha nodded grimly. *Sounds just like a stunt Lanäe would pull, but the girl has no sense of when to quit. This is going to be easier than I'd expected.* Räesha was sure she could convince Lanäe to admit to her theatrics and beg the Doyäenne's forgiveness. Perhaps they would give her latrine duty as punishment for a while to teach the errant girl her place among the Wushäen. The Sumäeri never tolerated such insubordination, either. *In this, at least, the Wushäen will have a Sumäeri ally.*

Räesha emptied the flagon of hot tisane she'd been served and wiped her mouth with the back of her hand. Standing abruptly, she adjusted her weapons and ordered Jäeden to take her to see the prisoner. Grabbing one last mouthful of meat, Jäeden nodded and moved toward the rope bridge that connected the eating area to the larger building bordering the commons.

"She'sh im dere," he said with his mouth full. He swallowed, nearly choking on the large piece of meat, and led her to the entrance. "Nobody's guarding her, but I'm sure you'll be safe. You're a lot bigger than she is."

Räesha smiled. The boy couldn't possibly realize that it wasn't her safety he should be worried about. If her baby sister wouldn't listen to reason and behave herself, Räesha was prepared to convince her with more stringent methods. "Just take me to her."

Jäeden led her through the passage that opened into an enormous chamber. Ornately carved beams and columns doubled as structural and aesthetic elements of the architecture. Räesha marveled at the beauty such simplicity offered. The chamber was round, with three chairs on a raised dais at one end and a smaller chair in the center. A gallery with rows upon rows of seats encircled the top echelon of the room. *This is where the tribunal will take place in just a few hours.*

A chill crept down her spine and she shuddered, rubbing the bumps that rose along the backs of her arms. At the far end of the chamber was a narrow door. It wasn't locked. Jäeden opened the door and held it for Räesha.

"I'll leave you to your work." He smiled, bowing. "Just call if you need anything."

Nodding, Räesha dismissed the boy and turned to peer inside the dim room. A few rays of afternoon light escaped the thickening clouds and slanted through the high windows onto the cot, catching the silver hair of the room's only occupant and reflecting it across the ceiling.

Lanäe sat cross-legged with her shoulders slumped, defeated. She didn't look up at her visitor. The room was narrow, allowing only for the cot and a chair. A plate of uneaten food rested on the chair in front of a cup full of water. Räesha frowned. *Lanäe is taking her theatrics further than usual this time.*

"Lanäe, talk to me," she said tersely, turning back to the door.

"Räesha!" The young girl gasped. She launched herself into her eldest sister, clinging to her as if her life depended on it. "How did you know? Oh, I'm so glad you're here. It's been just awful ... and they won't believe me ... Do you know they're having a tribunal for me tonight? My head is still throbbing from the vision, but..."

Räesha grabbed the young girl's shoulders and shook her firmly. "Lanäe! You must stop all this nonsense. We're not home anymore. These people aren't going to be taken in with your dramatics."

Lanäe stiffened. Her mouth clamped shut audibly and she ground her teeth. Amethyst and aqua eyes glinted at each other as the sisters faced off.

"You don't believe me?" Lanäe asked, incredulous. Her eyes narrowed and she pursed her lips. "You've never believed me. Why did you even come?"

Räesha put her hands on her hips and tapped her foot. "I came because father was worried about you. I came because I was asked to mitigate for you." She paced up the room once and back to her sister. "I came to talk some sense into you."

"Me? You came to talk sense into me?" Lanäe crossed her arms and regarded her older sister. She reached out and grabbed Räesha's hand. "You don't understand what's going on here or what's at stake. Come, I need to show you something."

Lanäe pulled Räesha out of her little cell, through the large tribunal chamber and out to the platform that held the ladders and bridges to the rest of the buildings. Wind whipped the younger girl's silver hair around her face, obscuring her features. Without another word, Lanäe took the ladder that went straight to the commons beneath the large building.

Not hesitating or waiting to see if Räesha was keeping up with her, Lanäe strode resolutely into the forest beyond the concentric rings of buildings. Räesha followed closely, her senses alert for pursuit or alarm from the Wushäen at the release of their only prisoner. Lanäe continued her march until she reached a grove of birch trees deep in the forest beyond the rings of huts. Standing in their midst, Lanäe placed her hands on the curling white-barked trunks and closed her eyes.

"Touch them yourself," she said to her sister. "Tell me what you sense."

Räesha raised an eyebrow at her sister's request, but decided to play along. She placed her palms on the trunk of one of the birch trees and, closing her eyes, slowed her breathing and lapsed into a meditative trance. Her awareness reached forward through her hands and into the tree, noting the myriad of crawling bugs that made their home in the bark or within the branches and leaves. Sinking deeper, she reached the inner core of the tree and could feel its energy pulsing joyfully.

The tree's song was one of health, of yearning for Lord Shamar's life-giving light and gratefulness for Lady Muralia's soil and water. The melody took Räesha along the branches to the miracle of new buds and unfolding leaves, the sighing of the branches in the wind and the digging of roots deep into the ground. Amidst its melody of harmonic well-being, Räesha sensed a counterpoint harmony of sadness, of longing that fueled the song of reaching both toward the light and into the darkness of the ground.

Räesha took a deep breath and opened her eyes. "I feel a reasonably healthy tree," she said.

"Ah, but reasonably healthy is unacceptable for Siläeri. The Wushäen's sole purpose is the nurturing of life. What does that tell you?" she asked, her eyes imploring her sister's.

Räesha thought for a moment. She considered a variety of sharp answers, but saw the pain etched on her sister's face and decided against it. "What are you trying to tell me?"

"Räesha, the forest is withering," Lanäe whispered. "Auräevya is covered with blight and has told me that a breach has been torn in Laylur's prison…Auräevya isn't strong enough to contain him much longer." Her eyes were wide and full of tears. "Our world is about to die."

"What? What!" Räesha sputtered. She grappled with her sister's terrifying words and her penchant for stretching the truth to her own ends. *Certainly I felt something sad in the undercurrent of the tree's song, but the end of the world?* "Wait, Auräevya *told* you? What do you mean Auräevya *told* you?"

Lanäe sighed again; her shoulders sagged as if weighted. "The spirit of the tree spoke to me. She appeared to me and gave me the warning." Lanäe looked up at Räesha, tears welling in her eyes as her emotions overtook her. "I've always been able to communicate with the spirits of trees. It's what gives me such great healing abilities and why the Wushäen accepted me. They don't believe that I talk to spirits, but they do see the results."

Räesha rocked back on her heels, absorbing her sister's explanation. "So, you're saying that the spirit of Auräevya warned you that Laylur was breaking free of his prison? Are you sure that you're not just making this up because the seniors threw you into the cesspool?"

Lanäe gasped, her head shot up, and she stared at her sister. "Who told you about that? How did you know?"

"It doesn't matter," Räesha said, her suspicions confirmed. "What matters now is that you stop this charade and apologize."

Lanäe inhaled, raising herself to her full height. Her eyes flashed in the light streaming through the boughs. "I didn't want the family to know of my pain and my humiliation." She fumed. "But the vision I had was real. The spirit of the Meq'qan girl who sacrificed herself with the Sceptre of Kulari spoke to me directly. Nobody else could hear her! She warned me of Auräevya's sickness and told me that the Sceptre of Kulari must be re-assembled to fight Laylur. Lesser demons are already free. We don't have much time!"

Räesha crossed her arms and paced around the glade. "Time? What time is it that we don't have? Even if I believed that Laylur was about to free himself from the abyss, what could we do? The Sceptre of Kulari requires the sacred elemental stones and wielders from each of the four lands. The old alliances are dead. The Askári lost their magical abilities when their sacred firestone was stolen. Who does the 'spirit' think could possibly wield the sceptre, should it be assembled?"

Lanäe watched her sister pace, holding herself still. "There is only one," she said quietly.

Räesha stopped mid-stride and looked at her little sister. "What *one*?" She strode back to Lanäe and grasped her shoulders, shaking her gently. "If this is another one of your stunts to put you in better graces, so help me I'll..."

Lanäe shook her head. "No," she whispered. "There is one who could wield the Sceptre of Kulari. The spirit told me...and I think he's related to us."

Räesha dropped her arms in defeat. *She isn't giving up as easily as I'd hoped. What is this other nonsense?* "Explain."

Lanäe walked slowly around the grove, her hand gently caressing each tree as she passed. "The spirit said there has been a child born to all the lands, one who has the innate ability to wield the Árk'äezhi energy of all five elements." Lanäe stopped and turned to face her sister. "You know our family's shame. Neräena was allowed to raise Maräera despite being a half-breed. Uncle Roväen went with her to Askáribai where she married some Askári-Tawali mixed blood. If there is anyone alive in Muralia today that has the blood of all the races, it will be Maräera's child. He could be the guardian we need to save us."

Räesha was stunned into silence. She had heard that Maräera had borne a son, but she didn't believe that it would have been allowed to live. Certainly not a mixed-blood with an Askári. It was bad enough that Maräera was half-Meq'qan, the result of Neräena's rape by her Meq'qan guards. *How could the Näenji Council have allowed such abominations to exist? They wouldn't. Lanäe must be fabricating all this stuff and I had very nearly been taken in by it.*

"Come with me." Räesha grabbed Lanäe by the hand and began walking back towards Siläeri.

"Where are you taking me?"

"You're going to apologize to the Doyäenne for all this nonsense and hope that they only banish you from Siläeri."

Lanäe yanked her hand free and stomped her foot. "I will *not* go back to that room. I'm telling the truth, whether you have the sense and foresight to recognize it or not!"

"Lanäe, I don't have time for one of your tantrums," Räesha scolded. "Now let's go."

"Never!" Lanäe screamed. She turned to run and froze, her eyes trained on a movement deeper in the forest.

Räesha followed her sister's gaze and inhaled sharply. A dark shape crouched between the trees across the grove. Fangs glinted in the fading light beneath the curling muzzle of the beast. A low growl escaped its chest. Movement to the left and right indicated at least two more of the foul creatures. More growls sounded behind them. *We are surrounded!*

Räesha slowly pulled her knife from her belt and the short spear she had draped across her back and held them in front of her. *We may be outnumbered, but I am Sumäeri!* She bared her own teeth in response to the threat. Not waiting for the demons to coordinate their attack, she lunged at the leader directly across from her. The beast hissed and swiped at the spear with its long claws. The sound of the sharp claws sliding down the metal blade caused a shiver to race down Räesha's spine.

"Räesha, watch out!" Lanäe cried as another beast launched itself from the right.

Räesha swung her spear around and pierced the beast's hide just behind the head. The monster twisted in mid-air, changing direction to avoid further damage and fell back on its haunches. More growls and roars filled her ears as the rushing of adrenaline heightened her fighting senses. There were at least seven beasts surrounding them. *Why aren't they all attacking?*

The Sumäeri's eyes shone brightly as she screamed a challenge to the demons. The circling creatures drove her mad. They were playing with her and Lanäe like they were some sort of prey. Räesha lunged at another beast while Lanäe shrunk behind her, whimpering.

As if in response to her earlier cry, Räesha heard the screech of her läenier as it approached. A fierce grin crossed her face. *These puny demons don't stand a chance!*

"Stay close," she yelled to Lanäe as she watched the dark shape spiral down towards them.

Lanäe turned to her sister, fear and horror registered in her eyes. Räesha heard her sister's soul-wrenching scream as she felt the presence directly behind her. Pain exploded in her head. Blackness enveloped her as Lanäe's screams echoed in her ears.

Chapter 3 - A Dangerous Proclamation

"He's over here!" an excited voice shouted as the pounding of feet roused Cédron's mind from the blackness.

The boy lay face down in the dirt. He didn't know how long he'd lain there, but his body was stiff and throbbing. He could hear cheers and shouts from the tournament grounds below the city. *I hope Tóran fared better in his battle.*

Something shifted in the ground near his head. Cédron opened his eyes slightly and watched as a tunnel snake slithered its way slowly beneath the tent flap where it found shade. He groaned, preferring the relief of oblivion to the pain of remembering why he was in this predicament.

"He's alive,"said a familiar voice, sounding relieved.

Cédron felt strong arms carefully lifting him up. His weight shifted slightly and he gasped in pain as he was raised to his knees. Shards of broken wood stuck into his ribs and back where he'd slammed into the barrel. Blurry figures were all he could see through his bruised and swollen eyes.

"Mijáko piles!" someone swore. "Look at his face!" Cédron recognized Zariun's voice as gentle fingers prodded his broken nose.

Cédron realized that Lord Shamar's rays had baked the sticky blood covering his face into a macabre mask.

"Eth nok ath bad ath it lookths," he said.

A cool, wet cloth was draped over his eyes and he was laid back gently, his head resting on something soft.

"Don't talk," Rováen said in his ear, then louder to someone standing above them, "I need some crushed willow bark in hot water."

The softness beneath his head shifted and Cédron realized that his head lay in someone's lap. He lapsed back out of focus as the conversation around him turned to who might have beaten him and why. Cédron hesitated to implicate his brother's friends, for to make enemies with the legionnaires would jeopardize his relationship with Tóran and certainly cause Kásuin problems. However, to stay silent would make him susceptible to future attacks. *Perhaps I'll tell Rováen when we're alone. Maybe he can help me figure out what to do about this.*

"Here Cédron, drink this." Rováen's words brought him back to his present situation.

Someone raised his head slightly and set a cup to his lips. The hot tea was laced with willow and he retched at its bitterness.

"I'm sorry I didn't specify to add sweetener," Rováen chuckled. "You'll have to take it the hard way."

The dried blood on Cédron's face cracked as he grimaced and took another swallow. He knew that the willow bark would help with the pain and hoped that Rováen hadn't snuck any valerian root into the mixture, as he planned to stay awake for the rest of the evening. Cédron hadn't heard any shouts or cheering from the tournament grounds and assumed the Warrior's Challenge was over and a champion determined.

"Who won?" he croaked.

"What did he say?" It sounded like Zariun's voice. "Did he ask who won?"

Cédron blinked in the afternoon light at the figure standing in front of him. He nodded slowly despite Rováen's hands holding his head still.

Zariun snorted. "Leave it to you to worry about the least important thing. We need to figure out who did this to you!"

40

"But…"

An enormous shadow leaned down over the boy and crouched down next to Cédron's head. Cédron recognized the caravan master Shozin Chezak by Lord Shamar's rays reflecting off his bald, ebony head. "Tóran won the tournament. It was a resounding victory and will make a very exciting story when he tells you about it. He broke his arm in the process, but was victorious."

Cédron relaxed slightly. *At least something good has happened today. Even though I wasn't able to see the fight, I'm glad for Tóran's success.*

Shozin looked at Roväen, his furrowed brow rippling dark wrinkles into his forehead. "We need to get him to a healer and get those shards of wood out of him."

"The willow should start to take effect in a moment," Roväen nodded. "Can you two help carry him?"

Shozin took Cédron's cloak and wrapped him carefully, then he and Zariun each grabbed an end. Shozin's powerful muscles bulged as he held Cédron's shoulders, while Zariun struggled to carry the injured boy's legs. In this most unflattering manner, the Regent's son made his way through his city to the healer's quarters. If others noticed who was in the makeshift litter and made any comments, Cédron was oblivious to them.

The willow bark had done its work, easing the pain in his body, and Cédron drifted into a waking numbness. His world was limited to senses other than sight with his swollen eyes. He could smell the pungency of unwashed bodies masked in perfumes and hear the buzzing of conversations as he made his way through the streets, but the colors and forms passing by him remained blurry and vague.

In due time, Cédron felt himself being lowered onto a cot. He removed the wet cloth from his forehead and saw that he was in the dimly lit quarters of the healers. Some of the swelling in his eyes had gone down and he could make out others filling the cots throughout the large bay.

Most of them wore the uniform of the Hármolin Legion, so Cédron assumed they were casualties of the day's tournament. He looked around but didn't see Tóran anywhere. *If he broke his arm, shouldn't he be here getting it set?* Cédron directed his gaze toward the master healer, an angular man whose sense of humor and flair for the dramatic offset his somber occupation. Cédron watched him as he tied off the thread in the head wound he had just finished stitching with an elegant flourish, then made his way to the cot where his newest customer lay waiting.

"What have we here? A brawl this early in the day?" he mused, observing the large splinters in Cédron's body and his broken nose.

Shozin stepped up on the opposite side of the cot, his dark eyes clouded with concern. "No, he was attacked behind one of the merchant's stalls. We found him lying in the alley."

The master healer's shrewd eyes raked his newest charge over quickly, barking orders to his apprentice with rapid fire. "Hot water, rags, honey, bandages, small tongs and willow bark."

"I've given him a draught of willow bark already," Roväen interrupted. "It should have already taken effect."

The master healer looked at Roväen and nodded. "That will speed things right along."

The apprentice ran quickly back to his master, his hands filled with the requested items. The healer made short work of pulling the wood shards from Cédron's torso and arms while Roväen daubed his face with witch hazel and water to clean off the blood. Cédron felt a deep crunching sound as the healer stuck two flexible sticks up his nostrils and pulled the bones into place. He felt as if he were simply an observer rather than the one whose nose was being taped and bandaged.

"These are fairly superficial and should heal quickly," the master healer noted as he slathered the thick honey into the lacerations on Cédron's body.

Cédron smelled the sweet floral scent of the honey and squirmed slightly as it tickled his skin. He sucked in his breath when the master healer wiped the sticky mound over the open wounds and plastered them with the bandages, binding them fairly tight. He was interrupted as a group of rowdy legionnaires banged open the door, carrying in their new champion amidst cheers and cat calls from the other patients lounging in the healer's care. Regent Kásuin Varkáras followed closely behind, worry etched deeply in his tanned face.

"Take this jar of honey and slather it thickly on your wounds every time you change the dressing." The master healer placed an earthen jar in Cédron's hands and, with a quick wink, tied off the bandage and attended the soldier who had entered the bay.

"Congratulations, Master Varkáras!" he said, bowing graciously. "Now, let me see the damage." The master healer reached for Tóran's arm.

Tóran retreated a step, pulling his arm from the healer's grasp. "We'll have to get this hauberk off first."

The master healer snapped his fingers. Two attendants, grim-faced and bloody from handling the multitude of injuries from the tournament, assisted Tóran with the removal of his hauberk and tunic. Cédron blanched when the armor was removed and he saw the compound fracture. One of the forearm bones protruded slightly from the bloody tear in the swollen, bruised skin.

Cédron was immediately nauseated and had to grind his teeth. Beads of sweat formed on his brow. Saliva began to flow in his mouth. His own injuries didn't bother him, but seeing his brother's grim wound made him ill. He looked away as the master healer grabbed the arm, grinding the wrist and elbow apart to set the bones.

Tóran retched drily. The master healer barked another list of ingredients to his assistants including willow bark and valerian tea. The healer daubed the wound with a rag soaked in calendula oil to both sterilize the wound and dull the pain.

Humming off-key while he worked, the master healer sprinkled powdered sulfur over the wound to prevent any further infection. He bound the arm tightly, wrapping the bandage over Tóran's shoulder to create a sling.

"That should do it for now," he said, eyeing his handiwork. "Don't move your arm for a fortnight or the bones won't set right."

Tóran nodded, sipping the painkilling tea gratefully. Cédron admired his brother's bravery, both in battle and in drinking the bitter tea. People would be talking about young Tóran Varkáras' triumph in the tournament his first eligible year. It was a rare achievement by such a young legionnaire and would be worthy of at least a song at the feast.

"You did well Tóran." Kásuin smiled, gripping his shoulder affectionately.

"Thank you, father," Tóran slurred, his eyes beginning to droop from the valerian root.

Cédron's stomach twisted in a painful knot. His father's obvious affection and pride in his adopted son caused pangs of jealously. Not only was the orphan Kásuin had rescued from the streets of Mítyon a full Askári, but he fulfilled the role as Cedron never could. Tóran was a legionnaire and had just won the Warrior's Challenge. Cédron was a Shäeli half-demon that Kásuin had to imprison in the castle for his aberrant magical abilities. Tears welled in his swollen eyes as self-loathing filled his mind. *How could my father have fallen in love with a Shäeli woman to begin with?*

Cédron turned his head away from the painful scene and hoped his father wouldn't realize he was here. He didn't want to spoil the special moment by making his transgressions and their consequences known. He closed his eyes. *He hasn't seen me. I know I'll have to face him for punishment later, but please don't let him see me now.*

Shozin Chezak cleared his throat loudly, getting Kásuin's attention. Startled by the sudden noise, Cédron opened his eyes to see Kásuin winding his way through the smattering of cots to his side. His hopes for escaping his father's wrath sank.

"Shozin! Rováen! Wasn't Tóran magnificent?" He smiled broadly, his grey eyes crinkling with the effort. "The youngest champion in history!" He noticed their solemn expressions and his smile faded. "What is it? Why are you both here? What has happened?"

Rováen stepped around the cot between Cédron and his father, blocking the boy's view. Although his voice was low, Cédron heard every word.

"Please stay calm and don't call attention to us. Our young miscreant Zariun here snuck Cédron out of the castle to wish Tóran well for the competition. I found them and was escorting Cédron to the tournament when we got separated. He was found behind the merchants' stalls a short while ago."

Rováen stepped aside and nodded down at the prone figure on the cot.

"No!" The color drained from Kásuin's face. The flush of pride from Tóran's victory faded to white pallor as he took in the extent of the injuries. "Laylur's beast! What happened? Who did this to him?"

"Cédron? Cédron is here?" Tóran staggered to his father's side and looked at his brother.

"I'm fine..." Cédron attempted to sit up, but was forced back onto the cot by Rováen's firm hands.

"We don't know. His injuries were severe enough that I administered willow bark and he's not been coherent enough to give any details," Rováen explained.

Shozin gripped Kásuin's shoulder, his frown underscoring the severity of the situation. "His wounds aren't serious, but the fact that he got them is. We need to get him to the castle immediately for his own protection."

The caravan master's eyes raked over the rowdy legionnaires meaningfully. "We don't know if his attack was a result of too much revelry or if he was targeted, but we can't afford to take any chances."

Kásuin's gray eyes hardened and he nodded to his large friend. Kneeling beside the cot, he laid his hand on Cédron's chest. "Are you alright, son? I'm so sorry I've kept you locked away from everyone and everything, but it's to prevent this sort of thing from happening. Can you forgive me?"

The tears in Cédron's eyes spilled down over his temples and into his ears. He lifted a hand to wipe them but his father's hands reached them first. *How can he be asking me for forgiveness? I'm the one who broke the rules and defied his orders. Father deserves better! He deserves a son he can be proud of, one who isn't a freak and who doesn't need to be protected like a delicate Yezman vase.*

"Nothing to forgive, father," Cédron said hoarsely, his eyes flicking from his father to Tóran and back. "I had hoped to support Tóran without being noticed. I'm sorry I've caused you problems, but I can't stay locked up forever. Please, just let me go to the Mage's Guild in Taksábai. Maybe there I'll learn how to manage my abilities and be less of a danger to everyone."

Cédron looked at his father and was surprised to see tears in his eyes. "I can't do that. I'm sorry, son. You are a Varkáras, and as such, it is time that I formally name you as my heir. I had planned to make the announcement at the end of the Festival of Narsham-Vu."

Cédron gasped. All of his hopes of studying at the Mage's Guild vanished in a gut-wrenching instant. His dreams of reconciling with the people of Dúlnat by learning how to use his powers for their benefit drained away. The simple realization that his father wanted to place him in a position of authority over a population bent on his destruction hammered through his pain-filled mind.

"No father, you can't! The people...they won't accept me. They'll kill me, and probably you, too." The boy tried to get up but was held down firmly by both Shozin and Rováen.

"Is that wise, Lord Regent?" Cédron heard Rováen ask his father. "Given today's events, perhaps you should reconsider our purpose here."

Tóran remained silent. Cédron raised his eyes to his brother's face. Tóran wore a mask of neutrality, but Cédron couldn't mistake the anger that burned behind his eyes. Cédron swallowed the bitterness of the truth revealed in Tóran's expression. *He's a legionnaire now. Any loyalty he ever had toward me as his brother has been annihilated.*

Kásuin sighed and scrubbed his weary face with his hands. His eyes hardened as he looked around the suddenly silent room. The rowdy legionnaires stood frozen at their Regent's proclamation. The tension in the healer's tent was palpable and the group from the caravan leaned in protectively around Cédron.

Regent Varkáras motioned for the healers to load his sons on litters and escort them home. "Let's get you two up to the castle and into the baths. We'll have much to discuss once you've rested."

CHAPTER 4 - DEMON BLOOD

Rováen closed the door to the bathing chamber behind him and prayed to Azria that the mineral waters would soothe and heal Cédron's wounds quickly. *At least the wounds of his flesh can be addressed by the baths. The damage to his psyche will require a different sort of healing.* Touching his forehead then his heart with his fingertips, the elder finished the prayer and turned, nearly slamming into Maräera, who had glided up silently behind him while he prayed.

"How is he?" Cédron's mother asked, worry lines etched into her pale skin.

Rováen shook his head slightly. "His wounds will heal, but his confidence in his ability to meet his father's expectations has been destroyed."

"What do you mean? Kásuin is just trying to keep him safe." Maräera raised an eyebrow, challenging her uncle to clarify.

"Expecting the boy to remain in the castle is one thing, but Kásuin has just told him that he plans to formally announce Cédron as his heir." The old man grasped Maräera's hand and placed it in the crook of his arm as he led her down the corridor. "The boy knows without a doubt that it is a losing proposition given the people's hostilities towards him. If he doesn't have the support of the legion, he will have no power to govern the city."

Maräera sighed. "He's such a gentle soul. I don't know if he'll be strong enough to challenge the legion…"

"No, particularly not if Tóran is against him." Rovaën finished her thought. "He loves his brother, and I think he would rather leave than risk alienating him."

The two continued down the hallway in silence, their thoughts still with the young boy floating in the geothermally heated pool. As they made their way through the living quarters and into the main areas of the castle, Rovaën continued to try and find a way of removing Cédron from Dúlnat that would appease the Regent. Each idea was discarded as impractical or improbable as he ticked them off in his mind. Maräera might be more open to letting her only son go, now that the threat of remaining outweighed the likelihood of the peaceful future they had so fervently hoped for.

Looking over at the younger woman, Rovaën squeezed her arm gently. "Listen, we both know now that staying here is too risky for him. He has to be able to work on his powers and get to where he can control them, or the danger he will pose to himself will be greater than anything the Askári can throw at him."

"Where do you propose he go?" Maräera asked, then inhaled sharply. "You couldn't be considering Samshäeli! Our people would slaughter him as an abomination without question. You know that."

Rovaën sighed and frowned. "Perhaps if we could convince my brother Räebin and his girls that he isn't as dangerous as his heritage makes him sound…"

Maräera whirled on him and stopped walking, her face pale and hands trembling. "I barely escaped my own fate. Cédron struggles to accept what he is, and the rejection of the other half of his family won't help him." Maräera's hands dropped to her sides, and her eyes grew wide. Grasping Rovaën's jerkin, she said, "If they ever found out about him, it wouldn't be rejection Cédron would face, but destruction. You must protect him. Promise me, you will always protect him!"

Roväen removed her hands from his jerkin and kissed each one tenderly. "You know how much I love the boy," he whispered. "You were right all those years ago, and I'm glad you stayed my hand. He's grown into a compassionate and intelligent young man who deserves the chance to make his own life. I promise you that I will watch over him and guide him as long as I am able."

Maräera collapsed into his chest, hugging him tightly about the middle. Roväen's heart squeezed with a pang of guilt. He had given her the only promise he could in good conscience. Although Cédron had grown into a good lad, there was no guarantee that as his powers grew, he wouldn't abuse them and take up the mantle his ancestors had unwittingly cast aside. Roväen would temper his oath with common sense. He closed his eyes and sent a prayer to Lady Muralia to watch over her half-demon son so that he would not be forced to carry out his original orders from the Shäeli Näenji Council.

They reached the double doors that let to Kásuin's megaron. Roväen halted before opening them. The elder Shäeli turned Maräera to face him. "Let me take him to Taksábai to the Mage's Guild. We can appeal to High Mage Ánderan Pól to see if they would accept him for training."

Maräera shook her head. "I can't let him go. He's still so young."

Roväen grasped her shoulders and shook her gently. "If you keep him here, you sentence him to death! At least give the boy a chance to grow up and become the master of his abilities. He can do nothing if he remains here."

Maräera raised her head and met Roväen's gaze. His guts clenched at the sight of tears in her eyes. He hated himself for having to be so hard on her, but the reality of the danger to her only child was not exaggerated. She had to support his position or risk losing the boy forever.

Slowly she nodded, the downward curve of her mouth displaying the misery she would not voice. "I cannot promise that Kásuin will allow it, but I will support you."

"That's all I ask." Rováen embraced her gently, then pushed through the megaron door.

Kásuin sat at his desk on the far wall across the room and barely acknowledged their entrance. Several sheaves of petitions littered the desk as the Regent ploughed through the unpleasant paperwork. The reasonably small, private room was large enough for the Regent to conduct meetings with his closest advisors, but not large enough to allow the influx of petitioners that vied for his attention. The floor was inlaid with the Askári compass rose, the symbol of the Konárras family crest, made of precious stones, with fiery veins of corundum offset against the golden topaz and orange carnelian of the center leaf designs. Lamps flickered around the room, their light reflecting off the white marble walls and causing the gemstones in the floor to gleam with an internal flame. The windows remained open in the Suntide heat, allowing the mountain breeze to cool the room and giving its occupants an unmitigated view of the city and its surroundings.

"Have you got them both settled then?" Kásuin asked without looking up.

Rováen made his way around the decorative flooring and pulled out one of the carved chairs for Maräera. She smiled slightly and sat, pulling her golden hair from behind her back and sending it cascading over the green brocade dress that fanned out around her. Rováen pulled over a matching chair and slumped into it, stretching his long legs out in front of him and crossing them at the ankles.

"Tóran was still sleeping soundly when I left him, and Cédron is reaping the benefits of the mineral baths." Rováen stretched his arms up and clasped his hands behind his head. "We should discuss what happens next."

Kásuin looked up. His grey eyes locked onto Rov`̈a`en's pale blue ones. The Regent set the stylus down on the table and folded his hands.

"You mean to talk me out of my decision to declare Cédron as my heir."

Rovären spread his hands out wide in surrender. "I only want what's best for the boy--what's safest and not going to get him killed."

"Mmm hmm." The Regent pursed his lips and turned his attention to Maräera. "And what are your thoughts, my love?"

Maräera glanced quickly at Rovären, who nodded slightly at her. "I think," she began, but her voice cracked. Clearing her throat, she raised her chin to face her spouse. "Although it breaks my heart, I think that we must at least consider postponing the naming ceremony until tensions have died down a bit. You saw what happened to him today." She rose and glided to Kásuin's side. Kneeling beside his chair, she placed her graceful fingers on her husband's forearm. "Please, hear Rovären out. His solution may not be ideal or permanent, but it is likely the best option for keeping our son safe."

Kásuin touched his beloved's cheek with the back of his hand, sliding an errant strand of golden hair from her eyes. "I'll listen, but I doubt you'll change my mind."

Rovären pulled on the end of his beard, glancing out the window toward the courtyard below as he gathered his thoughts. Kitchen drudges carried buckets of water from the well and small children played games with stones and short sticks. Beyond the gate, where guards no longer stood, life went on in the city. All seemed peaceful, normal. *That will all change if he continues with his plans. The legionnaires with revolt, along with the townspeople. Dúlnat and all Kásuin and Maräera have worked towards will be destroyed.*

"I suggest you let me take Cédron to petition High Mage Ánderan Pól in Taksábai," Rovären began, turning to face his friend. "Behind the thick walls of the Mage's Guild, the boy may have a better chance at learning how to use his gifts without persecution. I will monitor his progress there and…"

Kásuin slammed his hand down on the desk and rose, nearly knocking Maräera backwards in his ire. "He cannot go there!"

Maräera's face paled and she glanced at her uncle before speaking . "But why?"

"You *know* why! It wouldn't be any less dangerous for him there than it is here. Perhaps even more so." Kásuin paced back and forth over the Konárras compass rose embedded into the floor.

Roväen crossed his arms over his chest. "Algarik has not been heard from for years. He may not pose a threat any longer. What would it hurt to check with the High Mage and see? We certainly can't keep him locked up here forever."

"But he's my son and heir. He is the only one who bears the Varkáras lineage. He was born to this destiny, whether he embraces it or not," the Regent barked.

"What about Tóran?" Maräera asked softly. "We've raised him as a Varkáras and the people love him. He would be a strong leader and a fair Regent."

"How could you rob our son of his birthright?" The Regent gaped at his wife.

Maräera leveled her gaze at her spouse, her golden eyes hard. "The same way you do. I only suggested that he give up on the Askári half of his birthright, not the Shäeli side. He is gifted-"

"And it is those very gifts that endanger his life!" Kásuin interrupted, running his hands through his dark greying hair and pulling at his scalp with his fists.

"But only if he remains here!" Roväen argued, his chest tight. *Please let the man see reason!*

Kásuin squeezed his wife's hand in apology and slumped his shoulders. Glancing up at Roväen, he growled, "Don't think I don't know what you're up to. I appreciate that you're trying to keep the boy safe, but know that I do have a plan for encouraging the citizens of Dúlnat to accept Cédron. I've already spoken to him about it and he's in agreement."

Rováen's skin prickled and his eyebrows shot up. "What plan is this?"

Kásuin grinned and tapped his finger to his temple. "One that can't fail, if you'll just trust that I know what I'm doing."

Maräera narrowed her eyes and humphed. "Perhaps you should share your plans if you want us to support them."

The Regent's reply was interrupted by a knock at the door. Crossing the room, Kásuin opened it to a young runner who pounded his chest in salute. "You have a visitor from the Mage's Guild, sire." The boy handed the Regent a slip of parchment. Kásuin caught his breath as he stared at the sheet.

The Regent turned to face his wife and dearest friend, his face ashen. With trembling hands, he held out the sheet to Rováen. "My plans just became infinitely more complicated."

CHAPTER 5 - PRISONER

The swaying and bouncing motion jarred Räesha back into consciousness. Lying on her side with her hands tied behind her back, she could feel the hard wood of the cart pressing on her shoulder with each bump in the road. Keeping her eyes closed, Räesha assessed her situation as best she could. It was nearly dark, so very little time had passed since the attack. *What happened? Where is Yongäen?*

The sweet, coppery smell of dried blood filled her nostrils. She itched from the sticky trail that crept down her temple toward her cheek. Minus the splitting ache behind her ear, she couldn't identify any injuries on herself, but that didn't hold for the body thrown next to her. *Lanäe!*

Her thoughts turned immediately to her sister and her last moments of awareness before being struck. *What were those creatures that had circled us? Why am I not torn to shreds?* Räesha opened her eyes slightly and peeked between her lashes. In the pale light shed by the lantern attached to the corner of the cart, Räesha could make out Lanäe's body as it lay on the cart next to her. The Sumäeri's heart constricted and she clamped down on the sob that threatened to burst from her throat at her baby sister's sightless eyes. *No!*

Anguish filled Räesha's eyes with tears that she could not afford to shed. Glancing down without moving her head, the Sumäeri could see the shadows from deep gashes and spilled entrails of Lanäe's ravaged body that seeped fluids into the floor of the wooden cart. Räesha closed her eyes against the horror of her sister's corpse. *What happened back in the glade?* She racked her brain to remember, but nothing revealed itself from her memories after being struck from behind.

"The Sumäeri is awake," a deep voice stated above her head.

Räesha heard the shifting of another person above her and decided it must be the driver of the cart.

"Are you sure?" Another poked her with a blunt object, but she didn't stir.

"Her breathing has changed," the first voice said. "Be on your guard."

The muffled scraping of several sets of sandaled feet grated in her ear as they took their positions around her body. *At least my captors have the good sense to be wary. Not that it will save them.* Räesha smiled internally; they wouldn't be able to hold her for long. Still, she needed to determine who had killed her sister before she escaped so that the guilty party received the appropriate retribution.

Räesha's highly developed senses revealed the stench of her captor's evil in addition to the earthy scents of the forest they were riding through. It lay over the top of their musty, unwashed bodies and rough-woven shifts like a pungent film. They were all male and all armed.

A sharp cry in the distance followed by the clanging of a large bell announced the cart's return to Siläeri. The sound of scores of running feet and angry shouts alerted her to the imminent danger of her position. Räesha opened her eyes as two sets of rough hands pulled her to a sitting position. Overhead, lanterns were strung across the square, washing it in pale golden light. She looked around to a sea of livid faces and wails of despair as Lanäe's shredded body was displayed by the men in the cart.

"Murderer!"

"Lock her up!"

"No, stone her!"

Räesha watched patiently as the mob pushed their way to the cart and began rocking it violently. Her captors, cloaked against the night chill, made feeble attempts to prevent the riot from getting out of hand but were completely ineffective.

Räesha's eyes flashed at the men shoving themselves closer to her who had the temerity to grasp at her silver braid. They hastily retreated under the force of her glare, continuing their calls for her imprisonment and death for the murder of one of their own. A burly Wushäen with his hands still grimy from working the soil of Auräevya jumped onto the back of the cart and advanced. Räesha noted the sharp hoe he brandished and tensed to spring.

"Cease this nonsense," the Doyäenne commanded firmly from the back of the crowd. Bodies parted, allowing the matriarch to approach the cart unhindered. "What has happened?" She turned her amethyst eyes to the figures standing above Räesha.

As one, they all looked at the driver, deferring to him with their silence. The driver finished unhitching the 20 foot long saurian roshao from the cart, slapping the enormous reptilian beast on its long, indigo-spotted tail. He watched it amble over to a large patch of grass to graze with its flat, bill-like mouth before turning to the Doyäenne and pulling back his hood.

"We were returning from Suriyäeh when we encountered this Sumäeri attacking one of your Wushäen." He sighed and shook his head sadly. "I'm afraid she killed the girl before we could intervene."

Räesha's eyes widened. *I didn't kill my sister, those creatures did! These men weren't anywhere around when I was knocked unconscious, and Lanäe had still been very much alive at that point. Who are these men and why are they fabricating such lies?*

She turned her head slightly to look at her accuser. Her eyes were accosted by the man's disfigured visage. His squinty eyes were too small for the face that housed an enormous mouth filled with sharp, crooked teeth. One shoulder was hitched up higher on his neck than the other, giving him an unbalanced appearance. Behind his eyes, she saw a flicker of something foreign. She quickly scanned the rest of her escorts, noting similar deformities among the other rogues in the cart. Revulsion clenched in her stomach as she realized that these men were not pure. *The Shäeli are Lady Muralia's First People, made in the deities' images! These men may have been Shäeli once, but somehow they have become twisted and warped.*

Räesha scanned the myriad of faces surrounding the cart and was surprised that none of the Wushäen appeared to notice the distinct irregularities in her captors. *How do they not see the abhorrent features and the strange shadows flickering behind their eyes?* She watched in morbid fascination as the Doyäenne placed her delicate hand on the grimy shoulder of the driver and offered her gratitude for their services in this unpleasant situation.

The Doyäenne turned to Räesha. "How dare you murder a Wushäen?" she hissed, the light of the lanterns flickering across her face.

"I didn't!" Räesha cried. "We were attacked by creatures I've never encountered within our borders before." Her voice wavered and she stopped, taking a steadying breath. "We were surrounded, just beyond the trees there; did nobody see? One of the beasts launched itself at me when I was struck from behind. I awoke next to Lanäe's body in this cart." Räesha blinked and two large tears rolled down her cheeks. "I have no knowledge of these men, where they took us, or of how she was killed."

The Doyäenne raised her hand to quiet the protests of the outraged citizens. She turned to the burly Wushäen still holding the hoe. "Take her to the cell to await the tribunal. We will get to the bottom of this tonight."

"Wait!" Räesha cried. "Where is my läenier?"

The Doyäenne turned back to face the Sumäeri. "You released your raptor when you arrived. We have not seen it since." The older woman turned her back on the warrior and made her way through the crowd.

Räesha was pulled roughly from the cart and thrown over the large man's back like a sack of borage roots. Her mind spun as she realized her situation was careening out of her control. Anger fueled her pounding heart. Räesha looked back at the cart and saw the leer on the face of the driver. The repulsive man had the audacity to wink at her as she was being hauled away. Räesha didn't know who he was, but of one thing she was certain: he was no Wushäen.

Räesha didn't have long to wait before she was brought before the tribunal, her hands still bound behind her back. The young warrior blinked from the brightness of the room after the soft rose of the moonlit cell she'd spent the past hour in.

The murmuring voices echoed in her throbbing head. She still hadn't had an opportunity to clean or inspect her wounds after the attack. Though she was bloody and disheveled, her braid loose and tangled down her back, Räesha squared her shoulders and tilted her chin defiantly as she was placed before the tribunal and what appeared to be the entire population of Siläeri.

"State your name and station," intoned the bored scribe seated beneath the gallery to the right of the dais.

Räesha glanced up at the three chairs atop the dais. The Doyäenne was seated in the center and was flanked by two older men, probably high-level Wushäen. All three faces remained impassive, but the gallery was a storm of tossing, angry heads reflecting the hundreds of lights in silvery waves.

Räesha was certain that this idea of a tribunal was a sham. She had nothing to do with Lanäe's death. Her only goals were to learn what had happened to the two of them and to recover her sister's body for her family. Unsure how best to proceed, she decided to simply go along with the process...for now.

"Räesha Angäersol, Sumäeri and läenier rider," she said.

The buzzing from the gallery increased. Räesha could feel the tension level in the enormous round room increase. Clenching and unclenching her fists, she worked to loosen her bonds. She wished she had her spear or at least a stick to whack these idiots across their heads with. *How could the Wushäen become so far removed from their Shäeli brethren to hasten to such aggression? These people aren't warriors; they're gardeners!*

The Doyäenne stood and raised her hands for silence. She faced Räesha, stepping forward to the edge of the dais.

"You stand accused of murdering the Wushäen Lanäe," she said in a clear voice that easily carried to the furthest gallery seats. "If you are found guilty, you will be imprisoned for a fortnight, allowing your family ample time to pay restitution for your crimes. You will then be executed."

A cheer went up from all sides of the gallery. Räesha stared stonily at the Doyäenne. *If the Wushäen believe that the Sumäeri will stand for my imprisonment and execution, they are terribly mistaken. Although we Sumäeri haven't taken up arms against our kinsmen in years, there is a precedent.* The Doyäenne ignored Räesha's glare and raised her hands again.

"Bring in the first witness."

Räesha held her expression neutral as the misshapen cart driver shambled forward from the doorway in the back of the room. She did not look at him or react to his wheezing chuckle as he brushed past her.

"Ikäerin, your humble servant," he said, bowing to the Doyäenne.

The Doyäenne inclined her intricately-braided head slightly, acknowledging the man, and returned to her seat, indicating that he should tell his story. Ikäerin scratched the grimy tuft of hair that grew out of his chin as his beady eyes darted around the gallery.

"My men and I were returning from delivering a load of Auräevya's berries to the healers in Suriyäeh. We were just rounding the bend there beyond the groves when we saw the Sumäeri there," he inclined his head towards Räesha, "bring her blade up through that little girl's middle."

Shouts and angry murmurings swelled throughout the gallery as his words registered among the spectators. Räesha's eyes scanned the angry crowd. *How can they believe such a ridiculous lie? Sumäeri don't just attack innocent people for no reason, yet this tribunal is rapidly turning into a riot. What is going on here?*

Her arrival in Siläeri had not been welcome. She had sensed that when she landed. She couldn't figure out what could have possibly caused such increased hostilities between the Wushäen and the Sumäeri. Räesha looked around at the ledge of the gallery with its ornately carved banisters holding back the mob. Glancing out the window at the half-moon Orwena midway through her cycle, Räesha noticed a shadow briefly blot out the stars as it crossed the night sky. Clenching her jaw, she realized her time was limited and that she'd better make her move quickly before her one chance of escape eluded her.

The decrepit man sighed and shuffled closer to the Doyäenne, lowering his voice dramatically. "She made quick work of it, I'll give her that. She's an efficient killer, almost demonic. It's as if she was possessed or something."

More wails and shouts from the gallery at the man's theatrical pronouncement. The Doyäenne nodded at the man and thanked him for his testimony.

Räesha rolled her eyes and shifted her weight from one foot to the other. Her face flushed as her pounding heart thrust blood upward with the heat of her emotions. Taking a deep breath to try and calm her anger, Ikäerin's words struck her. *Demonic...possessed.* She looked at the cart driver, and her heart stopped. The unnatural flicker behind his eyes suddenly made sense to her. *He is possessed! Demons have infiltrated the Wushäen, and now they may know about Maräera's child! I have to get to him before they do.* Räesha knew she would never get a fair hearing from this tribunal, so her next maneuver would have to be gaining her freedom with the fewest casualties.

The Sumäeri warrior's eyes quickly darted around the room. She spied six armed guards, each bearing knives or short swords, but no long-range weapons. They were Wushäen, not warriors. They were ill-equipped to handle a Sumäeri; that much was obvious. Still, it wasn't in her nature to kill wantonly, especially since the Wushäen were already predisposed to violence and anti-Sumäeri sentiments. However, if they got in her way, she wouldn't hesitate to return their life's energy to Lady Muralia's bosom.

A movement to her left caught her attention, and she turned her head slightly to see the door to the chamber open as another witness was brought forward. Her breath caught in her chest as she watched little Jäeden being prodded to the center of the room. Fear was etched around his eyes and his throat bobbed as he swallowed nervously. He faced the Doyäenne and executed a cursory bow, as directed by his Wushäen escort.

"Runner Jäeden, ma'am," he squeaked, and then cleared his throat.

"Runner Jäeden," the Doyäenne said softly. "You were instructed to meet the Sumäeri and take her to the guest's quarters to await the tribunal, were you not?"

Jäeden's shoulders slumped and he hung his head. "Yes, ma'am."

"Yet she compelled you to take her to see the prisoner against my express orders."

Jäeden's head snapped up and he shot a terrified look at Räesha. He opened his mouth, and then shut it again. Räesha smiled benignly at him and nodded that he should proceed. Jäeden turned back to the Doyäenne and took a deep breath.

"She didn't compel me," he said miserably. "She was nice. She shared her food with me and...I knew she wasn't happy that she couldn't see the prisoner, but...well, she was nice about it and...I guess I just wanted...I wanted to impress her."

Räesha raised her eyebrows. She hadn't expected that from the youth. She looked at him again and saw the flush of embarrassment creeping up his neck to his cheeks. He kept his eyes averted and twisted his fingers as he awaited the Doyäenne's next question.

"After you led the Sumäeri to Lanäe's room, did you stay to hear their conversation?"

"Y-yes."

"And what did you hear?"

"W-well, at first Lanäe seemed happy to see her." Jäeden looked up at Räesha hesitantly, and then his shoulders slumped again. "Then they got into an argument and Lanäe took her to the groves. I followed them, but I wasn't close enough to hear what they said. I couldn't get any closer without being noticed, so I came back to wait for them." He looked up at the Doyäenne and crumpled to his knees. "I'm sorry I disobeyed you!" he cried. "She seemed so nice to me...I didn't mean to cause any trouble!"

"We understand, Runner Jäeden," the Doyäenne said as she lifted her head, allowing her voice to carry to the far recesses of the gallery. "The Sumäeri are treacherous, this one in particular. What is not common knowledge is that Wushäen Lanäe was this Sumäeri's younger sister."

Gasps and murmurings again filled the gallery, echoing throughout the round chamber. Räesha finally worked her bindings loose, keeping her hands hidden in the mass of tangled hair that tumbled to her waist. She checked the distance between her closest guard and her destination...it might work if she could distract him...

"Our young Lanäe came to us as the only member of the revered Angäersol family not to choose the life of the Sumäeri. She intimated to me upon her arrival her family's disapproval of her choice to become a Wushäen." The Doyäenne stepped down off the dais, turning to face the gallery behind her chair. "This Sumäeri came here today to change Lanäe's mind, and when she was unsuccessful, took matters into her own hands!"

The Doyäenne's accusations served to whirl the galleries into a frenzy. All eyes were on the Sumäeri, and she froze. Räesha realized that she couldn't escape if everyone in the room was watching her. She wouldn't make it three steps before the guards would be on top of her.

A loud shriek tore from the skies, startling the occupants of the tribunal. All eyes turned toward the large windows that opened out over the square. The stars were again blotted out behind the enormous shadow as screams of fear drowned out the Doyäenne's tirade.

Räesha didn't hesitate. She slammed her elbow into the ribs of the guard next to her, knocking him to his knees as she winded him. Grabbing the knife from his belt, she launched herself towards the Doyäenne.

Two guards charged her from either side of the matriarch, blocking her path. Sizing them up, Räesha determined that the larger guard would be the least likely to follow her successfully. She swept up little Jäeden and hurled him into the smaller guard, forcing the man to catch the boy rather than pursue her.

Brandishing the knife, she leapt over the cowering Doyäenne and sprang onto the large, ornately carved throne. Placing the blade between her teeth, Räesha leaped up to the gallery floor and pulled herself over the railings with her powerful arms. She felt the searing heat of a blade rake across her thigh.

Räesha hissed in pain through the knife in her teeth. The burly guard had thrown his knife well. It skimmed the back of her thigh before embedding into the wooden railing. It was a shallow but painful wound that seemed to glow brighter red in Orwena's scarlet rays shining through the window.

The lights of the hanging lanterns flickered eerily against her tattooed skin as she turned and threw her blade at the guard advancing towards her. It struck him neatly in the chest. More screams erupted around her as the guard fell over the railing to the floor below.

Baring her teeth in a fearsome grimace to intimidate any who might decide to impede her progress, Räesha charged along the railing towards the center of the gallery. She jumped over the three rows of spectators to the window sill. Hoping that she hadn't tarried too long, Räesha took a deep breath and leapt out of the window.

ChAPTER 6 - CONSPIRACY

Cédron floated on his back, alone in the deep, steaming pool carved from the rock beneath the private quarters of the castle. The mineral-laden water bubbled up from deep geothermal pockets and was siphoned into pipes which carried it throughout the castle. The steaming water was then used to warm rooms, fill baths, and provide the kitchens with hot running water on demand. Bathing was one of the greatest pleasures of living in the castle in Dúlnat, especially during the brutal mountain winters.

The wounded boy held his breath and rolled over, allowing the healing minerals into the abrasions on his front side. The willow bark had done its work. His skin tingled only slightly instead of stinging from the hot water swirling into the open wounds. He held his breath as long as he could, enjoying the weightless sensation as his body floated on the top of the water. Cédron wondered if the freedom in weightlessness was similar to the release of one's Árk'äezhi energy upon death. *I'll find out if I stick around here much longer.*

Cédron heard footsteps approaching. The denseness of the water made them sound close and loud, but he knew that whoever advanced toward him was still on the far side of the baths. He stayed in his position face down in the water, despite the burning in his lungs, to see what kind of reaction his visitor would give him. The interloper was barefoot, so probably not there to harm him, but it might be safer to play dead until his identity was known. If someone was going to try and attack him again, the baths would be the perfect place for it. His drowning could easily be considered accidental, especially after the beating he'd received and the willow-laced tea he'd been forced to drink upon his arrival at the castle.

Silence. Cédron waited. His heart began pounding loudly in his ears, blocking out any sound of approach from above the water. He hadn't heard retreating footsteps, so whoever was out there was either standing still or sneaking quietly up on him. Cédron's aching lungs screamed at him to roll over and take a breath, but his panicked mind urged him to stay still, pretending to have drowned.

He reached out with his consciousness, trying to discern the intent of whomever it was lurking behind the columns of the baths, silently watching him. Dead silence. His heart pounding in his head, Cédron felt a slight tremor in the air above him. Ice cold water poured onto the center of his back, shocking his skin in the steaming water and causing him to involuntarily inhale water as the attack registered in his brain.

Coughing and sputtering, Cédron rolled over and stood up defensively in the chest-high water. Unable to see clearly, he held up his hands and shot a spray of water in the most likely direction of his attacker. Calling on his magic, Cédron sent shards of water sharp as arrows. They pitted the quartz pillars surrounding the enormous bath. Shaking his head to clear the liquid from his bruised eyes while trying to isolate his quarry, Cédron inhaled deeply to quiet the throbbing of his pulse in his ears.

To his consternation, laughter echoed off the highly-polished rose quartz walls and reverberated into his ears. Looking around, Cédron found Tóran standing behind him. In his hand, an empty goblet dangled over the water, the condensation from the ice-cold liquid still clinging to the outside of the silver cup.

"I can't believe I got you!" Tóran chuckled as he set the goblet down on the rim of the pool and slid gingerly into the warm waters. "Sorry if I frightened you...I just couldn't resist the temptation."

Coughing the last of the water from his lungs, Cédron took a deep breath and yelled as loud as he could, channeling his built-up fear and aggression into sound rather than the more dangerous magical energy. The stained-glass windows shook, causing their figures to move as if they were alive.

"Mijáko piles, what were you thinking?" he sputtered finally. "I could have killed you!"

Tóran dunked his head into the pool and waved his good arm towards his brother, beckoning him closer. "Aw, I knew you were listening...and your sense of direction always was terrible. Besides, I just wanted to see if I could still sneak up on you, that's all." He lowered his eyes at Cédron's glare. "I didn't mean to scare you, you know."

Cédron gaped at his brother's easy posture, remembering the anger Tóran had worked so hard to hide earlier. He saw no trace of it now, only a mischievous glint that offered a challenge on several levels. Exhaling the remainder of his anxiety, Cédron moved closer to his brother and clasped his right arm. Tóran's left arm remained splinted and wrapped tightly.

"Good to see you, too. Oh, and congratulations on your win today," he added awkwardly.

Tóran raised his left arm. "It cost me though. The master healer said I'll have to wear this cursed splint until Autumntide!"

Cédron snorted. "That's unlikely. And how is he going to ensure your compliance?"

Tóran grimaced and sat down in one of the smooth carved benches along the inside wall of the bath. The water reached the top of his shoulders and he closed his eyes, laying his head back on the rim of the pool.

"I've been relieved of my legion duties for the next fortnight as a beginning."

Cédron nodded.

Tóran peered at his brother, his amber eyes contrasting Cédron's moss green gaze. Tóran's mouth opened wide in surprise. "Oh, what's this?" He grabbed playfully at Cédron's jaw.

"Ow, careful! It's just bruising, no big deal." Cédron tensed, trying to sense if a greater threat lay behind his brother's apparent teasing.

"No, it's...I can't believe it!"

"What?" Cédron asked, trying to catch a glimpse of his face in the reflective water.

"It's a hair on your chin!" Tóran chuckled. "You've grown up a bit this year."

Is that all? Cédron took a deep breath and allowed his shoulders to relax. He shoved Tóran away from his face, splashing water at his brother as he'd done when they were younger. "Stop teasing me. Having the body hair and bulging muscles of your monsaki brethren is nothing to brag about."

"Psht! At least the monsaki have tails and can swing from trees even with a broken arm." Tóran pursed his lips together and frowned. "I can't even pull on my own boots."

Cédron watched his brother silently as Tóran stood up from the submerged bench and launched himself on his back out into the middle of the pool. The young man floated to the center, his long dark braid dangling beneath the surface. Cédron knew how frustrating a broken arm had to be for Tóran. Forced inactivity for someone like him would be maddening, and Autumntide was just over a month away. Tóran would be like a caged animal.

Cédron leaned back into the seat and let his gaze wander to the murals on the bathroom's walls. He'd observed the vignettes of Muralian history hundreds of times growing up, but he'd never really paid attention to them until now. The first lancet depicted Lord Shamar and Lady Muralia in all their celestial glory, ruling the heavens from their seat among pearly-white clouds shaped like pillows. The subsequent lancets followed the story of how Lord Shamar's trusted advisor Laylur had fallen in love with the deities' daughter Hamra and plotted to take over the heavens with her as his queen. The battle scenes were brilliant in their displays of vibrant colors gleaming in the last rays of Lord Shamar's light.

Below the lancets, the deities' daughters Azria, Orwena and Hamra appeared in smaller scenes along the lintel, each adhering to her own specialty. Azria inspired healing, Orwena led the warriors, and Hamra tended births and deaths. Priestesses throughout the lands still filled the temples to serve these deities despite the fact that they'd abandoned the people of Muralia centuries ago. Only the Shäeli, the first people created by the deities, had maintained a connection with Lady Muralia and her daughters. The source of Árk'äezhi that lay deep within their borders had become forbidden to the rest of Muralia's lesser peoples after the War of Betrayal.

Lesser peoples! Cédron pounded the water. Just because he wasn't of pure blood, the Shäeli believed him to be an abomination. He'd overheard his parents speaking of it once when his powers first manifested. They knew that the superstitious Askári would fear him, but the Shäeli would simply kill him as an insult to their purity, rejecting him and his exceptional talents without consideration. *Aren't my talents worthy of embracing? Even the full-Shäeli only ever developed one talent from a small pool of abilities. I can harness all of the five elements...sort of. What gives them the right to perceive me as a lesser person or, even worse, an abomination?*

Cédron stared at the water in the pool and waved his hands in a small circle. He felt the energy rise from his chest and flow from his fingers. The water began to churn slowly.

Tóran's body spun gently in the current. With his eyes closed, the wounded legionnaire remained oblivious to the forces acting in the water.

The slender brother envied Tóran his muscular physique. Glancing down at his supple but thin legs and arms, he groaned at his inadequacies. *So much power in such a spindly body...Lady Muralia has a twisted sense of humor in allowing me to exist.*

Cédron's eyes again raised to the murals, following Muralian history through the ancient battle between Lord Shamar and Laylur. The scenes followed Laylur's betrayal and Hamra's despair. The final window depicted the sacrifice made by the deities that would imprison Laylur in his subterranean realm for all eternity. The decision forced them from their heavenly realm and into the celestial bodies they inhabit to this day. Cédron followed the story and wondered what circumstances caused Laylur to become a demon.

Perhaps he is just represented as demonic. After all, hadn't the occupants of the rapturous demesnes been beautiful celestial beings created by Lady Muralia? What makes some better than others, deities and demons, First Peoples and lesser peoples?

For the first time in his life, Cédron felt a pang of sympathy for the name that had been vilified by all Muralians since the dawn of time in their world: Laylur. *Was he really evil and imprisoned with his followers because he tried to destroy the world and sky as we've always been taught? Or was it because of his forbidden love for Hamra that he was cast down? Where was the justice in that?*

Righteous indignation flared in Cédron's chest as the similarities between his situation and Laylur's swirled around in his mind. *Is it my destiny to be killed or imprisoned for the good of the world as well, just because people fear and misunderstand me?* Anger built up in his body and bled into the current of Árk'äezhi energy being shot from his fingers into the water, causing it to swirl faster as his feelings intensified.

Tóran must have felt the increase in centrifugal force, for his eyes opened wide and he dropped his feet to the bottom of the pool. "What's happening? Cédron, what's the matter?"

Feeling the frustration and anger building at his impotence in shaping his future, Cédron snarled, "I've got to get away from here!"

The Árk'äezhi flowed from his body, causing the swirling water to burst forth with his cry and spin into the rose quartz columns that stood on each corner of the pool. Spray soaked the walls on the three sides that faced the boys, dripping quietly onto the marble floor. Tóran watched the angry demonstration with pursed lips, his good hand on his hip.

"That's why father is pushing to name you as his heir, you know. It's because you can do stuff like that. He thinks you'll be able to convince the people of Dúlnat that you'll be able to protect the city."

Cédron slumped his shoulders and snorted. "They want to kill me *because* of my magic. How can he possibly think that he'll convince them otherwise?"

Tóran's eyes hardened as he scrutinized his brother. Cédron sensed Tóran's disapproval but kept silent. The tension between the two brothers coalesced as Cédron waited to hear what Tóran knew of his father's plans.

"He's going to make you deceive them at the festival."

"What? How?" Cédron 's heart beat faster. *How has Tóran learned of father's plans? We only just discussed this!*

"By igniting Skáresk."

Cédron swallowed. *He knows about Skáresk.* The blade was believed to have beheaded Laräeith the Betrayer; it was the weapon inlaid with the sacred Askári firestone. Only a true Askári would be able to ignite the firestone, but the Askári lost their ability to access their magical energy centuries ago when Laräeith destroyed all but one of the sources of Árk'äezhi. Later, the sacred firestone was stolen by the monstrous Garanthian tribes of the north. The sacred firestone and its potent magic had been lost to the Askári ever since.

Now the Askári feared magic, allowing only those few trained in the Mage's Guild to wield their amulets and talismans under constant scrutiny and suspicion. It was Cédron's Shäeli blood that gave him the necessary access to magic that would allow his father to manipulate him for his own purposes. *Father has embedded a common firestone into the hilt of the sacred sword. Only a mage would really know the difference between a red stone and the sacred firestone now, since only a mage, or I, could ignite it.* Cédron thought about the implications of continuing to play innocent with Tóran and his brows furrowed.

"I could. In fact, that might work."

Tóran's eyes narrowed. "You wouldn't dare!"

Cédron shrugged. "I said I *could* do it. I didn't say I *would.*"

"I would kill you myself before I let you betray our people like that!" Tóran hissed, easing himself around Cédron to the edge of the pool where his clothing and weapon lay.

The hair on the back of Cédron's neck raised as his skin prickled. His blood seemed to turn to ice, flowing sluggishly through his veins and sinking his heart. Something was very wrong. It wasn't just Tóran's suspicion of him; it was his father's insane idea to even try to pass him off as heir to the Regency.

The Askári people of Dúlnat would never accept him as their Regent, no matter what Kásuin did or said. The vicious beating he'd gotten at the festival was proof of that. Even his beloved brother would turn against him if he went through with the ceremony. *What is father thinking?*

"Perhaps you have a better alternative?" Cédron asked Tóran, backing away from his brother.

Tóran walked up the short steps out of the pool, keeping his eyes on Cédron. He dried off as quickly as he could, using only his right arm, and struggled to pull on his pants over his damp skin.

"Get out of Dúlnat. It's the safest way for you," he said finally.

Cédron nodded. He climbed out of the pool and dried off while Tóran wrestled with his shirt and sling. He slowly approached his brother and pulled the sleeve out gently, allowing Tóran to slide his broken arm through the opening. Cédron helped Tóran re-sling his arm and tied the fabric harness behind his neck.

"Thanks," Tóran mumbled, avoiding Cédron's eyes.

Cédron sighed. "I wish things were different." He donned his own pants and shirt, pulling on his boots over bare feet. Cédron surreptitiously watched Tóran fight successfully with his own boots but lose the battle with his sword belt.

"Here, let me help you with that," the fair-haired boy offered, reaching for the belt.

Tóran grasped the hilt of his sword almost instinctually. Stunned, Cédron stepped back, his palms up in surrender. He held his breath, watching his brother's face.

"Old habits," Tóran apologized, his lips in a tight smile.

Cédron exhaled slowly, stilling his rapidly beating heart. The last thing he wanted to do was fight his brother, the winner of the Warrior's Challenge and hero of the people. Cédron stopped. His eyes opened wide and his jaw fell open. Thunderstruck, he reached out to one of the quartz pillars for balance as his thoughts coursed through his brain faster than he could process them.

"I've got it!" he breathed, eyes dancing at the epiphany.

"Got what?" Tóran fidgeted uncomfortably at his brother's sudden animation.

Cédron looked around, making sure nobody else was near the bathing room to overhear them. "I think I've figured out how to solve our problems. Father wants to name me heir

74

and he needs me to ignite Skáresk in order to get the people to support that decision-"

"Yes, but they'll never follow you," Tóran interrupted. "The legion won't support you. They hate the Shäeli. Without them-"

"I know." Cédron brushed aside the argument. "We're going to make *you* the heir to the Regency."

It was Tóran's turn to drop his jaw in surprise. "How are you ever going to accomplish that? Father has no intention of naming me heir. I'm not a Varkáras by blood."

Cédron grinned. "He won't get to. The people will. Look, you're heir in everything but name anyway. You look like a Varkáras, except you're too short and hairy." Cédron punched his brother in the shoulder. "The people adore you as the youngest champion of the Warrior's Challenge and, most importantly, you're full Askári."

"All true, but how are you going to get around Regent Kásuin's naming ceremony?" Tóran asked.

"Ah, now that's the best part." Cédron tapped his temple, grinning broadly. "I'll simply not ignite Skáresk until it's in your hands. I can cause the stone to flare even if I'm not holding it. We'll make it look like *you* ignited the firestone!"

Tóran sat down on a nearby bench, his eyes glazed over as he imagined the possible consequences of such a deception.

"Father would know."

"Father would *suspect*. He wouldn't *know*." Cédron gripped his brother's right shoulder. "He would never be able to prove it wasn't you, and the people would force him to acknowledge that it was."

Tóran was silent, his eyes focused on the intricate tiles of the floor.

"You can't tell me you don't want to be named heir," Cédron said, crossing his arms over his chest.

Tóran exhaled loudly. "No, I can't. I want it. I've always wanted it."

"And now you can have it," Cédron exclaimed, clapping Tóran's shoulder. "And maybe then I'll be free to go to the Mage's Guild."

"Aye, the Mage's Guild might be a more appropriate place for you," Tóran said. "But first we need to figure out how we're going to get you through the ceremony. The legionnaires want you and Rováen executed or exiled, and I've heard that they have a lot of followers among the citizenry."

"What? You mean...they would actually defy their Regent's orders?" he asked, incredulous.

Tóran's shoulders slumped. "I didn't want to have to tell you. I was hoping to convince you to leave Dúlnat quietly...and quickly."

"Tell me what?"

"Nobody's forgotten that you're half-demon, Cédron. People are terrified of you now that your powers have appeared." Cédron opened his mouth but Tóran raised his hand to silence him. "After father announced that he was going to name you his heir...well, you saw how the legionnaires reacted in the healer's hall. I don't know what prompted him to decide to make the proclamation now, but it wasn't the blessing of the people." Tóran grasped Cédron's upper arm and squeezed. "It's not safe for you here. You can't go through with the ceremony or you might get killed!"

Cédron frowned. *Has father gone mad? Why would he push for this now if I'm going to be killed at the ceremony...or during the festival...or in my sleep?*

"What can we do?"

"Maybe you could go in disguise?"

Cédron stood up and paced around the bench as he thought about it. "Yes, that might work. It would work better if we could convince father to cancel the naming ceremony and just end with the traditional presentation of Skáresk to the tournament winner."

"The trick will be convincing father," Tóran said, gingerly rubbing the skin that had been pierced by his broken arm bone. "I doubt we'd have trouble getting Rováen and Maräera to support cancelling the naming ceremony. They were arguing with father about it when I passed the megaron to bathe."

Cédron rubbed his hands over his eyes and face. The minerals of the bath had pulled his skin taut and caused the lacerations to itch slightly. "We'll have to be careful. If he knows we're up to something…"

"Maräera and Rováen will be discreet if we explain it to them, I'm sure," Tóran said quietly. "As long as it doesn't go any farther than the two of them. Otherwise we could both end up in the dungeon."

"What about Shozin? Do you think he'd help us?" Cédron asked.

Tóran snorted. "I'm sure he-"

The two were startled by a loud explosion outside the castle walls. Light flared behind the stained-glass windows as the staccato of more explosions rocked the evening sky. Panicked, the two raced from the bathing room and up the steps to the courtyard. Tóran stopped short when he reached the courtyard, and Cédron slammed into his rigid form. Both young men stared with wide eyes at the sight playing out above the ramparts of the castle walls.

Chapter 7 - An Unwelcome Visitor

Screams erupted all around the courtyard as another projectile shrieked up to the twilit sky and exploded into thousands of showering stars. Cédron nudged Tóran in the ribs and pointed to a large shadowy figure racing back and forth atop the ramparts of the castle. Another rocket whizzed through the smoke trail of the previous one and, with a loud *BOOM*, burst like a waterfall from its heavenly cliff. The brothers watched the figure for another moment before Cédron realized what was going on.

"He's launching them himself...from up there!" He pointed at the figure running around the ramparts. "See, he has some sort of small torch in his hands and he's lighting those things."

Tóran squinted to clear his vision through the billowing smoke. "You're right. I wonder why the legion hasn't stopped him yet." Tóran scanned the lower courtyard for signs of the city's defenders mounting an offensive but saw only awestruck spectators with their necks craned to the deepening night sky. Looking across the ramparts, he was surprised to find guards mounted on either end.

"Somebody knows what he's up to," he said to Cédron, nodding at the ends of the ramparts. "The legion has mounted guards on either end...but I'm not sure if it's to keep him in check or to prevent others from getting too close."

Cédron shrugged, frowning. "Maybe it's both."

The boys ducked as a large explosion echoed through the courtyard and a brilliant dome of red sparks cascaded from above, hissing as they hit the flagstones around them. The citizens below oohed and aahed their appreciation, once they realized that the explosions were for display and not an attack. Cédron and Tóran leaned back against the white stone walls and watched the following rockets light up the night, relegating Orwena's vermillion hues to pale shadows as the half-moon lifted above the trees. Both were completely oblivious to the figure inching up silently behind them.

"What are you two doing here?"

Cédron's heart jumped to his throat at the challenge from behind him. He spun to face their attacker just a shade faster than Tóran, but he was unarmed. Tóran pulled a blade from his boot and crouched into a defensive position as the gravelly voice that had startled them began to laugh.

"That's a pretty wonderful distraction, don't you think?" Zariun grinned as he stepped out of the shadows and into the illumination from the rockets. "I could have knocked both your heads together before either one of you would have known what happened." He clasped Tóran's forearm and smacked Cédron on the shoulder. "Good thing I'm a nice guy." He paused. His voice took on a more serious tone. "I was sent by the Lord Regent to find you two."

"Father wants us?" Cédron asked, exchanging a glance with Tóran.

"Yes, he's in the megaron with Rováen and Master Chezak." Zariun turned and headed back inside the bathing room. "They're trying to figure out what to do about him." He bent his elbow, raising his thumb to point to the figure on the ramparts.

"Who is that?" Tóran asked as he fell in behind Zariun.

Zariun rubbed his ebony chin, a slight frown creasing his forehead. "Some mage." He shrugged and led them from the bathing wing.

The trio hastened to the megaron. The boys could hear their father shouting down the corridor as they approached the heavy double-doors.

"...how he got access to the ramparts and why the Hármolin Legion didn't stop him. It's a matter of security!" Regent Varkáras slammed his fist down on the desk.

Master Chezak caught Kásuin's eye and nodded towards the door. Cédron watched his father take a deep breath before he turned to face them, but his face was still flushed with anger. Kásuin's grey eyes accentuated the silvering of his dark hair. His father had aged much faster in recent years, but remained vigorous. He rose from the small table the adults were gathered around and crossed the room in a few long strides.

"Thank you, Zariun. You may return to your duties." Kásuin dismissed the dark-skinned youth. "Tóran, Cédron, I'm sorry to have interrupted your baths." He gripped each of them affectionately on the shoulders. "I'm afraid we have a problem."

"Who is that mage, father?" Cédron asked, looking from Kásuin to Rováen for an answer when his father hesitated.

Rováen grimaced but said nothing, deferring to Kásuin to answer the question.

"It's Algarik...my brother," Kásuin said finally, returning to the table and slumping back into his chair. "He arrived a short while ago, claiming to be seeking new recruits for the Mage's Guild in Taksábai. I put him in the guest quarters and placed a guard outside his room, but somehow he managed to get onto the ramparts." He waved his hand in the general direction of the window and shook his head.

"Perhaps he has a contact within the legion?" Shozin Chezak suggested, wiping his hand across his dark, shiny, bald head and frowning. "That would explain his ability to move about the castle unchecked and unchallenged."

"Laylur's beast!" Kásuin swore, pounding the table again. "If he's compromised my legion, I'll...I'll...Ugh! I can't trust him, yet I have no real recourse against him!"

Shozin drummed his thick, calloused fingers on the table top for a moment, then folded his enormous hands together. "Is it possible that he's come to challenge your decision of ascension?"

Kásuin sighed. "I supposed it is possible, though unlikely. He relinquished his claim years ago when he left to join the Mage's Guild and took Muhr as his surname." He gave Cédron a feeble smile as he gently traced his finger along one of the scabs that lined his son's cheek. "Although I've caused quite a stir announcing my intention to name you as the heir to the Regency, I don't think that Algarik will have any support should he contest your claim."

Cédron glanced at Tóran and back to his father. "Why not? He's a powerful mage and your brother. Wouldn't he have a reasonable claim?"

A pained look crossed Kásuin's face. The older man ran his fingers along his short, silvering beard as he contemplated his next words. "Algarik is my *older* brother, and the Regency should have gone to him, but our father chose me instead."

Both Cédron and Tóran raised their eyebrows, Cédron's face blanching visibly. They hadn't heard this story before. They never knew their father even had a brother, let alone one who had a claim to the Regency.

"Why wasn't Algarik chosen?" Tóran asked.

Kásuin's eyes darkened and he let out a long, whistling breath. "Because he abused his powers."

"What, he pulled rank a few too many times?" Tóran asked, trying to hide his guilty expression.

Kásuin shook his head, his eyes not leaving Cédron's stony face. "No, not that kind of power. He was — is — able to access fire energy. His abuse of his *magical* powers caused our father to," Kásuin paused, "to exile him for his own protection and the safety of our people."

A wave of nausea crashed over Cédron as the meaning of his father's words sunk in. *That's what he's going to do to me! I thought he wanted to name me heir, but maybe he's changed his mind. I wanted to leave, but I wanted it to be my decision, not...*

Despite the churning in his stomach, Cédron knew that there was more to this story. His father loved him and had done everything in his power to protect him. Perhaps that was why they'd never been told about Algarik before. Father planned to name him his heir, regardless of how ill-advised such a move would be. *So why is he looking at me so strangely?*

"Cédron," Kásuin said urgently, grasping his son's arm. "I want you to stay away from your uncle. I don't trust his intentions, nor do I want him influencing you."

Cédron squirmed under his father's intense gaze. "I'm sure he wouldn't be interested in me."

Even as he said it, he hoped he was wrong. Algarik was a mage. He lived and studied at the Mage's Guild in Taksábai, the largest in the world. What Cédron wouldn't give to have the opportunity to go there to study, particularly if he could convince the people of Dúlnat to accept Tóran as the heir to the Regency. The Mage's Guild would give him the freedom to explore his abilities in a safe haven free from the prejudice that the majority of Askári still held for magic wielders in general and Shäeli demons in particular.

Rováen had been watching the boy and recognized his discomfort. Getting up from his seat, he walked over to Cédron. "Look, I know how enticing his status as a mage must be to you, and I know that you're interested in studying at the Guild, but this is not the way. He is dangerous, Cédron."

Cédron cast his eyes to the floor, observing the sparkle of the cabochon stones inlaid in the floor. He looked at Shozin, who nodded grimly in agreement with his father's and uncle's opinions. Swallowing his disappointment and frustration, he nodded mutely. *Perhaps now is not the best time, but I've just turned sixteen and am nearing the age of manhood. I* will *begin making my own decisions about my future.*

Tóran stepped over to the window and looked out over the ramparts. "It looks like he's done with whatever that display was." He turned back to face the others. "He's headed to the main hall."

Kásuin nodded. "Let's get to the feast then." He stood in between Tóran and Cédron and wrapped his arms around each of his sons' shoulders. "This has been a challenging day. I want you two to stay close and keep an eye on each other."

As the small group entered the main hall from the megaron, Cédron noticed that scores of tables had been set up to seat the hundreds of guests. The old tapestries depicting the seafaring Askári of legend had been replaced by a brilliant display of banners representing each regiment of the Hármolin Legion who'd sent a representative to compete in the Warrior's Challenge. Maräera was already seated at the head table with her ladies' maids arrayed behind her.

Candles burned at regular intervals across the long tables, and lanterns containing glow rocks hung from ornate holders suspended from the ceiling, filling the room with brilliant radiance. When the group entered the room, a loud cheer erupted from the excited guests.

"Tóran! Tóran! Tóran!"

Voices chanted, boots stomped, and tankards struck tables to accentuate the cheer. The entire hall vibrated with rowdy energy for the new champion. Cédron shrunk back behind Shozin as Tóran took his place at their father's side. Kásuin beamed with pride as they were met with swarms of well-wishers. Shozin maneuvered Cédron between himself and Rováen and skirted them around the crowd to the high table.

The caravan master stopped in his tracks when he spotted Algarik already seated, isolated as the other guests at the Regent's table avoided sitting next to him. Shozin steered the other two along the walls hung with tapestries to a small table recessed in an alcove behind the dais where the high table sat.

"We should be able to eat here in peace," he growled, glaring at the back of Algarik's head. "Mind you don't wander off, boy," he admonished Cédron as they sat down.

"Why would I leave such esteemed company and the promise of outstanding food?" Cédron joked.

Shozin pointed his forefinger at the youth's chest. "You know what I mean." The dark-skinned man's eyes shifted to the high table and the mage seated alone.

Cédron shrugged and glanced about the room. He was grateful that Tóran had distracted the guests from his entrance as he hated being a spectacle. It was bad enough that he'd have to present Tóran with the fire sword Skáresk at the festival in front of the entire population of Dúlnat, including Pánar and Jorrél. His throat caught for a moment when he thought of the two errant legionnaires, but a quick scan of the room put his mind to rest. They were nowhere to be seen, and he had the added protection of Shozin Chezak and his Uncle Rováen.

Servants came over and quickly placed steaming plates of food on the small table. Cédron picked at the plate of baked cámbor and borage roots, remembering with a pang the many adventures he'd had with Tóran hunting the vicious little shellfish along the shallows of the Shásti River. He peeled the flesh from the tail and dipped the white meat into the warm herbed oil. Picking at his food, he glanced up at the high table to where his Uncle Algarik sat. *I wonder what he's like. Why does everyone think he's such a danger to me?* He finished the rest of his meal while Shozin and

Rováen ordered several rounds of triticale ale and argued the finer points of brewing.

Cédron slumped down in his chair and crossed his arms over his chest, tapping his foot in annoyance. *Why is it that I'm treated as a child by some and a pariah by others?* He glanced over at the high table where yet another round of toasts was being made in Tóran's honor. He didn't begrudge his brother's popularity or success, but it rankled that his younger brother had far more control over his life. Lost in his thoughts, the rest of the noises seemed to fade away. The clinking of platters being scraped by utensils was muffled beneath the blanket of indistinct buzzing of conversations. Cédron stared into the flaming candle in the center of their table.

The dancing flame lulled the boy into somnolence and his eyelids grew heavy. Numbness began to spread throughout his body, and Cédron was mildly amused to find that he felt as if he was floating a few inches above his chair. His thoughts turned to the amazing explosions his Uncle Algarik had launched over the courtyard. The colorful sparks had been beautiful once the initial fear of attack had worn off. *Magic is wonderful!* He ached to speak with Algarik about the extraordinary display and have a conversation as equals about the various techniques of using fire energy.

"*I think that would be a marvelous idea*," a voice whispered near Cédron's head.

At first, Cédron thought he'd only imagined the voice. His eyes snapped open and he looked around, but nobody was near. Shozin and Rováen continued their heated discussion, ignoring the boy completely. Cédron shook his head and stared back at the flickering candle. He gasped. A face was staring back at him from the center of the flame!

Glancing fearfully at his companions, Cédron realized that neither Shozin nor Rováen could see or hear the image in the fire. Compelled by curiosity, he looked back at the face. It grinned at him. A scar pulled at the left side of the face, turning the grin into a grimace, but the eyes seemed to twinkle with amusement rather than malice.

"*You don't need to fear me*," the face in the flame said. "*I would welcome a visit with a fellow magic wielder.*"

Understanding struck Cédron like lightning. He turned his head to stare at his Uncle Algarik who was still seated at the high table, his right as the regent's kin and formal representative of the Mage's Guild. The mage seemed to ignore the attention, but his head nodded slightly. *Uncle Algarik can communicate through flame! What I could do with such a skill...even father couldn't deny the uses of such an ability. What else can he teach me? Perhaps father's fear and overprotective behavior stems from an envy of his brother's powers. He certainly is trying to keep my abilities stifled, at least from public view. Rováen has taught me some things, but also holds me back from reaching out and testing my full potential. What are they afraid of? Maybe Algarik has some of the answers. We have a lot in common; we were both born with innate talents that caused our fathers to exile or imprison us for our own protection.*

Cédron suddenly wondered whose protection the removal of the magic wielders had really been for. He nodded. He would meet with Algarik and decide for himself whether the mage was evil or if, like Cédron, he was just misunderstood.

ChAPTER 8 - ThE REd mAqE

Algarik paced back and forth across the thickly carpeted floor of his opulent guest quarters. His long legs made short work of the expansive room. His brother Kásuin had spared no expense to host him in a regal manner, and that was exhausting Algarik's patience. The legionnaires posted at his door, ostensibly for his protection, only served to prevent him from accomplishing his true purpose: observing Cédron.

The red mage had been waiting years for the opportunity to interview him. Only a short while ago, his master had alerted him to a powerful presence of Árk'äezhi in the world that he needed to seek out. When Algarik's spies reported rumors of Cédron's growing powers, he knew that the boy had come of age and inherited his dual birthright. It had taken longer than anticipated to work out an excuse to leave the Mage's Guild, abandoning his regular duties while he observed the boy, but the lost time would be worth it.

Algarik grimaced in frustration. He was less than thrilled to realize that the Shäeli protector was still staying close to the boy; in fact, he rarely left the boy alone. They had forbidden Cédron from using his Árk'äezhi at all to protect himself from the fearful Askári who were bent on the young heir's destruction. All the signs indicated that Cédron was the one his master needed in order to achieve his goals, if only he could get the boy to understand his potential. He continued pacing, trying to decide the best method of approach. *Kásuin has no intentions of allowing Cédron anywhere near me, and that simply will not do. My master's prison grows weaker by the day, and he needs the boy to protect him. Kásuin has no concept of what his son means to the world, but I do. Together, we will change the face of Muralia.*

Striding across the room, his eyes caught his reflection in the glass. The trademark Varkáras silvering dark hair and grey eyes were warped in his ravaged features, making him look far more than just three years older than his brother Kásuin. Years of studying the arcane arts and dealing with demons had taken its toll. Scowling, he left the glass behind and slumped into a chair next to the window.

Looking out, Algarik realized that the small formal garden he thought was restricted to the castle grounds actually extended throughout the entire city. The Maräera Gardens, named for Kásuin's beloved Shäeli wife, were filled with exotic trees, flowers, and bushes from all the different lands. Traveling with the Varkáras Caravan had afforded Kásuin the opportunity to see many strange things and trade for the exotic items with which he'd decorated both his gardens and his city.

A tiny twilling flitted up from the gardens below and landed on his windowsill. Algarik smiled crookedly at the sleek little bird that returned his stare with clever black eyes. The mage made some chirrup sounds with his pursed lips and coaxed the skittish bird closer. He carefully pulled his hands clear of the voluminous sleeves of his robes. The ruby on his right hand glowed softly as he held it out for the twilling's inspection.

The diminutive bird hopped closer to the shining stone and pecked at it tentatively. Its black-tipped brown feathers ruffled slightly at the hard resistance of the stone. Chirping, the twilling cocked its head sideways, looking at Algarik through one eye as if asking a question. The red mage chuckled softly and whispered 'maftah.'

The twilling's feet that rested on the back of Algarik's hand burst into flames. Flapping its wings frantically, the tiny bird squawked in panic as its feet were rooted in place. The flapping wings fanned the flames and soon the tiny bird was fully engulfed. With a final, agonized chirp, the lovely twilling was gone, and Algarik blew the small pile of ashes on the back of his hand out the window.

Watching the ashes float on the slight breeze, Algarik thought back briefly to the day he'd been banned from the Varkáras Caravan forever. Always in the shadow of his charismatic younger brother and ridiculed for his preference for books over swords, Algarik had grown up angry and resentful. A chance encounter with a rogue mage during his early youth revealed his own innate magical abilities.

Algarik's father, Górdan Varkáras, feared his son's powers but had failed to monitor his actions. Algarik had turned to the arcane arts early as a means to extract revenge against those who had tormented him in his youth. As a result of his illicit experimentations with forbidden magic, young Algarik frequently found himself in front of either his father or the caravan master. He absently fingered the long scar that ran from his left cheek to his chin, forcing his features into a crooked half-sneer whenever he opened his mouth. He'd never forgive Shozin Chezak for the insult of whipping him in front of the entire caravan.

Young Algarik had been practicing with firestones when the wind whipped the fire out of his control. He'd said it was an accident when the wagon caught fire and killed an entire family, but no one had believed him. His stomach roiled with regret and resentment for his father's fear and prejudice of his magic.

Algarik remembered the day his father banished him, imprisoning him in the dungeons beneath the Mage's Guild in Taksábai. He could still feel the sting and itch of the blood seeping down his cheek from where Shozin's whip had torn his face. He could feel the cold steel shackles on his ankles and wrists and the hard, wooden bench he sat on in the wagon for three days as they traveled to Taksábai. His eyes burned with unshed tears at the memories of loneliness and rejection.

It wasn't until the red mage, Bín Nétar, found him that his life turned around. Mage Nétar understood what a treasure the young Algarik was and released him from his torment. Algarik had served Bín Nétar faithfully over the past decades, scouring all the lands for magical resources until his more recent discoveries shifted the focus of his duties. He had a new master now, one that would not tolerate excuses or mistakes. This master would make him suffer for eternity if this mission didn't succeed.

Algarik knew he'd have to be careful while in Dúlnat, with the long memories of both Shozin Chezak and his brother. They didn't trust him or the Mage's Guild. Although he had declared the purpose of his visit as seeking new candidates for the Guild, he was sure he'd deceived neither the caravan master nor his brother.

His frustration at their campaign to prevent him from seeing Cédron added further weight to his theory. They were keeping an eye on the boy and had that ale-befuddled Shäeli elder always within earshot. *I'll handle that old fool when the time comes! If only the boy had responded more positively to my invitation. I thought I saw him nod his head, but I can't be sure.*

The mage sat at his table, distracted by his churning thoughts. He levitated the handful of black stones littered across the tabletop and burst them into flame. He was entranced in the spinning wheel of fire he'd created a foot above his table when his thoughts were disrupted by a knock at the door. Cursing the interruption, the stones fell and scorched the fine wood table. Algarik rose and answered the door.

A Hármolin Legionnaire stood in the doorway and saluted the mage. Scowling, the mage stepped back so the soldier could enter the room. *Now what? Another frivolous audience with some urchin with delusions of grandeur, I suppose.*

"Levirk Sirkran, at your service," the lean soldier announced. Under his breath, he muttered, "Please set up the sacred circle so we can speak privately."

Algarik looked more closely at the soldier, then grinned crookedly. He recognized the pointed goatee and the tiny, narrow-set black eyes of the Hazzara spy he'd sent to infiltrate Dúlnat's Hármolin Legion. Algarik was looking forward to the debriefing with this agent and quickly moved his chair out of the way to clear a space for the two of them.

The mage dug into the pouch at his hip and pulled out a handful of sparkling black powder. He scattered it in a circle around them, then removed one of the candles from his table and lit the powder. The flames burned instantly in a bright purple fire that consumed nothing but sound.

"Report."

"The Hazzara have successfully retrieved the Askári's sacred firestone from the Garanthian tribes to the north." He pulled out a bundle from his pack and handed the wrapped object to Algarik.

The mage unwrapped the stone, revealing the palm-sized cabochon ruby that had once been embedded in the sword Skáresk before being stolen during the Garanthian Wars. A thin smile tugged at the mage's scarred cheek.

"Excellent. Any casualties?"

The false legionnaire gave a high-pitched chuckle. "None from our ranks. The Garanthian tribes are marching south, slaughtering everyone in their paths in retribution for the losses they suffered."

The mage nodded. He held up the firestone to the glow stone's light and marveled at the internal fire the gem displayed. Sighing appreciatively, he returned it to Levirk Sirkran.

"I want you to hide this in Kásuin's armory. Put it in a box but place it away from the fire sword Skáresk," the mage instructed.

Levirk raised his eyebrows in question, but shrugged and re-wrapped the stone, placing it back in his pouch.

"I trust you can access the Regent's quarters without difficulty?" Algarik asked.

"I have enlisted two young soldiers to our cause. They are friends with Tóran and are usually the ones on guard in the Regent's private quarters. There is some history between these two legionnaires and the Shäeli boy. They gave that little demon a proper greeting at the Warrior's Challenge earlier today." Sirkran grinned.

"What have you heard of Cédron's abilities?"

"They appear to be quite significant, but at the same time, still largely uncontrolled. There was mention of starting fires and harnessing wind and water into funnels that did some damage, but no casualties. He's even been blamed for the increasing ground shakes, but there is no proof that he's the cause. He has shown some healing knowledge, but Kásuin is keeping him under close watch. He has been forbidden to demonstrate any of his talents publicly."

"Excellent. That is exactly what I'd hoped for. What about the legion? Do we have everything in place?"

The soldier's wicked eyes gleamed. "That part was almost too easy. We have exactly what we need. The Hármolin Legion will not pose a threat to us."

Algarik nodded. *I know better than to take all that for granted, but it won't behoove me to argue with this agent yet. I'll do my own assessment of the legion as soon as I finish with the boy.*

"Well done. You're free to return to your duties for now. Do not contact me until after the festival unless something comes up." Algarik dismissed him and waved his hands over the circle, extinguishing the flames. The soldier turned on his heel and left the room.

Algarik returned to the window and looked out at the waters rushing down the falls and into the basin below. The red half-moon Orwena was high in the sky now, and her blue sister Azria was just edging over the tips of the trees. *My plans are falling into place, but I need to remain vigilant. There are always ways in which things could go awry. I can't afford blunders now, given what is at stake.* His eyes involuntarily shifted to the carved black stone sitting on the end of his desk.

Algarik shivered slightly. He remembered the day he'd found the onyx obelisk and the demon imp trapped inside. The little creature had seduced him with its visions of conquest and control over the world's people and her elements. The knowledge and power it promised him had been so enticing for a price that, at the time, had seemed relatively small. Algarik had no visible scars from the payment the imp extracted, but the rent in his soul could never be healed. Still, it had been worth it. The imp had opened doors for him that would have taken a lifetime of sacrifice to achieve by himself.

Algarik wandered over to his table and picked at the fruit the servants had left while he'd been at the banquet. Sitting in the plush chair, he popped a few grapes into his mouth. Dúlnat was situated in a fairly harsh climate, so while grapes and berries were plentiful, Dúlnat was short on the citrus fruits he'd become accustomed to in Taksábai, or the succulents available only in Yezmarantha. Still, the tart berries and grapes were refreshing and certainly made excellent wines, as he had discovered during the feast. He would have to make sure that his armies of Hazzara spared the wineries and refrained from slaughtering the vintners on their way through the white city.

When he created the Hazzara, he'd recruited only the best and the brightest from each of the lands' guilds. From there, he sent them to Zen Hazad, known to most only as The Shadow, in the Zahili Desert for training. The Shadow had been training an army of mercenary assassins for decades. Forming an alliance with him had been one of Algarik's earliest coups.

Although Dúlnat didn't have any formal guilds to recruit from, there were many artisans who would be worth approaching. Winning their loyalty away from his blasted brother would only be the first hurdle. Everyone had their own price. The mage held high hopes for his nephew as well. *The boy has a heritage to envy. The potential is limitless, and I mean to have control over him. But…I'm running out of time.*

CHAPTER 9 - FUGITIVE

Räesha circled high above the clouds over her family's lands outside the Shäeli capital of Suriyäeh. The hard lump of emotion that she'd held at bay since her sister's slaying threatened to choke her, but she knew that her time for grieving had not yet arrived. Now a fugitive of her own people, every dream and ambition cast aside with her new purpose, Räesha allowed herself only a brief visit to her family's home to alert them to the corruption among the Wushäen and to bring them a warning.

The Sumäeri looked again over her shoulder. She wasn't aware of any signs of pursuit yet, but she knew it was coming. She hoped she'd have time to get her message to her family before the arrival of the Council Guard sent to apprehend her. Räesha hated to put her family at risk, but they had to be warned if their people were to survive this impending disaster.

Turning her attention back to the storm, she dug her knees into the Yongäen's neck and steered him down into the clouds. Räesha ignored the pain in her thigh and the chill of the rain and wind as the raptor spiraled tightly toward her family's ancestral home. Lights shining through windows illuminated the lawn through the storm, revealing the room that her family occupied.

Cold dread swept over Räesha at the thought, and she glanced back over her shoulder again. Her breath caught in her throat as a line of lights became visible on the road toward her house. Looking closer, she could make out a

domed carriage adorned with lanterns, the escorts mounted
and armed. Something powerful emanated from the domed
carriage, but she couldn't place its source. *The Council has
anticipated my plans and sent a contingent to arrest me!*

Landing, Räesha leapt from Yongäen's back and sprinted
into the house from the patio that held so many fond
memories of family gatherings. She spied the shelf where
her father had displayed her artwork from childhood and
vials of her sister Läerei's first experiments with toxins.
Shaking her head, she raced past the display, searching for
her family. She didn't have time to indulge in such
recollections.

"Mother! Father!" Räesha called as she charged up the
corridor from the kitchen to the study where she'd spotted
the lights from above.

"Laylur's beast, Räesha!" her father Räebin exclaimed as
he stuck his head out the door at the racket. "What...how are
you here?" He threw the door open fully and embraced his
eldest daughter.

"Father!" Räesha held Räebin tightly. She released his
embrace only to find herself in her mother's arms, then each
of her sisters in turn.

Elder Räelin kept his distance, his bushy eyebrows
knotted below the wiry silver hair that escaped the cap of his
station. "I don't know how you come to be here, my dear,
but it is good to see you."

Räesha broke away from the twins and stepped over to
Elder Räelin, clasping his arm in formal greeting. "Elder
Räelin, I'm glad you're here. I have very little time, but I
bring a warning."

Räesha bade her family sit while she quickly explained
the events that had taken place in Siläeri. She described how
Lanäe had been set to stand before the tribunal as a result of
her contact with the Meq'qan spirit of Auräevya and the
message the specter had given her. She wasn't sure of the
accuracy of the message, but she intended to seek out this

child of Maräera's and see if he had the ability to wield the Sceptre of Kulari.

Räesha's voice thickened as she recounted the attack and her discovery of Lanäe's body. Her mother squeezed her hand as she swallowed against the hard ball lodged in her throat. Sucking in a ragged breath, Räesha related how the Doyäenne had sent her before the tribunal and found her guilty of slaying her sister. Gasps erupted around the room at the unexpected turn of events.

"You mean the Doyäenne actually believed that cart driver over a Sumäeri?" Eläeni raged, crossing her arms and drumming her fingers along the tattoos lining her biceps.

Räesha nodded.

"Look, regardless of what Lanäe said she saw or what the Doyäenne believed, the fact of the matter is that we were attacked," Räesha said, turning again to Elder Räelin. "I saw the shadow behind the eyes of the driver of the cart. There was something inside him—something evil."

Räesha shuddered at the memory, then froze. Icy panic poured over Räesha as the implications struck her. *If the Wushäen are compromised and Laylur's minions know of my purpose, perhaps that contingent of Council Guard isn't just for me...*

"We have to get out of here, now!" Räesha said, her voice rising above the angry chatter of her siblings and parents discussing the temerity of the Wushäen. "There is a contingent of Council Guard on their way here now. I believe they knew I'd come here, but I don't think I'm their only target."

"What do you mean?" Räebin asked sharply, his eyes scanning the windows.

"I know this sounds impossible, but I just realized this is bigger than I'd thought," Räesha said, ushering her family out of the study and into the corridor toward the kitchen. "I will take Elder Räelin toward Suriyäeh on Yongäen, then head to Dúlnat."

Elder Räelin nodded, following her out to the patio. Eläeni and the three remaining sisters each grabbed their weapons and began filling packs from the larder, their countenances grim. Räebin rushed back into the room from the study, his eyes flashing with indignation.

"They dare!" The patriarch stormed at the brazen display of a lower-ranking Guard approaching his home. "I may be old, but I'm still a Angäersol! We are the greatest warriors the Sumäeri have ever seen!" He brandished the ancient sword that had been mounted on the wall in the study for over two decades since he'd retired from active service.

Eläeni walked to her husband's side and placed her hand on his arm. "We will stand together, as always." She bared her teeth.

"Come." Räesha motioned to her sisters. "I'll take you to your units. You must warn them of what's coming."

"No, we stand and fight," Läerei growled, her eyes glinting in anticipation of the challenge.

Räesha looked at her sisters; three sets of determined eyes set her teeth on edge. *They have no idea who is out there...or what. What will they do if it is their friends who have come to take us? Will they stand and fight? Any hesitation will kill us all.* Räesha nodded silently toward the back door, but her siblings stubbornly looked at their mother.

Eläeni placed her hand on Läerei's arm. "We can handle this. Go, warn your units."

"But we cannot abandon you," Läerei gasped.

Eläeni shook her head. "You aren't. You're preserving our future. Go." The Sumäeri woman pulled on the pendant that hung around her neck, breaking the clasp. She thrust the Angäersol crest and chain into her eldest daughter's hand, her eyes pleading.

Räesha nodded.

An explosion rocked the house to its foundations. The compression knocked everyone in the kitchen to the floor. Dense smoke filled the air, choking their lungs and stinging their eyes, blinding them to the terror that had just emerged from the domed carriage.

CHAPTER 10 - PLAYING WITH FIRE

Through his window, the pale cerulean glow of Azria cast its delicate light onto Algarik's hands. It was getting late for a visit. Algarik had begun fidgeting with the stones again when the onyx obelisk on his writing desk began wobbling. The stone transformed into an imp and hopped across the room. It scampered up onto the table top, its rickety legs and misshapen body hampering the progress of its sharp claws.

"The Master awaits your report," it hissed. Red eyes gleamed from deep within the jet-black stone.

Algarik stared at the figure for a moment, trying to decide his next move. *If my Master wants a report, I must give it. However, I don't want to risk scaring Cédron off either, should the boy decide to make an appearance.*

"He grows impatient with your delays." The tiny demon grinned, showing its rows of pointed teeth. The creature began preening its stubby horns with two-taloned claws.

"Be gone, churl!" Algarik spat at the little imp. It danced aside in hateful glee and returned to the desk and its original form.

Algarik sighed. He walked over to the looking glass and stared briefly at his image. The twisted, bitter mouth reflected his distaste for the task ahead of him as he poured a flask of liquid into the bowl resting on the table. He took two stones out of his tinder box and cracked them together, dropping the sparks into the bowl.

The liquid burst into blue flame. Algarik dipped his hands into the bowl, bringing them up with a flourish and wiping the looking glass with the liquid. The image of his reflection turned to flame as the liquid spread across the glass, engulfing it entirely. He focused his thoughts on the entity he wanted to contact. Slowly, another image appeared in the center of the glass. The tongues of blue flame licked greedily at the image from around the outside of the gilded frame.

"Master," Algarik whispered, bowing.

The entity in the glass remained shrouded in shadow, the flames the only illuminating element except for two exquisite, glowing eyes that took on the blue cast of the fire. The form floated amorphously in the mirror, blending in and out of shadow and flame. Cold from the depths of the ancient abyss seeped through the room and into the marrow of Algarik's bones.

"You have been strangely silent," the frigid voice rasped.

Algarik raised his eyes to meet his Master's unblinking stare. "I have been closely monitored, which has made it difficult to make any headway."

"There are none there who pose a threat to you, mage."

"No, but my objective requires finesse and tact. I don't want to arouse any suspicions or cause alarm. Our best outcome requires that our enemies remain oblivious to what is coming."

"What about the boy?" the creature hissed eagerly.

"He should arrive here any minute," Algarik assured the entity. "They suspected my interest and have warned him against me."

"You must bring him to me," the Master ordered.

"I will suggest that he visit the Mage's Guild in Taksábai. I'm sure that the idea will appeal to him. I don't want to use force until we know what he is capable of," Algarik replied.

"There is no time. The Garanth have slaughtered the Meq'qan tribes and are close to Dúlnat's borders. You must bring me the boy now!" the mirrored image demanded.

Algarik clenched his jaw and ground his teeth. *It is a fine line I'm walking. If I move too quickly, I could lose everything. If Cédron is even a fraction as powerful as we suspect he could be, having an adversarial relationship with him could ruin all our plans. If we want him under our control, we need him to be a willing participant; especially if the boy doesn't know exactly what it is he is participating in. I believe he is clever, and I don't want him asking too many questions.*

"I understand Master" Algarik bowed, knowing it was pointless to argue further. He would get Cédron to Thoromberk Fortress at his earliest opportunity, which, if everything went according to plan, might be sooner than expected.

A knock at the door caught them both off guard and severed the connection. The image evaporated, leaving only the blue flames burning merrily around the frame. Algarik rushed to the door and opened it, pleased to see his nephew waiting in the corridor. The mage smiled at Cédron and welcomed him into his chamber.

"I was wondering if I'd see you this evening," Algarik said. He kept his back to the mirror to obscure the flames still in evidence as he indicated Cédron should sit at the table.

Cédron's attention was focused behind Algarik on the flickering blue fire that was only just dying out.

"What is that?" he asked, crossing the room to the sputtering mirror. "How did you get the fire to burn without damaging the frame?" Cédron stepped around his uncle and ran his fingers along the wood.

"Ah, well now." Algarik hesitated, hoping to encourage interest without incurring fear. "That is one method of communication, like scrying. One focuses the mind on the flame and sends the intention to the other party."

"Like you did with the candle at dinner. I've only seen it done with stones or water. How can you scry through flame?" Cédron asked.

Algarik grinned. *The boy is starving for knowledge.*

"Well…" Algarik chose his words carefully. "We Askári live surrounded by the Sinharkon and Ronhádi mountain ranges. Both are volcanic, and historically we have held the sacred firestone in our care, which allowed us the ability to wield flame."

The mage wandered over to the window and folded his arms, staring at the blue cast of Azria on the courtyard and gardens below. "The Askári were all once natural fire wielders. Since the Garanth stole our sacred firestone during the wars, we have lost many of our abilities." Algarik paused and turned to face his nephew. "My heritage, as both Askári and Tawali, gives me added advantage. So, creating fire comes more naturally to me than to most. Perhaps you've noticed the same?"

"Hmm, it makes sense." Cédron conceded and shrugged his shoulders.

Algarik made his way to the large table and sat down, inviting Cédron to join him. The mage picked up an ebony carved pipe and lit it. Blue, sweet-smelling smoke circled around the mage's head as he exhaled.

Recognizing that his nephew was still unsure about him, Algarik decided to entice him with a more powerful demonstration. He pulled out three red tourmaline gemstones and set them, along with several yellow sphene crystals, in a circle in front of Cédron.

"I asked you to meet me because I suspect you may be what the Mage's Guild needs in these dark times. It is no secret that since Laräeith's Betrayal, the Mage's Guilds throughout Muralia have been in decline. There is little magic left in the world and even fewer still who have the ability to wield it for the greater good."

He watched the boy's face carefully to gauge any reaction to his words. Cédron remained guarded, his arms folded across his chest. Algarik was sure that the boy craved the freedom to pursue the abilities that he surely must have.

Algarik considered how he might convince Cedron to demonstrate his untrained skills.

"You," Algarik took out his pipe and pointed the mouthpiece at Cédron, "have Shäeli blood in addition to our Askári and Tawali heritage. I believe, therefore, that you may have the ability to become a great mage. You have the ability to work stone and fire, I assume, but I also suspect you could have access to the source of Árk'äezhi."

Cédron's eyes darkened. "The Askári call me a demon because of my mixed blood. It's why I'm imprisoned in the castle. Father doesn't want them to hurt me because of their fear."

"Your father is wise, and I'm sure he means well." Algarik winked, putting the pipe back into his mouth and puffing on it. Blue rings circled above the mage's head. "But I think that perhaps he is a bit overprotective of you. Let me give you a little demonstration, and then we can talk about your future, eh?"

Algarik pulled back the sleeves of his robes, revealing a large ruby ring on his right hand. The mage extended both hands and held them flat a few inches above the stones. Algarik closed his eyes and took a deep breath, exhaling slowly and concentrating. The ruby set inside the ring began to glow.

The yellow sphene crystals elevated slightly, bringing the red tourmaline along behind them. The stones began to spin in a circle in the space between Algarik's hands and the table. Then, clapping his hands once together, the red tourmaline burst into flame. The fiery vortex it created drew a slight smile from Cédron.

"Not bad." Cédron shrugged.

Chuckling, Algarik bent forward, putting his pipe beneath the swirling jewels. A thin spire of smoke wafted through the stones, spinning tightly as it rose. "I haven't found anyone, during the decade I've spent as Seeker for the Guild, that had even a fraction of what I sense in you," Algarik said, smiling. He thought he'd seen a flicker of interest in the boy's face as he worked with the crystals. "I want to see if you have what it takes to become a mage. If you do, I will do whatever is necessary to convince my brother that it is in your best interest to join the Mage's Guild and hone your skills."

Cédron stared at the red and yellow stones spinning a few inches above the table top. Algarik could tell that he was interested, despite his aloofness. He could sense Cédron's frustration with his father's restrictions. The freedom to study magic without prejudice would likely be worth some sacrifice to Cédron.

"What do you want me to do?" Cédron asked, his moss green eyes searching the grey depths of Algarik's.

The red mage smiled benignly. "Let's begin with some basic instruction, and we'll see where we land."

Algarik laid his pipe on the holder and turned his hand sideways, causing the circle of stones to fly vertically rather than horizontally. He waved the ring on his hand around, and the crystals mimicked his actions.

"It's all in the ring," he said. The mage turned his hand sideways so that the glowing jewel was clearly visible to the boy. "The ruby channels my Árk'äezhi energy into the stones, and my intention gives it direction."

"But why do you need the ring?" Cédron asked. "Can't you just move the stones yourself?"

"For those who are not inherently magical, the assistance of a talisman is required to collect, focus and channel the Árk'äezhi energy. One might use a wand, a ring, or even a staff." Algarik lowered his hand, extinguishing the tourmaline. He eased the swirling gems to the table where they continued to glow slightly with the residual expenditure of power.

"Many talismans were created with a specific purpose," Algarik continued. "The Rod of Shouman, for example, required the use of a firestone to harness what the Yezman called the 'fire in the skies.'"

Algarik noticed that Cédron sat straighter and seemed keen on this particular tack. He decided to continue with what he normally withheld for his more advanced students.

"There exists a field of powerful energy that is fueled by lightning. It circles the world, creating a buffer of power that is replenished by the lightning strikes. It is Lord Shamar's way of maintaining a lock over the land should the demon Laylur break through Lady Muralia's prison in the abyss. He would be alerted instantly by the change in the energy field."

"Doesn't Lady Muralia have any protection herself?" Cédron asked. "I know that there was a lot of magical energy lost after Laräeith's Betrayal, but we continue to live without the threat of demons."

Algarik was impressed with his nephew's astuteness for one so completely unschooled in the arcane arts and sciences. The mage took out a piece of parchment and began drawing on it. He created a sphere and roughly outlined the four lands for reference. Then, Algarik drew a circle around the world representing the atmosphere and a circle just inside the world's surface. He added sharp, jagged lines to indicate lightning between the barrier lines above the world to the line just beneath its surface.

"She does." Algarik turned the parchment around so that Cédron had a clear view as he pointed out the elements. "Lady Muralia has her own barrier of energy, what we call the Lluric Field. It runs beneath and within the land itself. It was also created as a warning system to alert the deities should the demons weaken their prison or escape."

Algarik pointed at the lightning strikes. "Lord Shamar replenishes Lady Muralia with his lightning strikes, which adds to the power of her Lluric Field, thereby maintaining the seal on the demon's prison." Puffing on his pipe, the mage blew several wispy blue rings into the air before returning his attention to Cédron and the lesson. "Now, the

Rod of Shouman was created by Laräeith's companion Salzem to counter the power of the Sceptre of Kulari that the Shäeli used to imprison Laylur in the abyss. The rod requires the use of a firestone to activate it because this staff is aligned to the fire element."

"What happened to the rod and the sceptre?" Cédron asked, placing his elbows on the table and leaning in closer to the drawing. "Do the mages use them anymore?"

Algarik shook his head. "The Rod of Shouman and the Sceptre of Kulari were the two most powerful talismans ever created. They have been dismantled, their parts hidden to prevent them from falling into untrained or unsafe hands."

Cédron pondered that for a moment. "Where is the Rod of Shouman now?"

"The pieces of the Rod of Shouman are in the vaults of the Mage's Guild in Taksábai."

"What about Skáresk? Did the sword get its flame from the fire within the stone, or did it harness lightning like the Rod of Shouman?" Cédron asked, studying the picture closely.

Algarik's eyes narrowed. He puffed on his pipe for a moment, causing Cédron to shift uncomfortably in his chair. "I believe that the firestone in Skáresk was the sacred firestone of the Askári. In that case, it would have drawn its flame from the Árk'äezhi of the wielder."

"The sword hasn't ignited for centuries. My father told me it was because the sacred firestone was stolen by the Garanth. Do you think that you or I could ignite the stone that's in it now?" Cédron asked. He looked up at his uncle's intense expression and gulped.

"It is a dangerous prospect on several levels. Is that how Kásuin is planning to convince the people to accept you as the heir to the Regency?" Algarik tapped the tobacco from his pipe into a plate and set the pipe down.

Cédron lowered his gaze to the floor. "Yes."

He scrutinized the boy for a moment, and then asked, "Is that what you want?"

Cédron shook his head and fingered the stones on the table in front of him. He picked up one of the yellow sphene crystals and held it to the light, noting its form and its flaws. Under his gaze and attention, the stone began to glow. Cédron quickly put it down and looked up to see if Algarik had noticed.

"No. I want..." Cédron took a deep breath and exhaled slowly. "Tóran should be named as heir; the people love him."

Algarik raised his eyebrows and sat back in his chair. *This is going to be easier than I'd expected.* "Which would free you from your father's obligation and allow you to study at the Mage's Guild?

"Yes."

Algarik drummed his fingers on the table, pretending to be lost in thought. His insides fluttered with excitement. *Everything is falling into place. My Master will be very pleased and will reward me generously.*

"Have you given any thought to how you might accomplish that?" the mage asked.

Cédron glanced at the closed door and the window. He nodded mutely but didn't elaborate. Algarik surmised his hesitation and patted the boy on the arm. Rising, he strode to his desk and pulled out a handful of powder from the pouch that still sat open on the corner. Sprinkling the powder in a circle around the table, he again called forth the flames that absorbed sound.

"None can hear us now." The mage winked at Cédron. "You can speak freely."

Cédron shifted uncomfortably in his seat. "I...I'm not sure I can trust you," he said, twisting a strand of golden hair in his fingers.

Algarik grimaced slightly. "You've been warned against me, I know. We are not that dissimilar, you and I. My father and my brother have always feared magic, which is why we have both been subjected to isolation and ridicule for our abilities."

Cédron twisted the hair tighter. "You abused your powers and hurt people."

Algarik's shoulders drooped. "The incident that caused my banishment was an accident that haunts me to this day." The mage's eyes flashed in anger at the memory. "My father had been waiting for an excuse to cast me out. His fear and vindictive prejudice cost me everything I held dear."

Cédron nodded, his eyes glistening in the moonlight. "That I understand."

Looking at the pale boy, so full of hope and promise, he almost relented. Sowing the seeds of distrust and severing the bonds of family had left the mage scarred and hollow, and he was now doing the same thing to Cédron.

The mage knew the pain and suffering the boy would have to endure once he realized the truth could destroy him. Still, the promise his Master had given him of the powers he would have at his command were more compelling. Algarik focused on the job at hand.

"My family misunderstood me," he began. "They rejected me. It was only when I reached the Mage's Guild that I found my true family, those who understood and appreciated my abilities." Algarik gripped the young man's shoulders and squeezed gently. "I can teach you how to harness your powers so that you don't make the same mistakes that I made. Let me help you."

Algarik locked his gaze on the boy's green eyes, willing him to comply. Slowly, Cédron nodded his head.

"Tóran and I decided that I would try to ignite Skáresk once I handed it to him, making it appear as if the sword was responding to him and not me," Cédron explained, his eyes focused on the flames encircling the table.

"Hmm, that might work," Algarik mused. "I think, however, that you would be wise to make sure that the firestone embedded in Skáresk was potent enough for you to ignite it at a distance. Do you have access to any of the stones coming from the mines?"

Cédron shook his head. "Father doesn't want to risk any accidents."

Algarik chuckled mirthlessly. "Yes, I'm sure that's true. Still, I would recommend that you search the castle and see what you can find. You will have only the one chance to convince the people of Tóran's abilities."

Cédron gave wry smile. "I'm not exactly allowed to wander aimlessly about the castle, going through my father's treasures."

Algarik stood. He waved his hands and the flames extinguished. "I may have a solution for that!"

The mage excused himself and strode to his sleeping chamber. He returned with a small creature tucked under his arm.

"A kesling?" Cédron laughed out loud. "They're good for sniffing out gas pockets, but not gemstones."

Algarik set the long-snouted rodent on the floor, maintaining a firm grip on its leash as the creature snuffled about Cédron's legs. The mage sat across from the boy and scratched the beast at the base of its neck, eliciting a pleased whine.

"What is not generally known about keslings is that they are also magical creatures," the mage explained in a low voice. "They can sense strong magic, so they would be able to identify stones that are more potent than others. Take it to the armory, for instance, and see how it reacts to Skáresk." He handed the leash to Cédron, who took it hesitantly.

"I'm not sure," Cédron said. "What if my father or someone found me snooping around?"

"Tell them the truth." Algarik smiled. "Tell them that you'd heard about the kesling's ability to sniff out magic, and you were testing it out. No harm in that." Algarik held his breath.

Cédron seemed to ponder the suggestion for a moment, and then smiled slightly. "Ok, I'll try it. If I find a powerful stone, all I have to do is replace the one in Skáresk, right?"

Algarik relaxed and smiled. "That's right. The sacred firestone was set just outside the guard in the pommel. The stone rotates in the setting to the left, releasing the prongs that hold it in place. I believe that a tourmaline now resides in the sword. If you can find a ruby or other charged firestone, it would be more powerful and allow you to ignite it from further away, making it seem as if Tóran activated the firestone himself."

"I understand." Cédron set his jaw. "Thank you, uncle, for your assistance. Now..." Cédron straightened in his chair and changed the topic. "Do you think that using a wand or ring like you do would help me focus my Árk'äezhi better than just a loose stone? Uncle Rováen has been guiding me. I've been trying to work with air, but I have had some trouble."

"Yes. I'll show you the basic principle of how they work." Algarik stood and waved the silencing fire away, then walked over to his desk and pulled out a crystal wand for Cédron to use. He handed it to the boy and explained. "First, you must quiet your mind, and then fill your thoughts with the desired outcome. See here..."

Algarik took off his ruby ring and put it into the folds of his cloak. He then closed his eyes and took a breath, focusing his energy on the wand, which began to glow with a soft light. He used the wand to raise the stones on the table and commence them to spinning individually on their own invisible axes.

The mage then lowered the wand and the stones and handed the glowing rod to his nephew. Cédron gingerly grasped the crystal wand and focused on recreating the swirling vortex his uncle had previously demonstrated. The wand glowed brightly and the stones easily lifted and spun.

Algarik's eyes sparkled with excitement. "Now, turn your intention to creating the flame of the tourmaline crystals," Algarik instructed.

Without any warning, the gemstones exploded in a red shower of powder and flame that shot shards of crystals throughout the room. The glass liqueur decanter that Kásuin had sent up for his brother's enjoyment shattered, spilling dark gold liquid all over the table.

"Oh, I'm so sorry." Cédron jumped up to clean the mess. The kesling squealed at the sudden movement and skittered out from under the lad's feet. Alcohol began dripping onto the floor in thick drops, and the kesling snuffled over to them.

Algarik's eyes narrowed as he watched his nephew. *The boy has far too much power to control through the wand. Certainly, he has more power than I suspected... I wonder...*

"I'm not sure what happened..." Cédron grabbed the platter with the remains of his uncle's meal and placed it on the floor under the table to catch the dripping liqueur. He shoved the kesling gently out of the way with the side of his foot.

"Please don't trouble yourself Cédron," Algarik said as he pulled the cord on the servant's bell, alerting the staff that their assistance was required. "I keep a man in the servant's quarters to assist me with things like this."

"I...I should go," Cédron stammered. "I didn't mean to ruin your robes, uncle."

Algarik smiled. The young man had proven to be a vast resource of untapped energy and had demonstrated that he could access it without the assistance of a wand or any other talisman. Algarik needed to soothe his nephew and maintain his confidence.

"I'm not made of sweetener, lad." Algarik shook his head. "I won't melt when I get wet. I also won't berate you for demonstrating your abilities."

Cédron smiled apprehensively. "Thanks, Uncle Algarik."

"Go on. Take the kesling and see what you can find. I'll handle this, and I'll discuss your future at the Mage's Guild with your father later tomorrow. You've demonstrated enormous talent. I'd like to see you in a place where you can learn to harness and master your abilities safely." Algarik grasped Cédron's arm and squeezed gently. "I'll do everything I can for you, Cédron."

Cédron smiled at his uncle and opened the door, shushing the squealing kesling as he stepped into the corridor.

"Mind you take care that you aren't followed," Algarik warned.

Cédron nodded and checked the corridor as his uncle had instructed. He picked up the kesling and scurried around the corner before the servant arrived to clean the mess. The baskets of glow rocks placed at intervals along the corridor gave him enough light to make his way to his rooms but were not bright enough to reveal the silent form, no more noticeable than a shadow, that lingered outside Algarik's quarters. It slipped away in the opposite direction once the young man left.

CHAPTER 11 - EMISSARY

Räesha flew above the Ronhádi Range, Yongäen's height flirting with the upper regions of atmosphere that barely allowed the two of them to breathe. There was little cloud cover this late in the Suntide season, so altitude was their sole option for camouflage. Pursuit would be close behind, and the Sumäeri didn't dare risk being caught out in the open.

Even though she was certain those who followed had no clear idea of where she was heading, she didn't want to make it easy for them to find her. Glancing behind her winged companion and down towards the green carpet of trees that lay spread out below them, Räesha allowed herself a full breath of relief. The squad of Council Guards which had nearly captured her at her family's home was nowhere to be seen.

Tears sprang unbidden to Räesha's eyes. *Now is not the time for grief. It is for vengeance.* The Sumäeri warrior swallowed hard against the tightness in her throat as a vision of her parents rose in her mind.

She would never forget how her father's eyes had filled with indignation at the Council's move against his family, or the frantic look on her mother's face as she broke her pendant and thrust it into Räesha's outstretched hand. *She must have known...but how could she have even imagined what they would be up against?*

Even before it had begun to overtake their home with its maelstrom of wild power, the Angäersols had felt its presence. Räesha had felt the first inkling of what the Council had set against them when she noticed the domed carriage. Whatever was being transported inside had great energy that had only barely been contained. She could sense the entity's rage at its confinement.

Only her fuzzy recollection of ancient history had allowed her to name the image of horror that had burst forth from the carriage: the Selväen. It was an ancient and fearsome creature of gnarled roots with a raging inferno in its chest. He had once ruled the forests of Muralia, until he had become corrupted with his own power. The Selväen had succeeded in laying waste to over half of the Ginäeyi Forest, what was now the Zahili Desert, before the ruling deities had stripped the immortal of the majority of his power and banished him to slumber in the deepest forest. *How could the Näenji Council awaken such a destructive force and let it loose on their own people? My life is forfeit for escaping the Wushäen, but to destroy my entire family...that doesn't make sense.*

The home had been razed to the ground, the gigantic wicker monster glowing from the feast fueling its internal blaze. Her parents would not have had any hope of stopping it. Only Yongäen's swift arrival had spared Räesha, Elder Räelin, and her sisters the same fate. Räesha had vaulted to her raptor's back, pulling her three sisters and the councilman up behind her with wrenching force. The läenier had escaped the destruction, but not before the group had one last look at the devastation. According to her memory, the Selväen was supposed to be a neutral elemental entity with no affinity for blessings or punishment. *How could the Näenji Council or the Wushäen have convinced it to destroy their home and kill her family?* The realization that such a force was loose and being used vindictively chilled her deeper than the frigid air that whipped against her skin.

Räesha didn't recognize any members of the Selväen's escort, and she wondered aloud to her sisters if they had really come from the Näenji Council. Although they hated to admit it, the Angäersol girls were in agreement. The unfamiliar unit had been wearing Council Guard uniforms, indicating that the Näenji Council must have become corrupted as well as the Wushäen. Their Sumäeri units had to be warned.

Räesha had delivered each sibling to her respective group before angling northwest to pursue her own overdue mission. Läerei had promised to look after Elder Räelin until he could be safely returned to Suriyäeh.

Yongäen altered his course slightly, dipping his left wing and nosing down into warmer air currents. Räesha spied the city of Dúlnat, a tiny sparkle of white between the two peaks in front of her. She still wasn't sure of what to expect upon her arrival, or whether Maräera's child would be the prophesied guardian Lanäe had promised, but it was the only lead she had, and there were few places in the world where she could go.

The Askári were ignorant and brutish, only marginally more sophisticated than animals. The thought of the only hope for her people coming from such an unlikely race fertilized the seeds of doubt that had sprouted in her mind. Her Uncle Rováen and cousin Maräera had lived among the Askári for nearly two decades and would be able to offer her better perspectives and sage advice. She would move on quickly, lest she endanger them as well. Räesha wasn't sure where her pursuers were, but she was convinced that they would hone in on her eventually.

The warmth of the air, as Yongäen spiraled towards the shining white tower, thawed Räesha's numb extremities. She'd pushed herself beyond reasonable limits to escape Samshäeli and was relieved to see her blue-tinged fingernails return to their normal pink. She rubbed her arms and legs to get the circulation back before landing. *No way am I going to appear weak in front of these lesser people.*

Yongäen screeched and extended his talons to grasp the battlements of the tower as it landed. Räesha felt a surge of pride for her fierce raptor as the Askári screamed and ran for cover. Surveying the city from her high vantage point, Räesha nudged the läenier with her legs, guiding him down to the courtyard below where she could dismount and leave Yongäen room to take off without causing any damage.

A small crowd of Askári gathered thickly around the edges of the wall to ogle the unfamiliar creature and its exotic rider. They kept their distance despite their curiosity, for the Sumäeri warrior and her beast were both foreign and fierce to behold.

None of Dúlnat's residents appeared brave enough to step within range of Yongäen's wicked beak or claws. The beast screeched loudly as he launched himself into the air to perch on the wall surrounding the castle. Half the spectators within a stone's throw screamed in terror when the he took off.

Räesha glared at the onlookers in contempt. *None of these stocky, ugly people are confident enough to look me in the eye.* Their stares were relegated to the foliage tattoos that fully covered her entire body, even around her face. She knew that she looked like a walking garden to them. *Ignorant kazan.*

The Sumäeri warrior hoped that Kásuin Varkáras would prove a more impressive specimen of the Askári people than those peeking at her from behind doors and windows like timid faerihks. She couldn't imagine a Shäeli woman forsaking her own people for such a mundane existence, let alone raising her child among such weakness and fear. The child would take on the attributes to which it was exposed. That was a dangerous prospect for the entire world of Muralia, should the boy prove indecisive or lacking a pure heart.

"I am Kásuin Varkáras, at your service Sumäeri," a strong, confident voice called from behind her.

Räesha turned as the charismatic Regent of Dúlnat stepped down the last stair and into the courtyard. He executed a gallant bow and held his hand palm up in her native greeting. She touched her downward facing palm to his.

"Well met, Kásuin Varkáras. I am Räesha Angäersol." Räesha met his gaze and was pleased to find both confidence and intelligence there. Noting his height and light eyes, she remembered he was also of Tawali descent. *Perhaps the boy will have the fortitude necessary to accomplish this task.* "I come with an urgent message from my people, one that requires a great service from you."

Motioning for the girl to follow him, Regent Varkáras turned and headed back up the stairs of the castle to his private chambers. Opening the door to his quarters, Kásuin pointed to a chair and suggested she make herself comfortable. He ordered refreshment be brought to his private quarters.

Kásuin closed the door after instructing the guard that they were not to be disturbed. Kásuin turned to face his visitor, noting the clear aquamarine eyes that regarded him coolly above her high, pale cheeks.

"How can I be of service to you?" he asked, bowing formally to his guest.

"Where are Rováen and Maräera?" Räesha asked, searching the large room for a sign of the only other Shäeli to have ever walked the streets of the white city.

"They should be here shortly," Kásuin said, crossing the room and checking the corridor. "Maräera was tending the gardens, but I'm not sure where Rováen has gotten to."

Kásuin closed the heavy wooden door again and turned to face Räesha. The Sumäeri smiled internally as his awkwardness became more pronounced. *He's not sure why I'm here and doesn't know what to do with me.*

Kásuin tried to engage her in conversation while they waited. He didn't ask about her family, an oversight for which she was grateful, if confused. He showed her around his room and pointed out the various artifacts he'd picked up in his travels with the Varkáras Caravan.

Räesha was impressed with the variety of decorations in the room as she wandered through it. She recognized the delicate glasswork of the Yezman artisans, the brightly woven tapestries of Datínai, and the grass mats of the Meq'qan tribesmen. She was particularly impressed with the small bust of Kásuin carved from onyx, probably from the Zaroon Quarry in the Zahili Desert. Its craftsmanship was exquisite. But there was something about the eyes. Her blood suddenly ran cold. *They're just like the cart driver's eyes, the one who accused me back in Siläeri,* she thought. *They flicker like ...like a demon's!* Räesha was loathe to touch the bust, but pointed it out to Kásuin. "That is an incredible likeness," she said. "Who made it?"

"Funny, I don't remember…" Kásuin was interrupted by a knock on his door and quickly let his oldest friend and wife in.

"Räesha! My, how you've grown." The elderly Shäeli man swept his niece into a tight embrace. "And your läenier is a formidable beast! He must be 40 feet long at least, and over half that high."

"He is," Räesha smiled slightly. "I've named him Yongäen." She squeezed Rováen tighter.

Rováen released her to step back, but the Sumäeri clung to him. She noticed the surprise in his eyes as she gripped his shoulders.

"Uncle Rováen, our family has missed you terribly," she said, her eyes tearing up. The questionable statue was momentarily forgotten.

Rováen's smile waned at the unusual display from the normally stoic warrior. "What is it, child? What has happened?"

Maräera embraced the Sumäeri gently, concern in her topaz eyes. "What news from Samshäeli, cousin?"

Räesha shared the story of her youngest sister Lanäe's encounter with the Meq'qan spirit of Auräevya and the fact that the Wushäen and the Näenji Council had chosen to ignore its dire warning.

"Then the rift between the Sumäeri and the Näenji Council continues?" Roväen asked, already knowing the answer.

"Indeed," Räesha confirmed. "Father sent me to mediate for Lanäe with the Doyäenne and the tribunal, but they refuse to believe there was any contact with the spirit of the tree."

"Where is Lanäe now?" Maräera asked.

Räesha grew somber again, her eyes full with the grief of her great loss. "She was slain by the demons that have already broken free of the abyss."

Maräera gasped, white knuckles clenching the armrests of her chair.

Roväen blanched and blinked his eyes rapidly in disbelief. "You have proof of this?"

"We were in the forest outside Siläeri when the creatures surrounded us. I fought them off briefly, but something struck me from behind," Räesha explained, her voice cracking. "When I regained consciousness, I was in a cart and Lanäe's ravaged body was thrown next to me. The Doyäenne believed the account from the cart driver that I'd slain my own sister. I escaped Siläeri, but not before I killed a Wushäen."

Roväen reached for Räesha and clasped her hands in his. "What of Räebin and the rest of the family?"

Tears flowed unchecked down Räesha's cheeks as she poured out the events of the past two days. She watched her uncle's face go slack with grief as she recounted the details of her parents' deaths. When she finished her tale, she sank into a chair, exhausted from her journey and the emotional trauma. Maräera got up and wrapped her arms around

Räesha's shoulders. The warrior leaned her head on the kind woman's chest, grateful for the comfort.

Roväen walked over to the large window that overlooked the Shasti Falls below. Kásuin's eyes followed Roväen's movements, but he took no step to comfort him or interrupt his thoughts. Roväen turned back to Räesha. He leaned against the carved window frame and crossed his arms across his chest.

"How can I serve you?"

Räesha stood. She glanced down at Maräera, over to Kásuin then back to Roväen. "If Lanäe is to be believed, and the preponderance of evidence suggests she is, then your son," she nodded to Kásuin and Maräera, "is the only hope for our world. I must escort him to the other major races and convince them to release their sacred elemental stones to him." Räesha adjusted the straps of her belt and spear harness. "I will then take him back to Samshäeli to train with the Sumäeri and be presented to Auräevya. If all goes well, then we hope the spirit of the tree will release the Sceptre of Kulari so that he can challenge Laylur. It is the only magic in the land strong enough to defeat him. Lanäe believed that because of his heritage, he might have the ability to wield the Sceptre."

"But how will you get past the Wushäen and the Näenji Council?" asked Kásuin. He remembered his own harrowing experiences dealing with the Näenji Council.

"We must use secrecy and stealth to keep them ignorant of our activities," Räesha acknowledged. "We do not have the support of the Näenji Council. We believe they are already compromised, as the Wushäen are."

Kásuin frowned. "I've dealt with the Näenji Council before and barely escaped with my life."

Maräera shook her head. "Cédron has some abilities, granted, but he's not strong enough to take on the Council."

Räesha nodded. "He will have the support of the Sumäeri; he won't have to challenge the Näenji Council alone."

"But to wield the Sceptre of Kulari?" Kásuin stood and slowly paced around the room. "That took the magic of all four sacred stones...and, if memory serves, the life of the last wielder."

Räesha's face hardened and she nodded.

"No!" Maräera cried, rushing to Kásuin's side. "Don't let her take him!"

"You're asking Cédron to sacrifice himself!" Kásuin crossed his arms and glowered at the Sumäeri. "He's just a boy, and not powerful enough to do what you expect of him." He looked at Roväen for assistance. "What you're asking would kill him."

"Your son's life was already forfeit." She leveled her gaze at the Regent. "That he's survived this long is an indication of his strength or - forgive me uncle - Roväen's weakness."

"What do you mean, forfeit?" Kásuin rounded on Roväen for an answer.

Roväen slumped in the chair, letting out a long sigh. He explained to Kásuin that Elder Räelin had charged him with the task of monitoring Maräera's unborn child for innate magical powers. They feared that his heritage would give him an inordinate amount of magical ability, powerful enough to destroy the world as his forbears nearly did. Roväen was to guide the child and teach it the values of life and to honor their deities. If the child proved intractable, he was to terminate it rather than risk releasing yet another destructive power on the land.

"Cédron has grown into a sensitive and loving young man." Roväen defended himself. "I never had cause to doubt him or our ability to guide him in the appropriate direction."

The slight hesitation wasn't lost on Kásuin. "But with Algarik trying to influence and impress him, the danger that he will choose the wrong path increases."

"Roväen has sworn to me to protect and guide Cédron for as long as he is able." Maräera stared at her uncle. "You love him and you love me. *This* oath you must not break."

"He must not be influenced by Algarik, or all will be lost." Roväen slammed his hand on the chair. "It is because I love him that I would kill him myself first."

Stunned into silence, Maräera sat down, her face blank and her fingers twisting themselves into knots.

"The risk of one life to save our world is a price I am willing to pay." Räesha stared at Kásuin steadily. "Do not forget that I have already lost half of my family, and the war hasn't even begun yet."

Kásuin stared at the two Shäeli in astonishment. "I will continue with my plans to name him heir to the Regency and keep him in Dúlnat where he will be safe." He paced to the window and looked out over the river and the falls. Turning back to his guests, he placed his hands on his hips. "Algarik can't touch him here, and the Council doesn't know of his existence, right?"

Räesha stiffened. "Don't count on that, Regent Varkáras. The demons know of his existence; that's why my sister and parents are dead. The Wushäen are compromised and the Council may be as well. Do not sit idly here thinking that your son is safe. Nothing is further from the truth."

Kásuin looked at Roväen, who nodded in grim assent. Kásuin turned his back on them and stared out the window. He drummed his fingers on his arms for a moment, and then turned to face the Sumäeri warrior. There was no compromise in the grey steel of his glare.

"I will not sacrifice my son. Your life may be forfeit in your own lands, but it is not here. You may stay and join Roväen as the boy's protector, but you will not spirit him away from the safety of Dúlnat. If you attempt to do so, my legionnaires will hunt you down." The Regent locked his gaze with Roväen's. "Cédron will be Regent after me. We will continue with the ceremony as planned."

Rováen held up his hands in surrender. "Of course, my friend. We will keep him as safe as if he was in Lady Muralia's own bosom, won't we?" He winked solemnly at Räesha.

What is he up to? Räesha hesitated a moment, then forced a smile and nodded to Kásuin. "As you command, Lord Regent." Räesha bowed. "Lady Maräera."

"I'm glad we understand one another." Kásuin dismissed them and returned to Maräera.

As Räesha turned to leave, her eyes raked across the statuette. *It hasn't moved. Perhaps I was mistaken.* An uneasy feeling stole over her as she passed the ebony figure, its eyes too vivid to offer her comfort. She stared at it a moment longer, daring it to move, then turned away.

Rováen escorted Räesha into the corridor and shut the door behind them. He led her silently down to his own chambers and out onto his balcony where the chances of being heard were significantly less.

"The stubborn old fool!" Rováen spat, glancing down into the courtyard. "He has no idea of the danger he's trying to ignore."

Räesha regarded her uncle for a moment, and then laid her hand on his arm. "We must act quickly," she said softly.

Rováen continued scanning the courtyard then straightened, his hand covering hers and squeezing gently. "I know. We'll do what we can...but first we have to find that boy!"

* * *

The onyx bust of Kásuin Varkáras sat on its lonely shelf while the Regent of Dúlnat and the three Shäeli argued over Cédron's fate. It maintained its position for the hour that the Regent sat at his desk, poring over papers and cursing to himself until he finally left. It held its form for a few extra minutes after the Regent's exit to ensure it was alone. Then, the bust vibrated until it returned to its natural form. The little imp cackled and clapped its claws. Its master would be very pleased with his report. He danced over to the open window and slid under the sill.

Algarik sat quietly at his desk, gritting his teeth with impatience as the imp slowly unfolded the report while it danced around, pleased with itself for succeeding in its charade under the scrutiny of the Sumäeri warrior. Its work completed, the Red Mage bid it back into its solid form, placing it on top of his desk.

Algarik was out of time. He couldn't let Cédron fall into the hands of the Sumäeri warrior; he had to get the boy to Thoromberk Fortress and his master before the ceremony this evening. *Where is that boy?*

Glancing outside at the bustle of the final day of the festival, a plan began to form in the mage's twisted mind. It would be dangerous and likely to result in many casualties, but that had never stopped him before. Gathering his supplies, Algarik swept out of his chambers, the fabric of his red robes billowing out around his legs in his haste. *This will be an evening no one will ever forget.*

CHAPTER 12 - SKÁRESK

Cédron crouched behind the large chest, holding the squirming kesling tight in his arms to prevent the little brown creature from scurrying away. Its nose twitched constantly and it flapped its wide tail against Cédron's arms, making a slapping noise. The boy was certain that its whines could be heard clear down the open corridor. He didn't dare release it yet, as the guard was due to return on his rounds through this wing of the castle in mere seconds. Cédron had just barely skirted into the armory and ducked behind the large chest before the legionnaire had swung through on his last pass.

The armory was an immense open chamber at the end of the southern wing of the castle's third level. At one time, it had served as an exhibition hall displaying weapons and fine artifacts from the merchant caravan's travels trading goods across the lands, but in recent years, the room had become more of a storage area. The morning rays of the daytime deity streamed through the leaded windows along the east wall, filling the space with golden light. Shimmering dust motes caught in the beam and caused the boy's nose to itch as much as the wiggling kesling's. He pinched it hard to prevent a sneeze.

As he peered around the room, Cédron could see piles of maps jumbled together on shelves. Rows upon rows of swords and decorative knives hung from their brackets along the far wall. There were three rows of long tables heaped with wooden boxes, services of dinner ware, goblets, and

126

silver carved with the Varkáras crest gathering dust atop piles of linens. Skáresk, the fire sword, held a place of honor high above the other swords on the far wall. *How am I supposed to replace the stone? I don't know if I can actually reach Skáresk.*

It had been surprisingly easy for him to slip away from his chambers unnoticed; his Uncle Rováen had already gone down to the main hall for breakfast. Keeping the furry kesling quiet during the night had simply been a matter of feeding it into somnolence, then hiding it under his bedding. Now it wiggled and squirmed while emitting a high-pitched whine through its rodent teeth that made Cédron wonder if it had been worth all the effort to bring it with him. He hunched down lower behind the chest and scratched the little beast behind the ears as the guard's boot steps approached from the back end of the wing. *Just a few more seconds, little one, and the armory will be ours.*

The guard strode into view, clad in the formal uniform of the Hármolin Legion, with the Konnáras compass rose in silver atop the dark blue tunic representing the Varkáras family. The steady beat of his footsteps faltered only slightly as it passed the main opening of the armory before moving on again. Cédron held his breath and clamped his hand over the kesling's snout. He knew something had caused the man to hesitate, but he couldn't be sure if the guard had heard them or if it was something else.

His heart pounding in his chest, he waited for several more minutes before carefully poking his head up from behind the chest. Nobody was in sight. The guard had gone on to the other wing, giving Cédron a few minutes to accomplish his task.

With a final pat on the head, Cédron released the impatient rodent to begin snuffling around the tables. Keeping one eye on the entrance and one ear cocked for sounds of the guard returning, Cédron followed the kesling as it rummaged through the piles of fabric on the tables.

Squealing with no concern for secrecy, the kesling charged over some haphazardly piled silver plates, knocking several to the ground in its haste to reach a small box atop what had probably once been a fine display of shields. Now jumbled on top of one another and covered with a layer of dust, the shields had lost all the luster of their former glory.

Cédron winced at the racket the kesling made as it scrambled over the shields and tore at the box. He glanced around to see if the noise had alerted anyone to his position and hastily gathered up the scattered plates. The kesling was whining insistently at the box, biting at it with its long front teeth.

Cédron gingerly grabbed the small chest from between the rodent's long claws and opened it. Inside, he found a large red stone nestled in the center of a black silk cushion. The fire deep within the cabochon filled the room with a scarlet glow as it caught the rays beaming through the window panes. Cédron's breath stuck in his throat. He stood mesmerized at the power and beauty radiating from this potent firestone. *This is it! I've never seen a more powerful stone in my life.*

Stepping over the kesling, which was still sitting up on its back legs trying to reach the stone, Cédron made his way over to the wall where Skáresk hung. He pulled the stone from the box and gave the box to the kesling to sniff around in while he sought a way to reach the fire sword.

Looking around, Cédron found a chair he could stand on to try to reach the sword. He put the stone in his pouch and began moving the heavy wooden seat toward the back wall. He was so intent on his work that he didn't hear the approaching steps. The kesling let out a little squeal and scurried past his feet into a corner, causing the boy to look up.

Cédron felt a jolt of panic to see his Uncle Rováen, the ebony-skinned, imposing caravan master Shozin Chezak, and a young Shäeli woman approaching from the back of the room. The woman was covered from head to toe in foliage tattoos, and carried enough weapons to intimidate a regiment of legionnaires.

"U-U-Uncle Rováen," the boy stammered. "Wh-what are you doing here?" He let go of the chair and stood up straight, wiping his sweaty hands on the back of his trousers.

Master Chezak crossed his arms and scowled while the Shäeli warrior stepped around the table, appraising him with her lips pursed.

Rováen raised an eyebrow. "I might ask you the same thing," the old man said, leaning back against the table and stretched his long, thin legs out in front of him. He crossed his legs and arms, appearing to relax, and waited for the boy's excuse.

Cédron swallowed hard. His mind raced furiously for a story that would be both plausible and give him reason for rifling through the armory's treasures.

"I, uh..." Cédron saw the Shäeli woman's eyes catch on Skáresk, inspiring him. "I just wanted to get a closer look at Skáresk...you know, to figure out how powerful the stone was and...um..." He shrugged, watching his uncle's face for his reaction to the partially-true tale.

Shozin Chezak clicked his tongue and moved his burly form back into the opening of the armory. "You need to come with us, now," he said gruffly.

Cédron looked from Shozin to Rováen, noting their grim expressions. The Shäeli woman's staring made Cédron uncomfortable.

Rováen seemed amused at the boy's discomfiture and waved an arm at the woman. "This is your cousin, Räesha," he said. "She brings us news from Samshäeli."

Cédron straightened his tunic and brushed off his hands against his trousers again. Stepping forward with his palms up, he offered his cousin the traditional greeting. "Welcome to Dúlnat, cousin. May Lady Muralia bless your steps upon the land."

Räesha covered his palms with hers and replied, "May our Mother grant you peace in these troubled times."

Cédron's hand went self-consciously to the lacerations healing on his face. *What does she know of my troubles?*

"Come, we must hurry." Shozin's black eyes were nearly slits as he squinted down the dim hallway. He leaned around a pillar to make sure the coast was clear, then motioned for the other three to follow him.

Rováen gestured for Cédron to precede him and, with a swift glance back towards the far corner, the boy sighed and left with his uncle and cousin behind him. *How am I going to replace that stone? The one in the sword isn't strong enough for me to ignite from a distance.*

Cédron knew he wouldn't get another chance to return to the armory before the festival. He felt a twinge of guilt for the kesling that still roamed around the piles of discarded objects. He hoped the little beast would find its way back to Algarik without further destruction of the armory. If not, he would have a lot of explaining to do once it was caught.

Shozin led them through the corridors and up to the highest tower, the crowning jewel of the Yezman glass workers Kásuin had brought to Dúlnat. The circular room was lined with stained-glass windows that splashed a myriad of colors on the white marble floors as the mid-morning light shone through them. This room also offered the best view of the entire valley, which was why it was chosen. Shozin ushered the group inside and shut the door.

"We will not be disturbed here," he said and walked over to the window to peer out on the festivities below.

Cédron watched his cousin in fascination as she, too, went around the entire wall, looking out the windows. Her movements were graceful yet filled with a tense purpose. He couldn't fathom what would bring her so far from home unless it was bad news. Word had recently reached Dúlnat that the Garanthian tribes had been moving south, but even they would hesitate before engaging the legendary Sumäeri warriors of Samshäeli. Watching Räesha was like observing a wild feline that had been placed in a cage. She paced around the room, staring out each window as if searching for something.

"They will be here shortly," she said, turning to Roväen. "I've sent my läenier deep into the mountains to hunt so they won't detect him, but we won't have much time."

Cédron's eyes widened with increased respect. *A läenier rider!*

Roväen nodded and strode across the room to Cédron. He propelled the boy into one of the chairs set up in a circle in the center of the room and sat down across from him. Shozin and Räesha took seats on the opposite sides. A sense of foreboding washed through Cédron, causing him to shiver slightly. *What's going on?*

He looked at his uncle, whose face remained solemn. Räesha glared at him with near hostility in her aquamarine eyes, and his cheeks began to burn.

"Why are we here?" Cédron asked.

Shozin drummed a staccato beat on the arm of his chair with thick fingers. "We're trying to keep you alive," he said.

Cedron's head snapped up to face the caravan master, his skin prickling. He opened his mouth to ask, but Roväen held up his hands signaling for Cedron to wait. "Let me start from the beginning." The old man looked over at his niece with a small, sad smile. "I never told you exactly why your grandmother, my sister Neräena, was banished to the caves. Well, not the whole truth, anyway. She had broken the Covenant laid down by the Näenji Council not to interfere with the lesser peoples of Muralia. She was a priestess of the goddess Azria and felt the calling to the Zig'orman Marshes, where a girl child had been critically injured. The child was one that Neräena felt strongly would make a good priestess if she recovered from her wounds, so she agreed to help heal the girl. My sister was returning with the child from the marshes, on her way to marry my closest friend, when she was brutally violated by one of the Meq'qan warriors of her escort. This vile man impregnated her with his seed and your grandmother chose to live in exile with her shame rather than kill the abomination that resulted from this union."

Cédron listened to this story, his ears burning as hot as his cheeks. *My mother isn't an abomination! She's beautiful and caring and...she's my mother!* He gripped the arms of the chair so tightly that his knuckles turned white.

Cédron knew the Askári had rejected him for being a half-demon, and he had been warned that the Shäeli viewed mixed-breeding as a crime punishable by exile or death.

Cédron looked at Räesha. "Are you here to kill me, then?"

"No. Oddly enough, I'm here to protect you." The Sumäeri woman grimaced.

Cédron looked at Rováen, then back to Räesha. "Protect me from whom? The rabble outside who want to stone me? Why would you care?"

Räesha regarded him stonily. "I'm here because my family...our family..." Her voice faltered.

"What about them?" he asked leaning forward in his chair. "Is my mother in danger?"

Rováen placed a hand on the boy's leg. "Most of our family is dead."

Cédron collapsed forward with his head in his hands. The angry words building in his mind disappeared along with all the air in his lungs. He slumped back in his chair, casting about for something that would connect the Angäersol deaths to him and explain Räesha's presence. *Somehow this is my fault, or Räesha wouldn't be here.*

"My youngest niece Lanäe was killed by demons," Rováen said softly. "My brother Räebin and his wife Eläeni were slaughtered by an ancient entity sent by our leaders."

Cédron's brow furrowed as he assimilated to this new information. "Demons? How could she have been killed by demons? They've been imprisoned for millennia by Lord Shamar and Lady Muralia."

He looked at his hands and thought about all the magic at his disposal – magic that terrified the Askári to the point of causing protests against his being named heir to the Regency. Jorrél and Pánar had made it clear that he was a Shäeli demon and should be torn to pieces for it.

"And you think that I had something to do with their deaths?"

"No, foolish boy!" Räesha stood and angrily paced the room. Turning back to the center where the other three were seated, she glared at Cédron with flashing eyes. "My family died *because* of you, because of their knowledge of your existence and your significance!"

"But what –"

Horns sounded from outside, interrupting Cédron's question. The blaring drowned out any further conversation as all four rushed to the windows to see what had triggered the Hármolin Legion's alarm.

"They're here," Räesha said, stepping back from the windows.

"Who's here?" Cédron asked, craning his neck to see the front gates and whoever it was that had caused the horns to sound.

Räesha shuddered. "The Council Guard. They are here to execute me, and likely you as well."

Cédron inhaled sharply. "Why would they want to kill me? What have I done?"

"You exist," Räesha said from the window and nodded to Rováen.

"You," Rováen pointed at Cédron's chest, "stay here and don't move. Whatever you do, don't use any Árk'äezhi, for they will sense it and seek you out. That would be most dangerous for you."

Cédron crossed his arms. "I can defend myself. I'm not completely helpless you know."

"Against a contingent of Council Guard? Yes, you are."
Räesha snorted. "Heed your uncle's warning. It will save
your life." She held him in her gaze for a moment, then
released him and followed Shozin out the door.

"But where are you going? How long must I stay here?"
Cédron asked his uncle, who was closing the door.

Rovären twisted his head back inside the room. "Räesha
must sneak out and find Yongäen. Even a Sumäeri warrior
cannot face an entire contingent of Council Guard alone.
Shozin and I will attend your father and see what we can
learn. Stay here, don't activate your magic, and don't worry.
I'll be back as soon as I can."

Rovären closed the door, leaving Cédron staring at the
wooden planking. As if in a daze, he stumbled over to the
window to catch a glimpse of his assassins.

CHAPTER 13 - SUMÄERI THREAT

Kásuin Varkáras banged his fist on the table, startling his advisers into silence. "He's my son, and a Varkáras!" he exclaimed. "My family was entrusted with the Regency of Dúlnat and we will not forsake that promise. You did not protest my ascendency and I'm only half-Askári. Have I not been a fair and just ruler?"

"Certainly, Lord Regent."

"Of course."

"All you say is true, but –"

Kásuin glared at the men. "But what? He is able to wield magic without a talisman or wand? So do some of the mages, yet you do not cry out against them."

"The mages are highly restricted and controlled by the Guilds," the nasally voice of the oldest advisor, Arís Tóque, intoned. "Your son has demonstrated a distinct lack of control and is not held accountable for his actions by this committee or any other. He's a danger to our society!"

Kásuin straightened and put his hands on his hips. He surveyed the room, taking in the slight nods at Arís Tóque's words. He paced back and forth for a moment before turning to his advisors.

"Is it not true that the Askári were once powerful magic wielders, harnessing the Árk'äezhi energy of fire at will?" He glanced around at the uncomfortable shifting stances and was unable to catch anyone's eyes. He continued to pace. "And isn't it true that we only lost our ability when the Garanth stole our sacred firestone?"

Arís Tóque's head snapped up. "What difference does that make? The stone has been gone for generations, our powers forgotten. Now we have no protection against one such as your son."

"Protection against him?" Kásuin shouted. "We've just learned that the Garanthian tribes are on the move. He is the only one who can counter them. You should be considering how best to protect him!"

"Lord Regent, with all due respect..."

The horns of the Hármolin Legion interrupted the minister's argument. The warning continued to blast as Regent Varkáras dismissed his advisors, promising to continue the discussion at a later time. He intended to name Cédron as his heir despite their foolish ramblings and unfounded concerns. It was the only way that Kásuin felt that he and Maräera could keep Cédron safe from the hostile world that kept trying to steal him from them. The Regent stepped into the corridor where a runner was racing to him with the news.

"A contingent of Sumäeri, Lord Regent," he blurted as he skidded to a halt outside the chamber door. "They arrived on foot and will attend you here shortly."

Kásuin smiled tightly at the boy and waved him away. Räesha had warned him, and now they were here. Even though he'd anticipated their arrival, a hard lump of stone sank in his innards. The Regent realized that the argument with the advisors was nothing compared to the battle he now faced.

Only once had he encountered the Council Guards, and he'd barely escaped with his life. Now they were in his land, under his jurisdiction, but he still felt a twinge of fear. Few could oppose the Council Guard of Samshäeli, recruited from the best Sumäeri warriors to defend the Näenji Council and unmatched in their ability to neutralize any threat to their society. Kásuin settled back into his throne to wait, his elbows on the arms of the ornately carved chair and his hands clasped in his lap. He did not have to wait long.

The legionnaires standing guard outside the small throne room entered and stood at attention. The herald announced the visitors and stood aside as the four men marched down the center aisle, stopping in the center of the inlaid Konnáras compass rose that took up the entire section of the floor in front of the throne. One young warrior came to the front and bowed to Regent Varkáras, his foliage tattoos sharp against his pale skin.

"I am Trilläen Villinäes, Captain of the Council Guard," he said. "We have come for the traitor Räesha Angäersol."

Kásuin stood and spread his arms out wide. "You are most welcome, Sumäeri, to my domain. But I'm afraid you've missed your kinswoman. She has come and gone."

An older, beady-eyed Sumäeri pushed past his captain and pointed a finger at Kásuin. "You lie!" he hissed. "We know she is here; we can sense her."

Kásuin's face remained calm despite the roiling of his stomach. To lie outright to these Sumäeri could be very dangerous. He knew they had the power to destroy his entire city, with their power over the forest threatening all the plants surrounding and filling his lovely white settlement. He'd seen the Ginäeyi Forest come to life at their command and had no desire to watch his city crumble under the very flora he and Maräera had nurtured. He knew the game he was about to play was risky, but he didn't feel as if he had a choice. Kásuin smiled and tried to appear relaxed.

"Most esteemed Sumäeri, your kinswoman was here this morning. She arrived on her läenier and met with her uncle, my wife and myself briefly," he continued. "She left only within the hour and was headed north to the Meq'qan tribes."

Trilläen Villinäes stared at Kásuin Varkáras with his emerald eyes, searching the man's demeanor for the truth. His brow furrowed.

"Why would she go to the Meq'qan?"

They're biting! Now to reel them in. Kásuin shrugged his shoulders. "She is seeking sanctuary. I could not, in good conscience, offer it to her here after her admission."

"Lies!" the older soldier spat. "Your wife and her uncle are the only family the girl has left. She is here, and we will find her!"

Captain Villinäes put his hand on the older warrior's shoulder, holding him back. "Peace, Bräentu, let me handle this."

Bräentu shrugged off his captain's hand and jabbed a finger towards Kásuin. "Make no mistake, *Regent*, that we will find her and we will hold you accountable for your deception. Your entire family will pay the price of your decision."

Kásuin stared placidly at the man, refusing to be baited by his threats.

"Did Räesha tell you she was a fugitive?" Captain Villinäes asked quietly.

Kásuin ran his long fingers through his dark hair. "She did," he said. "But I have no jurisdiction over her for any crime she may have committed in Samshäeli. I could not bring myself to hold her against her will or punish her simply because I did not like what she had to say."

Bräentu stiffened with indignation, his eyes bulging. "How dare you! Her very presence here makes her a traitor and you know it. I was at your tribunal; you are familiar with our laws and know why you were sentenced to death...and Maräera with you. How you escaped..."

"How we escaped is no longer important," Kásuin interrupted. "You said you were here for Räesha. What other purpose brings you to Dúlnat?" The Regent looked at Captain Villinäes, ignoring the posturing Bräentu and incensing the man even further.

"The Näenji Council would like to interview your son; to observe him and to assess for themselves whether he poses any potential danger." Captain Villinäes sighed, wiping his hands over his face. "We know of your heritage. The boy's mixed blood makes him an abomination, but to be of the Varkáras line makes him an even greater threat."

"So, what you're saying is that you want to take my son back for his own execution, is that correct?" Kásuin asked with an edge to his voice.

"For lack of a better term, yes."

Ok, here we go. Kásuin chuckled. He clapped the young captain on the back and called for refreshments. Captain Villinäes' jaw slackened and he looked at his men for guidance. They all either just shrugged their shoulders or shook their heads. None had any idea what would cause such a strange reaction in the Askári ruler.

"Captain Villinäes, please accept refreshments for you and your men." Kásuin herded them over to a table that had just been erected at the far end of the throne room and was being laden with food. "As you know, we are celebrating the final day of our festival of Narsham-Vu. Tonight, we honor the winner of the Warrior's Challenge, and I name the heir to the Regency."

The Regent seated himself at the head of the table and began heaping food onto his plate as if he'd not eaten all day. The Sumäeri looked to their captain, who nodded, then began loading their own plates with the sumptuous fare. Kásuin smiled pleasantly and popped grapes into his mouth as he continued with his explanation of the festival.

"I intend to present Cédron as my heir, even though he isn't well-favored among my people. They have always feared him because of his Shäeli blood, but really there is no danger. He has no magical abilities." Kásuin winked at Bräentu and stuffed a large meatroll into his mouth.

Captain Villinäes shifted uncomfortably in his chair. "We have heard accounts to the contrary, you understand," he said.

"Of course! Rumors abound when one is different," Kásuin said indulgently. "But I assure you, he has no innate talent whatsoever."

"We have our orders," the captain said, taking a drink of the triticale ale that had been poured in the tankard placed before him. "We cannot just forsake it on your word alone."

Kásuin nodded, wiping his beard with a napkin. "Agreed. I want you to attend the festival this evening, as my honored guests. Cédron will present the fire sword Skáresk to the winner of the tournament. The blade will remain dark, you will see. If he had any latent magic, the fire stone would ignite."

Captain Villinäes pondered the offer for a moment, chewing the unfamiliar fruit as he did so. Finally, he raised his tankard to the Regent. "Agreed. I would not spill any Shäeli blood unless it was warranted, even as diluted as your son's is."

Kásuin returned the toast, exhaling the tension that had built up during his charade. He wasn't sure if the Council Guard actually believed him, but it didn't matter. What he most needed now was time; time to come up with a new plan to both save his son and convince his people to accept him. As he watched Lord Shamar advance overhead in the sky, Kásuin Varkáras knew that his son's time was running out.

CHAPTER 14 - IMP'S IMPUDENCE

Algarik stared out the window of his chambers, his jaw clenched as he watched the progression of the Sumäeri contingent through the portcullis and into the courtyard of the castle. *What are they doing here? Why now?*

The red mage knew instinctively that they were here for Cédron and would want him dead. He knew of the Shäeli Covenant against interbreeding with the lesser races. His nephew would be considered an abomination, a crime against the deities.

How they had missed his existence all of these years was a mystery, but they were here now, and that fact changed everything. A dark cloud of dread blanketed the mage's mind as he considered the price he would pay if he failed in his mission. *I have to get Cédron to Thoromberk Fortress tonight. I'll use force if necessary!*

If the Sumäeri were here for Cédron, then the boy's plan to ignite Skáresk for Tóran would only alert them to his powers. Given their knowledge of his heritage, Algarik knew the Sumäeri wouldn't allow the boy to live out the day. He had to come up with another plan, one that would keep the boy safe, yet give him the impetus to leave with him.

Algarik paced the length of the room, his crimson robes snapping as he moved. He glanced out his window, noting that Lord Shamar was now well above the tree line. The parade would take place at dusk; that would give him about eight hours to put some sort of plan in place. Folding his arms across his body, he drummed his fingers along his

upper arms as he thought. *My original idea might still work;*
I'll just have to make a few slight modifications. I'll need to
contact Levirk Sirkran and see what we can come up with.
But first, I need to see what those Sumäeri are up to.

Algarik turned and walked over to his desk where the imp
sat in its obelisk form. The mage held his right hand over the
top of the obelisk, his ruby ring glinting in the light shining
through the windows. Closing his eyes, he willed the imp to
awaken.

His ruby ring glowed brightly as the Árk'äezhi flowed
from the stone towards the obelisk, calling forth the sleeping
demon inside. The obelisk wobbled slightly as it changed
form, the hideous grin of the imp a precursor to the twisted
deformity of its body.

"What is your wish, mage?" it hissed, licking its talons
with its long, forked tongue.

Algarik regarded the disgusting creature for a moment,
and then gave his command. "Go to Kásuin's chambers
again. He will be receiving a contingent of Sumäeri warriors
shortly, and I want to know how he plans to keep Cédron
away from them. Be discreet and do not give yourself
away."

The ebony imp lashed his tongue out towards the mage,
then continued to preen its talons. "Sitting still in that room
bores me. I won't do it."

Algarik smiled dangerously, his eyes flashing at the
insubordination. "Truly? You would prefer something a little
more exciting then, yes?"

The imp caught the edge in the mage's voice and looked
up. He regarded his keeper with his wicked black eyes then
gave an insolent nod. The little demon sat back on his
haunches and began cleaning his tail, running his tongue
down the length of it.

Algarik cleared his throat and sat down at the desk.
Grabbing his pipe, he knocked the old ashes out of the bowl
and filled it with a pinch of new leaf from his pouch. The

mage put the bit into his mouth and held his right hand over the bowl, his ruby ring glowing with growing power.

"Maftah," he whispered as the flame shot from his fingertip into the tobacco.

Algarik pulled on the pipe for a few moments, blowing smoke rings into the air as he waited for the tobacco to burn hot. Seeming to relax, the mage stretched out his legs, crossing them at the ankles as he took steady pulls on the pipe. The imp watched him surreptitiously as he continued to groom himself.

Without warning, Algarik blew through the stem of the pipe, shooting the bowl of burning embers into a plume over the imp. The embers sprouted wings and teeth and dove at the impertinent demon, biting and burning every inch of its little body. The ebony creature shrieked in pain, hopping around and swatting helplessly at his attackers.

"All right, I'll go!" it screeched, ducking for cover beneath a sheaf of parchment.

Algarik smirked and waved his hand. The embers burned themselves out and turned to dust. "I thought you'd see it my way," he said. "Don't hesitate to defy me again; I am always open to devising new ways of causing you pain."

The imp gathered its tail into its claws and wiped at the scorch marks. "Indeed you are, you vile man," it whimpered, then scampered to the window and leapt.

"You have no idea," Algarik muttered after the retreating demon.

The mage watched as the imp raced along the wall, his claws carving holds in the smooth marble as he made his way to Kásuin's chamber and through the open window.

Algarik glanced down and watched the men below erect the dais on the tournament grounds for the closing ceremony of the festival. Rows of lanterns were being placed along the parade route that led from the village to the dais, allowing the internal glow rocks to absorb Lord Shamar's rays so they would be bright when the deity retired that evening.

The sweet scent of breads and pies wafted into his window from the bakery below, causing Algarik's stomach to growl for the second time that day. He would need sustenance for the journey he was about to make and decided that he'd work on his ideas over a hot mug of adzuki and some fresh sweetbreads.

The mage had turned and made three strides towards the door when he stopped short. Wheeling back to the window, he stared out at the parade route. *Of course! Why didn't I think of that before?* Closing his windows and shutters to the heat of the day, Algarik strode out of his chambers, whistling a lively tune as he made his way to the kitchens.

Chapter 15 - Festival of Narsham-Vu

Lord Shamar's waning rays retired behind the rim of the Ronhádi Range that surrounded Dúlnat, heralding the evening and the beginning of the Narsham-Vu parade. In the highest tower of the castle, Cédron grimaced as he pulled off the heavy Aruzzi costume's headpiece.

The young man had never had to wear it before, with its headdress of glass tiles from the desert land of Yezmarantha and the tail with eight long, curling feathers that were forbidden to touch the ground. He wasn't sure he had the stamina to wear the awkward outfit during the entire parade without collapsing. Beads of sweat were already forming along his hairline and trickling down the center of his back.

"Do you really think this is necessary?" Cédron complained to Shozin Chezak, who had so generously offered him the disguise.

A frown creased the dark-skinned man's face as he folded his arms across his chest in irritation at Cédron's apparent disinterest in performing the Aruzzi legend proudly with the appropriate bearing. He appealed to Roväen and Kásuin. "Perhaps something a little less ornate?"

Cédron's eyes lit up.

"I'm sorry, Cédron, but it is for your own safety." His father sighed at the unfortunate necessity for such drastic measures. "The Sumäeri will be searching for you and waiting for you to use your powers. This disguise will give you added protection from them and from others who wish you harm."

"This whole thing is a mistake." Cédron grimaced as he hitched the straps for the heavy tail feathers over his shoulders. "What if I can't get Skáresk to ignite in Tóran's hands?"

Kásuin started at the comment, but Shozin placed a warning hand on the Regent's shoulder, shaking his head. "Our apologies, my Regent, but given the current situation, we have changed the plan without your consent. The contingent of Sumäeri must believe that Tóran is the one the stone lights for, or they will kill your son." He turned to Cédron. "You have demonstrated your ability to control your powers fairly well. The Council Guard will sense the presence of Árk'äezhi energy when you ignite the firestone within the sword, but they won't be able to figure out where it's coming from. If we're going to convince them that it is Tóran's Árk'äezhi, we have to have you close, but unseen. We all believe in your ability to do what you must tonight." The bald man smiled. "Keeping you alive and unsuspected is our first goal. We can decide what you will do tomorrow once it arrives."

Chuckling at the youth's discomfort, Roväen helped attach the shoulder harnesses and arranged the bright gold, blue and green feathers appropriately in an array behind him. "Besides," he interjected, "you make such an attractive Aruzzi. All the lady Aruzzis will be cawing their appreciation for you tonight."

Cédron made to swing at his mentor's shoulder for teasing him, but his hand got tangled up in the feathers of the headdress and he knocked it off his head again. The glow rocks in the corner flared brightly and crackled audibly with magical energy as Cédron's frustration mounted.

"Easy, lad." Roväen placed his hands on his nephew's shoulders. "It'll all work out."

Breathing deeply to calm his growing annoyance, Cédron blew a long, whistling breath and closed his eyes. He reminded himself that this was a special night for Tóran, and his discomfort was secondary to the honor being bestowed on his brother at the festival. Cédron stomped around in the heavy, talon-shod leggings, trying to get used to the idea of strutting like the proud fabled beast he was portraying.

"Let's get this over with," he said to his entourage, waving Shozin Chezak in front of him.

"I will have three caravan members surrounding you at all times. You have the steps for the dance down?" Shozin asked as they made their way to the staging area for the parade.

"Yes, Zariun led me through them this afternoon. He said I moved like a drunken legionnaire, so I guess I'll fit right in by the end of the evening."

"You'll be fine," Rováen encouraged him and fluffed the tail feathers one last time. "I'll be nearby."

Making his way down the back staircase to avoid being seen, Cédron began to have second thoughts about attending the festival, even disguised as he was. Everyone had to go through such great lengths to protect him, and it seemed extremely inconvenient. He was about to say as much when his father took him aside.

"I appreciate your willingness to risk exposure. I had truly hoped to name you as my heir, but the deities are conspiring against that. Your mother and I are very proud of you. We will make it up to you someday." Kásuin clapped his son on the shoulder in farewell and made his way to the stands with Rováen to watch the parade and enjoy the festival as best he could.

Shozin herded the boy through the courtyard and over to where the other Aruzzi dancers were in position for the parade, practicing their moves. "Just keep your head on and your feet apart and you'll be fine." He winked and melted into the crowd.

Out of place and uncomfortable, Cédron stood watching the other dancers. He spied the Aruzzi riders practicing their jumps and spins and envied them their lack of ornate costuming. He knew that the rider's face mask and hat wouldn't hide his height or his inability to perform the grand leaps, so that costume was out of the question.

I wish Zariun would get here and tell me where to stand. Suddenly, he was struck from the side. Cédron nearly lost his footing as the impact to his ribcage knocked the wind out of him and caused his headdress to wobble dangerously. *If that thing falls off again, I'll be completely exposed.* Cédron twirled around, extricating himself from his attacker and still maintaining a firm grip on his headdress.

"Nice tail feathers." A familiar voice laughed.

Cédron looked up to see a big, familiar grin peeking out from under the mask of an Aruzzi rider's costume.

"Zariun, you pile of kazan droppings!" Cédron exploded, releasing the adrenaline built up from the impact and the relief that he wasn't under attack. "You nearly caused me to blast you!"

"Yeah, maybe so." His friend laughed. "But someone had to get you moving!"

Zariun stepped out in front of the performers, tossing his head and leaping in the air with the dancing prowess gained from nearly two decades of practice. His family had all been acrobats and dancers with the Varkáras Caravan, and Zariun had begun tumbling even before he could walk.

Cédron followed shortly behind, not nearly as smooth or confident in his portrayal of the legendary Aruzzi, but enjoying himself more as the procession wore on and he became more comfortable with the dance. He got so caught up in his steps that he didn't notice that one of the attendants marching along with them quietly slipped away into the crowd.

* * *

Levirk Sirkran waited patiently in the city gardens for one of his spies to find him. He'd placed them in every possible group attending the festival to find the young Varkáras boy. He figured they would try to disguise him for his own safety, especially after the arrival of the Sumäeri Council Guard.

Their presence had increased the anti-Shäeli sentiment of the growing protesters who opposed Kásuin's decision to name Cédron as his heir. It wouldn't take much for the seeds of distrust that had already so conveniently been sown by the boy himself to blossom into full-blown violence, making his job that much easier.

The Hazzara agent was enjoying the reverie of the mayhem his master's plans would cause when he was interrupted by the patter of running feet. Levirk stood to await his spy, confident that his master's plans were going to unfold without a hitch.

"Sir," the young man gasped, catching his breath from his sprint across the gardens from where the festival was taking place. "He is in the Aruzzi dancers…the one that stumbles over his own feet."

Clever! Who would have thought to put him in such a high-profile position? Full body costumes, too. The soldier handed his scout a small pouch that jingled with flecksun coins.

"Oh, and where is the old Shäeli? He is never far from the boy's side." Levirk didn't expect much trouble from the old man, but he'd learned to never underestimate an adversary on his own turf.

The runner snorted in amusement. "That one already has several sheets to the wind. I saw him near the dancing square demonstrating some steps to the caravan master. The pair of them were staggering around like husan racers newly arrived in port."

"Well done. Back to your post, and I'll give you a bonus at the end of the night." Levirk dismissed the man, who saluted and turned, sprinting back to his place among the dancers' assistants.

Levirk Sirkran walked slowly toward the back side of the dais where the ceremony would take place shortly. A huge tree sat imposingly over the dais and recently constructed stage, casting long shadows over the entire area. Algarik sat high in the boughs of the tree, waiting for his agent.

"He's with the Aruzzi dancers," Levirk Sirkran whispered as he settled himself in on the sturdy branch just below the red mage.

Algarik's eyes glittered in the soft light of the glow rocks lining the parade route and circling the dais. "Even better than I'd planned. He'll be right in the thick of things when the chaos commences."

The two settled back in their perch to watch the parade and wait for their moment.

* * *

Cédron's breath had shortened to gasps after dancing the entire parade route. His costume was heavy, and the effort required to keep it balanced and hop around in the dance became much more audible to his fellow costumed Aruzzis. Luckily, the troupe slowed their steps to a more formal procession as they made their way down the aisle illuminated by lanterns. The dancers reached the end of the aisle and stationed themselves on the dais facing the crowd.

The stage had been set up with long, white curtains that reflected the colorful plumage of the Aruzzi as they arranged themselves along the back wall. The fabled beasts provided a regal and colorful backdrop for the ceremonial presentation of Skáresk to the tournament winner. Cédron perched himself behind Zariun where he could still see the stage but not be noticed by the crowd.

Regent Kásuin Varkáras took his place on the stage and clapped his hands twice. The drums boomed out again in a steady cadence as the priestesses of the warrior goddess Orwena began their procession towards the dais. Their flowing red skirts glowed ephemerally in the torchlight, and the tiny gold medallions in their bodices glittered with each twist and turn of their intricate dance.

Just before they reached the stage, the dancers all drew two hidden sai's from straps attached to their thighs and began an intricate mock-battle with the ornate short spikes. Cédron watched in awe as the graceful priestesses demonstrated their martial expertise, blades flashing so quickly that the individual strokes couldn't be seen.

"Wouldn't want to have one of those girls annoyed with you, huh?" Zariun grinned as he poked Cédron in the side.

"That curly-haired one there would keep Tóran interested," Cédron mused out loud. "Of course, they'd probably just argue strategy all the time."

Zariun chuckled and nodded, his eyes trained down the street where the priestesses of Azria were getting into position.

Cédron turned his attention back to Orwena's priestesses, whose pace had picked up with the pounding drums, whirling in a frantic climax to their battle. The drums boomed, all together in one final explosion of sound that the spectators felt through to the core. The dancers froze in their final pose, each sai poised to strike a mortal blow to their opponent. The wild cheering and applause of the crowd as the girls gracefully exited the stage made Cédron's ears ring.

Azria's priestesses began their procession towards the dais. Cédron was surprised to see them beginning their dance without any music, and then he realized that his ears were still ringing from the final booming of the drums. As the Azrian priestesses drew closer, the crowd around him quieted down and he could hear the delicate strains of the flutes and woodwinds that accompanied them. Azria's healing blue aura was reflected by her priestesses' layers of gauzy scarves.

The dancers began their delicate steps, changing position frequently. Then the priestesses began to sing. Their song was high and light and matched the airy movements of their dance perfectly. People sighed as the girls floated past, emitting the calming scents of lavender and jasmine and orange blossoms. Each acolyte wore a wreath of the fresh flowers in her hair and tossed garlands into the crowd. Next to him, Zariun let out a long sigh.

Cédron glanced at his friend and rolled his eyes "Someone's got it bad," the disguised heir whispered into his friend's ear, causing Zariun to jump. "Which one is it?"

Grinning unabashedly, Zariun winked and poked Cédron with his elbow. "Don't you need to change or something?"

Smiling beneath his headdress, Cédron slowly inched his way between the other Aruzzi dancers and backed up to where the curtains hung around the dais. Ducking behind the curtain, he found a stool with his clothing laid out on it and three of Zariun's troupe, their dark faces nearly invisible in the fading light, waiting to help him change. Cedron nodded to them and they silently helped him out of the heavy costume, hanging the plumage and headdress on hooks attached to the curtain rods.

Cédron wished he had the opportunity to bathe before dressing in his finery. The sweat made his shirt stick to his body uncomfortably, but he knew that he had to be back on the stage in minutes. Running his fingers through his damp hair and arranging the Varkáras medallion chain that draped across his shoulders, Cédron nodded his thanks to his assistants and stepped back through the curtain behind the dancers. He stationed himself closer to the Azrian priestesses and Zariun stepped in front of him, keeping him from view of the festival goers.

Hamra's priestesses completed their demonstration with a cloud of lavender smoke, and the crowd silenced. Regent Varkáras took the stage once more, this time bearing Skáresk. The Regent beckoned Cédron and Tóran forward amidst scattered booing and cat-calls from the crowd. Kásuin turned to face the citizens of Dúlnat and raised his hands for silence.

"Good citizens," he announced. "I give you all that I have to give: my sons and greatest treasures. Together they will lead this city and her Hármolin Legionnaires to greatness. We are on the brink of war with the Garanth, yet these two stand as a beacon of light and pillar of strength in the face of this great challenge. They have set aside their differences and embraced their respective talents. I command you do the same, for together we may survive where divided we will all surely perish."

Cédron's cheeks burned. He was uncomfortable being put on display and terrified of the hostilities he could sense from the people of Dúlnat. The crowd watched silently as the Shäeli boy took the Askári symbol of power from his father. A few angry cries of protest were heard from the back of the mob, but the drums began, drowning out any further noise from the otherwise silent crowd.

Kásuin bowed, then exited the stage to sit in the ornate box at stage right with Maräera while the boys continued with the ceremony. As Tóran approached, Cédron knelt, holding the sword above his head for Tóran to grab. He caught his brother's eye and shook his head slightly, trying to convey the message that he wouldn't be able to ignite the stone.

"When does it ignite?" Tóran whispered.

Cédron looked around for the Sumäeri, fear etched on his features. "I don't know if I'll be able to do it. I couldn't replace the tourmaline with a firestone."

Tóran grasped Skáresk by the hilt. "I'm sure you'll figure it out." He winked at Cédron and slowly began the steps of the dance that depicted the battle between the Hármolin Legion and the forces of the Shäeli traitor Laräeith. Áreon Kírsis, Tóran's final opponent from the Warrior's Challenge, stepped forward in his costume of shame, his sword poised to engage his enemy.

As Cédron released the blade, he backed up into the curtains and pulled out the potent firestone from his pouch. Concentrating his Árk'äezhi through the stone in his hand, he willed the tourmaline in the hilt of Skáresk to glow. Pearls of sweat formed on Cédron's upper lip as he kept the flow of energy high enough to keep Skáresk glowing but low enough not to draw attention to his activated Árk'äezhi.

According to legend, the crystal gained strength from the wielder and its power increased as the dance progressed. The spectators all watched in awe as the red glow of the crystal embedded in the pommel of the famed sword grew intensely, causing the metal blade to appear ensconced in flame as Tóran and Áreon circled and swung at each other in their mock battle. Cédron watched as the sword glowed brighter and brighter. *I'm not doing that!*

Cédron glanced down at the firestone in his hands. Its glow remained constant and he knew that his focus had been true. Cédron looked around. Skáresk was shining like a small sun beneath Tóran's hands. Cédron's heart began beating faster as he willed his Árk'äezhi back. The stone in his hands dimmed, but Skáresk continued to blind him with its power.

The drums beat in time with the battle unfolding on the stage. Louder and louder, they beat until Cédron felt like the ground was rumbling. Glancing around, he noticed that the curtains on the dais were swaying. Two of the Aruzzi dancers lost their balance and fell over, their glass and feathered headdresses crashing to the ground. People started murmuring in the crowd.

Cédron looked around in panic, trying to determine what was causing the shaking when it struck him. *Another ground shake! Did my Árk'äezhi do that?* Loud creaks from the loosening structure above his head reached his ears. With a crack, the frame holding the curtains split and crashed towards the box where his parents sat, immobilized by shock. The drummers ceased their playing, but the rolling thunder of the massive ground shake continued. Cédron shoved the firestone into his pouch and threw himself down, placing his hands in the dirt and willing the ground to calm itself.

As the Árk'äezhi flowed through his fingertips and into the ground, he felt a sticky, dark ooze just beneath the surface. It was as if the ground itself was decaying. People started screaming. The ground shake increased, causing the curtains to fall behind him. *Mother! Father!* Leaping to his feet, Cédron edged his way down towards the box where his parents had been sitting. Maräera was helping a young child into her mother's waiting arms. Kásuin was nowhere to be seen.

Cédron saw the contingent of Sumäeri stationed at the back of the crowd begin to make their way toward the dais. *They think I'm using my magic to cause the ground shake! Maybe it did, but they're going to kill me if I don't get out of here!* His thoughts were interrupted as a flock of twillings were stirred up from the trees behind the stage. Cédron turned to see what had startled them and was surprised to see the glint of something glowing in the boughs of the center tree.

On the dais, Tóran continued the dance, his face exultant with the blazing Skáresk in his hands. The boy seemed oblivious to the chaos surrounding him. The sword flared blindingly as Tóran poised it above Áreon, preparing to execute the final blow. *I'm not lighting the sword. How is it still glowing? Somebody else must be doing it.* Making his decision, Cédron turned his back to the stage and motioned to Zariun that he wanted to check out the trees.

He'd taken only three steps when a blinding flash lit the sky from behind him and a huge explosion threw him forward. Shards from the tourmaline embedded in Skáresk rained down on the dais as the powerful energy radiated out into the crowd. More explosions rocked the night as the ceramic pots lining the parade route burst into flames. Screams erupted all around him, and the smell of burning flesh and melting fabric singed his nostrils.

CHAPTER 16 - TRAGEDY

Cédron lay on his back in the center of the dais and conducted a rapid internal check. He realized he'd mostly been bruised from falling. Something had cut him above his right eye; blood dripped down his temple. The body of a man had fallen on top of him during the explosion. He heaved it off and got shakily to his feet.

Looking down, he was knocked back to his knees as the charred face of his best friend stared sightlessly back at him. Blood from fragments of the exploded glow rocks and ceramic from around the dais were embedded in Zariun's head and neck. Blood pooled beneath him, spreading its vermillion stain across the stage.

Anguished, Cédron put his hands on Zariun's chest, calling forth the healing energy to try and revive his friend. There was no spark, no glimmer of life left in the body for his healing magic to respond to. He laid his head across his friend's body and wept. He had begun to gulp his breaths to quell his grief, when a blast of cold knocked him to the side. Cedron scrambled to his feet and into a protective crouch above his friend's body. He saw nothing. Glancing to either side, he saw only the horror of the destruction. Turning back to Zariun, he faced instead the sheer, elongated face of a screaming Mäuli.

Mäuli. The vicious, troubled spirits of those ripped violently from their bodies without the benefit of transition from physical to astral. These spectres, the victims of the crimes that took their lives, refused the call to Lady

Muralia's peace. Instead, they were compelled to right the injustice caused them and would hunt any in their path until their appetite for hatred was slaked. Cedron's heart thumped loudly in his chest as he faced the warped apparition, whose scream thrummed with hate and retribution. The spirit reached out towards him and the boy went numb. Fear rooted him to the spot and stripped him of all thought but the white rage that burned within it. Cedron's heart pounded faster. The Mäuli stretched her mouth as if to devour him whole when something flashed behind the large tree near the pavilion. The Mäuli stopped and turned, distracted by the light, and gave a shriek of triumph. Dropping Cedron, the spectre streamed towards its next victim.

Cedron sank to his knees. His hands shook as he bent again to his friend's body. He knew that Mäuli were usually helpless victims whose life had been taken by force. Most of the stories included an element of love and betrayal, but this was a mass event. Cedron wondered why there weren't more of the ghosts. Perhaps he didn't know all there was about how the Mäuli were created. He was grimly thankful that the one that had captured him had gone in search of another. Perhaps it knew who caused the explosion. Cedron thought about it some more as his heart began to slow its pace. If some spirits had stronger ties to their lives, then perhaps those were more susceptible to becoming Mäuli. Cedron stiffened as a new thought struck him.

Mother! Reeling in shock, he left his friend's side and lurched over to the right side of the stage where he'd last seen Maräera. He let out a strangled cry as his mother's pale arm stretched out from under the fallen stage. Blood was splattered across her skin. He heaved at the heavy timbers, but they wouldn't budge. Cédron cast about, seeking anyone who could assist him, but could see little in the billowing smoke around the stage. *I could try lifting them with my Árk'äezhi, but I can't tell if father is under there. I could end up hurting them more.*

The wails of confusion became screams of terror at the destruction the explosion left in its wake. A slight evening breeze had begun to blow, clearing out sections of smoke and revealing the horror of the scene. Panic abounded, hampering the efforts of the healers and legionnaires that swarmed the area trying to treat the injured and restore order.

"You there, are you hurt?" a healer yelled at him, obviously trying to identify casualties.

"No, but my mother is buried under here. Help me!" he cried, still pulling futilely at the timbers.

The healer whistled and another burly man joined him. Together the three of them lifted the heavy framework off Maräera's body. Cédron crouched down and gently rolled Maräera over onto her back. The boy smoothed her golden hair away from her face, praying to Hamra for the impossible. Her sparkling golden eyes had gone dim and her gaze was fixed.

"Mother!" the boy sobbed, throwing himself onto her chest. "No, I'm sorry, so sorry! Please no! This is all my fault."

The healer reached over and closed the woman's eyes, his face a grimace of disgust for the demon woman as he pulled his hand away.

Cédron sat unmoving. The loss of his dearest friend and his mother siphoned the remaining strength in his body. He could only stare blankly at the healers picking their way through the wounded spectators, their faces bound hastily with fabric against the smell of scorched flesh and hair.

"I'm so sorry, lad," the healer said softly as he motioned for the soldiers to carry the body away. "Get yourself to the healers and have them look at that cut."

Cédron nodded mutely and stood. *I have to find Tóran and my father.* Cédron shook himself and began searching among the chaos for the familiar long, dark braid or the curved blade of Skáresk.

Cédron found Tóran slumped beneath Áreon's hulking frame. Shoving the unconscious legionnaire off his brother's chest, he scanned Tóran's face and body for injuries other than his broken arm.

"I'm fine," Tóran croaked. "Just help me to my feet and I'll find father."

Cédron squatted down and threw Tóran's good arm over his shoulder. Straining with the effort, Cédron lifted the much sturdier young man to his feet.

"Are you sure you're not hurt?"

Cédron's worried expression and tone caused Tóran to smile weakly. "I'm tougher than I look."

Cédron wobbled a little and grabbed his brother's shoulder to hold himself steady. "Mother and Zariun are dead. The Council Guard are sure to think I've caused this." He shook his head. "Go find father. I need to…"

Tóran gripped his shoulder, his face pale and grim. "You need to get out of here. Go!"

Cédron turned away and staggered to the end of the burning dais, averting his eyes from the twisted and blasted bodies that littered the parade route. Behind him, the winds had blown the flames from the dais into several of the vendor's stalls lining the parade route. In a few moments, the entire festival area would be burning out of control.

Legionnaires raced up and down the route, barking orders to form a water line. Those not injured began hauling buckets of water from the Shasti River to put out the blaze. Cédron turned to the trees behind the dais where he'd spied something earlier and saw his Uncle Algarik making his way through the healers towards him.

"Cédron," the mage called, beckoning him with his hand. "Come with me!"

Cédron took a step towards his uncle, then halted. The ruby on his hand was glowing brightly. *Laylur's beast, could he have caused the explosion?* Cédron didn't know the extent of the mage's magical skills, but it was entirely plausible that Algarik had caused the explosion or the ground shake. Cédron knew the mage and his father had quarreled and that his uncle bore no love for Maräera and her Shäeli brethren. The more he thought about it, the more plausible the thought became. Anger burned in his chest. Cédron felt the wash of flame course through his veins as he called up the Árk'äezhi energy.

"You killed my mother and Zariun!" he screamed. "I'll…"

Algarik raised his hands to shield himself, waving them in front of him in negation. "No, I only helped ignite Skáresk for Tóran," he yelled at the boy. "I knew the tourmaline wasn't powerful enough…but the ground shake you started…"

A movement in the shadows behind the mage caught Cédron's attention. Three of the Sumäeri Council Guard emerged from behind the trees, weapons drawn and advancing. What plans he might have had died in that moment. Cédron knew that he couldn't face all of them and survive, even if Algarik chose to help him.

Suppressing his energy, Cédron turned and fled into the billowing smoke and chaos of the parade grounds. *Where can I go? Where are my father and Uncle Rovӓen?* Cédron looked around frantically, trying to decide which direction to turn when a pair of strong arms gripped his shoulders, dragging him into the throngs of people out of the Council Guard's line of vision.

"Don't struggle," a deep voice whispered in his ear. "Just put this on and follow me."

Cédron felt a hooded cloak being placed over his head and shoulders and realized that Shozin Chezak had found him. Relief washed through him, causing his knees to weaken and collapse.

"Hold on there, no fainting allowed yet, my boy." Master Chezak hauled him to his feet and half carried him down the water line. "Here, get in line and help with the water. Just keep your head down and pass the buckets." The burly caravan master stood next to him, passing the buckets of water along towards the dais.

"What about my family?" he asked, looking around.

Shozin shoved his head back down. "Shh! Don't worry, we'll find them. Just keep moving, and keep your head down!"

After three buckets passed their hands, they moved down the line, exchanging places with a couple of men further away. Cédron kept his head down and fought the urge to look for the Shäeli guards he knew were searching for him. He focused on suppressing his emotions and steadying his breath so that he didn't give away his position. *Just pass the buckets. Don't panic. Pass the buckets.*

The two of them continued with this method, passing buckets, then exchanging positions with men further down the line, until they were within sight of the river. Cédron's mind was numb from shock. Losing Zariun sucked the joy and color out of the world, and Maräera's lifeless eyes continued to stare at him in his mind, accusing him of murder as if Cédron had caused the explosion himself. *I never should have tried to interfere with Skáresk. Now I've killed my mother, my best friend, and probably my father.*

Tears welled up in Cédron's eyes but refused to fall. Anger and doubt warred within him as he tried to piece together the events of the evening. He mulled over Algarik's insistence that he'd only ignited Skáresk for Tóran. *What if he is right and somehow I caused the ground shake?* His hand went to the pouch and he felt the bulge of the powerful firestone that rested within it. *What if this somehow ignited the glow rocks and caused that explosion? Maybe the Shäeli are right; maybe I don't deserve to live.*

Morbid thoughts of his father lying dead among the twisted and burned corpses on the dais filled his mind and tightened his chest. Cédron struggled for breath as the panic of his predicament closed in on his mind, like crawlers weaving a tight web of hopelessness and desolation.

Moving further down the line towards the river, he tasted the coppery tang of blood from the cut above his eye as it trickled into his mouth. *The blood of a monster, of a demon. What a boon it would be to the world if it were me lying on that stage instead of Zariun. He deserved better!* The tears that had threatened on the edge of his eyelids fell unchecked into the cloak as he stifled the sobs that swelled in his chest.

"It's time to go," Shozin muttered next to him.

Cédron passed the last bucket to the man next to him in line and took a ragged breath, wiping his eyes with his sleeves. Remaining hunched over to hide his stature, Cédron shambled along next to the caravan master as the two made their way to the staging area where the caravan was preparing to leave after the festivities. He resisted the urge to look over his shoulder repeatedly as the two picked their way among the empty wagons. If the Council Guard were close, Shozin wouldn't have brought him out into the open like this.

"My mother is dead," Cédron repeated, still coming to grips with the horror of his reality.

Shozin nodded and continued to pick his way through the caravan in the darkness. "The bodies will be prepared for burial tomorrow." The glow from the fire east of them in the parade grounds was dimming as the flames were tamed by the well-organized waterline.

Cédron raised his eyes to the sky and saw the comet Haeris, the herald of the skies, streak across in his semi-annual trek. He wondered if the deity recognized the tragedy that had occurred on his rounds and would report it to Lord Shamar, but the deities hadn't interfered in the events of the lesser peoples for over a millennium, and there was no reason to think that now would be any different. He continued on behind his escort.

Cédron was still watching the skies when Shozin approached the largest wagon in the caravan and stopped directly in front of him. He walked right into the large man's backside and fell backwards.

"What the…?"

Shozin turned to him with his finger to his lips. Pulling the young man up with his other hand, he motioned for Cédron to wait. Shozin quietly climbed the short steps up to the dark window of the enormous wagon and opened the door. Cédron held his breath as the caravan master crept inside and shuffled about. After a few moments, the boy heard the unmistakable clinking of flintstone being struck. Shozin held up a tiny candle and motioned to Cédron to make his way into the wagon.

Releasing a little of the tension in his shoulders, Cédron scrambled up the ladder and shut the door behind him. Shozin pulled down two bunks that were chained to the wall, then went over to his cabinets. He pulled out a couple of blankets and tossed them onto the bunks. Cédron watched him numbly, his mind still churning over the evening's horror. At some point, Rováen and the gemcutter Sahráron joined them; one of them forced a steaming cup of tea into Cédron's unresponsive hands. He'd managed to swallow a few sips when Rováen, looking as haggard and miserable as he'd ever seen his uncle look, pulled off the boy's boots and laid him down on the bunk.

The three of them laid in their bunks, unmolested by those pursuing Cédron, but not free from the terrible events of the day. Each time Cédron closed his eyes, he was tormented by the images of Zariun and his mother. Their visages stretched in eternal agony, blaming him for their deaths. After a while, the boy quit closing his eyes. He gazed at the elaborately painted murals that covered every inch of the inside of the wagon illuminated by the flickering candles. Flowers in a riot of shades and shapes assaulted his eyes with their vibrant colors. The oil-painted garden was so exquisitely done that the boy thought he'd caught the scent of several of the blossoms. Few of them were familiar to him, and he wondered if the gardens of Yelandi were Shozin's inspiration.

Cédron let his mind wander for hours, avoiding sleep and the nightmares he knew stalked him. After a while, Shozin and Rováen's breathing became more regular, and he knew they'd finally succumbed to their exhaustion. Rolling carefully off of the bunk and stepping on the edge of Rováen's bunk beneath him, Cédron tip-toed over to his boots and grabbed his cloak. With a final look at his uncle and the caravan master, the boy almost lost his nerve. *No, I can't stay here another moment. Every minute I stay endangers the rest of my friends and family. I'll grab a husan and make my way into the mountains.*

Keeping to the shadows, Cédron ran, hunched over, to the paddock where the racing husan were kept. Nickering softly to the skittish equines, he chose a likely beast with curved talons and long back legs. The beast stood twelve feet at the shoulder, and Cedron grabbed a stool and placed it next to the husan. Leaping onto the beast's back, Cédron grasped two handfuls of the midnight blue mane and gripped the beast between his legs with his knees.

"All right boy, let's see what you've got."

Cḣapter 17 - Missing

Rovärn woke from a fitful slumber and stared out above him at the unfamiliar flowers and foliage painted in garish colors all across the ceiling of Shozin's wagon. The emptiness in the pit of his stomach returned with his memories, then filled with the dull ache of grief for his beloved Maräera. He had given up his life in Samshäeli to be with her when she chose exile, and a life with the man she loved, over her own people. Rovärn had witnessed the pledging of her life to Kásuin and the birth of their only son. He'd helped her raise the boy and fulfill her dream of creating the most exquisite gardens in all of Askáribai. The thought of his days not being filled with the joy of her laughter or the beauty of her smile sharpened the ache in his chest to a jagged edge.

Rovärn knew that Cédron would need to escape the city secretly and as soon as possible. Not only did Algarik and the Council Guard seek the boy, but the legionnaires had decided that the young Shäeli demon was responsible for the death and carnage of the festival. Rovärn and Sahráron had said as much to Kásuin when they'd found him helping Tóran back to the castle after the fires had been put out. They had assisted the Regent in preparing Maräera's body for burial before he and Sahráron left to find Cédron.

Not since the death of his sister Neräena had the old Shäeli felt so empty and hollow inside. When they'd found Cédron in Shozin's wagon, he'd still been in shock. Rovärn had left him out of the discussion of their plans, but now he had to get the boy up and moving before anyone else found where he'd been hiding.

Rováen rolled his legs over the suspended cot and sat up. Looking above him into the bottom of the cot that held the boy, he noticed that it lay flat. The old man gasped, his chest suddenly too tight to allow air. *Cédron, no!* He stood quickly and glanced into the bunk, his suspicions confirmed. *Where could he have gone?*

"Shozin, wake up," he cried shaking the enormous man's shoulder as he slept in a permanent bunk along the back wall. "Cédron's gone!"

The large man slid out of bed and yanked his boots on, glancing out the small window to try and see the boy. "Do you think he might have just gone to relieve himself?"

Rováen sighed and touched the blanket on the top bunk. "No, the blanket is cold and his boots and cloak are gone. He hasn't been here for some time."

Shozin rubbed his ebony head, his throat rumbling deeply as he thought. "It's more likely that he's gone off alone rather than having been taken by someone else. We can't let anyone know that he's missing."

"Agreed." Rováen nodded, pulling his boots and cloak on. "I'll see if he's gone to the castle. You see if Sahráron or Zariun -" he winced at the sudden memory "-or if the rest of the acrobatic troupe has seen him."

Shozin nodded and tucked his knives into the sash wound across his waist. "I'll keep an eye out for him while you search. In the meantime, I have a caravan to get on the road."

Rováen clasped arms with the caravan master, stepping out of the wagon and heading up the winding road toward the castle. He thought of Maräera's recent conversation with him. Her last request was to make him promise to guide her son and keep him safe. *I fully intended to keep my promise, but I can't if Cédron has run off or been spirited away! If Algarik has gotten his hands on the boy...*

The old Shäeli raced up the deserted streets, checking doorways and open spaces for the errant boy. He nearly got stabbed in the chest by a loose husan when he poked his head into the stables. Roväen spent an increasingly frustrating and unfruitful hour tearing through the castle corridors, seeking the boy in all the rooms and places he'd always loved to hide, but there was no sign of him. He closed the door to Cédron's old room and leaned against the wall with his eyes closed. *I have no choice but to tell Kásuin.* With a heavy heart, Roväen sped off down the corridor to the main reception room of the castle

"My Lord Regent," he gasped, skidding into the hall crowded with retainers and petitioners. "A word, please."

Kásuin raised his hands for quiet and addressed the room full of people. "We will adjourn for today."

There were a few disgruntled petitioners, but most were anxious to return home to their loved ones after the recent disaster. The guards escorted the last few stragglers out of the room and positioned themselves outside the door. Kásuin and Roväen waited until the last person had left before addressing the problem.

"He's...he's gone. Cédron is gone."

"Gone?" The Regent stood, his face paling at Roväen's words. "What do you mean gone?"

Roväen took a deep breath to slow his breathing. "I mean, when I woke up this morning, he had already left. His boots and cloak were missing, but there was no sign of a struggle or that anyone had taken him out from under our noses."

Kásuin frowned and sat down hard on the large throne. He put his head in his hands and shook his head. "I can't lose him, too."

Kásuin raised his head, and Roväen was shocked to see how haggard the man had become overnight. Dark circles shadowed his eyes and accentuated the hollowness of his cheeks. "Where do you think he might have gone?"

Rováen shrugged his shoulders. "I've searched much of the town, the caravan, the stables and everywhere in the castle that I could think of except…"

Kásuin nodded. The Regent motioned for one of his personal guards. "Bring Algarik to me at once." The guard saluted smartly and turned on his heel to fetch the Regent's brother.

"When was the last time you saw Cédron?" Kásuin asked, one hand on the older man's shoulder.

Rováen sighed and said wearily. "Last night after…everything. The boy was in shock. He wouldn't eat and he barely drank, so I put him to bed. He was gone before I woke early this morning."

The rays of Lord Shamar were peeking through the early mists. They sparkled through the ornate panes of stained glass, warming the room slightly. Kásuin paced before the window, and Rováen wondered what direction his thoughts had gone. The Regent opened the panes to let in some fresh air and turned to face Rováen.

"Algarik will arrive in moments and I don't want him to know that he was being watched," Kásuin explained to Rováen. "I need him to keep his guard down as long as possible if I'm going to get any answers from him. Don't let on that we know he spoke to Cédron." He looked up sharply as the guards entered with Algarik behind them.

"Ah, brother, thank you for joining us on such short notice." Kásuin smiled tensely, clasping Algarik's arm. "I apologize for the early hour. I trust you slept well?"

"Never mind the niceties Kásuin," Algarik growled. "What do you want?"

Kásuin glanced at Rováen, who nodded in reassurance. "Cédron is missing. We're not sure when he left, where he was going or with whom. We had hoped he might have left word with you?"

"Me? I've barely spoken to the boy," Algarik lied.

"Well, we...ah..." Kásuin faltered, not wanting to admit his knowledge of the illicit meeting between the mage and his nephew.

"Mage Algarik, the boy is fascinated with you. Make no mistake," Rováen said. "The draw of wielding magic without prejudice is a powerful one."

Algarik raised his eyebrows but returned his attention to Kásuin. "No brother, I haven't spoken with him since our very brief conversation in my chambers the other night, of which I'm sure you are very well aware." Algarik held up his hand forestalling the budding protests on Kásuin's tongue. "He certainly hasn't given *me* any indication of an interest in joining the Mage's Guild." He frowned slightly at Rováen. "Nor is he likely to, considering the events of last night."

Kásuin dipped his head in acknowledgement and glanced at Rováen. The old Shäeli was sure the mage was lying to them. He was also fairly certain that Algarik was suspicious of this whole interview. Still, he did seem sincere about not knowing the whereabouts of his nephew, so it was likely that the young man had taken off on his own for some reason.

"If you will excuse me, I have much work to do today." Algarik bowed curtly to his brother, turned and left the room, his crimson robes flowing behind him in the current of his swift stride.

Kásuin watched his brother's hasty retreat then turned to Rováen. "I want you to ride up into the mountains and see if he is in his usual haunts. I'll alert Tóran to keep an eye out for him while he's on patrol. Let's try to keep this as quiet as possible for now. I don't want Algarik to think he's gone too far from home until we have a better sense of what he's planning."

Rováen placed his hands on his hips and frowned as he stared out the window. "I don't like the idea of putting Räesha in danger, but it might make sense for her to join the caravan in Cédron's place as a decoy for the Council Guard.

It might throw them off long enough for us to find him. I just hope they don't pick up Cédron's trail if he has left the confines of the castle."

The Regent frowned at the necessity of using such a ruse, but nodded his head. "Please do so and convey to her my appreciation for her willingness to take this risk, should she do so."

The old man nodded. He fervently hoped that Räesha would be able to fool the Council Guard for a bit. He wasn't sure how far she'd get before they discovered the ruse, or if she'd survive their wrath once they did, but he had no choice. If, for some reason, they followed Cédron's trail, things could get messy in a hurry. He shook his head to clear his mind of such ugly thoughts and headed upstairs to find the Sumäeri warrior.

CHAPTER 18 - AN UNLIKELY ALLY

Cédron stretched out along the back of the mighty racing husan, wedging his legs into the beast's haunches to slow its stride. They'd been running hard since before Hamra settled down behind the trees, the clouds still bearing the lavender traces of her light as her father began his daily sojourn across the skies. The husan snorted and slowed its gait to a loping stride, allowing the boy to loosen the grip he had around the long, midnight mane.

Inhaling deeply to clear the nightmares in his head, Cédron closed his eyes and let the astringent scent of evergreens fill his nostrils. The road he was on was well-traveled and led past the mines before angling up towards the northern watchtower. After the festival and the carnage from the explosion, Cédron figured that the people who would normally be traveling this path would be staying in the city to assist with the clean-up and burials.

The lump that had still not left the boy's throat strangled him. He swallowed hard to push it down, along with the tears that stung his eyes, and he felt sick. *I've always been an outcast, but at least I'd had mother and Zariun.* Tears splashed down his cheeks and seeped into the large husan's deep blue hide. *They're gone, Tóran will turn against me if forced to pledge his loyalty, and father...* A twinge of guilt twisted in his guts. *I can't stay here and jeopardize everything father has worked so hard to accomplish.*

The long, curved talons of the husan thudded heavily in the dirt with a regular cadence. Cédron listened to the twillings chirping in the trees and tried to count the beast's steps to clear his mind. *One, two, three, four; one, two, three, four; one, two, three, four; five-six...wait, what?* Cédron pulled on the husan's mane and leaned back, forcing the equine to a stop next to a large atoca berry bush. He listened. *Thump-thump. There it is again!* Beads of sweat prickled around his forehead and between his shoulder blades. His heart beat faster in his chest. *Thump-thump. Who is all the way out here?*

Sliding off the husan quietly, Cédron led it over to a patch of grass growing alongside the road and pulled a length of rope from his pack. He looped the line over the husan's horns and slid it down its long neck, then wrapped the other end around the base of the atoca bush. *This won't hold him for long, but the berries should keep him interested until I find out who is up ahead.*

Cédron stepped off the road and climbed up the back side of the hill to his left. He followed a small path that led him onto a promontory that sat above where the *thump-thump* came from. He crawled slowly out to the edge of the rock and peeked through the bushes that hid him from view. Cédron's breath caught in his chest as he spied his company. *A legionnaire! How am I ever going to get past him?* He held his breath as the young soldier stopped on the path just below the promontory where he sat. From his perch, Cédron could hear the legionnaire muttering under his breath as he paced back and forth.

Cédron rolled over onto his back. The soldier stomping around below him didn't seem to have any purpose, and Cédron still couldn't determine what caused the thumping sound. There was no other mode of transportation visible, so the soldier probably walked here, meaning that he may not have been at the festival or have heard about the explosion. Feeling slightly hopeful about his chances, Cédron turned back over onto his stomach and peeked over the edge of the rock.

The legionnaire didn't look much older than Cédron. He had wispy dark fuzz on his upper lip, but none on his chin. His dark hair was loose rather than braided, and it blew across his eyes as the breeze caught it. The soldier wore the dark blue tunic, grey trousers, and black boots of the Hármolin Legion, but the silver overlay with the circular Konnáras compass was missing, as was the customary short sword. No rank insignia was showing. A light breeze blew the scent of the pine and juniper across the promontory where Cédron lay hidden from view. Below him, on the trail behind the young soldier, little rodents skittered up the trees. The legionnaire started at the sound. He kept looking around, as if he was afraid of being followed. Nothing moved on the road behind him.

Appearing satisfied, the young man walked over to the cliffside and pulled out a brace of daggers from the wall, then stuck them into his wide belt. Cédron watched as he pulled two from the sash and weighed them in his hands, walking away from the sheer rock face. After a moment, he began throwing them, two at a time, at the cliff face beneath the promontory where Cédron lay. *Thunk-thunk. Ah, so that's what he's doing. Odd that a legionnaire would be practicing with throwing knives, but then again, that's probably why he's doing it out here, away from everyone else.*

The legionnaire continued practicing his intricate knife-throwing routine. He faced away from the wall, and then threw two knives as he turned, *thunk-thunk*. Next, he threw two from a backwards spin, *thunk-thunk*. His movements were graceful and very deadly. Cédron was intrigued. *I wonder how accurate he is.* He didn't dare make a sound for fear of startling the soldier and earning one of those small knives in his head.

Sliding backwards down the hill on his stomach, Cédron decided that he would have to face the legionnaire and hope for the best. Tóran had always boasted about the weapon's master and their sword training; legionnaires never used throwing knives. Such a practice was considered vulgar and beneath their station. *Maybe this guy is different from the rest of the Hármolin Legion. I just hope he doesn't try to kill me first and ask questions later.*

Rounding the hill, Cédron stepped out from the boulders hiding him from the soldier's view just as the dark-haired lad was getting ready to throw his dual knives. Instead of aiming for the cliff wall as he'd done previously, the legionnaire spun towards the sound of Cédron's approach. He leveled his aim and let both short knives whiz through the air at his adversary's head. Cédron's eyes widened at the incoming projectiles. He took a deep breath and blew out towards them. His right hand swung up straight in front of him to block the knives and his left swept out to his left, where he hoped to direct them. One blade turned and sunk hilt-deep into the cliff wall. The other spun out of control and headed back the way it came.

"Watch out!" Cédron cried as he realized the knife was going to strike the soldier in the face.

The legionnaire ducked to his left as the knife flew past, narrowly missing his forehead. The young man pulled two more knives from his belt and prepared to throw them at the interloper, but Cédron held his hands out, palms up, both in greeting and to show he was unarmed.

"I mean you no harm," he said watching the legionnaire's eyes. "I'm sorry for the knife. It was supposed to follow the other blade over there." Cédron jerked his head to the left indicating the cliff face. "I am unarmed."

The legionnaire's eyes narrowed, distrust flickering in his dark gaze. "Just what are you doing up here, anyway? Didn't your father just name you heir to the Regency? Shouldn't you be in Dúlnat learning how to ruin your citizens' lives or something?"

Cédron felt like the air had thickened, making it difficult for him to breathe. His breath became shallow as he fought back the emotions that ran so close to the surface. *He doesn't know! What can I say to him that will gain his trust but won't scare him away or be a lie?* Cédron cast his eyes downward.

"There was a…a change of plans," Cédron stammered. "After Tóran won the Warrior's Challenge, father decided to name *him* as his heir to the Regency instead of me."

The legionnaire guffawed loudly and slapped his leg. "Tóran won the competition? Mijáko piles, I'd leave too! That conceited monsaki always strutted around like he was better than everyone else. I can't imagine how puffed-up his head must be after winning the tournament!"

Cédron laughed nervously. *Looks like I don't have to say anything. I'll just run with this guy's assumptions for now.* "Well, he's out of commission for a while – Áreon Kíris broke Tóran's arm in the final round, and he's been relieved of every duty except patrol until Autumntide."

The smirk on the legionnaire's face disappeared, replaced by a fleeting expression of guilt. "Patrol, huh? Well, guess I'd better pack up and get out of here before he finds me."

"Where are you supposed to be?" Cédron asked, glancing around to see if any patrols could be spotted from their current position.

The legionnaire gathered up his knives from the ground and wall and placed them back into his sash. He hefted a large pouch hanging at his side. "Technically, I'm not on duty until day after tomorrow. I wasn't supposed to leave for the northern watchtower to relieve my father for a couple of days, but my mother asked me to go early and take him his herbs that he'd forgotten." The young man shrugged. "Besides, I didn't have anything better to do. I hate crowds."

Cédron nodded and stepped towards the legionnaire to introduce himself. As he reached the soldier, a pair of twillings rose from the bushes beyond the bend in the road towards Dúlnat. Afraid he'd been discovered, he whirled around and stared down the road where the shuffling of someone's approach could be heard.

Cédron clasped his hands together, calling up his Árk'äezhi energy to defend himself as the stranger approached. *They may kill me, but I won't go without a fight.* Cédron raised his hands, the fire building in his palms, throbbing in tandem with his racing heart, when the midnight blue head of the untethered husan wandered into view. Cédron blew out the breath he hadn't realized he'd been holding and clapped his hands together. Sparks jetted out from his fingertips, causing the legionnaire to duck again.

"Hey, watch it!" the dark-haired soldier exclaimed. "Wait, you have a husan? Why didn't you say so?"

Cédron grabbed the rope and led the beast over to where the legionnaire was gathering his things. "Um, didn't really come up in conversation?"

"Do you think you could give me a ride to the watchtower?" the soldier asked, pulling his hair back and tying it with a leather thong. "I was supposed to have gotten there yesterday, but I took my time leaving town."

Cédron scrutinized the young man. Although slightly shorter, he wasn't as heavily muscled as Tóran. The husan could probably handle carrying the both of them as long as they didn't push it too hard or too long. Cédron weighed the risk of traveling with this unknown soldier more slowly versus hastening across the mountains on his own. He really didn't have a destination in mind that would be safe. Besides, having a legionnaire at his side should the Sumäeri find him might be an advantage.

"Sure!" He smiled and clapped his new companion on the shoulder. "The northern watchtower it is."

Cédron held the rope and bade the husan to sit back on its haunches, allowing the two of them to scramble onto its long back. He dug his heels into the beast's side, prompting it to stand and begin its loping canter up the valley and into the pass. The husan's long front legs strode out several yards and his powerful haunches propelled them up the mountain pass at a decent clip. Their journey would take several hours, putting them at the watch tower before dark if their pace remained steady. They rode in silence, still unsure of each other and of what to say.

The shadows deepened as the husan and its burden climbed higher in the pass where the walls rose steeply on both sides. Cédron peered into the afternoon gloom, the skies hiding Lord Shamar's rays behind ever-thickening clouds. He watched the little puffs of dust the husan's curved talons stirred up as they struck the ground. The sweet scent of the dry grasses and mountain heather thickened in the late afternoon air.

"We're going to get wet before we reach the tower," the boy riding behind him said, glancing skyward.

Cédron nodded. "Yes, you're probably-"

A loud screeching and the flapping of hundreds of tiny wings above them caused the two to duck and cover their heads. A small cloud of pale white diclurues whirled around them from behind and passed the boys as they made their way into the skies. The sound of their clicking, leathery wings and gnashing fangs were the most prominent noise until even that faded, giving way to the thumping of the husan's heavy talons as it plodded down the center of the pass in the otherwise still evening air.

"That was unexpected," the young man said, flattening his hair where the breeze from the diclurues had ruffled it.

"Yeah, for a moment there, I thought they were going to attack." Cédron's hand was still at his chest, his heart beating irregularly. "One time, I was too close and they all crapped on my head as they flew over."

The soldier let out a single bark of laughter. Then he fell silent. Cédron wasn't sure if the young man wanted to continue the conversation and just didn't know what to say, or if he'd rather be left alone. He took a deep breath and decided to try a different approach.

"So, what's your name?" he asked.

The legionnaire continued his silence. Cédron turned his head slightly to look at him. The young man's eyes were on the ground. Cédron could tell he was uncomfortable and that he was holding some sort of debate within himself, but he couldn't fathom his continued stubborn silence.

"Anéton," he answered. He looked up at Cédron, reconciled to whatever his inner struggle had revealed to him. "My name is Anéton Bessínos."

"I'm Cédron Varkáras."

"I know."

Cédron felt the too-familiar shame of being different and he clenched his teeth. He remembered Shozin's recent reprimand to not make assumptions, especially when it came to how others thought or felt until asked directly. Cédron wasn't quite ready to confront the young man on his personal feelings about Shäeli 'demons,' so he decided to test the legionnaire's willingness to engage in conversation.

"That was a pretty amazing knife technique you did up there," Cédron began.

Anéton shot a sideways glance at his companion and smirked. "It's not something I'm commended for in the legion. In fact, your brother Tóran lets me know how cowardly knife-throwing is every chance he gets. It's ok for him to use his acrobatics, but I'm chastised for my special talent."

Cédron stiffened. *Again with the hate towards Tóran. What's this guy's problem? I've never heard of anyone disparaging Tóran before, certainly not for his behavior on the training field. I wonder if this guy's goading me into saying something incriminating. Maybe they have some sort of history together.*

"Tóran does have a talent for unconventional fighting techniques," Cédron commented, watching Anéton out of the corner of his eye. "It seems to work well for him."

Anéton snorted and shook his head. "Sure, sure. It's just that he's the *only* one who gets to try something different."

Cédron raised an eyebrow. *So much venom.* "You don't think much of my brother, do you?"

"Well, let's just say it's hard to keep up with such an outstanding example of legionnaire bravery and determination. He was annoying before the Warrior's Challenge, but now that he's the youngest soldier to win it, he'll be impossible."

Cédron grimaced. "Try living with him."

"No thanks." Anéton held his hands up in mock surrender. "I had to deal with him every day in training."

"He does have a tendency to make everyone around him feel inferior, doesn't he?"

Anéton gave a jaunty salute. "An excellent trait for our future Regent to have, don't you think?"

They both laughed, releasing a bit of the tension that surrounded them. Each had borne the brunt of Tóran's attitude and was thrilled to have found a sympathetic ear. During the trek up the mountain astride the lumbering husan, the young men got to know each other better.

Cédron shared with Anéton how Tóran had been found by his father as an orphan in the wilds of the Tália Jungle. Cédron's mother had been unable to bear more children, and Kásuin thought a brother would be a welcome companion for Cédron when other boys his age tended to shun him.

Over the years, it became apparent that Kásuin and Tóran had much more in common than the biological father and son. Cédron had become an outsider in his own family. This was a situation that Anéton understood better than Cédron would have thought.

Like most boys in his situation, Anéton was forced into the Hármolin Legion because his father was a legionnaire, not because he was interested in it. There was a certain philosophical difference between the young soldier and his superiors that kept him in trouble on a regular basis. Anéton was more than happy to share his unscrupulous fighting philosophy and knife-wielding skills at Cédron's prompting.

"So now Tóran is the heir to the regency and I'm a fugitive," Cédron finished his tale as the rode. "The Sumäeri can only track me if I use my powers, so I figured it was better to leave than risk the lives of anyone else I care about."

The first large drops of warm rain struck the ground as they neared the summit of the pass. The sweet scent of the dry grasses and mountain heather thickened in the warm evening air as the humidity rose with the coming storm. The last rays of Lord Shamar were streaking along the horizon beneath the clouds in a palette of bright reds, oranges, and, near the treetops, deeper purples. Cédron glanced over his shoulder at the eastern horizon and could see a sliver of Orwena in her red glory cresting the trees. They would be to the northern watchtower soon, hopefully before the deluge began and soaked them completely. The husan wandered over to the taller grasses and began to eat. Cédron pulled at the rope and dug in with his heels again, spurring the beast back onto the road.

"We'll have to let him graze once we reach the tower, or he'll start nipping at us," Cédron warned.

"No problem. There's a grassy knoll by the tower that should suit him just fine," Anéton replied.

A thick torrent of rain beat unceasingly on the companions as they began the last, steep grade of the trail to the guard tower. The grass was slippery and the musky aroma complemented the delicate scents of the lavender and pink sweet peas that grew thick among the rocks. Cédron thought their grasping tendrils on the rocks were probably the only reason the larger boulders hadn't lost their precarious hold on the hill and rolled down. The young men approached the base of the tower unchallenged, which was unusual for a guard tower, but Anéton shrugged it off.

"I'm relieving my father," he explained. "He's better known for his drinking than for performing his duties."

The circular tower stood several stories high and was made of white stone, like one gigantic turret. Battlements along the top allowed archers to shoot at any surrounding enemies if necessary, but the towers hadn't been staffed with more than one or two guards since the end of the Garanthian Wars. There were long, narrow windows at uneven intervals around the tower that were used as lookouts during a siege when the top was too dangerous. Oddly, no life stirred from either the top or the windows. Anéton called out for his father several times but got no response.

"Do you think he's ill?" Cédron asked, sliding off the husan's back and holding out his arm for Anéton.

"No, he's probably asleep." Anéton smirked, grabbing the rope from Cédron and releasing the husan to roam free in the grass and sweet peas.

"How can we get in if he doesn't open the door?" Cédron pulled on the iron ring as hard as he could, but it wouldn't budge.

"Not to worry." Anéton winked. "A legionnaire is always prepared." He pulled out a metal pin and began working on the locking mechanism.

Cédron shook his head. *I didn't know lock picking was a skill taught in the legion, but I guess there's no point in arguing.* Cédron watched in fascination as Anéton turned and twisted the pin, his tongue sticking out slightly between his lips. Cédron looked around for signs of any trouble, struggle, or a returning guard while Anéton worked.

The rain had already begun letting up as the clouds moved swiftly overhead in the air currents. Although the area was clear and quiet, the hair stood up on the back of his neck. Cédron glanced up and scanned the tree line below the tower for signs of movement, but there was none.

"Got it!" Anéton clicked the lock and swung the door open, bowing at the waist and waving Cédron in like visiting royalty.

"Quit goofing off and find your father," Cédron ordered, grinning.

The two young men climbed the circular stone stairs that wound around the inside of the white tower. They reached the guard room and saw immediately that it was empty. Heavy tapestries hung along the windows and back wall, providing the only color in the otherwise cold and gray room. Large woven baskets hung from hooks along the center beam. The table and chair were pushed in neatly, the fireplace was cleaned up and the kettle sitting over the ashes was cold. The weapons rack was empty except for a pair of broken spears, a crossbow with bolts, and an old sword. Nobody had been there recently. The air smelled stale.

Anéton swung off his rucksack and dropped it onto the table. The package that he had attached to his pouch rolled out. He untangled the ties that held the package and showed it to Cédron.

"Herbs and stuff that my mother makes for my father. She insists he eat the ground flax and barberries for his heart. I keep telling her that if she'd just quit haranguing him, his heart wouldn't keep beating so fast." He grinned.

"Really, a weak heart?" Cédron asked. "That's unusual for our soldiers, isn't it? They are conditioned to be in such good shape."

"Well, he looks alright from the outside." Anéton chuckled. "But I wouldn't put too much hope on his insides. I imagine they're pretty pickled at this point."

Cedron opened his own pouch and produced a small round of cheese, slices of smoked mijáko and hard rolls. He dug deeper for the flask of ale. The two sat and ate in companionable silence, both famished after their long trek. Finishing their meal, the boys made a cursory inspection of the tower and found it lacking in amenities like stores of water, clean rushes for the bed and weapons.

The two decided to continue their inspection up to the roof and battlements, which were at the top of the winding staircase, ending in a trap door. Anéton grasped the iron ring to push the trap door open but found it too heavy to lift on his own. He called Cédron up next to him and together they pushed. The trap door creaked and grated as it inched open slightly.

"Apparently, nobody has used this door recently," Cédron puffed breathlessly.

He continued to grunt and struggle, finally putting his back to the door and using his legs to lift it. Anéton joined him and, with both of their backs against the rusted trap door, the protesting hinges were worked free. Both young men nearly fell backwards as the hinges broke and the door slid off to the side.

Standing up, the afternoon breeze blowing across the top of the tower was welcome to both sweat-drenched young men. They stood in the open crenels between the thick merlons and enjoyed the view. Off to the north side, just opposite the trap door, were several Yezman jars.

"What's in those jars?" Cédron asked, wandering over to the vessels that were nearly as big as he was.

Anéton glanced over. "Oil for the signal fires, should we need one. It's one of the ways we let Dúlnat know if there's an enemy approaching." He inhaled deeply and ran to the edge of the battlements, looking around frantically. "Speaking of smoke, I smell some!" he cried. He scanned the horizon for the telltale wisps of grey against the dark sky.

Cédron leaned out over the edge of the battlements to the west as if he'd spotted something. "I don't see any smoke, but there is someone coming, quickly. It looks like…but it can't be…"

"What is it?"

"I think it's some Meq'qan tribesmen, but they never leave the marsh unless they're migrating, and that isn't until after the harvest." Cédron said, squinting into the waning light.

Anéton joined Cédron on the western edge of the tower and they watched together. Through the gloom and drizzling rain, they could make out a man running along the tree line and two more behind him carrying a litter. As he ran, the first man kept turning around to look behind him. The two in the tower looked further west to see what the runners were fleeing, but could see nothing in the forest behind them. The first Meq'qan made it through the trees and into the clearing below the tower.

"He's been injured!" Cédron pointed at the blood on the man's shoulder.

The two yelled to get the runner's attention and waved for him to seek safety in the tower. The tribesman looked up and nodded. He sprinted up the hill towards the tower door, swinging his right arm powerfully to propel himself forward. The other two Meq'qan had just cleared the tree line and were making their way up the hill towards the tower.

They both sprang to the trap door and raced down the stairwell to open the tower door for their visitors. Cédron unlatched the door, and the wounded man fell heavily into their arms. He was gasping for breath, with blood soaking his entire chest area, making him slippery to hold on to. The man turned around and yelled at the remaining tribesmen to hurry with their burden.

The feathered shaft of a thick bolt stuck out above the wounded Meq'qan's left shoulder blade, and the blood was welling up around the injury and seeping into their clothes. Anéton scanned down the hillside for any evidence of the tribesmen being followed. The two tribesmen carrying the litter reached the top of the hill and were ushered into the tower. Cédron bade them head up the stairs and lay the litter and a small bundle onto the floor, then he tended the wounded warrior. Anéton shut the door and locked it before turning to help his wounded guest.

The two young men half carried, half stumbled with the Meq'qan up the stairs to the living level where they sat him on the bed and began to carefully pull off the clothing so they could get a better look at his injury.

"Garanth!" the injured man gasped. "They are coming!" Weakened from the run and loss of blood, the man slumped backwards and lapsed into unconsciousness.

CHAPTER 19 - MEQ'QAN WARNING

Garanth! Anéton and Cédron stared at each other, their eyes wide. Each understood what the Meq'qan's warning meant for them and for Dúlnat. If the Garanth were this far south, their home would be their next stop. Shozin Chezak had mentioned rumors of Garanthian armies moving through the Tek'kut Marshes, but Regent Varkáras had been confident they would stay to the west and bypass Dúlnat. Cédron knew the fearsome tribes would destroy everything in their path. The white city with her thousands of people, stained glass, and beautiful gardens would be obliterated.

"I will need to get word to my father," Cédron gasped, easing the wounded Meq'qan onto the cot. "Just as soon as we take care of him."

Anéton nodded, grabbed one of the small, tightly-woven baskets from the hanging rack, and filled it with water from a jug near the window. Bringing the water to the side of the bed, he tore a strip from the end of the bed's blanket with his knife. Throwing his uncle's words of caution about using his Árk'äezhi aside, Cédron pulled out a bloodstone from his pouch and nodded to Anéton. The legionnaire pulled the bolt from the Meq'qan's shoulder, earning only a small moan from the unconscious man. Blood surged from the ragged flesh and ran in rivulets into the cot and onto the floor. Cédron quickly placed the bloodstone over the wound, activating his Árk'äezhi.

The blood welling out of the wound was sucked into the stone with a force that caused Anéton to gasp and step back.

Cédron held his concentration on healing as the crimson stain turned dark and began to dry up. Anéton cleaned the wound with the water and applied a dressing using the strip torn from the bed, watching Cedron with respect in his eyes. The other two Meq'qan tribesmen had set their litter down carefully on the floor and stepped behind Cédron to inspect their work. Once the wound was cleaned and dressed, they laid the wounded man back down on the cot and covered him with a light woolen blanket.

"We are grateful for your assistance." The younger warrior nodded to Anéton as he tossed the bloodied bolt onto the table. "Those Garanth scouts would have killed us if they'd caught us. We are all that's left of our tribe."

"Just the three of you?" Cédron gasped at the idea of nearly an entire race being down to three individuals.

The young men nodded, their eyes cast down. "The three of us and our Seeress are all that survived the slaughter in the Tek'kut Marshes. I am Chem'ewa." The young man clapped his chest. Pointing to the other two in turn, he said, "And this is Dir'iq. Ta'riqk took the bolt in the shoulder, and our Seeress remains removed from this world. None of the tribes remain."

Cédron glanced over at the small form lying on top of the litter. "Your Seeress? Is she hurt?"

The young Meq'qan placed a hand gently on top of the woman's shoulder. "She is old and has been ravaged in spirit, but her body is unharmed. She is resting now, and so must we."

Anéton nodded as he got up from the cot and crossed the room to look out the window. "How many Garanth are on the move, and where are they headed? Do you know?"

Chem'ewa glanced at Dir'iq, who shrugged and sat down on a woven mat near Ta'riqk. "It looked as if the entire Garanthian Nation was upon us." The boy shrugged, his yellow reptilian eyes haunted. "At first, they pretended to want to trade with us, but then the warriors poured out from the hills and slaughtered everyone…only the Seeress's foresight saved us."

"The *entire* Garanthian Nation?" Anéton asked, scratching the back of his neck.

Dir'iq narrowed his slanted eyes. "Do you think we lie?"

"No, no!" Cédron raised his hands out, palms up. "I need to get word to the Hármolin Legion in Dúlnat, and I need to know how many Garanthian warriors they need to prepare for. Were there only bulls, or were there females and young among the warriors?"

Dir'iq's brows furrowed as he pressed his lips together. "There were only bulls, hundreds and hundreds of bulls who cut down our people like grass. They burned our homes. We have nothing left and nothing to return to."

Anéton turned away from the window and faced the two Meq'qan. "You are welcome to stay here. We will protect you until we can get you to safety."

The two Meq'qan tribesmen nodded their thanks and laid down on the floor, one next to Ta'riqk's bed and the other next to the Seeress who now slept on the litter. Cédron looked around the sparsely furnished quarters and, spying a wooden bowl, dumped the contents of his flask into it and began concentrating. Anéton watched as the water in the bowl began to spin slowly.

"You can't keep using your Árk'äezhi!" he gasped. "The Shäeli guards are still tracking you. You'll bring them right here if you're not careful."

Cédron opened his eyes and drummed his fingers quickly on the table in frustration. "Look, we have no other choice. I have to warn my father so he can get word to the legion. I don't want our people to suffer the same fate as the Meq'qan!"

Anéton followed Cédron's gaze out the narrow window at the darkening sky, both watching the sliver of orange along the horizon as Lord Shamar retreated below the trees.

"If they catch me, it's ok," Cédron said. His golden hair caught the last rays of light through the window, making his hair appear to be aflame. "So many have lost their lives on my account. I can't be responsible for the loss of any more."

Anéton nodded as Cédron turned his attention back to the water and closed his eyes. He slowed his breathing and relaxed. The waters began to churn again slowly and Cédron opened his eyes, focusing on the water.

Cédron held his hand up for silence and focused on the water again. The waters swirled faster, and this time the Maräera Gardens appeared in the bowl.

"Father," Cédron called softly into the bowl. "Father, I need you." He stared into the bowl, focusing his power on the summoning.

Suddenly, the face of Kásuin Varkáras was staring out at the boys from the depths of the bowl. He looked both shocked and afraid at hearing his name called from the fountain in the gardens.

"Cédron? Is that you?" Kásuin hissed, his eyes wide. He looked around to see if anyone else had noticed the unfortunate display of magic.

"Yes father," the boy answered. "Listen to me. The Garanthian army is headed south. They may be moving towards Dúlnat. We have Meq'qan survivors who informed us that hundreds of bulls have annihilated the Meq'qan tribes of the Tek'kut Marshes. Warn the legion."

"Cédron, where are you? What has happened to you?" Kásuin beseeched his son.

"I'm at the northern watchtower, but I have to go." Cédron winced, rubbing his forehead. "Scrying takes too much energy, and I can't stay in one place too long, or they will find me. I will come home as soon as I can, father. Warn the legion. Evacuate the city."

Cédron broke the connection and slumped back into the chair. He gulped the water from the bowl and rose, throwing his cloak over his shoulders despite the muggy heat of the evening. He knew he'd need it later in the chill of night.

"My father will make sure Dúlnat is safe. You wait here for me or your father." With a nod, he indicated the wounded Meq'qan. "They need to stay here and recover. I'll go see if I can figure out which direction the Garanth are heading."

Anéton opened his mouth as if to protest, then shrugged and nodded. Cédron clasped his new friend's arm in farewell as the first howl of the Garanth's mulark dog pierced the air, freezing him in place.

"It's too late," Anéton gasped. "They're already here."

* * *

Regent Kásuin Varkáras marched purposefully in from the gardens to his megaron, where he hoped he'd find Rováen waiting for him. Cédron's face still swam before his eyes, his son's warning echoing in his head. He didn't know exactly who Cédron was with, but he'd said he was at the northern watch tower, which meant the Garanth would be advancing from the north. The idea of his son charging into their midst in order to gain intelligence terrified him. He and Rováen had faced danger before, but nothing like this. *The stakes feel higher when it's your own child.*

Kásuin nodded at Rováen as he entered the megaron. He sat down wearily on the ornately carved chair behind his desk and laid his dark head in his hands. The guilt and sadness over Maräera's recent death resurfaced with a vengeance, and he knew that her spirit would torment him for the rest of his days if he let anything happen to their only son. He had to protect him from all the forces that seemed allied in their efforts to destroy the boy, but Kásuin was beginning to realize that the only effective way to keep Cédron safe was to let him go. The Regent of Dúlnat, for all his power and prestige, had no inkling of how to do that. *How do you just let your son go and trust that he will be ok?*

Kásuin raised his head, the few strands of silver sprinkled in his dark hair catching on the rays of light that poured through the window. His grey eyes were shadowed as he exhaled slowly and raised his gaze to Rováen, who remained standing silently at his friend's side.

"Cédron is at the northern watchtower. He used some sort of scrying to let me know that the Garanthian tribes are advancing. I have to inform the legion."

Rováen sagged against the window and exhaled slowly. "Well, at least he's safe."

"Safe!" the Regent cried. "How is being in the direct path of the Garanthian tribes safe?"

Rováen stepped towards his friend and placed his hand on Kásuin's shoulder. "He's far enough from Dúlnat that the Council Guard won't sense his Árk'äezhi, and he's beyond Algarik's reach. I'd say the Garanth are the least of the evils the boy can face right now."

"Hmph." Kásuin shook his head and headed for the door. "Come on, let's get the legion mustered before we're overrun."

Kásuin's thoughts were dark as he stormed out into the fading afternoon light seeping beneath the clouds and reflecting off the white marble of the courtyard. He knew the legion opposed his decision to make Cédron his heir, but he hoped they could at least agree that the city would need to be defended from this new threat. There had been rumors and threats of open rebellion in some quarters. Kásuin hoped that this meeting wouldn't be the one that drew battle lines in the sand between the legion and their sovereign. He glanced up at the darkening clouds and grimaced as the first drops of the Suntide storm fell onto his shoulders. The Regent and his best friend moved into the streets of Dúlnat, waving with brusque gestures at the greetings of those they passed on their way to the northern quadrant of the city where the legionnaires' barracks were housed.

The cobblestone streets were filled with folks on their way to and from the market, their baskets held firmly on their heads or hips, small children in tow. The two men wove their way through the throngs of people, many of whom would have stopped the Regent to speak with him had he not been in the company of the outlandish Shäeli. People's faces went either slack or dark as the two approached. Kásuin's anger grew as he noted his people's reactions to Rováen's presence. *Public protests indeed! If the legionnaires are leading the anti-Shäeli sentiment, I'll demote Captain Sórsen and replace him with Rováen myself!*

Kásuin reached the end of the tower where the legion made their home. He walked through the gated arch that separated the legion from the rest of the city's inhabitants, and up to the stone building that doubled as both watch tower and residence for the Captain of the Legion. Kásuin's ire hadn't abated, and he pounded on the door with the full force of his indignation and rage.

"Captain Sórsen, come out here and answer to your Regent!" Kásuin shouted at the barred door.

Legionnaires came running from the training field behind the barracks, the stomping of their heavy boots in the dirt and on the flagstones offering counterpoint to Kásuin's pounding on the door. A few dark heads poked out from the barracks windows, marveling at the scene below them.

The tension in the air was palpable as the legionnaires surrounded the two men. Kásuin stopped pounding the door and turned to face the men who stood silently watching him. Their faces were a mixture of expressions, ranging from impassive to indignant to angry. Never before had their Regent been forced to invade their demesnes, and Kásuin felt the hostility radiating out of these men as the remains of the day's heat rose up from the flagstones beneath their feet.

"Where is your captain?" Kásuin asked the front line of men facing him, their swords still drawn, though not held aggressively.

"You're not welcome here, Regent Varkáras," a voice drawled from the center of the group.

Bodies parted slowly as the speaker made his way through the ranks to the front of the crowd. Kásuin beheld Captain Sórsen in sparse combat gear as if the man had been practicing on the field with the rest of his men.

The stocky captain was shirtless, wearing only his black leather trousers and boots, but he had his sword belt and scabbard hanging on his right side. He held his sword in his left hand, his short bristling hair sticking up despite the sweat covering his head. Kásuin had never really liked the Captain of the Legion, but he'd felt at the time that following tradition and supporting the winner of the tournament was more important than imposing his own will. He was beginning to see the error of that decision.

Captain Sórsen glared at the Regent, his ruddy complexion as much a result of his recent efforts on the training field as the enormous quantities of ale he was reputed to enjoy.

"You've overstepped your bounds bringing that Shäeli here," the captain growled.

Kásuin reached for Rováen's shoulder and gently pulled the Shäeli back behind him. Rain fell steadily from the darkening sky as the Regent gathered his thoughts. He placed his hands on his hips, taking a moment to survey the faces surrounding him and to choose his words carefully. He stepped forward to face Captain Sórsen and offered his hand up in the traditional greeting.

"Captain Sórsen," he began. "I beg your forgiveness for this intrusion. I have just learned that the Garanthian army is on the move. They have destroyed the Meq'qan villages of the Tek'kut Marsh and are moving southward. We need to prepare the city for siege."

The angry murmurings and shifting of feet and weapons stilled at Kásuin's words. He had their attention now.

"I need you and your men to organize a quick and safe evacuation of the civilians, and then report to me for further instructions. I expect to have more information on the size of the army and their route shortly," Kásuin said loud enough for all assembled to hear.

"Do you now?" Captain Sórsen spat into the dirt at the Regent's feet. "And where would this information be coming from?"

Kásuin groaned internally. *Mijáko piles, I can't lose them now!* He made a decision not to deceive his legionnaires, but he couldn't be completely truthful with them either.

"I have word from those at the northern watchtower that the Garanth are on the move," he answered, his eyes holding the insolent gaze of the captain. "A small group of Meq'qan survivors made their way there."

The legionnaires muttered loudly within the ranks, their leaders calling for order and silence. One legionnaire, a thin man with wicked black eyes and angular features, spoke up louder than the others.

"Old Bessínos is manning that tower. There's no way he's gotten word to you that quickly."

Captain Sórsen motioned for silence, compelling even the rowdiest to obedience. He turned to Kásuin and Rováen, his eyes reflecting the revulsion he felt for his sovereign.

"True, how did you get word from Bessínos so quickly?" he sneered. "Did a little bird fly down and whisper these lies to you?"

Kásuin's face flushed. Anger flared through his body at the insolence and temerity of his legionnaires. He clenched his fists, wishing he could wipe the sneer off the face of the cochäera-snouted man in front of him. Kásuin knew he had to work with the captain if he was going to get the cooperation of the entire Hármolin Legion. He took a deep breath and was about to tell them of Cédron's message when Rováen stepped forward.

"How the warning was brought to us is not the issue," the Shäeli said, addressing the ranks of soldiers. "The fact that we will be facing a horde of Garanthian bulls shortly, is."

Captain Sórsen's eyes narrowed. "How do we know you're not just trying to get us out of the city? I'm not naïve enough to think you don't have spies among us that have informed you of our concerns about your ability to rule." The captain leered at the Regent, his neck craning up at the taller man.

The men roared their support for their captain. Swords clashed on shields, feet stomped and Kásuin felt his control of the situation and his future slipping through his fingers. He raised his hands for quiet, trying to address the soldiers who refused to listen to their Regent.

Captain Sórsen fanned his arms to incite his men to greater heights of frenzy. The legionnaires pressed in around Kásuin and Rováen, pushing the two against the wall of the barrack's tower. A few stones were hurled in their direction but failed to hit their mark.

Kásuin looked helplessly at Rováen, hoping the other man might have a solution. Rováen hung his head, defeated, and shook it slowly. Kásuin stood straight and faced the angry mob. He wouldn't show any fear to these men who had forsworn their oaths of loyalty to him.

"String them both up!" shrieked Captain Sórsen at the men.

Rough hands grabbed Kásuin and Rováen and forced them to their knees. Mud splashed all around them as the men jostled for position. Ropes were being wrapped around their arms and binding their hands when the watch tower bell began to peal.

The legionnaire manning the tower leaned out and shouted at the captain, who couldn't hear amidst the chaos of the lynching. He jumped up on a barrel that was sitting beneath the eaves of the barracks where it could catch water. Straddling the edges, he hollered at his men for silence.

Between peals of the warning bells from the tower, everyone assembled below heard the same message: THE NORTHERN WATCH TOWER IS UNDER ATTACK!

CHAPTER 20 - WAR APPROACHES

Räesha ran her fingers through her close-cropped hair and tried to get used to life without her long braid. She felt almost naked without the weight of her waist-length tresses. She shook her head, marveling at the feeling of the air blowing through clear to her scalp. As much as the change had seemed distasteful at the time, she realized the soundness of R"oväen's argument. If she was going to successfully decoy as Cédron, she'd have to look like him.

The Sumäeri had allowed her traveling companion, the famed gem cutter Sahráron, to cut off the long silver braid and dye her remaining hair golden with walnut extract. Sahráron was renowned for her exquisite wares and had a near magical ability to bring out the beauty in both her stones and their wearers. Her eye for color and form made Räesha's transformation complete. The resemblance was remarkable, particularly after she'd donned Cédron's clothing and the chain of state, the heavy gold medallions bearing the Varkáras crest that draped across her shoulders over her cloak.

"It suits you," Sahráron said, startling Räesha from her self-conscious fidgeting.

"What?"

"The golden hair," Sahráron explained, smiling and pulling at her own dark hair as the breeze loosened it from the thong. "It goes well with your skin tone."

"Um, thanks." Räesha smiled shyly at the older woman.

The two women continued on in silence, Sahráron clicking her tongue at the four husan pulling her wagon as the caravan wound its way through the mountain pass towards the Dagán Valley and their ultimate goal of Taksábai. Kásuin and Rováen had decided that sending Cédron's cousin with the caravan as a decoy was the most believable deception they could pick, given the circumstances.

They knew that both the contingent of Council Guard and Algarik continued to pursue Cédron and traveling with the caravan would give 'him' complete and constant protection. Both parties would have to use stealth and cunning to reach the decoy and discover the deception, occupying their efforts for the longest period of time and giving Rováen and the Regent more time to find the missing boy and get him safely out of Dúlnat.

Disguised as Cédron, Räesha had been sitting in the front of the wagon with Sahráron as the caravan slowly made its way through the city of Dúlnat, through the mourning crowd, and into the narrow pass that wound down the mountainside. There should be no doubt to anyone that Cédron had gone with the caravan since the entire city had turned out for the first of many funeral processions and then to see the caravan off.

They had been traveling for one day and Räesha was already feeling a sense of frustration. It would take at least a fortnight for the Varkáras Caravan to meander its long way through the mountains to the valley near the capital city of Askáribai. Yongäen kept out of sight, following the caravan well above the clouds or, when the skies were clear, high enough in the atmosphere not to be noticed by any on the ground.

Räesha missed the exhilaration of flying with her raptor, the beating of his strong heart beneath her legs, and the wind in her hair. *Well, at least I won't have to worry about getting whipped in the face for a while.* She twisted a short piece of hair near her ear, then patted it smooth again.

She glanced skyward, trying to spot her steed, but he was too high. She could sense him on the very outskirts of her awareness, so she knew he would come to her if she needed him. Räesha was relieved to know that he was safe high above her where the other, more fearsome predators couldn't reach him. This train of thought brought her to her sisters. She wondered how they were faring within their Sumäeri units.

Her insides twisted, remembering their narrow escape from the Selväen and the contingent of Council Guard that had been sent to destroy her entire family. She closed her eyes and swallowed the lump of grief that remained unresolved. She couldn't afford to indulge her sorrow at the loss of her parents and their home yet. First, she had to keep Cédron safe, then get him to accept the quest that he seemed destined to undertake.

Räesha still wasn't completely convinced that the young man could handle what she was going to ask of him, but events had spiraled out of their control in recent hours. He was Muralia's only viable option at this point. If Cédron refused this task or couldn't handle it, then all would be lost. Her parents and her sister would have died in vain. Räesha knew that she would quickly follow them back to the Valley of Souls, where the remainder of her people would flee from the ravaged destruction that their world would become if the demon Laylur was allowed to escape his prison and wreak his vengeance upon the deity who held him for millennia.

Räesha drummed her fingers on the wooden bench. She itched to be astride her beast and facing an enemy rather than running and skulking and hiding. Sahráron noticed her agitation and shook her head, smiling slightly.

"This must be difficult for you." Sahráron pulled her shawl tighter about her bony shoulders, shivering slightly in the breeze. She offered the warrior rolls of spiced mijáko and atoca berries and smiled when her offer was accepted.

Räesha stared out at the horizon, chewing on the savory roll and watching the endless wave of evergreen trees tossing amid the sea of blue sky. She spied a small herd of mijáko ambling their way down the rocks above them, their cloven hooves catching holds in the tiny fissures that creatures with thicker hooves would find impossible to navigate. Even their precarious march wasn't enough to distract her from her irritation.

"I feel like I'm at the edge of a storm. I know that it's coming. I just don't know where the first bolts of lightning will strike," she said. "I hate feeling unprepared."

Sahráron nodded.

"I wish I knew how my sisters were faring with their units," Räesha continued. "I hope they're safe and their leaders listened to them."

Sahráron glanced at the Sumäeri warrior in surprise. "Can't you scry them?"

Räesha let out a rueful laugh. "Normally, yes, but using my Árk'äezhi will alert the Council Guard to my position and my identity." She drummed her fingers again. "We're trying to avoid a confrontation for as long as possible."

"Hmm." Sahráron frowned, her dark eyes regarding her companion. "I wonder if this would work."

Sahráron held up her left hand. Räesha had noticed the array of silver chains connecting the rings of aquamarine gemstones with the turquoise in the center of her hand, but she didn't think that the trinket was anything other than an ornate piece of jewelry.

"What? Does it have some sort of practical function?" the Sumäeri asked.

Sahráron's mouth twisted slightly and her freckled nose wrinkled with the expression. "Yes, you could say that."

Räesha watched the gem cutter, her eyebrows raised expectantly. Sahráron handed the warrior the husans' reins and turned to face her.

"I created this arrangement of stones to communicate with a Meq'qan of the Tek'kut Marsh at Kásuin's request," she said, rubbing the stones with her right hand. "I was able to scry the village Seeress without using any Árk'äezhi other than that of the stones themselves. Perhaps you could use them without using your own Árk'äezhi?"

"You have the ability to access your Árk'äezhi energy to activate the stones?" Räesha asked the Askári woman.

Sahráron smiled wistfully. "No, I have no innate ability…only the knowledge of how to access the stones' energies. That's why I thought it might be a reasonable alternative for you – especially if you don't want to attract attention to your own Árk'äezhi energy."

Räesha nodded. She pondered the viability of using the stones. The Shäeli didn't utilize talismans or amulets or other such accoutrements for their magic. They simply tapped into the natural flow of Árk'äezhi energy flowing from Lady Muralia through their world and used it to enhance the living things around them.

Most Shäeli had one particular gift that they used their Árk'äezhi energies for. Hers was the ability to interpret animals' thoughts, which made her a logical candidate for a läenier rider. Her sister Läerei was skilled in making toxins from plant extracts that the Sumäeri used to paint on their arrows and spear heads. She was talented enough to create gradations of toxin that could run the gamut between rendering the recipient unconscious for several hours or dead within seconds. Her twin sisters Läenshi and Säeshi had complementary gifts of identifying and enhancing Árk'äezhi, which made them a particularly effective team.

Räesha thought about her pursuers, wishing she had a vial or two of her sister's potions handy. *Just in case this doesn't work. I don't want to kill anyone if I don't have to.*

Räesha looked back at the older woman and nodded. "What do I do?"

"Just keep the husan following the other wagons for a bit."

Sahráron turned and climbed down the side of the wagon. Räesha could hear her climb the ladder on the back end of the wagon as they continued their slow march through the pass. She heard the gem cutter open the door and then rummage around through her wares.

The jingling of the harnesses on the husan and the enormous, bovine kazan pulling the wagon ahead of her momentarily overpowered the sounds of cursing that came from the back of the wagon. Räesha smiled. *She sure is a feisty woman.*

The warrior held the reins evenly, guiding the four husan along the trail behind the wagon in front of them as if she'd been doing it for years. She doubted if the beasts had any sense of the change in masters, but it didn't matter. Sahráron returned and climbed up the stairs, sitting down on the hard bench and holding out her left hand.

"I replaced the turquoise with aventurine and the aquamarine with peridot, since the Shäeli are aligned with terran Árk'äezhi and not water," she said.

Räesha marveled at how quickly the woman had replaced the stones in their setting. "How does it work?"

"Well," Sahráron began, "it's pretty simple, really. I stumbled on the phenomenon accidentally when I was working on a necklace. It's just a matter of clearing your mind and focusing on the properties of the stones." She hesitated for a moment, her eyes shadowed and tense. "Then there is the fact that it will drain you of your physical energy if you're not careful."

Räesha glanced up from the stones and into the slender woman's face. "What do you mean, exactly?"

Sahráron sighed. "The cost of activating the stones without using your Árk'äezhi is the depletion of your strength. I was able to scry for only a few minutes before becoming exhausted." The gem cutter had her elbows on her knees and placed her chin in her hand.

She tapped her jaw with her finger as she thought briefly, the motion drawing attention to her dark freckles that accented the angle of her face.

"Perhaps knowing what will happen and preparing for it will help. Maybe if you try to control your thoughts and the flow of your energy, you will have better success at it than I did...I really wasn't sure what was going to happen, and it took a lot out of me."

Räesha stared at the stones for a moment, then nodded slowly. She slipped the rings onto her fingers and closed the clasp on the bracelet, securing the center stone to the back of her hand. Closing her eyes, she concentrated on the stone's properties while simultaneously blocking her natural flow of Árk'äezhi. The Sumäeri was surprised to feel the vibrant pulse of the stones on her hand without the warmth of Árk'äezhi flowing from deep within her heart.

In her mind's eye, she could see the stones vibrating softly with their viridian glow. The green of the stones focused and became the leaves and undergrowth of the Ginäeyi Forest where her sister Läerei was on patrol. She opened her eyes and saw the same scene in the large aventurine nestled on the back of her hand. As her sister's face came into clearer view, Räesha gasped.

"Läerei!"

Räesha watched the image in the stone stop and look around. Obviously, her sister had heard her cry. Räesha called to her again, this time more insistently. Läerei grabbed her knife and crouched into a defensive position, her eyes darting as she tried to locate the source of the voice calling her name.

Räesha concentrated harder, willing the vines near her sister to create a vessel that would allow her sister to see her face and converse with her. She felt the muscles of her back and legs becoming weaker as her energy poured into the stones, but she ignored it. *This has to work. I need her to see me!* Räesha created a circle of vines that surrounded the broad, waxy leaf of a taro plant and projected an image of her face into the shiny surface.

"Läerei, hear me!"

Räesha watched as her younger sister located her image on the plant. Her eyes widened into saucers.

"Räesha?" she gasped. "Is that you? What sort of sorcery is this?"

"I'm being hunted by Council Guard," Räesha explained, combing her short, golden hair back from her face. "This Askári woman is helping me contact you without using my Árk'äezhi so that they can't track the disturbance in the energy."

Läerei nodded her understanding. "We heard that Trilläen's group had been sent to get you."

Räesha blanched. "Trilläen? Are you sure?"

Läerei's face saddened. "I'm sorry. This has to be difficult for him as well."

"Not as difficult as you might think." Räesha's face hardened. "They have also been charged with capturing our cousin, Maräera's demon-child. I wonder how much information they've been given about the situation in Siläeri."

"I don't know," Läerei replied. "All we have been told is that our borders have been compromised and that we need to double patrols." Her brows furrowed and she crossed her arms. "You also need to know that Thoromberk Fortress is occupied again."

Räesha inhaled sharply. "That evil place was abandoned. Even the Garanth fear it."

Läerei nodded grimly. "Yes, and the patrol that reported it has disappeared. We don't know if they were captured or killed, but we cannot sense their Árk'äezhi."

"Do you know who…?"

The ground beneath the wagon started to pitch and roll, causing the husan to spook. Räesha pitched forward on the bench and Läerei's face wavered. The warrior grabbed the bench seat with her free hand and ground her teeth, little beads of sweat forming on her top lip as she concentrated on maintaining the connection.

"Räesha! What is happening?" Läerei's eyes widened.

The terran thunder rumbled just below the whining of the husan and the creaking of the wooden-spoked wheels, making it difficult to hear. Räesha poured all her effort into the stone, focusing on keeping the connection to her sister active.

"Ground shake," she grunted as the wagon lurched sideways.

Läerei wrapped her arms around herself and rubbed the prickles on her biceps. "I wonder if there is a connection to Thoromberk Fortress."

The ground shake slowly subsided and Sahráron got the husan under control. Räesha nodded her thanks to the woman and took a deep breath. "Do we know who is occupying it?"

"We haven't been able to tell and we've been forbidden to leave the borders by the Council." Her sister frowned. "There have also been reports of black-clad warriors in the desert. All we know is that they originated near Yelandi and are headed west. We don't know who they are or what they are doing, but if you see them, stay clear."

Räesha rubbed her forehead. "The Näenji Council has forbidden the Sumäeri to investigate, haven't they? All these threats to our lands and still they keep our borders closed as if ignoring the problems will make them go away." She looked into her sister's eyes, the furrow in her brow deepening. "What of the ground shakes? Have you noticed any changes? They are quite severe here in the north, as you see."

Läerei nodded, her face grim. "They are worsening. Whole sections of land have been swallowed in the chasms broken open by the shakes. Lady Muralia is weakening and our hands are bound from doing anything about it."

"I just don't understand it." Räesha pressed her index finger to her now-throbbing temple. "How can the Näenji Council be so passive in the face of such obvious danger?"

"Something isn't right. It's like the Näenji Council has been corrupted, but nobody sees it. You need to be careful." Läerei reached out towards the leaf. "Be on your guard. Trilläen and his men have been ordered to execute you if you don't return to Samshäeli with them."

"I can handle Trilläen," Räesha said softly. "I'll get the boy to you as soon as I can. Then we can see if he's worth all the sacrifices that have been made to this point."

Läerei's face stiffened with grief. She reached up to the leaf and touched her sister's face. "Be careful, Räesha," she said. "Come back to us soon."

Räesha nodded and let the connection lapse. She slumped in the seat, exhausted from the effort of maintaining the scrying energy. The stones on her hand dimmed and went dark, their energies also depleted. With shaking fingers, she unhooked the clasp and slipped the peridot rings off her fingers.

"Thank you for sharing your stones." Räesha handed the jewelry back to the gem cutter. "I should probably leave the caravan soon, just to be sure you aren't in greater danger than we anticipated."

Sahráron nodded, placing the rings and bracelet back on her right hand. "You'll need some rest before you go, and some food. There's fruit and bread in the wagon. Go rest. I'll keep a look out."

Räesha handed the reins to Sahráron and stood. Lord Shamar dipped down behind the trees, filling the skies with the fiery shades of his farewell to his beloved wife while Orwena began her evening vigil to the east. A gentle breeze blew the Sumäeri's hair back off her face and she turned to inhale the evening's scents of warm grass and wildflowers. Suddenly a wave of power rolled out of the northeast struck her like a blast, nearly knocking her out of the wagon.

Her eyes shot open as she grasped the back of the bench for balance. "Laylur's beast, what was that?" The warrior stared at Sahráron for answers.

The gem cutter looked up at Räesha, her sharp eyes curious. "I only feel bumps on my skin, but you've nearly fallen off the wagon. What's going on? What is that energy I sense just outside my awareness?"

Räesha closed her eyes and focused. The strength of the Árk'äezhi was greater than anything she'd ever felt before. *Whoever it is, he or she is extremely powerful!* She reached out with her mind, trying to locate the source of the power. Her awareness raced along the stream of power back to its source. She felt her skin begin to burn as the heat from the fire assaulted her senses. *This is nearly unbearable, but I must find out who is behind this.* She gritted her teeth against the increasing pain and stretched her mind further. On the edges of her awareness, she felt a presence. The being was raw, like a force of nature that was untamed and unpredictable. She skirted around the glowing source of power, trying to find a way closer without damaging her psyche. As she circled around the radiating being, she saw its eyes open. *It cannot be!* The connection was broken and her awareness flooded violently back into her mind.

"Cédron, no!" Räesha gasped, her hands grasping the bench to steady herself.

"What is it? What has happened to Cédron?" Sahráron's voice cut through the Sumäeri's inner turmoil.

The warrior returned her stare with haunted eyes. "He has turned himself into a beacon for all to see. I must get to him before Trilläen and the Council Guard find him!" Räesha stood and swayed, the dizziness forcing her to sit down hard on the bench.

208

"You can't go after him in your weakened state." The older woman laid a hand on Räesha's arm. "Perhaps you should get help. Rovän can stand with you against the Council Guard should you be forced to make a stand. You can't do it on your own."

The wave of nausea that accompanied the weakness slowly subsided, but Räesha knew that Sahráron was right. "I'll pick him up in Dúlnat on my way into the mountains. The boy is going to need all the allies we can muster if he continues to flaunt his powers like that." She stood again and, holding onto the wagon frame for balance, turned to go down the steps.

"Wait!" Sahráron held up her hand. "I have something I want you to take to him. I'll be right back."

The gem cutter handed the reins to Räesha and scurried into the back of her wagon. Räesha kept one eye on the husan while whistling the high-pitched note for Yongäen. The husan ignored the shrill sound. The Sumäeri scoured the skies for signs of her mount, the pounding in her chest increasing with every second she wasn't in the air. Sahráron climbed up onto the bench in front of the wagon and held out her hand. Räesha raised an eyebrow. In the woman's hand was a small octagonal box.

Sahráron showed Räesha how to open the ivory lid that was inlaid with lapis around the outside representing water and the Konnáras compass rose inlaid with onyx in the center. Inside, a smaller working version of the compass was carved with magnetic arrow ...actually floating inside a crystal casing! Around the outside of the compass was the face of a clock carved in ornate detail and colored with vibrant blue and green dye. A piece of golden twine was attached from the bottom of the compass casing to the top of the lid, creating the line for the sundial.

"This is a diptych sundial," the older woman explained. "An adept wielder can determine the longitude and latitude in degrees using the chart inside the lid. It must always face north when taking a reading. The twine catches the rays of Lord Shamar, casting a shadow on the dial face. The calculations can be determined by adding or subtracting from the chart in the lid."

"Fascinating!" Räesha smiled slightly at the complicated instrument. "Do you think the boy will figure out how to use it?"

"Yes, you Shäeli are an ingenious people." Sahráron smiled wanly. "I'm sure with Rováen's help, he'll soon be quite adept. May it always help him find his way."

Räesha took the compass and stuck it inside her pouch. A shriek from the skies informed her that her mount had arrived. She took a deep breath, gathering her strength in spite of her exhaustion. With a nod to her hostess, she leapt from the wagon and ran to her beast. Vaulting to his back, she hugged her raptor fiercely.

"Up, my friend. We must away before it is too late!"

Chapter 21 - Garanth Attack

Cédron watched Anéton's face turn chalky as another piercing howl of the mulark split the air. His blood turned to ice at the sound of certain death. *That beast is tracking the Meq'qan's scent straight here!* They stayed at the window just long enough to see several large shapes crashing through the trees nearly half a mile away, heading straight for the tower.

Anéton broke out of his stupor first. "Weapons, I need weapons. Mijáko piles!" he cursed, dodging the exhausted Meq'qan as he scouted around the room. "The only weapons here are that crossbow, a couple of broken spears, and a sword. My throwing knives won't be much use against the thick hides of the Garanth and certainly not against the scales of those mulark dogs."

Cédron glanced out the narrow window to mark the approach of the enemy. Spying the splash of color among the large boulders that surrounded the hilltop on which the tower was built, he tapped his temple. "I have an idea. Follow me."

Cédron and Anéton raced back up through the trap door and onto the top of the tower. Cédron pointed to the enormous jars of Yezman oil.

"Help me dump this over the side and into the flowers," he grunted as he tried to lift the half-filled jar.

"You can't lift it," Anéton pulled Cédron's hand off the jar. "You have to roll it like this."

Anéton grasped the tall jar around the widest point in the center and tilted it towards himself slightly, spinning the jar on its bottom edges. In moments, the legionnaire had the half-full jar balanced precariously on the edge of the crenel, where it would barely squeeze through the opening. Cédron's jar didn't move as easily. He'd never spun the liquid-filled jars before and the more he spun it, the more the liquid sloshed the opposite direction, making the jar wobble the wrong way. Cédron tried to imitate Anéton, but he kept losing his balance. He cursed as he scraped his knuckles on the stone walls. Finally, bloodied from the scrapes and muscles twitching from the exertion, he rolled the half-filled jar next to its mate.

"Go get the crossbow and that quiver full of bolts from below," Cédron shouted from across the roof. "We'll try to slow them down."

Opening the lid from his Yezman jar, Cédron tore two strips from his shirt and soaked them in the oil before throwing them on the rooftop and sealing the jar back up. He heaved with his fatigued arms, but the jar was too full and wouldn't budge.

"Hurry!" he cried as Anéton sprinted back up the stairs and through the trap door. "Help me push these jars over the edge."

Anéton tossed the crossbow and quiver behind the closest merlon and raced over to Cédron. Together, the young men pushed with all their strength, knocking the large jars over the edge. They watched with grim satisfaction as they smashed upon the rocks below. Oil splashed all over the flowers and flowed down the hill, bringing a grim smile to Cédron's face. *Excellent. I hope this works.*

"Come on, let's get another jar over to the other side of the tower." Cédron waved Anéton over to the remaining jars. He grasped the first jar and easily lifted it over his head. "Mijáko piles, this one's empty!" he cried. "Grab that next one."

Anéton raced to the next jar. It too was empty. "How are we supposed to light the warning beacon or torches if there isn't any oil?" Anéton cursed his irresponsible father for the tower's unpreparedness.

The young legionnaire reached for the last jar. He couldn't lift it. "Cédron, this one's full. I need your help!"

Cédron grabbed the enormous jar from the opposite side. Grunting and straining, the young men tried to roll the jar like they'd done the other. It wouldn't budge. Straining and swearing, they pulled and tugged on the earthenware with all their strength. Nothing. Cédron ran his hands over his face, wiping the sweat from his eyes. *This isn't working, and we're running out of time!*

Making a quick decision, Cédron whispered a prayer to Orwena. "Let's try to lay it on its side and roll it."

Anéton shook his head. "We can't! The lid will fall out and all the oil will spill all over the battlements." He scratched his dark head, looking around for an alternative. "Let's try using the baskets to fill an empty jar halfway."

Another howl tore through the air, raising bumps on their arms. Cédron's eyes widened. "We don't have time for that! Just try laying it over and rolling it to the other side."

Anéton nodded and positioned himself on one side of the jar. The legionnaire pulled the jar towards himself as Cédron pushed it away. Gently they laid the jar on its side. The lid held in place. Sighing with relief, Anéton rolled the jar to the far wall of the tower. Lifting with all their strength, the two of them tipped it over the battlements. It smashed on the ground below. Slowly, the oil drained its way into the boulders, saturating the remaining plants. Cédron hoped it would be sufficient to catch the wet foliage on fire.

Running back over to the stack of jars, Cédron picked up the two strips of oil-soaked cloth. "Grab the crossbow and those bolts," he ordered and jogged over to the edge of the battlements. Handing the cloths to Anéton, he instructed the soldier to wrap two of the bolts with the fabric and stand back.

"Maftah," he whispered, drawing forth the Árk'äezhi from within and igniting the first deadly projectile.

Anéton looked out beyond the battlements and could see the searching Garanth. "They're getting closer. If the grass and flowers catch fire quickly, we may have a chance." He shot the bolts into the oil-soaked sweet peas and dropped to his knees. "You'd better pray to Orwena for a miracle."

The lads watched the bolts hit the ground with a squelch. They held their breath, praying for the oil to catch fire. Nothing happened. Cédron's heart sank. "The plants are too wet from the rain. We're trapped in this tower with nowhere to go and no aid coming!" He slumped to the floor, his back resting against the battlements. Anéton slid down next to him and pounded the floor with his fist.

A slight breeze ruffled the forelock of his golden hair, tickling his cheek and bringing with it the scent of fresh smoke. Startled, Cédron stood up and looked over the side of the battlements.

"Look," he cried pulling Anéton up beside him. "It worked!"

"Yahaa!" the young soldier shrieked and brandished the bow at the rising flames below him.

The mulark was getting closer, it's howling more insistent. Cédron could see that the beast was still too far away for Anéton to hit with accuracy. The four Garanthian bulls following it were still way behind, moving much slower with their armor and weapons hampering them. Cédron squinted, trying to sharpen his view of the distant pursuers when the hound bounded through the last of the trees and into bow range. Its thick, sinewy muscles corded as it launched itself towards the tower. Bile filled Cédron's mouth as he watched the slavering canine race toward them.

Its head had a rounded sheet of black, plated scales that sloped into a massive square jaw filled with enormous fangs. The plates extended down its twelve-foot length, protecting it from attack. A long reptilian tail whipped out behind it in agitation as the mulark began scrabbling with its long claws against the walls of the tower, looking for a purchase. Mijáko piles! *That thing is bigger than a kazan bull, easily seven feet tall, and covered with overlapping scales. We don't stand a chance!*

The young men watched in horror as the mulark's claws tore holds into the smooth siding of the tower and began to scale the wall. Adrenaline pumped Cédron's heart faster as he tore from the battlements and raced down the stairs to find something to slow the beast with.

Returning to the main quarters of the tower, he searched the room for anything he could throw at the mulark that might knock it from the walls. Nothing caught his eye until he turned toward the sleeping Meq'qan. The table next to the cot had two chairs pushed in beneath it. The young man grabbed one of the chairs and headed towards the stairs.

Climbing back to the battlements as quickly as he could, Cédron threw open the door and prayed that he wasn't too late. He glanced around carefully, half expecting the mulark to be waiting at the top, ready to pounce on his exposed head. Cocking his head sideways, he could hear the beast's claws still scraping along the wall as it continued its climb. Anéton was racing back and forth along the battlements with the cocked crossbow in his hands trying to find a good shot.

Cédron stepped through the trap door and pulled the chair after him. He raced to the edge of the battlements and looked over the side, his heart in his throat as he came nearly face to face with the clashing jowls of the massive canine. The boy swung the chair at the beast, knocking one of its claws loose.

The mulark slipped down the side of the wall a few feet, then gained holds with its claws and began climbing again. The beast's long tail whipped up and knocked the chair from Cédron's grasp, throwing him back from the edge. Cédron quickly got to his feet and picked up the chair, his only barrier from the advancing canine.

Returning to the wall, Cédron jabbed the chair legs straight down at the monster, banging it in its smooth, scaled head. Anéton fired a bolt at it, but the sharp metal simply glanced off the beast's scales.

"Mijáko piles," Anéton swore. "Will nothing stop it?"

Cédron knew that their feeble efforts wouldn't stop or hurt the beast, but maybe they could knock it back from the wall enough to prevent it from digging its claws into the stone. The boy swung the chair at the mulark's snapping jaws. The mulark swiped at the chair with one of its muscular forearms. In doing so, it compromised its hold on the wall. Anéton grabbed the legs of the chair and together the boys pounded the shoulder of the loose arm with the chair, banging it repeatedly while dodging the whipping tail.

The mighty beast snarled and snapped at them with its gnashing maw. Cédron could see the frustration in the beast's eyes at it took another swipe at him, so he pressed his advantage and pounded the beast again in the shoulder. The chair angled slightly, glancing off the forearm and striking the heavily-scaled shoulder.

The beast howled in pain as the foot of the chair caught on a loosened scale and tore it from the shoulder, exposing pink flesh at the top part of the mulark's chest.

"Anéton, if you can get a shot at that open area, maybe you can kill it!" he yelled, pointing at the wound.

Anéton let go of the chair and grabbed the crossbow. Cédron slammed the chair into the mulark again, but the enraged beast clamped down on the legs with its enormous jaws and broke the weakened chair into pieces. The boy's grip on the wood was lost as the monster shook it from his hands. Cédron leapt back from the advancing beast as Anéton grasped a thick, metal bolt from the quiver. The soldier slid it into the channel just as the mulark crested the top of the battlements and landed on the flagstones, the beast's eyes nearly level with Cédron's.

Cédron gulped, his palms instantly clammy from the panic rising in his throat. *I sure hope he's as good with the crossbow as he is with those throwing knives.* Anéton raised the crossbow and aimed it at the mulark's chest, his hands quivering slightly. The beast must have sensed his prey's apprehension as it reared up on its sinewy hind legs, howling in triumph.

Anéton pulled the trigger and launched the bolt at the mulark, but the beast dodged the projectile and swatted the weapon from the soldier's trembling hands. Anéton's eyes widened and Cédron knew this was his friend's last moment. The snarling animal stalked the legionnaire warily, his yellow eyes gleaming with the anticipated kill. Cédron inched his way closer to the Yezman jars, hoping to find something to fight the mulark with. He glanced over at Anéton and saw him hunch down to make himself a smaller target. The monstrous dog's long tongue hung through its slavering jowls, tasting the fear and smoke in the air. Growling, the mulark tensed its legs and crouched down to spring.

Anéton's hands felt around the ground near him and Cédron hoped he would find something that he could use to fight the beast. The legionnaire's hands raked over the quiver that had been knocked off his shoulder. He pulled out another short bolt and held it firmly in his hand. *Oh man, he's only going to get one shot. If that doesn't work, that creature is going to eat both of us!* Cédron snuck around the back side of the stand of jars where the wisps of smoke from the fire below had begun to swirl.

Anéton got to his knees and raised the bolt just as the mulark sprang at his head. Cédron gasped aloud as he plunged the bolt into the beast's shoulder as it struck him. The two combatants rolled backwards on the flagstones, Anéton's arm holding the mulark's neck as far away from his face as possible while shoving the bolt into the tough hide. Cédron fought down the terror that threatened to root him to the spot and grabbed the empty Yezman jar. He lifted it over his head and began staggering towards the mulark.

The mulark screamed and loosened its hold on the legionnaire's shoulders. The beast spun around and whipped the young man with its long tail, sending him flying across the battlements. Dazed, Anéton shook his head and tried to get his bearings while Cédron struggled to get the enormous jar closer to the beast. Cédron ignored the screaming panic in his mind and inhaled a deep breath. Exhaling and shaping the intention of his Árk'äezhi with his mind, he willed the clay jar to fly into the monster's side. The force of his Árk'äezhi enhanced the wind, barreling the container into the beast much harder than he would have been able to on his own. The mulark howled with murderous rage and turned to face this new threat. Anéton got shakily to his feet.

Glancing over to Anéton, Cédron's heart leapt to see the crossbow with a loose bolt lying next to him. "Grab the crossbow!" he screamed at the legionnaire. "At your feet!"

Anéton looked down. Grinning with the unholy joy of the warrior facing impossible odds, the legionnaire grabbed the crossbow and loaded the bolt.

"Come on, my pretty," he crooned at the beast. "Let me send you back to the depths of the abyss where your spawn came from!"

The mulark turned at the sound of his voice and bounded towards him from across the flagstones, his claws scrabbling on the stone in his rush to attack. Anéton let the arrow fly. The string twanged as it zoomed straight and true into the chest of the advancing beast. The vicious hound sprawled across the stones just a few feet short of the soldier, the arrow sticking out of its chest.

Anéton took a shuddering breath and stepped back from the corpse of the mulark. Cédron's heart pounded in his chest, causing the blood to throb in his ears. The look on Anéton's face told him that he felt the same. Both incredulous that they'd survived the mulark's attack, the young men made their way to the edge of the battlements and tried to determine the location of the advancing Garanthian warriors.

The smoke from the flowers below was getting thicker and would soon obscure both the keep and the boulders from view.

"We need to keep them away from the tower," Cédron said as he bounded down the winding staircase. "The fire should loosen the boulders from the flowers so we can roll them down on the Garanth as they climb the hill."

The two young men landed in the living quarters. Grabbing the broken spears as they passed, they charged out into the raging inferno of sweet peas. Cédron pulled his shirt up over his face to filter the thickening smoke, his eyes watering in the acrid stench. Using the broken spears as levers, they loosened the lower boulders from their flowery prison.

As Cédron levered the large rocks that he intended to roll down onto the advancing Garanth, he realized that there was a major flaw in his plan. Although the Garanth couldn't see him through the thick screen of smoke, Cédron realized that he couldn't see them either. They would have to listen for the warrior's passage and hope for success. Not good odds for two young men against four Garanthian scouts and no visibility, but it was the best he had come up with, and it would have to do.

Cédron and Anéton crouched behind the largest boulders above the watch tower and waited. It wasn't long before they heard the guttural language of the Garanth as the brutes navigated their way through the smoke. Heaving with all their strength, the two friends lifted the first boulder with the shafts of the broken spears and rolled it down the hill. It bounced a few feet then stopped, lodged in between two smaller rocks. Cursing, Cédron left his hiding place to loosen the boulder again.

The smoke was curling before his eyes, causing them to sting and water. Cédron couldn't be sure, but he thought he saw a dark shape move off to his right towards the tower. Creeping as stealthily as he could, he made his way to the large boulder again and put all his weight behind lifting it. It wouldn't budge. Cédron strained his already exhausted muscles. Sweat rolled into his eyes, adding to the smoke sting. In front of him, a dark shape with curved horns loomed in the billowing smoke. *These Garanth are bigger than Shozin Chezak!*

Cédron ducked down, hating his luck and frantically trying to think of an escape. He couldn't move because the swirling smoke and sound of his running feet would give away his position. He couldn't stay put because the Garanth were heading straight for him. More grunting and stomping of heavy feet came from the southwest. *I'm surrounded!*

Cédron crouched into a ball, trying to make himself as small as he possibly could in the hopes that the Garanth would overlook his position behind the rocks. *I should try to use the bloodstone to make myself invisible. Uncle Rováen showed me how to do that once.* He carefully inched his hands over to the flap of his pouch and reached inside for the bloodstone. He grasped the first stone he felt and pulled it out.

The firestone flared instantly to life, filling his body with the warmth and power of the Árk'äezhi through the stone. His skin began to glow with the brilliance of the energy pouring through him, leading the Garanth directly to his position.

"Cursed mage thief!" the first Garanth roared when he reached the glowing boy. The warrior, easily seven feet tall, swung the flat of his blade at Cédron, knocking the firestone from his grasp. Instantly, the glow subsided and the stone went dark, rolling into the smoldering grass.

Cédron gasped, holding his bruised hand into his body. "Thief! What…?"

220

The second, stockier Garanth charged through the grass from behind him, knocking him flat onto his face. Cédron lifted his head and watched the tall warrior search through the grass and floral vines for the firestone while the shorter one yanked Cedron's pouch from his shoulder. They dumped everything into the grass, poking through the meager foodstuffs and gingerly pushing the rocks to the side. The two conferred in their guttural language for a moment, casting dark glances at him.

"You, mage." The taller Garanth addressed him, holding up the firestone. "How did you get this stone?"

Coughing from the smoke, he was unable to answer. The stocky Garanth pulled him up by the scruff of his neck and shook him. He set Cédron down on his feet, which nearly gave way from the shock of being captured by the fearsome warriors.

The boy's glazed eyes went from one Garanth to the other, his tongue stuck to the roof of his mouth. The taller warrior took a step closer and backhanded Cédron across the cheek. An explosion of pain cleared his mind as the coppery taste of blood filled his mouth. Cédron spat, glaring at the warrior.

"How did you get this stone?" the Garanth roared again, raising his fist.

Cédron cowered as the second blow struck his jaw. His teeth clamped together as the force of the blow lifted him from his feet and knocked him to his backside. The stocky Garanth kicked him in the back, causing the boy to gasp in pain. Cédron could feel his lower lip swelling as his vision blurred from the puffiness below his right eye. *I can't tell them where I come from or they'll certainly march on Dúlnat, but I have to think of something. Where is Anéton?*

The two Garanth argued over him for a few moments, gesturing wildly with their hands. Even though the smoke swirling around got thicker, making it difficult to see, it was obvious to Cédron that the stockier warrior wanted to kill him outright, while the taller one had some other plan in mind. He wished he knew what Anéton was doing. He had hoped that the smoke screen would give them an advantage over the Garanth, but it hadn't succeeded. Cédron hoped that his friend hadn't decided to send the boulders cascading down on top of all of them. The smoke burned his eyes and stripped his lungs raw.

The taller Garanth knelt down to look at Cédron directly. He stared at the boy with surprisingly intelligent eyes. Cédron squirmed uncomfortably under the scrutiny, but refused to answer the warrior's question. The Garanth nodded curtly at the second warrior who stepped up behind him.

Cédron felt the strong grip of the Garanth on his forearms. He tried to struggle, but the Garanth was too powerful for him. The warrior facing him tied his hands together and gagged him. From behind the Garanth came a fearsome growl. The shadow of a third enormous warrior loomed up, twice the size of a man, from behind the screen of burning grasses.

The two Garanth turned and grunted at the third. The larger warrior growled back, his grunts deep and agitated. Waving his arms, the huge bull motioned for his tribesmen to follow him down the hill. Grabbing their captive, the two Garanthian warriors followed their leader. The three Garanth had nearly reached the bottom of the hill where the smoke had begun to thin when they heard a cry of agony from the tower. Cédron's two initial captors turned to go back up the hill, Cédron in tow, but the larger warrior grunted again. Holding out his hands, the third enormous Garanth reached for Cédron. As he pulled the boy away from his captors, he waved his hands towards the tower and grunted. The first two Garanth nodded and began making their way up the hill.

Clearing the base of the hill and getting his first breath of fresh air, Cédron blinked the stinging tears from his eyes and gasped. The enormous Garanth in front of him was removing

222

his head from his shoulders. Choking back a scream, Cédron's knees weakened with relief as Anéton grinned from underneath the large makeshift disguise. The clever legionnaire had turned a large woven basket upside down and stuck the broken spears on either side to make horns. He had then draped his cloak over the third spear that was stuck horizontally through his jerkin, making his shoulders enormously broad. Using one of his throwing knives, the young man cut Cédron's bonds.

"Well done!" Cédron said weakly, still tingling with relief. "I thought I was done for!"

Anéton shoved the disguise back onto his head as the two large shapes loomed closer in the smoke. "You may be yet. I have to get the other two Garanth away from the tower before they kill the Meq'qan. Go to the woods and hide." The legionnaire lumbered back into the smoke, stomping and grunting in his best Garanth impression.

The two Garanthian warriors had realized they'd been fooled. They circled around the boulder just as Anéton lumbered away, trapping Cédron between the fire and themselves. Panic squeezed the boy's lungs, making breath nearly impossible. Cédron turned and started to run, but his legs bound up beneath him. He fell forward, his hands reaching out to catch his fall. As his fingers dug into the ground, the boy was hit with a sudden inspiration. He closed his eyes and called forth his Árk'äezhi which began flowing through his body and out from his hands. Invoking the energy in the land, he willed the ground to swallow his captors.

The Garanth were both startled as the ground opened up beneath their feet and swallowed them to their waists. Dirt continued to flow slowly up their bodies, encasing them in the soil. The stocky Garanth roared in anger as he tried to wade through the dirt to reach his weapon. As he reached the hilt of his blade, the dirt rose up beneath the grass and trapped his arm. Cédron watched in fascination as his body swiftly became covered in dirt, rocks, and grass.

The second Garanth managed to get turned around before his legs locked up in the rock and he hurled his sword at Cédron. The boy ducked and the blade spun over his head, but the tip sliced open the back of his shoulder as it flew behind him. Cédron screamed in pain as the end of the blade scored his flesh, but knew that he couldn't release his hands from the ground or the magic would retreat. The Garanth roared at the boy and reached for Cédron's pouch, which lay near where his legs were encased in the ground. He quickly picked up the pouch and the firestone, hurling one, then the other at Cédron's head in an attempt to break the spell.

Cédron ducked away from the pouch, but lifted his hands to catch the firestone. The Árk'äezhi shifted from the ground to the stone, causing the firestone to glow and releasing the warriors from their terran prisons. Bursting out of the ground like angry kazan bulls, the two Garanth charged Cédron, their rage completely unrestrained.

Terrified, Cédron aimed the firestone at the stampeding warriors and willed the energy of the fire to burst forth. He felt the scorching heat coursing through his body and out his palms into the firestone. The ball of fire shot out from the stone and slammed into the first Garanth. The mighty warrior was lifted several feet into the air and thrown down the burning hillside. His companion was struck down by the wave of heat that came from the blast.

Cédron looked around wildly for his attackers. Neither moved from where they'd been thrown, but Cédron couldn't tell if they were dead or just unconscious. The stone glowed brightly in his hands but remained only warm to his touch. He raised his hands to send another blast into their bodies when the screams from the tower reached his ears. *The other Garanth must have reached the Meq'qan!*

* * *

224

Anéton peered through the billowing smoke and twilight haze. Fragments of two twisted, hulking bodies among the rocks below revealed themselves briefly before another swirl of smoke devoured them from sight. *Nice job Cédron. Two down, two to go!* The young legionnaire scurried around the back of the tower to entice the remaining two Garanth away from the keep.

Focused on the ground and the placement of his feet, he didn't see the first Garanth looming up in front of him until it was too late. Anéton banged right into the warrior's thick torso and bounced backwards. Anéton's makeshift disguise slipped sideways on his head then slid to the ground. The two adversaries stared at each other in surprise before the huge bull launched himself at his now-puny foe.

Anéton ducked and rolled beneath the legs of the seven foot-tall warrior before sprinting further down the hill. *Mijáko piles, he knows where I am now!* Anéton searched frantically for a better hiding place, the wind blowing the sparse cover of smoke away from his current location.

The Garanth turned around and chased the boy down the hill, bellowing to his companion in their guttural tongue. Anéton was watching the bull that was pursuing him and didn't see the heavy blade from the second swing down towards his head. The whistle of the two-handed sword registered in the back of his mind and he instinctively ducked. The blade swung harmlessly over his head but the Garanth on the other end of it was nearly on top of him. Anéton tried to scramble away, but the Garanth caught him in the chest with the backswing of his blade.

The blunt edge slammed into his body, hurling him several feet away. The young soldier crashed into the rocks, knocking the wind from his body. He fought the wave of nausea and blinked against the stars circling before his eyes. Anéton looked around. There were no weapons within reach and the bull was approaching with its inexorable, lumbering steps.

225

Groaning and nearly blind, Anéton remembered the brace of knives in his sash. He grabbed at his waist, slicing his hand in his haste. The young man knew that he'd have only one chance to incapacitate or kill the thick-skinned creature. It was a risk, but he'd have to lay still and let the Garanth get close enough that he could assure his aim.

The monstrous warrior bellowed a challenge as it reached the young legionnaire. It raised its enormous, wicked blade over its head to strike Anéton down. As the blade swung down and the Garanth's head followed it, Anéton flung the two knives he'd hidden in his right hand at the mighty warrior's head. He rolled out from under the swinging blade and leapt to his feet.

Casting a backward glance to check his handiwork, Anéton was pleased to find the Garanth bellowing and screaming like a kazan bull. One of the blades had bounced harmlessly off the warrior's thick forehead, but the second had embedded itself deep within the Garanth's left eye socket.

The howling beast staggered around the knoll for several steps before tripping over the loose boulders and crashing face-first onto the rocks. The Garanth lay still. Anéton realized that the hilt had pushed through the socket upon landing, as he could see the tip of the blade protruding from the back of the skull.

Relieved at his momentary victory, Anéton staggered back up the knoll behind the fiery inferno that surrounded the watch tower. He glanced toward the structure and gasped. *The whole building is on fire! The Meq'qan will be roasted alive! I hope Cédron got away because I don't have time to look for him, too.*

Racing as fast as he could on his weakened legs, Anéton sought the door to the tower. The heavy wooden door stood ajar, its hinges broken. Anéton's hopes sank. *We're all doomed.*

He knew that the remaining Garanth was inside and had set the blaze, trapping the wounded and exhausted Meq'qan. Anéton charged into the fire, determined to take the last surviving Garanthian bull with him to Lady Muralia's bosom.

Anéton raced up the steps, undaunted by the massive warrior looming at the top of the staircase. The Garanth was facing the room and didn't hear Anéton's approach in the roar that echoed throughout the tower. The stocky soldier careened into his enemy, sending his adversary sprawling into one of the burning tapestries. The Garanth tried to turn as it stumbled forward and wrapped some of the burning tapestry around one shoulder. It forgot Anéton and yanked at the burning fabric, causing the tapestry to catch more firmly in its armor and one of its horns.

Coughing and sputtering in the thick smoke, Anéton wiped his eyes with his shirt sleeves to clear his vision. Glancing around the room for anything he could use, Anéton spied the lone sword hanging on the wall. He grasped it and slashed at the remaining rings holding the tapestry against the window, causing it to wrap the Garanth completely in its flaming embrace. The bull bellowed and thrashed about, its skin scorching as the burning fabric of the tapestry ignited the flailing warrior's hair.

The acrid stench of charred Garanthian hide caused Anéton to retch, his nostrils flaring in protest. The Garanth stomped his way out of the burning wall hanging and looked around for his opponent. He spied the wounded Meq'qan on the cot and took a step in his direction.

Anéton gulped. *I can't let that monster kill the poor Meq'qan; the man hasn't even regained consciousness yet.* The legionnaire held his breath, grabbed the ceramic bowl that sat on the table and hurled it at the monster's head with all his might. The bowl shattered against the warrior's thick skull, causing the Garanth to change the object of his attention. The brutish warrior let out a roar and charged towards Anéton.

The young man spun on his heel and slid down the banister to the broken entrance. He raced down the hill towards the smoldering remains of the first two Garanthian casualties. Anéton could hear the enraged bull close on his heels, the panic of his desperation nearly incapacitating him. *Keep moving, keep moving, don't let him catch you!* Anéton chanted to himself as he ran. He looked around desperately for Cédron, simultaneously hoping for help and relieved that his friend seemed to have fled to safety.

His boots slipped in the slick grass and he lost his balance, rolling down the hill. He crashed into a large boulder. Bruised and weakened by the fall, Anéton struggled to pull himself to his knees. The fourth Garanthian warrior was still behind him, charging down the hill for the final blow that would end this skirmish. Anéton lurched to his feet and staggered to the far side of the boulder, placing the enormous rock between himself and his foe.

Anéton spied the large ax that the first Garanth had dropped when the fireball slammed into him. The legionnaire grabbed it and hefted the blade in his hands. *It's so heavy, I don't know if can throw it accurately.* Stepping out from behind the boulder, he aimed the ax at the oncoming Garanth and threw.

Anéton heard a squelching sound and then the shuddering inhale as the ferocious bull struggled for breath. He peeked around the boulder to find the blade sunk deep in the fleshy part of the Garanth's neck, right at the shoulder. Blood pumped from the wound, running in thick rivulets down the Garanth's jerkin and pooling on the ground. Although his opponent hadn't died instantly, Anéton knew that it had been a lucky shot.

The Garanth spotted Anéton and staggered towards him, a burning madness smoldering in its beady eyes. Anéton turned to run but his fatigued legs gave out beneath him. The strain of battle coupled with the continuous inhalation of smoke had weakened him beyond his limits. Anéton fell.

The huffing warrior behind him stumbled and reached out to steady itself on the boulder. Anéton could hear the bull's labored breath as it struggled for life. The massive beast's hand failed to find purchase in the rock, slippery from the stream of blood pouring from its neck. The bull wavered for a moment and then toppled forward, landing across Anéton's legs and torso.

Anéton was sure his legs were broken. He couldn't breathe beneath the Garanth's crushing weight. The legionnaire expended the last reserves of strength to try to move the heavy corpse from his body, but to no avail.

Lying back breathless, he watched the stars begin to peek through the billowing clouds of smoke, cleared away by the wind. Belatedly, he realized that it was the lack of air causing the stars. Anéton felt his life ebbing away. *Warrior Goddess, I hope I've earned my place at your table this night.* Anéton sighed his last prayer and slipped into blackness.

CHAPTER 22 - ALIGNING WITH THE FIRESTONE

Algarik slammed his door shut behind him once he reached his quarters. The errant kesling huddled between his legs, nearly tripping him. Swearing loudly, he shoved the little creature into the corridor, where it wandered after new scents. The mage gathered his few belongings together and shoved them into his upholstered bag. He knew his brother and that Shäeli were lying when they'd pretended Cédron was missing. Obviously Kásuin had spirited Cédron away quietly with the caravan, but perhaps all was not lost. The boy couldn't be too far ahead of him, and Algarik was certain he could handle Shozin Chezak once he caught up to the caravan. Still, he would have to report to his master and explain the change in plans before he left.

Muttering angrily under his breath, Algarik found the vial of firewater from his desk and poured it into the bowl at the base of the mirror. He dipped his hands in the flaming liquid and swept them around the frame of the mirror, causing the bright-blue flames to lick greedily at the wood. The demon appeared immediately, as if expecting the summons.

"What news of the boy?" it hissed behind the mirror.

"He has eluded me momentarily." Algarik fumed, drumming his fingers quickly on the desktop while he reported. "I am setting out immediately to retrieve him."

The demon stared him silently for a moment, his unblinking gaze squeezing icy fingers around the mage's insides, freezing his anger to sharp icicles that stabbed at his heart. Algarik clamped down on his internal weakness and continued with his report.

"I gave him the Askári firestone, which he carries with him." Algarik smiled slightly. "I will be able to sense its power if he uses it. There is a Sumäeri warrior who has attached herself to him that may prove problematic, but..."

"The Shäeli are of little concern to us," the demon spat impatiently. "Their Näenji Council is under my influence and in complete denial of any danger. It is the boy I need now."

"Understood, Master." Algarik bowed and assured the demon he would begin his pursuit immediately.

The demon vacated the fiery surface, leaving only the wisps of colored flames dying slowly around the frame. The red mage completed his packing, shoving the onyx imp unceremoniously into the bottom of his bag. Algarik paused mid-pack and stood up straight. *Kásuin doesn't trust me. He lied about Cédron.*

Algarik sat down at his desk and pondered his next step. He knew that Cédron was likely further out of his reach than he could reasonably find. He couldn't afford to waste time searching in the wrong direction. He didn't know where the boy was or where he was headed, and the mage couldn't be certain whose company he was in. Algarik was certain that wherever the boy was, the Sumäeri was likely with him.

If Cédron was truly with the caravan, he would be heading southwest. Since Algarik felt that Kásuin had lied to him, he discarded that option almost as he thought it. The boy's most likely path would be south to the Tádim Pass; that would be the quickest route to Samshäeli. The only other option would be for him to head north to Lake Juláni, then south via the Rabe'en Plains to Samshäeli.

The red mage knew that he couldn't cover both routes alone, and his resources were spread thin with the coming war. If he didn't find Cédron and get him to his master soon, he would have to face consequences that were too dire to contemplate. *I haven't worked this hard to have everything destroyed before it even begins! I've sacrificed too much to turn back now.*

Algarik's attention was broken by a slight movement on the floor near his chair. A small ubrick beetle was crawling across the floor. Its hard, black wings were folded smoothly against its long-shelled body. A grin twisted the mage's face as he grabbed the tiny beetle and put it on the table.

He pulled out an ebony wand with black crystals embedded along its shaft and a red tourmaline mounted on the end. Waving the wand, he shouted, *"Tezra!"*

The ubrick beetle swelled until it was as large as Algarik's fist, its pincers clapping menacingly at the mage. With the red stone glowing brightly, Algarik instructed the creature to find his agent that had infiltrated the Hármolin Legion and have the man report.

The mage was certain that between the two of them, the Sumäeri wouldn't stand a chance at preventing Cédron from joining him at Thoromberk Fortress before the season of Suntide ended. Satisfied that he had an advantage over the Sumäeri and anyone else protecting the boy, Algarik shouldered his pack and made his way to the stables.

* * *

Screams echoed in Cédron's ears as he raced up the hill, dodging the dark shadows that loomed towards him. Smoke filled his lungs and he choked, his eyes nearly blinded by stinging tears from the acrid air. Heat from the blaze made reaching the tower nearly impossible. The boy paced back and forth trying to figure a way in. *I started this fire to try and save those poor Meq'qan; now I've roasted them alive!*

Smoke swirled and billowed in the breeze, clearing just enough for Cédron to spy a gap in the flames where a large boulder had been uprooted from its perch. The dark hollow was devoid of grass and would provide him a haven of clarity amidst the raging inferno that encompassed the entire hilltop. The boy pulled his shirt up over his face and sprinted for the clearing. The screams from the tower grew more insistent. His heart pounded in his chest as he pondered the best approach from his new vantage point.

Flames licked the outside of the watchtower and smoke trickled out the upstairs window. Cédron realized that even if he could get through the burning door, he wouldn't be able to get all four of the Meq'qan out by himself. *Anéton is dealing with the Garanth, I hope, but I'm not strong enough to lift that injured warrior myself.*

His attention on the tower, Cédron didn't notice the hand reaching out from the smoldering brush behind him. Feeling the grip on his ankle and certain that one of the remaining Garanth must have found him, Cédron screamed and lurched forward. The grip on his ankle was like a vice, unrelenting and desperate. The boy fell on his face and called forth his Árk'äezhi as he was being dragged back. The earth rumbled and bucked beneath him and he felt the grip loosen. Cédron jumped to his feet and turned to find one of the Meq'qan tribesmen laying on the ground.

"What have you done?" the the young tribesman gasped, his eyes wide as he stared up at the boy.

Cédron squelched the energy flowing from his hands and the ground ceased to rumble. "I'm sorry, I thought you were one of the Garanth."

"I am Chem'ewa of Ta'voran Marsh." The man slapped his own chest.

The Meq'qan got to his feet and grabbed Cédron by the front of his jerkin, shaking the boy slightly. "The fire has trapped my clansmen! We have to get them out of there!"

Guilt stabbed Cédron in the heart as he grabbed the young man's hands and pulled them from his chest. He glanced back at the burning door to the tower, still shut tight. Looking up, the only other exit he could see was too high for a man to jump without causing serious injury.

"How did you get out?" he asked the tribesman.

Chem'ewa's eyes brightened for a moment and he straightened up slightly. "I found a tunnel."

Cédron frowned. "Why didn't the others just use the tunnel?"

"Ta'riqk is still unconscious." Chem'ewa shook his head. "Dir'iq won't leave our Seeress, so it's up to us to help them. Come, follow me!"

The warrior waved for Cédron to follow him. The young man got back down on his knees and crawled beneath the layer of heavy smoke towards one of the smaller boulders. Cédron shrugged his shoulders and got down on his hands and knees. Following the Meq'qan down the hill and away from the tower, he prayed that they'd be able to get back to the tower before it became fully engulfed in flames.

Ahead of him, Chem'ewa had gotten to his feet and skirted the boulder. Cédron came up behind him and shook his head. Buried in the side of the steep hill, well away from the burning tower, was a slatted wooden door covered with sod into which a thicket of sweet peas had grown. Their vines and suckers held the camouflage flawlessly as the tribesman swung the door outward. *The Askári of Dúlnat are miners to the core. They sure love to make tunnels!*

Chem'ewa beckoned Cédron inside the tunnel, then he closed the door. The sod door muffled the roaring of the fire above; their labored breathing was deafening in the void. Surrounded by total blackness, Cédron fished in his pouch for glow stones. Charging the stones with the warmth and energy of his hands, the boy held one out to the Meq'qan. Extending the second stone out in front of him, Cédron saw that the walls and floor of the tunnel were paved with stones. Crawlers skittered away from the light as he raised the glow rocks above his head, where their sticky, decorative webs adorned the corners.

"Come." Chem'ewa began walking up the inside of the hill towards the tower. "We must hurry before my clansmen are overcome with the smoke."

Cédron nodded and followed behind. He wasn't sure how they were going to get all of the Meq'qan out of the tower and into the safety of this tiny tunnel, but maybe by the time they reached it, Anéton would be able to help. *I hope he's still alive.* The boy stayed close behind the tribesman as he led the way back to the secret door into the weapons room of the tower. Pulling the lever, the door grated open and the two emerged into a smoke-filled room.

Cédron muttered a prayer to Hamra, hoping to encourage the deity to stay her hand from taking the lives of the tribesmen, and hurried up the stairs after the Meq'qan. When they reached the landing where the living quarters lay, they found the smoke from the burning door thicker. Ta'riqk remained unconscious on the cot, while Dir'iq was hovering over the squirming bundle on the litter. *That must be the Seeress. I wonder if she can "see" a way out of this mess.*

"Get off of me!" the old woman cried, her gnarled hands pushing at Dir'iq's chest.

Dir'iq stepped back and offered the old woman his hand, his brow furrowed. "You must let me protect you from the smoke and the fire."

The diminutive woman turned her pointed chin towards the taller man. "There's only one who can save us now." Turning to Cédron, she hobbled over to the boy and surveyed the young Shäeli.

Cédron squirmed under her scrutiny. Her yellow reptilian eyes saw straight to his soul. Although she was tiny, Cédron felt power radiating through the woman and he knelt before her, his eyes cast down.

"I am Cédron Varkáras, at your service."

The Seeress grasped his hands and knelt in front of him. Cédron was surprised at the steel in her grip.

"You must put out this fire," she demanded, her hands trembling slightly.

Cédron gaped at her. He glanced out the window at the inferno raging all around the hilltop. The breeze continued to fan the flames, spreading them towards the forest.

"I have no water," he gasped. "There is no way to stop it now."

Ta'riqk moaned from the cot where he lay. Chem'ewa grabbed a bowl and water skin and tended to the wounded man. Dir'iq stood behind the Seeress and scowled at Cédron. *What do they expect me to do? I can't stop the fire with the water skin I have!*

"You must align with the firestone and call the flames back into it," she stated flatly, encompassing the area with her outspread hands.

Cédron's head spun. *How can I do that? I don't know how to call flames into the stone. How does she know I have a firestone anyway?*

"Look, I don't know how to do that, and we don't have time for me to learn." He coughed as the smoke scoured his lungs. "We have to get everyone into the tunnel. We can stay there until the fire burns out."

The Seeress shook her head. "No, you started this blaze with the firestone. It will burn until it is called back by the same Árk'äezhi, or we will all be lost."

Cédron's head shot up. He stared at the Meq'qan Seeress in disbelief. *How could she possibly know that?*

The lines on the old woman's face deepened as she smiled. Folds overlapped around her eyes and mouth. "I know a great many things, boy. Now get up and use your firestone before the entire mountain is destroyed."

"How…what…I…I can't control it," Cédron stammered, staring at the crone.

The old woman held his gaze, the fiery light reflecting in her strange eyes. "You called it forth, and now you must quell it. There may be more of my kinsmen out there fleeing the Garanth. They are doomed if you cannot stop the blaze!"

Cédron stared at the woman, prickles of sweat beading across his forehead. "I don't know what to do!"

The Meq'qan woman placed her weathered hand over Cédron's. She clasped his hand tightly in hers, closing her eyes and breathing deeply. Cédron felt the rush of strength pour into his body through the woman's hand. He saw a vision of himself holding the firestone over his head and willing the fire to return into it. His mouth dropped in disbelief. *She's got the ability to share thoughts!* The Seeress released his hands and nodded.

"Yes, it is one of my gifts as a Seeress," she said quietly. "And you are much more powerful than you now realize. You have the ability to control the flames. Do so, now! You have seen what must be done."

Cédron pulled out the firestone from his pouch and hesitated. "But if I stop the fire, any Garanth out there will be able to see us."

The Seeress leveled her reptilian gaze at him. "Perhaps. But more of my kinsmen and women will be lost if you don't. The stone has come to you for a reason. You must use it."

Cédron swallowed hard. He didn't know who or what was out there, hiding in the smoke, that would be able to find him should he expend so much Árk'äezhi. *What if the Sumäeri are nearby and have isolated my energy? Or the Garanth? I'm sure they're still looking for me.*

"You must align yourself with the sacred firestone," the crone said. "It will guide you once you've surrendered yourself to its power."

Cédron was sweltering as the walls of the room seemed to close in on him. He stripped off his torn, bloody shirt and grabbed the firestone from his pouch. Running up the stairs, he lifted the trapdoor and strode out onto the battlements on the roof of the tower. Chem'ewa and the Seeress followed close behind him. Holding the stone above his head, he closed his eyes and willed the fire back into the stone.

Cédron felt the heat of his Árk'äezhi rising from deep within his chest, flowing out of his palms and into the stone. The force of the blast of energy rocked him back on his heels, but he refused to open his eyes or lose his concentration. The power of the stone increased, causing a similar response in his Árk'äezhi. In his mind's eye, Cédron could see the fire returning to the stone, the power of the wind pushing the flames and smoke towards him and into the large gem. His hands throbbed and burned as the stone's power melded with his own. Cédron nearly cried out as the heat moved down his arms to his chest, where his flesh seemed to burn from the inside out.

Cédron started to panic. He saw visions of Meq'qan refugees screaming and twisting in pain as the fire ravaged them. Digging deep within his mind, he sought the confidence he needed to wield the firestone. Images of Jorrél and Pánar swam before him, taunting his weakness and blaming him for the deaths of the townspeople, his mother and Zariun. He shook his head to expel the images, knowing deep in his heart that the explosion had not been his intention or his fault. Cédron felt his energy weaken, his focus falter.

The burning sensation threatened to overpower him and he knew that he was about to succumb to the stone's fire. If only he could reach his pouch and the wind or water stones. Maybe he could blow in some rain clouds to ease the scorched land and his smoldering skin. To his surprise, Cédron felt the grip of the Meq'qan Seeress on his arm. Then he felt the hands of her two male companions on each shoulder. *They're giving me their strength!*

Overwhelmed at their gift and confidence in him, Cédron strengthened his resolve and focused on generating the properties of air and water with his own magic. He felt the cooling sensation almost immediately. He could hear the hissing of steam on his flesh and feel the droplets of water

238

on his nose as the rain began in earnest. Wind whipped through his hair and he felt himself being lifted off the roof and into the vortex of smoke and steam as the vacuum extinguished the flames. The firestone continued to pulse in his hands, recalling all the energy of the wildfire into its midst, while the rain brought healing to the land. *This is impossible! The power of this firestone must be equal to that of...Laylur's beast, it can't be!*

Realization of what he held dawned on the boy's face and tears filled his eyes. *That's what the Seeress had said; she already knew. Somehow, I'm holding the Askári's sacred firestone! I feel like I can do anything!* A wave of power coursed through his pounding heart and rippled out across the land. The raw energy flattened grass and bent trees in its wake. The Árk'äezhi had barely left his fingers when the ground began to shake. The tremors built into sharp rattles, causing the Meq'qan to fall to the floor of the battlements below him. Their cries of fear barely registered in Cédron's ears above the roar of the land.

Slowly, the firestone eased its throbbing and cooled in his hands. Cédron felt his body lower back to the roof as the winds died and the rains ceased, but the pulsing around his heart seemed to continue unabated. *What's happening to me?* Cédron opened his eyes and saw that he stood on top of the one of the merlons above the fallen Meq'qan. His skin glowed from the added energy of the firestone. He bent down to assist the Meq'qan Seeress when another violent ground shake boomed across the hillside. Cédron looked into Chem'ewa's eyes as the young man reached over the Seeress to protect her, his yellow, reptilian eyes nearly orange with fear.

The ground shake continued to rumble across the hillside, causing the watchtower to lean and groan. Without further warning, the floor beneath their feet began to crumble. Cédron dove for the Meq'qan, raising the firestone above his head to form a barrier of energy around them. The battlements collapsed. Cédron felt a brief moment of panic, the screams of the Meq'qan faint behind the rushing in his ears as the compromised tower imploded. The world went dark.

Chapter 23 - Alliances

The darkness was a void with no sight or sound to disrupt the stasis. Cédron tried to reach the light and wind and sound of life, but he was trapped. A twinge of panic gripped his chest. *I can't breathe! Have I been buried alive?*

Cédron struggled to free himself from the leadened sensation. He couldn't feel his body or extremities. He thought his eyes were open, but the blackness made it impossible to tell. *Wait, I think I see a light.* Cédron tried to move towards the brighter spot in his vision, but his body betrayed him and refused to move. Icy tendrils of fear crept down his spine, making him shiver. The boy fought the urge to scream as the brightness moved closer. The light elongated as it neared him, becoming a recognizable form.

Cédron's breath caught in his throat. *It cannot be! Mother?* The slender figure before him stood with her back turned. Her thick golden hair, so similar to his own, cascaded down her back in waves. Surrounding her body was an ethereal glow that wasn't quite as peaceful as Cédron would have expected.

"Mother!" He attempted to call out to her, reaching for her shoulder. *"I'm so sorry! I didn't mean to cause the ground shake. It was an accident. Please forgive me!"* No matter how loudly he yelled, no sound emerged from his closed throat.

Reaching out as far as he could, Cédron tried to touch his mother's shoulder. The very tips of his fingers touched her skin. The figure turned to face him. The joy swelling in Cédron's heart at the opportunity to speak to his mother and ask her forgiveness disintegrated into terror as the creature faced him. Rather than his mother's beautiful smile, Cédron found himself face-to-face with the demon Laylur. His long nose and sharp chin accentuated the narrow placement of his eyes and the gaunt cheeks that screamed of deprivation. *Where is my mother? She was just here, where did she go?*

Cédron reached out to the demon and grabbed it by the front with both hands. As he shook the body in his frustration, the demon's mouth opened and an enormous pointed tongue lolled out the side of his mouth. Wicked dark eyes taunted him as the demon's laughter echoed in the deep recesses of Cédron's mind. The demon's sharp tongue pierced Cédron's chest, causing a dull ache. The boy shook the demon harder, causing its mirth to become hysterics and the ache in his chest more insistent.

The boy tried to release his hands from the demon, but they were fused together. The more he tried to extricate himself, the harder the demon laughed, and the deeper the tongue pressed into his sternum. Cédron realized that the more the demon laughed, the brighter it became. With a flash so blinding that Cédron shrank back, Laylur exploded into thousands of pieces. Shards from the demon embedded themselves into Cédron's chest and the dull ache in his sternum increased to a sharp pain.

The force of the explosion and the pain forced Cédron to open his eyes. His breath caught in his chest. He was face-to-face with the sharp beak and fierce golden eyes of a läenier. The raptor nudged his bruised chest again and screeched. Behind him, Cédron heard footsteps running in his direction.

"Laylur's beast, boy, what happened here?" Räesha gasped.

More footsteps thudded as Rováen and Tóran reached him. Cédron nearly cried from relief to see their welcome faces.

242

"Garanth attacked," Cédron croaked, trying to sit up. Rováen squatted down and lifted the boy's shoulders. "I stopped the fire, but the ground shake collapsed the tower."

Rováen nodded to Räesha. "It's a good thing you could bring us so quickly."

"Is he hurt?" Räesha's forehead wrinkled as she looked the boy up and down.

Rováen felt Cédron's head and down his chest. He shook his head slightly. "Not badly, but we can't take him back to Dúlnat."

"We need to get back to help father and the legion," Tóran glowered mutinously.

Rováen shook his head. "Kásuin will have his hands full evacuating the city while the Hármolin Legion musters to face the rest of the Garanth army. He sent you with me for a reason." Rováen jutted his chin towards the sling on Tóran's arm. "We need to go."

Cédron stood up and looked around frantically. His legs gave way beneath him, but Rováen held him up. "Easy lad, you're ok now. Let's get you out of here."

"No!" Cédron cried and lurched several steps towards the collapsed building. "We have to find them!"

"Find who?" Tóran asked, scratching his head with his unslung arm as he scanned the hilltop. "There are others here?"

Cédron nodded. "Anéton lured two of the Garanth away from the tower so they wouldn't get the Meq'qan they were hunting. The Meq'qan were on the top of the battlements with me when-"

"Anéton Bessínos?" Tóran asked sharply. "What was he doing up here?"

Cédron nodded. "He was going to relieve his father from duty, but his father wasn't here. Then we saw the wounded Meq'qan running from the Garanthian patrol. We have to find them!"

Räesha and Yongäen started searching the rubble from the tower. The great beast moved large stones and brick with his talons, rolling them off piles to search beneath them. Rováen and the boys moved to the opposite end of the tower closest to the downward slope. Tóran shielded his eyes from Lord Shamar's rays.

"What's that down there?" he asked, pointing to a shard of metal glinting in the light.

The three of them slipped down the hill to find the remains of a monstrous Garanth bull draped across some what they took to be some stones.. Beneath the warrior's thick legs lay a small knife hilt, the blade glinting in the light.

"That's Anéton!" Cédron cried and began lifting the Garanth.

Rováen and Tóran each grabbed a leg and shoulder respectively and helped Cédron roll the mammoth Garanth over. In the grass beneath the Garanth, curled up next to a boulder, lay the unconscious legionnaire. Blood seeped from his nose. Cédron knelt at his friend's side and laid his hands on the legionnaire's chest. He could feel his heart beating faintly and nearly collapsed with relief. Calling forth his Árk'äezhi, he willed the spark of life that lingered in Anéton's chest to swell and grow. Charged with the radiant energy from aligning with the firestone, Cédron's Árk'äezhi filled Anéton's body and caused it to glow from within. The young man's breathing deepened and his eyes fluttered open.

"Anéton!" Cédron crouched at his side, shaking the young man gently. "Anéton, are you ok?"

"I'm still alive?" Anéton croaked, his eyes squinting against the late rays of Lord Shamar's light.

"Thanks to your friend here." Tóran grimaced. "I'd stick pretty close to him if I were you."

Tóran shifted around to Anéton's left side and used his good arm to stabilize the young legionnaire. Rováen slipped his arms under the soldier's shoulders and heaved with his legs, lifting the young man to his feet. Anéton wavered for a moment, his eyes unfocused. Cédron bent down, picked up the throwing knife, and handed it back to the legionnaire with a wide grin.

"I don't know how you did it, but the Garanth are all dead."

Anéton blinked and stumbled forward a few steps. He grasped the hilt of the blade and slid it back into his sash with his remaining knives. Glancing down at the huge warrior he'd killed, the young man shook his head. "I shouldn't be alive."

Tóran nodded. "You're right, you shouldn't. Where was Álraun? Wasn't he supposed to be manning the tower?"

Anéton shrugged.

"Fine time to desert his post," Tóran muttered under his breath.

Cédron watched the exchange and noticed Anéton's cheeks flare crimson. The legionnaire fingered the sash with the knives as Cédron cleared his throat. He felt compelled to defend his new friend. "We were lucky Anéton was here instead."

Tóran didn't catch that he'd embarrassed Anéton. Still staring at the Garanth corpse, he evaluated the situation like a military commander. "Killed four Garanth single handed? Amazing." He looked at Anéton. "Good work, Legionnaire."

Cédron, normally eager for his adopted brother's approval, saw Anéton's pride and felt no need to correct Tóran's count. He looked around, seeking to break an awkward silence. "It looks like Räesha has found something." He nodded at the bundle near the Sumäeri's läenier. "I hope the Meq'qan survived after all they've already been through."

The four made their way up the hill and stopped in their tracks. When they reached the top, they found Räesha ministering over Ta'riqk's wound. The light from her hands was just receding as they approached.

"Is that what you did to me?" Anéton gasped, turning to Cédron.

The boy shrugged. "Something like that." He gazed out across the mountain range, his face grim at the memory of his mother. "At least I still had something to work with." The boy cleared his throat and blinked back the moisture that threatened his eyes. There had been no spark in Maräera's body by the time he'd found her and the feeling of helplessness continued to plague him. "Let's get out of here before the Council Guard finds me."

Ta'riqk responded to Räesha's touch and leapt to his feet. Drawing his blade, he placed himself next to Chem'ewa, who blocked the Sumäeri from the Seeress. Cédron noticed Dir'iq's body lying a few feet away, twisted at an odd angle.

"Keep your distance, you Sumäeri demon," Chem'ewa spat at Räesha through narrowed eyes as he noted her markings.

Cédron held his breath. *This is not a fight we should be having right now! They have to set the old hatreds aside.* Räesha regarded the tribesman's short dagger and defensive positioning and laughed. Cédron thought the sound was like the rippling of a stream.

"Do not trouble yourself." She smiled engagingly at the young Meq'qan. "We are here on similar purpose."

The Sumäeri angled past Chem'ewa and Ta'riqk to kneel in front of the Seeress. Ignoring the men's protests, Räesha offered her open palms. "Greetings, wise one. May Lady Muralia's bounty forever bless your people."

The Seeress stepped forward, impatiently batting away Ta'riqk's restraining hands to place her palms on the upturned hands of the Shäeli woman. "May Lord Shamar bear the light of your people to the land."

Cédron and the others watched in awe as the Seeress and Sumäeri's hands began to glow softly. The Seeress's eyes closed during the exchange, as did Räesha's. The two women concentrated on sharing their energy and knowledge.

The silence on the hilltop was interrupted only by the rustling of small insects returning to the grasses and the heavy breathing of the Meq'qan held at bay by the energy field as they struggled to separate their Seeress from their enemy. The Seeress sagged wearily as the bond was broken, and Ta'riqk and Chem'ewa were able to step in and assist her, glaring at Räesha for her contact.

"Release the hate and the worry from your hearts." The Seeress sighed heavily to her companions. "The Sumäeri is no enemy of ours. She seeks the salvation of our world, as we do."

The two men glared at Räesha but did not press the attack. Instead, they guided the crone to a large rock and seated her there before turning back to Dir'iq's body.

"We must bury our fallen brother," Chem'ewa said, his face as stiff as his voice.

Cédron's guts twisted. *He died in the ground shake that I caused! Is nobody safe around me?* Guilt assailed his senses and he cast his eyes downward in shame. "I will do it. It is because of me that he perished."

"Wait," Räesha commanded sharply.

Cédron paused, his hands on his hips. Räesha strode over to him and placed her hands on his chest.

"How did you come by these markings?" she asked, her hands following the outline of flames that covered his skin.

"The boy has aligned with the sacred firestone," the Seeress announced. "He has proven his Askári blood."

Cédron felt the skin on his chest over his heart, then looked down and gasped. His chest was covered in strange, bright tattoos. A circle of orange-red flames surrounded his heart and seemed to flick towards the edge of his chest as they reduced in size. The significance of the tattoos struck him like a thunderbolt. *It really is the Askári's sacred firestone! How did it end up in father's armory? The Garanth stole it generations ago!*

Digging deep into his soul, Cédron felt the rise of Árk'äezhi as it flowed with his thoughts and intentions. Using the residual power of the firestone coursing through his veins, Cédron lifted his hands and placed them on one of the large boulders. Lifting the boulder as if it weighed nothing, the lad carried it to Dir'iq's body and gently laid it beside the fallen warrior. His companions watched silently as he continued moving boulders until he'd built a sturdy cairn over Dir'iq's corpse. At last depleted of his residual Árk'äezhi, Cédron slumped against the cairn and wiped the tears from his cheeks.

"I am sorry for the loss of your kinsman," he choked, meeting the Seeress's yellow gaze. "Though I did not realize the significance of the stone or its power, I hope you will accept as an offering the use of the last of my connection to the stone. He was a devoted warrior and will be honored at Orwena's table, I'm sure."

"So, you see." The Seeress smiled kindly as she hobbled to the boy's side. "You are the one who can wield the sacred stones. Your father was right."

Cédron stared at her, the words not registering properly in his brain. "My father? What does my father have to do with this? What are you talking about?"

The Seeress turned her yellow gaze upon the boy and smiled. "The Regent suspects the part you are to play. We spoke about it at great length."

Cédron stared at the tiny woman, a pain in his temple beginning to throb. "What part? What is going on here?"

Räesha turned to the Meq'qan Seeress. "Mother, perhaps I can be of assistance to you. I told you earlier that we had similar purpose."

The Sumäeri shared the recent events in Samshäeli, including the loss of her youngest sister to the demons already loose in the land. She recounted the hard decision her family had come to by agreeing to defy the Näenji Council and seek out Cédron, whose ancestry could be their only salvation. She concluded with the tragic deaths of her parents and her mission to seek out the sacred elemental stones with Cédron. With the help of the Sumäeri, he could reassemble the Sceptre of Kulari and battle their foe, as it appeared inevitable that Laylur would soon escape the abyss and be loose upon their land.

"Blasphemy!" shouted Ta'riqk, jumping to his feet and brandishing his fist at the Shäeli woman. "Only the Meq'qan priestess can wield the power of the sacred aquastone."

"You Shäeli plan to strip us of our power!" Chem'ewa scowled at Cédron and Anéton for their betrayal of his trust.

"I can't save Muralia," Cédron gasped, horrified. "I have almost no control over my Árk'äezhi energy. You saw what happened at the watchtower. I was barely able to contain the wildfire I started. I can't wield the most powerful sceptre ever created!"

"We will guide you, train you, and prepare you for what you must face." Räesha nodded towards her uncle. "Rováen has taught you much, but even he believes your abilities are far greater than you realize."

Cédron looked at Rováen, then at his adopted brother. His breathing became shallow and sweat had formed along his upper lip

"What about the explosion at the festival," he asked, his eyes pleading with Rováen's, "and the ground shakes that killed my mother and your kinsman?" Cédron glanced at the Seeress. "I nearly burned the entire hillside around the watchtower with the firestone when I attempted to use it. I'm not able to do this! I don't have enough control." Cédron turned to Räesha, placing his left hand on her shoulder as he hung his head. "I'm sorry, I just can't risk it. I'd probably cause more damage than good anyway." Turning to his brother, Cédron said, "Tóran is more able to lead the fight against a demon army. You're putting your hopes on the wrong person."

"Refusing this quest is not an option for you now," Räesha said savagely. "My sister and parents have already died. I will not let their deaths be for nothing!"

The Seeress stood, her reptilian eyes fixed on Cédron. She placed her hand on his forehead and closed her eyes, muttering words of power.

"He is the one I spoke of to Kásuin last Dormantide. He has the heart, but not the courage to achieve this task," the Seeress declared. "He does not understand or believe." She turned to Rovaen. "It is as you feared."

Cédron turned to his uncle. "What is she talking about?"

All eyes were on Rovaen, whose face clouded as he considered his next words. "Your father had a dream...a premonition the night after your powers manifested." He turned and faced Cédron, who was standing taut as if about to spring away if he didn't like what he heard. "He told me that Lady Muralia had come to him. She told him that you would face the greatest challenge of our time, and that you would need help to prevail or all would be lost."

As Rovaen faltered in his tale, the pieces fell into place for Räesha. She whirled on her uncle. "You had Sahráron make those stones to contact this Seeress, didn't you?"

When Rovaen didn't answer, Räesha turned to the old woman. "What did you see? What counsel did you give the Regent?"

The Seeress sagged back and took a ragged breath. "I couldn't see the future of this boy or interpret the dream clearly," she said. "There were too many variables clouding my vision to be sure."

"So, you hid him in Dúlnat and forbade him from using his Árk'äezhi to keep him safe," she hissed at Rovaen. "Lock him away where nothing could reach him and maybe this whole thing would just disappear, is that what you thought? You cannot hide him from his destiny! It is an imperative from the deities!"

250

Rovāen had tears in his clear blue eyes as he nodded at the fuming warrior. "We've lost so many already...and he's so young."

Rovāen glanced over at Cédron, who was slumped back against a large boulder. The boy could feel Räesha's eyes on him, and he refused to return the gaze. Instead, the young man looked at Anéton, whose expression was a ridiculous mixture of chagrin and awe.

"Wow, the Sceptre of Kulari." Anéton blinked and shook his head. "And to think, I thought you were just a caravan freak." He grinned.

"Don't be ridiculous," Cédron snapped. "I can't wield that thing and you know it. Just imagine what I could do with a weapon like that."

"Yeah." Anéton winked at him. "Think of what you could do to that pie hole of Pánar's."

"This isn't funny." Cédron turned to Räesha and Rovāen. "My place is in Dúlnat alongside my father and my brother. I will defend my city and my family, not waste my efforts on this ridiculous...quest. You're a great Sumäeri warrior; you fight Laylur!"

"Boy, you are the only one with the blood to wield the Sceptre of Kulari." Räesha rounded on Cédron, grabbing him by the front of his shirt and shaking him slightly. "It is only by the providence of the deities that you've been allowed to live this long." She glared at Rovāen before returning her fierce gaze at Cédron. "I don't know that you're worthy of this quest. Maybe the Council is right. If you won't take up the Sceptre of Kulari and face Laylur, then you are too dangerous to have just wandering around. You know what happened the last time!"

Cédron's eyes hardened to green ice. "I know that I'm called a demon and an abomination, that everyone wants me dead because I'm different and because I have powers. What nobody understands is that I'm trying to use my abilities to help, to heal and to support my family. I didn't mean for that wildfire to get out of control. It was an accident."

"That's not what I meant. I was referring to-"

"Let's just take this down a notch," Rovaën interrupted. "Our tempers are getting the better of us and nothing will come of us talking over one another...." He shook his head in warning to Räesha. "...or speaking out of turn."

Räesha gritted her teeth and bit down on the angry revelation she'd been about to make.

The Seeress cleared her throat. "The ground shakes are not all your doing, boy." She patted Cédron's hand. "Our priestesses have felt Lady Muralia's weakness for some time now. We have noticed the decaying of her terran body. The ground shakes are but a symptom of her weakness and the demon's growing strength."

Räesha nodded. "It was the spirit of the Meq'qan priestess, inhabiting the dying Auräevya, who told my sister Lanäe about a powerful guardian who could wield the Sceptre of Kulari. You are the only one alive who has the blood of all races. It is you who must do this."

"But I can't challenge Laylur!" Cédron shouted, then clamped his lips shut.

The Seeress shook her head. "No, you are right. You cannot stop the great demon yet, but perhaps you can slow him down."

Cédron put his head in his hands. "How in our Lady's name do you expect me to do that?"

"You can heal the land where the demon has weakened it with his poison." She smiled and pointed a gnarled finger at the young boy. "You have already proven yourself by aligning with the sacred firestone. If you could get the Meq'qan's sacred aquastone from the priestesses of Lady Muralia in the Zig'orman Marsh and take it to the Shaláen Falls, the source of water Árk'äezhi, you could heal the land. The demon's prison is deteriorating, and he sends his minions through every time the ground trembles. Heal the land, and you strengthen the ties that bind him. This will also strengthen your own powers, bringing you closer to your ultimate challenge."

Cédron bent down, placing his palms on the boulder, and looked at each member of the party in turn. "I will go to the Zig'orman Marsh with you and discuss this with your priestesses. I make no promises."

"Agreed," Rovaën said and looked around. "We should build a fire and some shelter for the night. We can begin our journey to the Zig'orman Marshes in the morning."

Räesha frowned and turned to face Cédron. "No, we must leave immediately. You've all but lit a beacon for anyone to find you. What were you thinking? I felt your Árk'äezhi from the Dagán Valley and left the caravan to find you, and I was followed."

Cédron blinked. "I...uh...well."

"We must leave," Räesha said, handing Cédron a shirt from her pack. "My raptor can get us over the Tádim Pass. The journey isn't too far."

The läenier let out a screech and raised back on his legs, wings fanning in agitation. Räesha looked off into the sky, trying to see what Yongäen's eye's had detected. Her countrymen were too far away for her to spot them, but she trusted her läenier.

"It looks like we may already be too late."

CHAPTER 24 - PURSUIT

Algarik felt the ripple of power deep within his body. It vibrated every fiber of his being with the force of its blast. *Cédron has aligned his Árk'äezhi with the Askári firestone!* A slow grin pulled at one side of his face. The other side twisted in a grimace from the old scar. The second phase of his plan was now complete. The untrained boy had enormous power at his command and no proper guidance in how to use it.

The red mage had figured out early in his journey with Levirk Sirkran that Cédron hadn't gone with the caravan. However, it wasn't until he felt the ripple in the Lluric field that Algarik realized Cédron was much too close to the advancing Garanthian army approaching Tamóna.

"Mijáko piles! He's just east of Tamóna," the mage cursed, wheeling his husan around from the southward path they were taking. "He's going to run afoul of the Garanthian horde, if he hasn't already."

Levirk Sirkran pulled back the reins on his husan and waited. Glancing backwards, he followed Algarik's gaze northward through the Tádim Pass. "Shall I retrieve him for you?"

Algarik turned and regarded his companion briefly, the tic in his left cheek twitching slightly. "No, I'll head towards Tamóna. You stay here. I'm sure that eventually they will make their way south, and I'd like to have you on this end to catch them in case they slip through my grasp."

Levirk Sirkran's thin lips twisted as he chuckled softly. "That has happened a lot lately."

The red mage's eyes flashed dangerously as he turned his attention to his Hazzara spy. *He's right, it has happened far too frequently, but that is about to change.* Algarik smiled, his bared teeth more warning than friendly.

"Perhaps you are right," Algarik agreed. "I think I need a new mode of transportation – one that will allow me to cover greater distances at speed."

Algarik pulled out his pipe and lit it with his ring, sucking hard to get the tobacco burning brightly. Levirk Sirkran watched him smoke, his black eyes glittering with thinly-veiled impatience. The Hazzara agent drummed his fingers on his thigh and patted the husan's thick neck as the ten foot long beast sat back on its muscular haunches.

Algarik watched him through partially-lidded eyes as he enjoyed the calming sensation of the leaf. He knew that his agent was anxious to get on with his journey. The sharp-featured man loved the hunt and thoroughly enjoyed the kill. He was one of the best Hazzara agents the Shadow had ever trained, but Algarik still wasn't sure he could trust Sirkran to capture Cédron rather than torture and kill him, should he encounter the boy first.

"Come here," the mage said suddenly, acquiring Sirkran's immediate attention. "I'm going to give you a tool to help locate the boy should I miss him. Hold out your talisman."

Sirkran hesitated only briefly, then walked his husan over to Algarik. He removed the leather thong that held the torus knot talisman. The ruby in the center gleamed as he held out the symbol of the Hazzara affiliation. Algarik grabbed the talisman and held it in his left palm. He twisted the ruby on his right hand to face his palm and held the glowing stone over the amulet, muttering under his breath. The large stone of the talisman began to hiss and glow. The intertwined metal of the torus knot churned and writhed within its form like a living being. Satisfied, the red mage handed the amulet back to his agent. Sirkran's eyes flicked to his master's before grasping the sinuous metal. He stared at it in his hand, transfixed on the two bright pinpoints of light deep within the center stone. Algarik heard his agent's sharp intake of breath as the magic awakened the creature.

From the the center of the Hazzara's ruby slithered a glowing red fire snake.

The six-inch reptile wriggled out of the stone and onto Sirkran's arm, burrowing into the skin. The flesh on Sirkran's arm smoldered as the fire snake wormed its way in, then it cooled. Sirkran gritted his teeth against the pain, his muscles flexing as he stared down at his arm with wide eyes. Glaring back at him were two glowing red eyes from the center of his forearm, with the red outline of the interloper pulsing like a living tattoo. The small man gulped.

"Yes, it lives inside you," Algarik crooned. "It will alert you to the power of the firestone or the boy's Árk'äezhi." The mage stroked the skin above the snake fondly, his fingers causing the creature to wriggle beneath the skin. "Remember, detain only. Do not kill the boy."

"What about those who travel with him?" Sirkran asked, pulling his arm back and covering the unwelcome addition with his sleeve.

"They are not my concern." Algarik shrugged. He grabbed Sirkran's forearm again and squeezed. "I will know if you harm him."

Levirk Sirkran grimaced as the burning snake beneath the red mage's palm protested the constriction by scorching the underside of his flesh. "Of course, I understand."

"Excellent. Now I'm off." Algarik wheeled his husan around, the beast's tusks nearly goring Sirkran's leg with the maneuver.

The red mage spurred his mount into a loping gallop, riding hard southwest towards his home and the monster he'd spent years growing and modifying. Laräeith's Codex hadn't been the only treasure he'd found on his travels. The discovery of a clutch of eggs suspended in the crystal pillars of the Zaroon Quarry had filled him with wonder. It had taken the young mage years of studying the codex and decades of practice before he'd been able to coax one of the deviant embryos to life.

The spawn of the corrupted Aruzzi were called rinzar, and the beast had been next to useless to the mage until he'd stumbled upon a breeder in Taksábai whose enhancement program provided him with the knowledge to enlarge his creature into a monster capable of both transportation and rampant destruction. Algarik didn't know if he would be successful in subduing the enormous raptor enough to ride it, but he knew that the risk of not pursuing Cédron outweighed the logical choice of staying with his spy.

Levirk Sirkran wouldn't cause him any trouble now; he'd insured the Hazzara agent's compliance with his little implant. The man wouldn't be able to harm Cédron, even if he wanted to. Algarik would know instantly the moment the fire snake was in close proximity to that Askári firestone. Whistling a pleasant tune, the mage charged through the trees of the pass towards the Dagán Valley. He knew what he needed and where to get it. Pursuing Cédron would have to wait just a little while longer.

ChAPTER 25 - NEAR ESCAPE

"They're nearly here," Räesha gasped, her eyes fixed on the treeline below. "We have to go. Now."

Rováen held up his hand. "Wait, you two should go in separate directions. They will have to choose which quarry to hunt."

Räesha stopped in her tracks. She turned slowly to face her uncle. Still a fugitive, she couldn't yet take Cédron to Samshäeli without assistance. Yongäen could only carry three passengers, and then not too far. She needed a midway point that both groups could reach in short order, yet still be protected from the Council Guard. After a moment, she nodded. "I'll take the Seeress and her kinsmen to the marshes." She'd have to risk separating herself from Cédron so she could try to earn the marshlanders' trust before he arrived and asked for their aid.

"Good," said Rováen, glancing briefly at Cédron. "We will be there only a few days behind you. Go now and fly high!"

She embraced her uncle and gave the Seeress's arm to Chem'ewa.

"Dress as warmly as you can, it will be cold at the heights we must fly."

The young man nodded and pulled a heavy cloak from his pack. After securing the garment over the old woman's head, he guided the Seeress towards the agitated läenier. Räesha turned to Cédron. The Sumäeri warrior pulled out a small box from her pouch and handed it to him.

"This is a compass that your friend Sahráron made for you. She asked me to give it to you."

She quickly showed Cédron how to open the ivory lid and briefly how to read the sundial. "Sahráron said that it would always show you the way."

"Thank you Räesha." Cédron 's voice cracked. "I will use it well, I hope."

"See that you do."

The Sumäeri warrior pulled her cloak out, threw it around her shoulders and adjusted the new riding straps she'd rigged for her passengers. Yongäen fidgeted, shifting his weight from one foot to the other. *If we're still within bow range of the Council Guard when we take off, we'll never make it.*

The thought of the golden-orange feathers of her beloved beast stained with blood brought on a wave of nausea. Räesha swiftly belted the final strap in place and ushered the Meq'qan Seeress and her two tribesmen up onto the back of her raptor.

"Come, we have to hurry," she said, holding the straps out for the Meq'qan to climb up with. "The group of Council Guards is nearly here."

"We are too late," Chem'ewa cried, looking wildly around for the elite warriors. "They will kill us with their bows if they spot us in the air!"

Ta'riqk held the Seeress back from the raptor. "We can't risk losing our Seeress. They're seeking you, not us. We'll find another route."

The Meq'qan turned to go, urging the ancient Seeress to come away with them, when the old woman held up her hands.

"No," she said in her quavering voice. "We must ride with the Sumäeri. She is the only one who can get us to the Zig'orman Marshes in time." She turned her yellow eyes on her kinsmen and nodded. "War is coming to all our people. We have to let them know before they are slaughtered as our tribes were."

Räesha's body was taut with frustration as the Meq'qan argued. They didn't seem to realize that every second wasted reduced their chances of escape. Finally, she vaulted to the back of her mount and held out her hand.

"I'm leaving," she seethed through clenched teeth. "Any who want to join me need to get up now!"

Ta'riqk scowled. After a final word from the Seeress, he and Chem'ewa gently lifted the old woman into Räesha's waiting arms and scrambled up behind her. Yongäen stepped forward, spreading his wings wide and stretching them in preparation for flight. Räesha scoured the forest and large clearing for any sign of the Council Guard, but saw no trace of her pursuers.

Nudging the raptor with her legs, Yongäen hunched down, bunching his muscles for the mighty leap he needed to spring airborne with the extra weight. His wings extended fully, he beat the air and rose slowly above the ruined tower.

Räesha had Yongäen circle the ruins once as it spiraled into the darkening clouds before heading northeast. She thought she heard a cry from below, but she couldn't be sure this high up. She was craning her neck around her raptor's head to see what was below her when an arrow whizzed by, narrowly missing her cheek. Räesha lurched back and veered the beast off to the right over the trees, away from the direction of the volley of arrows.

"Duck!" she cried to her passengers. "We're being shot at."

The three Meq'qan followed Räesha's lead, lying down as flat against the raptor's back as they could, each body stacked upon the back of the other, making them a smaller target. Räesha hugged her läenier's neck tightly and directed him with her legs. She wheeled him around, then zigzagged him through the steady barrage coming from the four Council Guards below.

Don't get hit! She sent the mental message to her beast, who rumbled in return. Räesha offered a prayer to Orwena for their safe deliverance from the hunters and was rewarded with a scream from her beast. Looking back, she saw the shaft of an arrow protruding from Yongäen's orange-coated leg. It hadn't hit any vital areas, but it was causing the avian a great deal of pain. Räesha fervently hoped they hadn't used any of her sister Läerei's toxins, or their flight would be a short one.

Glancing toward the ground, she spotted two of the Council Guard as they emerged from the forest just to the west of the tower. Although far away, there was no mistaking the set of the shoulders and waving hair of the man who'd most recently shot at her. *Trilläen! How could he? He swore to me that-* Räesha clamped down on the rest of that thought. It didn't matter what Trilläen had promised her; she'd made her choice, and now she'd have to deal with the consequences.

Räesha closed her eyes and lent her strength and Árk'äezhi to her struggling mount, willing the beast to fly east and out of bow range. The raptor made steady gains in altitude as it carried the group out over the vastness of Lake Juláni. Once they'd put a few leagues between themselves and their pursuers, Räesha felt comfortable taking a break. They would fly for some time before reaching the eastern edge of the lake and the final pass through the Ronhádi Range, but she wanted to take a look at the injured raptor's leg. As Lord Shamar's light rose higher in the sky, Räesha's wind-whipped face soaked in the feeble warmth. Urging her beast onward, she scoured the landscape for a shoreline large enough to set down. She wasn't sure if he would be able to land without doing more damage to Yongäen's leg, especially considering how loaded down he was with passengers. She knew that there was nothing more she could do for him except lend him her energy.

"Look for a beach long enough to land," she yelled at the Meq'qan behind her, noting the fear in their eyes and the white-knuckled grips they had on the flying straps. "We should be able to rest a bit and see to that injury before reaching the Zig'orman Marsh."

The Meq'qan simply nodded, their faces telling Räesha that the reprieve from flying would be welcome. The Sumäeri marveled at their tenacity, especially that of the old Seeress. These people had been through so much in the past few days, losing their tribes to the Garanthian slaughter, being attacked and buried in the watch tower, and now riding astride a flying monster. Still, they had accepted the necessities of the last two with stoic silence and a grim determination that would rival any Sumäeri patrol.

Räesha empathized keenly with their recent losses, the agony of her murdered family still raw around the fringes of her mind where she kept it at bay. She had to convince Cédron of the importance of his role in this war, or her family's deaths would have been for nothing. *That boy has got to at least attempt to obtain the aquastone from the Meq'qan priestess. If he can heal the land of ground shakes, we will have more time to work with him before he must face the great demon.*

Räesha believed that accomplishing this first mission would give Cédron the confidence he'd need to complete the greater quest of securing the other sacred stones and acquiring the Sceptre of Kulari. She and her Sumäeri brethren could train him to do the rest. If Laylur's minions succeeded in freeing the fallen deity from his prison, then their world and all those who lived in it would be faced with ravaging and destruction worse than what they had faced with Laräeith's Betrayal. *I won't let that happen!*

The Sumäeri warrior reached deep inside herself to that place where the greatest strength resided. She thought of her sister Lanäe and her parents, now gone, but with love rather than the guilt and grief that had previously been her overriding emotion. Räesha knew that she would do anything, sacrifice everything, to do right by her family.

Happy memories of her first trip to Auräevya, the Tree of Life, filled her mind and brought an unbidden smile to her lips. She and Läerei had been young and unruly enough to exasperate their parents with their disobedience. They'd chased each other through the gardens, tearing through piles of recently gathered leaves and roots that the Wushäen had stacked for disposal, earning stern looks from the Wushäen and sharp words from their parents. Räesha's grin grew wider. *Even then, it was apparent that we didn't have the temperament for docile activities. Läerei and I are Sumäeri to the core.*

Räesha's first trip to Suriyäeh, at the tender age of 11, had given her a taste of what her life was to be like. She remembered the thrill of watching the warriors training with their staffs and their magic, dueling each other with the combination of martial and arcane arts. As a young girl, Räesha had always thrived on the challenge of tracking. She could identify the person or beast she was after by sensing of their emotions. That's what had made her and Trilläen such excellent partners – his ability to read sign and her keen sense of where the prey was and what condition it was in. It had saved their skins on more than one occasion.

The two young Sumäeri had learned quickly not to attempt to capture the fierce kessäeri if it was mating season. The indigo males were more aggressive than usual, charging anything that approached the flock of females they were attempting to woo. Trilläen had sported the lump on his head from that adventure for nearly a week. Memories of her former partner sobered her instantly. She knew that he'd been sorely disappointed with her decision to join the ranks of the läenier wings, but she also knew that he loved her enough to let her go. *How could he agree to this mission? I could understand if he'd learned to resent and hate me for my rejection, but to harm Yongäen...that's not the Shäeli way.*

Räesha's eyebrows knit together as she tried to work out what could have happened in Suriyäeh to convince the Näenji Council to take such a departure from their foundation and teaching. The creating deities Lord Shamar and Lady Muralia had been cut off from regular contact with their First Peoples since Laräeith's Betrayal and the shifting of Árk'äezhi energy, but that should have inspired the Näenji Council to adhere even more carefully to their basic charge of caring for Muralia and all the lesser beings. *How could*...then the thought struck her like thunder. She nearly slipped off her mount as the shock of understanding made her dizzy.

If Trilläen had been ordered to burn the enormous city-tree of Suriyäeh by one of the council members, he would have done so without question, even though it meant the lives of hundreds of thousands of his kinsmen. Räesha closed her eyes and buried her face in her raptor's golden neck feathers. *There will be no reasoning with Trilläen or the other members of the patrol. They will capture both of us and kill us with no compunction for us or our mission. They do not see the bigger picture here.*

It had become clear to Räesha, after the death of her parents, that some demons had indeed broken through Lady Muralia's wards and were running amok throughout the land. Certainly, she had seen them in Siläeri. One, at least, had been working within that cart driver. It stood to reason that Laylur had instructed his minions to infiltrate the governing bodies of the land first. The likelihood of at least one council member being influenced, if not outright possessed by a demon, was exponentially higher than she had originally surmised. She saw evidence of it everywhere, even in Dúlnat. She shared her uncle's distrust of that red mage. That, coupled with the Council's decision to release the Selväen on her family in opposition to the basic Shäeli teachings, convinced her that the council had to be exposed to demonic influences. *But can I convince Trilläen of all this? Will he even listen to me?*

Räesha had been so lost in her ruminations and focused on sending her Árk'äezhi energy to Yongäen that she was oblivious to her surroundings. The läenier had flown nearly to the southeastern end of Lake Juláni without her realizing it. The gray skies had turned the clear waters of the lake a matching cloudy slate, blending them together into a cineral landscape. The rains had continued to pelt the group, but Räesha ignored the discomfort. Dark skies turned to darker thoughts and brought to mind the gray eyes of the rogue mage Algarik who had arrived in Dúlnat just before she did.

Räesha had known from the moment she'd laid eyes on Algarik that the man was evil. He was the epitome of what the council feared in Cédron, and he had the same frightening heritage. It was no wonder the Shäeli had closed their borders. After the woman, Laräeith, took advantage of her Shäeli teachers, warping the magic she'd gained into something twisted and evil and completely upsetting the balance of Árk'äezhi with her war, none of the lesser peoples were allowed into Samshäeli again. If Cédron were to be enticed to the more powerful negative influences as his uncle most certainly had been, then Laylur would win. She shook her head. *That must not happen.*

As if in response to her train of thought, Yongäen plunged through the air, his wings failing to catch the updraft that held them aloft. Räesha felt the death grip of the Seeress's hands around her middle and heard the terrified screams of the Meq'qan at the sudden loss in altitude. Even though they'd reached the foothills below the Ronhádi Range, the damage had been done. The warrior reached out to her raptor, tried to soothe his mind, but all she sensed was the haze of pain and exhaustion. She'd pushed him too far, having asked him to bear the weight of passengers for long flights in the thin air of the mountains. Wounded as he was, the regal bird had reached his threshold and couldn't stay in the air. Räesha's mind raced. *Where can we land that won't kill Yongäen and us as well?* Her eyes scoured the sides of the mountains, seeking a grassy valley or anything that would allow a reasonably safe landing.

Ahead, just beyond the foothills, Räesha spied the swampland grasses of the Zig'orman Marsh. If the raptor could glide, perhaps they could make it to the softer ground below. She sent a mental picture of what she intended to her beast, praying that he'd understand. Yongäen faltered as he tried to spread his wings. He flapped and squawked weakly. Räesha poured the remaining Árk'äezhi she had for her own strength into her mount's, fervently hoping it would sustain the beast the several hundred yards they would need to make a safe landing. Yongäen spread his wings and caught the updraft. They glided over the scrub trees that dotted the hills and approached the marshlands.

The raptor back-winged to slow his descent and reached for the ground with his legs. The wounded leg buckled, sending the beast crashing into the ground on his chest. The force of the impact launched Räesha and the Meq'qan from Yongäen's back, scattering their bodies in front of him like so much flotsam on the tide. Räesha lay on her back and closed her eyes, taking a slow inventory of the damage. She carefully turned her neck and spotted the body of the Seeress crumpled in a heap next to her. The force of the impact could have easily broken every one of the fragile woman's bones.

The Sumäeri felt like she'd broken several bones herself, not to mention internal damage and bruising. She groaned and tried to roll over onto her knees and see to Yongäen, but her view was blocked. Shadows of several people crossed the ground as Räesha realized she was surrounded.

"Don't move, Shäeli demon," a man's voice growled. "Or we'll make an offering of your hide to the goddess."

266

CHAPTER 26 - ROKNAAR

Rováen led the small group down the hill and into the next valley. They moved quickly, not worrying about covering their tracks. They scrambled up the next rise, grasping the bushes to keep upright and to propel them forward on the ever-increasing grade of the slope. Nobody spoke. They made no sound other than the puffing and blowing of their breath as they jogged along the ridge of the mountains. Cédron couldn't help but glance behind him every so often, certain that pursuit and death awaited him each time he did. Still, he saw no signs of the Sumäeri hunters and that continued to give him the strength to keep going.

By midmorning the next day, they seemed no closer to the Tádim Pass than when they started. Sitting by the first fire and warm food they'd had in two days, Cédron pulled out his compass to see what might be the best route over the mountains. Holding the device up, he scowled and turned it back and forth, trying to get a better reading. After working with the device for several minutes, he realized it operated on intention. He would hold the image of what he wanted to find and the needle would point him in the right direction.

"This can't be right," he muttered under his breath, turning around in circles.

"What is it?" Tóran asked as he peeked over his brother's shoulder at the compass.

Cédron held the compass lid for Tóran's inspection. "See, the needle is pointing into the mountainside when I ask which direction will get us to the Zig'orman Marsh. That can't be right, can it?"

Roväen turned around and walked back to where the boys were hovered around the compass. "What's the hold up?"

Tóran shrugged his shoulders as Cédron held out the compass for Roväen's opinion.

"His compass is faulty." Tóran winked, looking around the clearing they'd stopped in.

Roväen took the compass and held it, turning several directions and surveying the lay of the land before handing it back to Cédron.

"I think that perhaps there are tunnels riddled in these mountains that we could use." He pulled at his beard and scanned the horizon. "I wonder…"

"What's that up there?" Anéton asked with his mouth full of dried fruit. "Looks like the entrance to a cave to me."

The other three looked in the direction he was pointing and saw an opening in the mottled and scored side of the mountain. Uneven stalagmites and stalactites gave it an ominous appearance, but Cédron and Anéton decided to check it out anyway. Roväen assisted Tóran with packing up their supplies and looking for a source of water to refill their flasks. Hiking up to the cave opening, Cédron noted that the ground was soft around the cave entrance, rather than solid stone as he would have anticipated. He shared his observation with Anéton who was at his side flipping one of his throwing knives, oblivious to the changes in the terrain.

"That's probably from the moisture trapped inside." Anéton shrugged. He shoved the knife into his sash and continued inside the mouth of the cave.

"Anéton, come here a second," Cédron called to his friend, now deep inside the cave.

"Why? What's the matter?" Anéton turned around to see what Cédron wanted.

"I just have a funny feeling…"

Anéton began walking back to the mouth of the cave when the floor tipped up at the entrance and knocked him backwards, deeper into the cavern. Cédron jumped back away from the mouth of the cave and yelled at Anéton to run out. Anéton couldn't get to his feet as the floor continued to heave and roll, like an enormous kazan tongue. He began to crawl forward on his hands and knees to maintain his bearings, but as he got nearer the mouth of the cave, the stalagmites and stalactites began closing in on each other.

"Help!" Cédron screamed to Rováen and Tóran. "Bring me my stones!"

Rováen was across the narrow defile and peeking into the mouth of another cave when he heard Cédron's call. The old Shäeli leapt down to the trail below and raced to Cédron's pack, as nimble as a man half his age. He quickly rummaged around until he found the pouch he was looking for. Sprinting up the hill, he tossed Cédron the bag. Tóran arrived right behind him.

"It's some kind of cave creature, and it's got Anéton!" Cédron cried, yanking the bag open and dumping out its contents.

Rováen cursed as he peered into the creature's maw. "It's a roknaar, a burrowing cave worm. I thought they'd all died out years ago."

Cédron gaped at his uncle. "You mean you knew about them and didn't say anything to us?"

Rováen shook his head. "I thought them extinct. I didn't realize the danger. We'd better get Anéton out of there quickly or he'll be this one's meal."

"Maybe if I send a wind tunnel into its belly, it will hold the mouth open long enough for Anéton to make his way out." Cédron grabbed the sphene crystals and raised them into the air in a vortex.

Rováen nodded and closed his eyes, placing his hands on Cédron's shoulders and adding his Árk'äezhi to the boy's power. Cédron focused his energy on the air properties of the stones and pictured what he wanted them to do in his mind. The stones began spinning faster and faster, floating just above his right hand, and they created a whirlwind that set down just in front of him and caused the trees and bushes around them to whip and break.

"Get down!" Rováen yelled at Tóran to keep him from getting hurt in the wind storm.

With Rováen's help, Cédron used his other hand to guide the cyclone to the roknaar's mouth and forced it between the stalagmites and stalactites that had nearly sealed. The rock shuddered as the opposing forces clashed, and the roknaar was unable to force its mouth shut on the whirling storm of crystals. Images of Anéton's body being impaled by the roknaar's stalactite and stalagmite teeth filled his mind's eye and caused the magic to flare.

"Cédron, focus!" Rováen cried, gripping his shoulders.

"I can't!" Cédron sagged against the older man. "All I can see is Anéton's death."

"You must quit resisting!" Rováen shook the boy firmly. "Relax and allow the Árk'äezhi to course through you. Project with your mind what you want it to do – give it direction. Do not let it control you!"

The boy nodded and closed his eyes. "Anéton, try to crawl out! Stay as low to the ground as you can while we hold it off," Cédron yelled at his friend while trying to maintain focus.

Anéton nodded and put his head down, crawling forward slowly against the wind whipping his hair and pushing him backwards. Cédron watched his friend's progress and lost focus on the stones for a moment, and their intensity lessened. The roknaar began closing its mouth again, rumbling its triumph and rolling its tongue, nearly throwing Anéton back deeper into its throat.

"Cédron!" Rováen screamed above the howl of the wind and the rumbling of the roknaar.

Quickly closing his eyes, Cédron tried to see only the glowing yellow crystals of the sphene as they spun with their frantic pitch while aiming the whirlwind inside the mouth of the roknaar with his left. He saw, in his mind's eye, the cyclone holding back the crushing stones in the cave's mouth, and prayed that Anéton would be able to make it out before the roknaar overpowered them. He could feel the cold fingers of doubt squeezing around his head and breaking his concentration.

Cédron opened his eyes and saw the cave mouth closing on his friend. The floor of the roknaar cave began to grind back and forth, causing the stalagmites rising up to crunch together. Anéton's trousers got caught in between the grinding stones and he began pulling frantically at his pants and grunting in pain as the stone tore the skin off his shin.

The fear of losing another friend threatened to unnerve Cédron completely. He had pushed his mind as far as he was able and began to slip into the dark abyss of grief that losing Anéton promised. He felt Rovaën squeeze his shoulder, offering his strength and reminding the boy that he wasn't alone. He closed his eyes again. Together, they held the roknaar's mouth open until Anéton was able to free his leg and crawl over the last of the jagged, stone teeth. He fell heavily outside the mouth of the cave. Tóran pulled him from the rolling lip and onto solid ground. Cédron opened his eyes and relief flooded him as he saw his friend lying on his back, panting from the exertions. The roknaar began heaving angrily, causing the rocks above it to cascade down upon the terrified group below it. The whole buried creature was lurching out of the mountain towards them.

"We have to stop it!" Cédron yelled at Rovaën.

Cédron, in his panic, pushed both hands toward the roknaar. This caused the sphene crystals to fly into the roknaar's gaping maw, embed themselves within the rock walls, and explode. Shocked, Cédron stared at Rovaën, then turned back to the cave mouth. The beast was seething loudly, the rock around the sphene crystals steaming as if the stones were burning it. The rumbling quieted as the sphene crystal evaporated all the moisture in the walls around it. The creature settled. Everyone in the group stood still, not daring to move or breathe for fear of awakening the monster again.

"It appears to be appeased with your crystals," Tóran whispered.

Cédron's shoulders relaxed. He turned to assist Anéton who was sitting on the rocks, still catching his breath and staunching the blood from the scrape on his leg. The legionnaire was still shaken up from nearly being swallowed by the stone monster, but otherwise appeared in good shape. He bound his wounds tightly and assured his friends that he was fit to travel.

Rováen pulled out a small piece of valerian root from his pouch and gave it to him. "Chew this. It will help calm your racing heart. It's not everyone who can escape the belly of a roknaar and live to tell the tale."

"A what?" Anéton asked, his mouth full of the root.

"I believe that creature is called a roknaar or cave worm," Rováen mused as he eyed the mouth of the cave. "I'd heard of them, but never in my life have I ever encountered one. They were thought to have died out years ago. They are quite lethal."

"Do you think there are any more?" Cédron asked, searching the area for suspicious cave entrances.

"Not likely. They were prevalent once, but it's been decades since I've heard any rumors of their existence. This does, however, solve the riddle of your compass."

"How so?" Cédron asked.

Rováen sat back on his haunches and laid his arms across his knees. Pointing at the compass, he grinned. "Roknaars move by eating through the rock of mountains. We can use that compass to follow their tunnels to the Zig'orman Marshes. Which direction does it say we go?"

Bemused, Cédron opened the compass and watched as the needle settled on a direction. He pointed to the cave opening just to the east. "Up there."

"Well, let's get going." Rováen rose and helped Anéton to his feet before leading the group up to the cave entrance.

Cédron and Anéton didn't move. Rováen clapped Tóran on the shoulder and gave him a gentle shove, but the young legionnaire turned to face his brother.

"It's the fastest route," he said, grasping Cédron by the shoulder with his good arm.

Cédron's face was pale, more white compared to Anéton's greenish complexion. Cédron disliked caves, the spinners made his skin crawl. But he'd never felt mortally threatened by them before now. There was no way he was going into one of these caves.

"No," he shook his head and saw Anéton's echoing shake next to him. "We will have to go over the pass. I am not stepping into another cave. Anéton was nearly eaten by that...that roknaar thing!"

Rováen sighed and nodded his head at the boys. He reached up and scratched his beard and shifted the pack on his shoulder.

"This was my fault," he said softly. "I should have made sure that none of the creatures remained. I should have warned you of the potential danger. I was wrong. I beg your forgiveness." He turned and gazed over the mountains towards the pass. "It will take us several days at the very least to traverse the mountains. Räesha will be waiting." He turned back to his nephew. "And do not forget that we are being hunted. Cedron, we don't have the luxury of time. We have to go through the caves."

Cedron stared at his uncle in disbelief. He was arguing for certain death. He felt the prickle of sweat along his hairline and the tightness of his chest. Another look at Anéton convinced him and he shook his head.

"No, it's too dangerous."

Anger flashed briefly in Rováen's eyes. "It's dangerous either way, true. It isn't nearly as dangerous in the caves if you know what to look for." He held up his hands, one over the other with palms facing each other and his fingers curved like claws. "The roknaar caves will have stalactites and stalagmites, essentially their sharp teeth. The caves that we will be traversing are smooth. We will check them out thoroughly before we enter any, ok?"

Cedron turned to Anéton who shrugged slightly, keeping his face neutral. Cedron looked out over the broad expanse of mountains before exhaling the breath he realized he'd been holding.

"Agreed," he nodded, stabbing his uncle in the chest. "You go first."

The tunnels were fairly smooth, as if they'd been polished. Several of them angled steeply in other directions. As they wandered further in, they found debris littering their way. There were arched plates that were several feet across and would stretch to more than a man's length if they could be pulled flat.

"What is this stuff?" Tóran asked skeptically, kicking at a few plates and finding them extremely hard and painful to his toes.

"I think it may be the skeleton of the roknaar," Rováen speculated. "The worms are soft on the inside and have these hard plates like a shell on the outside. The plates are probably shed as the roknaar grow."

"Yes, and they are very light and strong." Tóran smiled, holding one out for Rováen to test. "They would make great sleds."

Rováen took the plate and placed it on the ground upside down, with the curve of the shell on the ground and the edges facing the top of the cave. The semi-circular plate wobbled on its edges until the old man jumped onto the center. The plate held his weight even as he continued to jump on it, until it slid sideways. Rováen fell off, laughing.

"Well, they certainly seem durable enough." He chuckled, picking himself up off the ground and rubbing his sore backside. "Perhaps we should take them with us. If we continue southwards, we may need them to slide down the angled tunnels."

Cédron pulled out his compass and got a reading before heading out, verifying that the tunnel was indeed heading the appropriate direction. Hoisting the shells onto their shoulders and clutching glow rocks in their hands, the four travellers began the long, dark trek beneath the Ronhádi Range.

CHAPTER 27 - BETRAYAL

Captain Trilläen Villinäes surveyed the remnants of the northern watchtower. Acrid smoke filled the air as the small contingent of Council Guard searched for signs of the wielder of such a massive amount of Árk'äezhi energy. They had been following the Varkáras Caravan under the false assumption that the boy, Cédron Varkáras, was among the travelers. They realized their error when they felt a phenomenal burst of power to the north.

Trilläen knew instinctively that it was the boy's Árk'äezhi that caused this devastation, but he couldn't be sure that young Cédron had done it without help. It broke his heart to think that Räesha was involved, but he had to put his personal feelings aside and fulfill the task he'd been given by the Näenji Council.

"There are two dead Garanth under those boulders on the far side," one of the scouts reported to the amethyst-eyed captain.

Trilläen gritted his teeth, his chiseled features tightening with the effort. *That makes a total of four dead Garanthian warriors. It is unlikely that a boy of only sixteen could handle four full-grown Garanth bulls on his own, regardless of how much innate magic he has at his disposal. Räesha! Why are you doing this?* Trilläen nodded to his scout and waved him away to search the rest of the plains.

The elite warrior walked through the scorched grasses, noting the various signs of passage as he made his way towards the interior of the tower. It was clear that the boy hadn't been alone. There had been several others with him.

At least three sets of bare footprints indicated Meq'qan tribesmen, while the rest were booted, leading the captain to think that the Askári legionnaires were guarding the tower when the Garanth attacked. *That would make more sense. Four Hármolin Legionnaires along with the boy's magic could reasonably handle the Garanthian patrol.* Trilläen didn't know how long Räesha had been at the tower or whether or not she had participated in the battle against the Garanth. What he did know was that she'd fled with at least three others from the tower, forcing from him the last shred of hope that perhaps there was an explanation for her apparent treason. Trilläen sighed as he walked, thinking about how their futures might have turned out differently had he not been tapped to join the Council Guard. Trilläen and Räesha had been friends since their Sumäeri trials as children. Both had excelled in their specialties – Räesha won all trials with animals, including the taming of the läenier, while Trilläen won the tracking exercises. Together they had made an unbeatable team, their complementary skills earning them the admiration of their peers. It wasn't until Räesha had saved Trilläen from an aggressive flock of kessäeri that he'd truly come to appreciate her.

Trilläen smiled as he remembered how Räesha had swung down from the trees in front of the indigo avians that were tearing at his back with their heavy beaks. She'd mimicked their cacophonous call and distracted them while the rest of their patrol put them to sleep with her sister Läerei's sleep-toxin darts. She'd never let him forget the humiliation of having to be rescued.

As their friendship blossomed, so did his feelings for her. He remembered the day he'd asked her to join him at the crystal bridge, the multi-hued stone monument erected centuries ago to celebrate the blessings that Lord Shamar and Lady Muralia had bestowed upon their First Peoples. He had planned to ask her to be his wife, to share her life with him for the rest of their days.

She had arrived, her aqua eyes shining with her own news: she'd been tapped to be a läenier rider. Trilläen knew that nothing in the world would make Räesha happier than joining one of the airborne wings of läenier riders. It had been her life's dream. A pang of regret and sorrow filled his chest as he played out the scene in his mind, like he'd done hundreds of other times since. *If only I'd spoken first and told her I loved her, she might have chosen me.* He still could have married her and become a tracker or maybe a weapons master, but those were not the roles he was suited to, and Räesha might have given up her dreams to prevent him from giving up his own. He knew he could never have made her choose between her love for him and her innate talent. That was against the Shäeli teachings. Every Shäeli was born with a gift that was expected to be utilized for the good of the land. Räesha was no different. For him to wish otherwise would have been selfish and would have eventually caused Räesha to resent him.

The young captain had never been able to fill the void she'd left in his heart when she assumed her new role, and he still wasn't sure how he was going to be able to convince her to return to Samshäeli with him to face the Council. Secretly, he hoped that she'd realize the error of her ways and seek him out, trusting that he'd treat her fairly. He told himself that he would do everything in his power to help her, and he prayed she would realize that once he caught up with her.

"It appears that our quarry is headed over the mountains," he said, nodding at each man as he approached the circle. "I think they've headed to the Zig'orman Marshes."

"What makes you so sure, *Captain*?" Bräentu sneered, placing his beefy hands on his wide hips.

The captain knew Bräentu resented that Trilläen had been placed in charge of this expedition, especially since the other had far more experience. Trilläen would never admit that he'd used his family's contacts within the Näenji Council to receive this assignment. He trusted none of the other Council

Guards to be as fair or sympathetic to his oldest friend, so he tolerated the hostility with as much humility as he could muster. *For Räesha's sake.*

"Several of the tracks around the tower were barefoot," he explained, casting his gaze northward. "The Meq'qan of the Tek'kut Marshes were slaughtered by the Garanthian tribes. I believe she may be taking the survivors to their kinsmen."

"Her treachery knows no bounds!" Bräentu exploded, his complexion reddening with his ire. "When I get my hands on her-"

"We will take her into custody and return her to the Näenji Council for a tribunal as we were directed," Captain Villinäes interrupted the older man's tirade. "Make no mistake; I will not tolerate any vigilante justice in my patrol."

Bräentu glared at his captain and muttered under his breath as he moved to gather his things. The other two, younger scouts and less interested in the quarry than in the chase, nodded their acquiescence and shouldered their packs. The four elite guards set out in a new direction, their Árk'äezhi giving them the stamina and speed to run from the northern watchtower towards Lake Juláni and through the mountains without tiring. They charged through the underbrush and trees that shaded them from the worst of the Suntide heat. They had been trained extensively in focusing their Árk'äezhi energy on tracking the signature energy expenditure of others.

Although Trilläen could tell that Räesha had not caused the explosion of fire energy that started the wildfire, he knew she had been there, and traces of her essence filled his nostrils. He would catch her, and he fervently hoped that he could control his errant sergeant when their paths finally crossed.

ChAPTER 28 - CAVE SURFING

Cédron kept his compass handy and checked it frequently, admiring the complexity and workmanship more each time he used it. The instrument indicated their continued progress southward and slightly east as they followed the tunnels deeper into the Ronhádi Range. They had been traveling for several hours without rest and none in the group had any idea how far they had actually gotten towards their goal.

Fortunately, the roknaar armor was light, for all its durability, and didn't increase their burden other than the discomfort of keeping their arms overhead, holding the plates on top of their shoulders. Still, after walking for what seemed to be an eternity, their bodies and minds began to become weary with the unending and unchanging journey.

The air was damp and slightly stale, an indication that vents providing fresh air were becoming less frequent the deeper they went. The temperature, however, remained constant and added to the sensory deprivation that befuddled their body clocks. Cédron didn't know whether it was night or day, warm or cold, rainy or dry. He wished fervently that the marvelous compass, which had so many amazing features, could indicate cycles of Lord Shamar and his Moon Daughters. It had a barometer, but the constant climate deep in the tunnels negated its ability to determine what was happening outside in the world.

Cédron disliked closed-in spaces as a general rule, particularly after the ground shake that had claimed his mother. They could easily die under the crushing weight of the mountains should another ground shake occur while making their way beneath the peaks of the Ronhádi Range. At least the tunnels were sanded smooth from years of the roknaar's passage through them, stripping them of the sticky webs of the cave crawlers that were usually prolific in areas like these.

"What do you think is happening back home?" Anéton asked, startling Cédron out of his thoughts.

Cédron knew immediately that Anéton was referring to the invading Garanthian army. "I don't know. I hope that the Hármolin Legion can hold off the Garanth attacks. The army will go through the city of Tamóna after the Tek'kut Marsh. I don't know if any there will survive, or if the Garanth will push all the way to Dúlnat before they're repelled." He shook his head, eyes downcast.

Cédron was so deep in his thoughts of his father and the Garanthian threat against Dúlnat that he didn't notice Rováen had stopped in front of him. He banged the armored shell heavily into the old man.

"Hey, what are you-"

"The tunnel has dropped off here," the old man explained. "There has been some sort of ground tremor or some other disaster that caused it to break away."

Cédron's fears gripped his heart and squeezed the air from his lungs. The four peered into the darkness with their glow rocks extended as far out as their hands could hold them, but the gloom of the darkness surrounded them after a few short feet. What if they were trapped beneath the mountains? Cédron laid down his roknaar armor and pulled out the firestone. Closing his eyes, he went deep into himself to the source of his energy, then, reaching out through the stone, cast forth a beam of light.

The stone in his hands glowed brightly. The ray of light broadened and extended a bit out from the drop off, proving that they were indeed trapped. As the energy of the stone increased, the tunnel burst into light as if Lord Shamar himself had entered the cave. The ground protested the offensive brilliance of the firestone and trembled slightly. Cédron's eyes widened.

"Ground shake!" the boy gasped. "And this time, I think I really *did* cause it!"

Tóran blinked and lost his balance in the sudden onslaught of light, sound and shifting ground. He stumbled into Anéton, who reached out to the wall for balance.

"We have to get out of here before the tunnel collapses!" Rováen yelled, pushing the three young men against the smooth wall as trickles of dirt began filtering the firestone's light.

Cédron slid out from Rováen's protective arm and stared out over the edge of the tunnel. Once his eyes adjusted to the light, he could see that the tunnel continued on after a gap of over ten feet across and nearly five feet down, where the section of the tunnel had collapsed. The gap between continued down into the depths further than Cédron could see, and he nearly jumped off the edge and into that abyss when Tóran sidled up next to him unexpectedly.

"I think I could jump it," Tóran said, eyeing the distance for a leap while holding the wall for balance as the ground shakes increased.

"Hmm, it will be dangerous," Rováen frowned, noticing that the tunnel continued in a steep downgrade on the other side. "But how would you stop?"

Cédron looked at the cleft briefly before Anéton crowded him on the edge for his own peek at the challenge. The chasm could be jumped with some effort, but the landing would be difficult. The tunnel sloped downward and curved out of sight after only about thirty feet. There was nothing but empty space on either side of the collapsed tunnel, apparently where a river of molten lava had run its course millennia ago and cooled, settling deep into the bowels of the mountain.

"If you jump high and over rather than straight across, you'll come down at a better angle to stop," Rováen stated, fingering his silvery beard as he considered the possibilities. "But without momentum, you'll probably miss the landing and slip into the crevice."

Cédron pondered the jump from every angle he could think of. It was hard to concentrate as the ceiling of the tunnel continued to shift and trickle dirt into his eyes. One way or another, they were going to have to make the jump or die. If he did a forward flip in the air, as Zariun had taught him, he would land with the momentum throwing him backward away from the slope, and that might work. If he landed wrong, he could tuck into a ball as he landed, rolling safely down the incline until he could stop himself. That might prevent any serious injury.

Suddenly, he was knocked aside into the wall as Tóran charged past him.

"Yaahhh!" Tóran ploughed between Cédron and Rováen with the roknaar shell held out in front of him.

As the young soldier leapt, he positioned the shell beneath his feet with the curves extending in front and in back of him, holding onto the curved front end with his good arm like a forward rudder. The shell landed on the smooth tunnel below them and Tóran skidded it, leaning to the right as the sled scraped around the corner.

"Woo hoo!" Tóran yelled as he slid around the bend and out of sight.

Cédron grinned. "It sounds like he made it around the corner okay. We'd better join him before this whole tunnel collapses on our heads!"

"Crazy bugger!" Anéton scratched the back of his neck and went back to grab his shell.

Rováen shook his head. "I think I'd rather risk the ground shake." Sighing, he grabbed the sled and nodded to his companions.

Cédron motioned for Anéton and Roväen to precede him in this newest madness and held his breath as the old man launched himself across the chasm. Landing easily and steering the sled around the bend, Roväen hollered for Anéton and Cédron to hurry up or they'd get left behind.

Ducking as a large piece of the tunnel fell to the floor and shattered at his feet, the slender boy picked up the armor and held it in front of him. Cédron nodded to Anéton to take the first position, and he watched as the legionnaire sprang into the air and across the chasm. Taking a deep breath, Cédron ran the five steps needed to reach the end of the drop off and sent a quick prayer to Orwena as he jumped into space. His knees and ankles were jarred on impact, but his Shäeli reflexes quickly took over, and Cédron steered the sled around the corner and down the tunnel. He could see the light from Roväen's glow rocks ahead of him where the old man had strapped them to his jerkin to allow both hands to steer the sled.

Cédron grinned tightly against the wind rushing into his face as he raced down the tunnel. His face was flushed as his heart pounded in his chest. The roknaar had smoothed out the tunnels beautifully, making their descent almost flawless, if somewhat faster than he was comfortable with. *At this speed, I don't even notice the ground shake!*

He could hear Anéton whooping ahead of him, obviously enjoying the rapid descent into the dark unknown. He held up his stones higher to see how far ahead Tóran had gotten and spied the outline of his brother's head and shoulders just ahead of Anéton. Cédron turned slightly to see Roväen right next to him, maneuvering his own shell expertly. Anéton had passed Roväen, so either Cédron's friend knew how to make his plate of shell move more quickly, of his uncle knew how to slow down. The boy grinned at his uncle and received a nod and a chin jut telling him to pay attention to what was in front of him.

284

Rováen had noticed the boulder just off the center of the tunnel as Tóran hit it and spun out of control. Without the full use of both arms, the wounded legionnaire struggled to get control of his sled. Rováen warned Cédron to avoid it just in time as the boy leaned to the left and skidded, clipping only the edge of his sled. Rováen steered to the right of the boulder and continued unhampered down the tunnel.

Tóran, however, wasn't faring so well. His sled had become airborne when he hit the boulder, and he spun around before returning to the tunnel floor. Cédron watched him trying to decide whether to spin his shell around to face forward again or simply let go of the one side and try to grasp the other forward-facing end. Tóran couldn't quite reach the opposite side of the shell without losing his balance and falling out of the sled. Cédron realized that any injuries his brother would sustain, should that happen, would be painful, if not life-threatening, given his current speed.

Cédron hunched down in his shell to make it go faster, but his brother outweighed him enough that he couldn't get close.

"Anéton," he screamed. "Get to Tóran! I can't reach him."

"Right." Anéton nodded, grim-faced.

Anéton leaned forward and pulled up along next to the backwards facing Tóran, steering his sled until the sides touched.

"Jump onto mine!" Anéton yelled to Tóran. "Grab my hand and swing over!"

Tóran looked over his shoulder at Anéton, his long dark hair blowing into his face and obscuring his vision. "I can't! I'll lose my balance!"

Cédron kept his eyes on the tunnel in front of them. He called out obstructions for them to avoid. Rováen followed behind, waiting to catch them should one fall. Anéton unbuckled his belt and yanked the scabbard from the leather.

He held the scabbard below the hilt and stretched out the tip of the sheath to Tóran.

"Grab the scabbard, quickly!" Anéton cried. He noticed the great open end to the tunnel getting closer and the black abyss yawning beyond it.

The young man reached for the scabbard. His fingers brushed the end of it, but his sled hit some loose gravel. It slipped to the side just a bit, knocking him off balance and preventing him from getting a good hold of the sword.

"Come on, try again!" Cédron screamed. The opening was growing bigger by the second.

Cédron held his breath as Anéton stretched his arm out again. Tóran grasped the tip of the scabbard, swinging himself behind Anéton and onto his sled just as they hit the end of the tunnels and flew out the side of the mountain and into open space. Cédron's stomach lurched as his sled reached the cave opening a moment after theirs and he sailed blindly into the darkness beyond.

He let go of his sled and threw his arms over his head in panic as they fell towards the valley below them. He couldn't see what was beneath him in the darkness, but he knew that landing from this height wouldn't be pleasant. *Now would be a good time to know how to fly. I wish I'd had a chance to try that!*

Cédron's breath was knocked from his body as he plunged into the frigid mountain river flowing out from beneath the mountains. His initial response to the shock was to inhale, and he quickly wished he hadn't. The water was numbingly cold as he sucked it into his mouth and lungs.

Kicking to keep his head above the water, Cédron heard splashing around him and knew that at least two other members of the group had landed in the water. He cast around but he couldn't see them. Someone splashed near him. Cédron tried to call out, but water kept sloshing into his mouth and forcing him to cough. Cédron lost all sense of direction as the water crashed down, tumbling him back into the swiftly flowing river.

"It's Cédron," he finally gasped. "I'm over here."

As he squinted in the dark, trying to see where the splasher was, he didn't notice the dark shape swiftly approaching him from the side. The smooth object struck him in the side of the head. He saw bright spots for a moment before reaching out and grabbing the curve of the roknaar shell that was floating next to him. Tóran was lying on his stomach inside the shell with his feet and legs dangling in the water. His broken arm was twisted at an awkward angle. He was unconscious.

"Anéton! Rovänen! Tóran's here on the shell," he called out to the other two who had surfaced near him. "Grab onto the other side."

Cédron swung the shell around, pushing it through the current to the other two treading water near the opposite curve of their makeshift raft. Cédron hauled himself onto the floating shell and felt the armor sink beneath the water, submerging Tóran into the turbulent water. He quickly jumped off and treaded water next to his wounded brother.

"It won't hold us if we try to get on." Cédron panted from the exertion.

Cédron could see Anéton's face across the shell and realized that Lord Shamar had crested the horizon. His light filtered through the clouds, bringing the light of day with him.

"I can see the bank just over there." He pointed with his free arm. "We need to get him onto dry land."

Anéton swam around to the same side as Cédron, while Rovänen held the end of the shell steady, like a rudder. Together they pushed the shell towards the bank, kicking with all the strength they had left.

Long minutes ticked by as they pushed their leadened limbs into navigating through the freezing water. Ignoring the numbness in their bodies, Cédron and Anéton continued to fight the current. With lungs burning from the cold and the effort, they gasped for air as waves and spray crashed over them repeatedly.

The three swimmers were walking on pebbly soil before they consciously realized it. They had finally reached the shallows of the river after their long struggle. Calling on reserves they didn't know they had, they hauled the shell, with its wounded burden, onto the river bank.

"Gently with him," Cédron cautioned Anéton. "We don't know what kind of injuries he sustained in the fall. He still hasn't opened his eyes."

The two carefully pulled the shell back from the bank and into where the tall reeds and grasses lined the river. They set Tóran down and stamped down a circular area that would provide a softer cushion for their wounded companion. Rováen staggered out of the water and collapsed down next to the boys.

"This will keep us from being easily spotted," Anéton said as he peered through the tall cattails for signs of anyone following them.

Cédron and Rováen knelt down at Tóran's side and removed the young man's pack. Cédron pulled out a blanket from the pack and rolled it into a pillow to lay his brother's head on. He then pulled out a blanket from his own pack and was pleased to find it still reasonably dry in its wrapping. Rováen began gently probing Tóran's body for injuries. He moved slowly and methodically down the body, his expression grim.

"We need to get him out of these wet clothes and warm him up," Cédron said, eyeing his uncle. "As do you. What did you hurt in the fall?"

The old man winced. "Not fooling you, am I?"

"No."

Rováen tried to inhale, but the ragged breath caused him too much pain. "I think I've broken a couple ribs."

"Anything else?"

Roväen shook his head, saving his breath.

"We can bind you up once we've taken care of Tóran, ok?" Cédron decided.

Roväen nodded and continued his probing of Tóran's body. Dark purple splotches stained his chest. His breath was shallow and gurgling. "He's got several broken ribs, internal bleeding and, if I'm not mistaken, he's punctured a lung. I don't know if I can save him."

Cédron blanched. "Wh-what do you mean, you don't know?"

Roväen just shook his head and emptied his pouch. He sent Anéton to scavenge for herbs while he mixed a poultice from his stores and the water from the river. The old man smeared the poultice across the Tóran's body, then placed all the bloodstones from his and Cédron's pouch on the largest of his wounds.

"Now we wait," he grunted through the pain of his own injuries. "Hopefully, the bloodstones will siphon enough of the blood to allow him to breathe."

Cédron nodded silently and quickly bound his uncle's ribs as tightly as he could with strips torn from his cloak. Anéton returned from his search empty-handed, and the three of them sat in vigil while the activated bloodstones cleared Tóran's body cavity of excess liquid.

Cédron dozed off and on throughout the midday heat, glancing periodically for any changes in his brother's shallow breathing. After several hours, with the only difference in the world being the angle of Lord Shamar's light, Roväen sent the boys off to forage for cámbor, the river shellfish that dwelt around the rocks near the bank. The weary travelers feasted on the bounty that the boys produced and took turns standing watch over Tóran throughout the night.

Cédron had third watch and gazed out over the grasslands as Hamra sank down beneath the horizon, painting the skies in a swath of lavender and plum as her father brightened the opposite horizon. Twillings were awakening, starting the day with their songs and flitting among the reeds in search of insects. For a moment, Cédron was at peace. He was startled to hear the sudden rattle in Tóran's labored breathing. Shaking Rovāen, who had succumbed to sleep next to him, Cédron scooted around the grasses to get a closer look at his brother's face.

"What is happening?" he asked his uncle. "Why can't he breathe more easily? The bloodstones have kept his lungs clear of fluid, haven't they?"

Rovāen placed his hands on Tóran's chest and muttered under his breath. The old Shäeli then turned to his nephew and placed a hand on his shoulder. "Cédron, he's not going to make it. His injuries are too extensive without using all the Árk'äezhi I have."

"Then do it!" Cédron cried. "We can't just let him die. He's my brother!"

"Listen," Rovāen began, wincing with the extra breath needed for arguing. "If we use any Árk'äezhi, everyone in the known world will know where we are."

"So what?" Anéton shrugged. "I can take them."

Rovāen sighed, slumping his shoulders in defeat. "You don't understand. It isn't just the Council Guard that is pursuing you. I believe that Algarik is as well. He is vastly more dangerous than you imagine. If we attract him here, we all die." Rovāen pointed at himself and the two soldiers. "And you will be warped into something terrible. He wants your magic, Cédron, and he'll stop at nothing to get it."

"I don't care." Cédron set his jaw. "Even if you're right, Tóran is my brother and I can't abandon him to die like this. Not if I have the power to save him." He looked at Rovāen. "Will you help me or not?"

Cédron held Rovāen's gaze. An unfamiliar hesitation and fear were apparent behind his blue eyes. Cédron had never known his uncle to be frightened of anything before, and it unnerved him slightly, but it wasn't enough to deter him from whatever was necessary to save Tóran.

Slowly, the old man nodded his head. Rováen took out his knife and cut Tóran's sodden shirt away from his body to expose his wounds more clearly.

"Mijáko piles!" Anéton hissed as he spied the deep purple bruises on the legionnaire's torso. "Do you really think you can save him?"

Rováen shrugged and told Cédron to get the firestone. "We'll do our best. Keep your eyes open. This is going to be like a signal fire."

Anéton stood, weaving slightly from weariness, and drew his sword. "No problem."

"Now Cédron," Rováen began, instructing him on healing his brother. "First you need-" He pulled the firestone out of the bag.

"No! The firestone?" Cédron asked angrily. "I don't want to kill him!"

The old man placed a hand over Cédron's and squeezed gently. "You don't understand. Fire doesn't just create devastation and destruction. It gets its power from passion and love. Fire, more than anything, is fueled by our most ardent emotions. It is your love for Tóran that will lend the power to the firestone necessary to save him by speeding up the healing processes. Does that make sense?"

"Oh. Yes, I think I understand." Cédron nodded slowly. *I don't know if I can do this, but I have to try.* Cédron felt the knot of panic tighten in his stomach. Uncertainty stayed his hand as he warred with his conscience over attempting to use the powerful stone. If Tóran died from his injuries, it would be easier to take than if Cédron killed him in an ill-advised attempt to heal him. Cédron looked at Rováen.

"I'm not sure where to start."

Rováen nodded. "Just close your eyes and let the stone do its work. See your brother's wounds healing and his body revitalized, and the stone will guide you the rest of the way."

Cédron closed his eyes. Anéton and Rováen watched as his pale hands began to glow where they rested on Tóran's chest. Cédron could sense the Árk'äezhi flowing from his heart, pounding and throbbing with each beat as his desire for Tóran's well-being charged the firestone and spread like a pool of light into the wounded young man's body.

Cédron tried not to imagine hordes of Sumäeri warriors converging on their position as he accessed deeper stores of his Árk'äezhi to save his dying brother. His hands began to shake from the depletion of his energy, and his breathing became shallow, but he could sense that it was working. Opening his eyes, Cédron watched Tóran's ashen complexion in the rosy light of the glowing rock, willing him to heal.

"I'll help." Rováen placed his hands over Cédron's, lending his Árk'äezhi through the firestone.

Cédron felt his power bolstered immediately. A wave of power surged forth from his hands and into his brother's body, radiating sufficient power to flatten the grasses around him. He coaxed the warmth and rejuvenating strength from his body and the firestone to enter his brother's body and mend the organs. He could see in his mind's eye the knitting of tissue and the coursing of blood as it pumped properly through his veins. The heat from the stone warmed Tóran's skin and spurred the healing, returning a healthy color to his face and producing deeper breathing. Tóran's eyelids fluttered briefly, then he opened his eyes.

"What happened?" he croaked. "What's going on?"

Cédron's concentration was broken and he dropped the firestone to the ground at Tóran's side. Sucking in a deep breath, he grinned. "You nearly died from your crash landing. Are you able to move?"

Tóran closed his eyes a moment, then ran his hands over his body. "I-I think so. Hey, my arm is healed!" Tóran got up to a sitting position, using both hands to pull his body erect.

"Outstanding! Well done, little brother." He grinned, twisting his arm around and flexing it.

Cédron grinned, punching his brother in the shoulder. "Glad I could be of service."

"Uh guys," Anéton said quietly. "There's someone out there."

Instantly, the small group was silent. All their senses were alert to the sounds of approaching steps, faint as they were. Fear gripped Cédron's heart as his innards turned to ice water. *We've been discovered!*

"They're here," Anéton said, brandishing his sword and stepping out from their curtain of reeds. Cédron peeked through the cattails and gasped as one of the Council Guard approached from the bank of the river. Three more revealed themselves from the surrounding grasses. A smirk played on the lips of the burly Council Guard that stood in front of Anéton.

"Well, well, well," he sneered. "Look what we have here, Captain."

CHAPTER 29 - SUMÄERI BATTLE

The morning mist lay heavy over the wetland grasses as Räesha swatted again at the eternal clouds of biting insects that swarmed around her and Yongäen. The Sumäeri warrior had risen at dawn to see to her läenier's healing wounds. As she pulled back the wrappings from around his leg, she cringed. *This isn't healing like it should. What am I doing wrong?*

Frustration mounted as she swatted again at the tiny gnats and biting flies to cleanse the pus that oozed from around the puncture where the arrow had pierced the skin. The fluffy orange feathers of Yongäen's legs offered scant protection from such weapons.

Räesha wiped the sweat that had formed along her forehead despite the chill of the early morning air. Once the wound was cleaned, she slathered it with the poultice that Zale'en had given her. The high priestess had done everything she could to assist the warrior out of gratitude for Räesha's safe delivery of the Seeress and remaining Meq'qan survivors of the Tek'kut Marsh. The tribal warriors had nearly killed her, but Zale'en saw that they transported their kinsmen. The high priestess had convinced them to hear their story first. Räesha knew she owed the woman for her life and that of Yongäen.

The news of the Garanth's genocide of their people devastated the priestess and her tribe, many of whom had begun voicing their outrage by calling for retribution. Caf'iq Mak'ki, the chieftain of the tribes of the Zig'orman Marshes, supported the younger warriors' calls to war, a move diametrically opposed by his spouse, the high priestess Zale'en. As a warrior herself, Räesha tended to sympathize with the angry men, but as a Shäeli, Räesha also valued life and understood Zale'en's devotion to Lady Muralia and her reticence for bloodshed.

Räesha slapped the bloodsucking insects on her thigh and decided that sometimes killing was necessary, particularly if it meant her survival versus the feasting of the swarm. She enjoyed the company of the Meq'qan, but Räesha was anxious to leave the marshes – to escape the bugs, if nothing else. She frowned as she tied off the fresh bandage on Yongäen's leg. *Hopefully he'll heal with this dressing and we can be off. I don't like leaving Cédron out there, with both the mage and the Council Guard hunting him.*

"How is your raptor this morning?" a voice dry and withered as Autumntide leaves called out from behind her.

Räesha spun around to see Zale'en and two of her novices approaching from the village. Räesha had been so deep in thought that she hadn't been paying attention to her surroundings, and the women had nearly reached her before she knew it. Räesha let out a long breath and smiled slightly.

"He'll make it," she said. "The wound continues to fester, but perhaps with the additional poultice you made for me, it will improve."

Räesha bowed low to the priestess as she approached, her hand extended. She grasped Zale'en's hand and squeezed gently in gratitude. She chuckled quietly as the two novice girls eyed the raptor with fear. She knew that they would not have ventured nearly as close if they hadn't been in the company of their high priestess.

Räesha reveled in the fact that she rode such an intimidating beast. She loved Yongäen and he returned the sentiment. They were a bonded pair, dedicated to each other completely. Räesha patted the bird on the neck and stroked him gently. The beast nuzzled her shoulder with his enormous beak, eliciting squeals from the young girls.

"What news have you of the boy?" Zale'en asked, stroking the raptor bravely.

Räesha grimaced. "Nothing, for which I'm sort of grateful. If he uses his Árk'äezhi, then I will sense him, but so will those who hunt him." She scratched the top of Yongäen's head, and the läenier crooned quietly. "I don't know if we could handle another battle right now."

Zale'en nodded, leveling her reptilian gaze upon the Shäeli's blue eyes. "He must be brought to me as soon as you can find him. I will see if he is worthy of the goddess's aquastone. If he has a pure heart and true need, he will be able to claim it from her."

Räesha nodded her acquiescence. *Perhaps facing the mage and the Council Guard are the least of Cédron's challenges. If the boy has to face either the great deity herself or her guardians, he had better know what he's doing.* "I will set out tomorrow and head east to seek-"

A wave of power radiated across the marshes, causing the bulrushes to flatten and the women's hair to fly skyward as the shock of energy crashed through them. Despair washed over Räesha as she felt the power of the firestone and recognized Cédron's Árk'äezhi behind it. *The boy must be in grave danger to use his energy like that! He's sending out a signal for all to see!*

Zale'en's yellow eyes widened as she felt the power. "Was that the boy? He is strong!"

Räesha pursed her lips. "Yes, and I must go to him immediately. The fool has alerted the whole world to his position!"

The warrior vaulted to Yongäen's back and urged the beast skyward. She knew that Zale'en could feel the strength of his power, so she knew he had to be fairly close to her current position. Wheeling Yongäen eastward, she directed the läenier forward.

Räesha felt the pulses of power even high above the land, its essence charging the Shouman field like Lord Shamar's lightning storms. Static crackled in her short hair as tiny sparks stung her cheeks and neck. *I've never known anyone's power to affect the Shouman field like this. I've always been taught that only Lord Shamar had control over the field.*

Räesha realized, as she continued seeking the boy, that Cédron did indeed have the potential to heal their world of the ground shakes and seal the breach in the demon's prison. She had to get him to Elder Räelin and the Sceptre of Kulari. She was certain now that he could successfully wield it.

It felt to the warrior as if only a few moments had passed when she found Cédron and his companions beneath her. They weren't alone. Räesha's heart leapt into her throat when she recognized the tall, rangy figure of Trilläen Villinäes. The Council Guard had the companions lined up along the river bank on their knees.

Her heart beat faster. It looked like the Council Guard were going to execute the entire group. Räesha closed her eyes and sent a fervent prayer to Orwena to let her land in time to prevent her brethren from making a catastrophic mistake.

Yongäen's scream rent the skies and caused the figures on the ground to look up as one. Räesha wasn't sure how she was going to deal with Trilläen, but she hoped that he would value their previous relationship enough to hear her out.

Pounding her thigh impatiently while her beast spiraled to land, she thought quickly of how best to approach her former paramour. The raptor dug his claws into the soft ground near the bank of the river and she slid quickly off his back and strode over to where the two groups waited, watching her approach.

"And look here, it's the traitor as well," Bräentu sneered. "We can complete both missions in one fell swoop."

Trilläen scowled at his men. "Hold. We will hear what the Sumäeri has to say first," he ordered and turned to Räesha, his eyebrows raised.

297

Suddenly awkward, Räesha hesitated for only a moment, then brushed past the Council Guard and held her hand out palm up in greeting. Trilläen covered her hand with his and the warmth of his skin sent shivers down her spine. Her eyes opened wide and she looked into Trilläen's eyes to see if he'd felt the exchange as well. His unusually dark, plum-colored eyes softened as she looked at him, making her even more uncomfortable.

She could have spent the rest of her life basking in the adoration of this exceptional man. Räesha shook her head slightly to dispel the temptation of pining over what could have been.

"Thank you Trilläen," she said softly, then glanced over to the river bank at the four figures still on their knees. "Are you all ok?"

As one, they nodded but kept their eyes on the group of Council Guards. The three warriors stood to one side, but kept their weapons drawn as if they anticipated a fight. Räesha looked at them and realized that the heavier-set one who'd called her a traitor was the most dangerous. His eyes were filled with loathing, and he hefted his sword as if itching to swing it.

Räesha didn't know how much control Trilläen had over the man, but she didn't trust him. The way his beady eyes raked over her made Räesha's skin crawl. She turned her attention back to Trilläen.

"I understand that the Näenji Council has charged you with returning me to face the tribunal after my escape from Siläeri, and to bring this boy to be evaluated," she began, gesturing to Cédron as she spoke. "I will agree to accompany you and bring Cédron with us as long as you hear me out first. Is this agreeable?"

Trilläen opened his mouth to speak, but Bräentu interrupted him. "Shut up, wench. You are in no position to negotiate." The large man lowered his spear to her chest and poked her menacingly, his grin widening. Yongäen screamed in protest, charging the man threatening his rider. Räesha knew that killing him wouldn't help her cause, so she raised her hand to halt the raptor's attack. With her left hand, she grabbed the shaft of the spear behind the metal tip and pulled it away from her chest.

"I don't need you to call your beast off," Bräentu snarled. "I'll kill you both without breaking a sweat."

"Bräentu," Trilläen barked. "Stand down. I'm in charge here and will listen to what this rider has to say."

Bräentu glared at his captain but lowered his spear. He returned to his companions behind the kneeling prisoners but remained within earshot. Trilläen apologized for his patrol's behavior and invited Räesha to tell her story.

The läenier rider shared the reason for her visit to Siläeri as mediator for her youngest sister Lanäe's tribunal. Trilläen listened without expression to the story of how Lanäe had been approached by the Meq'qan spirit trapped within Auräevya, the Tree of Life, and her warning. His eyes shifted to Cédron briefly at the mention of the one born with the blood of all races, but he returned his gaze immediately to Räesha.

She took a deep breath, then shakily told the story of Lanäe's death and her horror at realizing that it was indeed demons that were loose and had infiltrated the Wushäen. Räesha watched Trilläen's face for any sign that he understood the danger to their world, with the breach in the demon's prison, but his features remained impassive.

"I am not positive," Räesha said, her voice hardening. "But I fear that the Näenji Council may be compromised as well. They awoke the Selväen and sent it to destroy my family."

Trilläen's jaw dropped. "The Selväen?" The color drained from his face and he grabbed Räesha by both shoulders. "Why would they do that? How did you survive?"

Räesha's face darkened at the memory. "My sisters and I were able to escape on Yongäen." She glanced at Bräentu and decided to keep the rest of her knowledge to herself.

"But your parents?" Trilläen gasped.

Räesha shook her head, her eyes filling with tears.

Bräentu's laugh sawed down her nerves. "That's right, we razed the place to the ground," he sneered. "The Selväen doesn't tolerate traitors. He destroys them. He stoked his fires with plenty of traitor blood before we were done."

"You were there?" Trilläen turned to his second-in-command. "You condoned this?"

"Of course." Bräentu shrugged. "I *obey* my orders, unlike some." The thick man glared at Räesha and spat. "I don't buy this pile of kazan dung she's spouting, either. Let's just kill her and the rest and go home."

"Our orders were to bring Räesha and the boy to the Council," Trilläen reminded him. "And since you are adamant about following orders, that's what we will do."

Bräentu stared at his captain, his body tensed for conflict. At his sides, the other two Council Guards shifted uneasily, unsure of what to make of the tension between the two men.

Behind them on the river bank, Räesha watched Rováen nudge Cédron and Tóran, who were on either side of him. He nodded at the Shäeli arguing and mouthed silently for them to prepare to fight. The two legionnaires returned his nod, but Cédron's eyes were wide and his head shook slightly.

Räesha realized that this was the first time Cédron had been faced with Shäeli opponents. He'd told her earlier that he would rather go with them peacefully than attack his own people. *Well, if he wants to live, he may not have much choice.*

Räesha lifted her chin and addressed Trilläen. "Please, you know now how much I've already lost. Help me save our world," she pleaded.

300

Trilläen shook his head. "The boy is powerful and very dangerous," he said slowly. "The Näenji Council knows his heritage, and I believe they are wise to be cautious about him."

"He's an abomination," shouted Bräentu. "We should kill him now before he can cause any more harm! I'm tired of talking!"

The stocky warrior raised his spear and thrust it towards Cédron's heart. Rováen saw the strike coming and knocked Cédron backwards onto the ground. Tóran and Anéton pulled their swords from their scabbards and fell upon the two guards while Rováen grabbed Bräentu's thrusting spear.

The old man forced the stouter man off balance. Räesha rushed to Cédron's side, pulling him up and assuring herself that he was unharmed.

"See how the traitor protects the little demon," Bräentu screamed, spittle spraying from his lips. "She deserves to die!" He dropped the spear and charged the woman, grabbing her around the throat with his beefy hands.

Trilläen tackled the two of them, knocking Bräentu's hands free from Räesha's neck but eliciting the ire of her raptor. Yongäen screamed and charged into the fray, talons raking friend and foe alike in his haste to assist his rider.

Cédron rolled to the side and fished the firestone from his pouch. He shot two bolts of fire over the läenier's head, hoping to distract the beast from his attack, but it served only to infuriate him further. The raptor's talons scored into Tóran and the Sumäeri; attacking him on its way to reach Räesha.

Rováen grabbed the spear that Bräentu had abandoned and swung it towards Räesha's attacker. It struck Bräentu in the knees and the burly warrior howled in pain. He turned to Rováen, rage burning in his eyes.

"I'll kill you all!" he screamed, pulling a knife from his belt.

301

Bräentu smashed Räesha across the face with the hilt of his blade, knocking her backwards. He charged Rováen with an insane fire burning in his eyes. Anéton and Tóran continued to fight with the other two guards, neither gaining the upper hand.

Tóran's acrobatic skill served him well as he easily kept his opponent at bay, flipping backwards when the Sumäeri pressed the attack. Anéton managed to catch his attacker with his throwing knives, wounding the older Sumäeri, who limped over to a fallen log.

"Cédron," Rováen shouted over the chaos. "Use the firestone to increase this one's anger."

"What?" Cédron gasped. "Why? He's already half mad!"

Rováen grinned and grunted as he whacked Bräentu on the side of the head with the wooden shaft of his spear. "Exactly. Just a little push and he'll lose all control."

Räesha sat up and shook her head, the ringing in her ears distorting the sounds of fighting all around her. She watched as Cédron aimed the firestone at Bräentu and closed his eyes to concentrate.

"No Cédron!" she screamed. "Don't kill him with your magic or Auräevya will reject you!"

Cédron hesitated. Trilläen rolled away from Räesha and leapt towards Cédron, knocking the stone from his grasp. Räesha recovered the stone, but was shoved back down as Tóran slammed into her while fighting the other guard. Trilläen got to his feet and raced to Räesha.

"Give me the firestone," he yelled.

"Never!" she screamed back and got to her feet.

Trilläen jumped toward her and caught her around the waist, dragging her to the ground. The läenier glared balefully at the warrior with his amber eye and launched himself skyward. The raptor circled once, then extended his talons as he dove towards the captain.

Räesha realized that Yongäen was about to gouge her friend, so she lunged in front of him, waving her beast off.

Both Räesha and Trilläen were watching the raptor and didn't see Bräentu poised to throw his spear. The grizzled guard screamed his war cry and threw the shaft. The point thrust deep into Räesha's chest, knocking her back into Trilläen's arms. The two Sumäeri fell to the ground together, Räesha on top of Trilläen.

Pain exploded in her chest, making breath impossible. "That's twice you've saved my life," Trilläen whispered into Räesha's ear as he gently nestled her head in his lap. Tears streamed unheeded down his cheeks and onto her forehead.

Räesha looked into her former love's face and smiled weakly. "You owe me," she sighed and rolled her head to the side, the fire gone from her aqua eyes.

CHAPTER 30 - RÄESHUN

Cédron stood, staring dumbly at the spear sticking out of Räesha's chest. He was frozen. Blood pounded in his ears, drowning out the sounds of the battles continuing around him. *She can't die!* The boy raced to Trilläen's side and pried the firestone from Räesha's grasp. Cédron held the stone over her body and willed the fire to heal her. The magic flared through his hands, strengthened by the force of his emotions. The burning light engulfed him in its brilliance, scorching his skin as the Árk'äezhi poured forth from his hands, through the stone, and into Räesha's body. Nothing happened.

Cédron's breathing became shallow as his inability to save her struck panic in his heart. *This is all my fault! Her whole family has died because of me! Please Azria, if you can hear me, give me the power to save her!* Cédron's prayer to the goddess of healing went unheeded. The life had left Räesha's eyes, never to return. Cédron dropped his hands and sobbed.

Bräentu sauntered over to Räesha's body and pulled the spear from her corpse. "No sense in losing a good weapon." He grinned, winking at Trilläen.

Rage boiled over in Cédron. The firestone responded instantly to the force of his passionate hate, glowing brightly in his hands. Cédron stood and faced the rogue guard, who hefted the bloodied spear over his shoulder. Cédron didn't think about his next move. He just reacted.

Fire thundered through his veins as the power of his Árk'äezhi coursed through the firestone. The heat burned the skin on the palms of his hands, but Cédron was oblivious to the pain. He saw nothing through the haze of red except Bräentu's leering face. Cédron wanted revenge for his cousin's death, and he meant to have it. Raising the firestone over his head, Cédron directed the flow of energy towards the burly man.

Bräentu's grin vanished as the power struck him full force in the chest. Shock registered on the guard's face as his blood began to boil. His skin turned red and steamed as the water evaporated from within, his body shrinking and shriveling as it dehydrated. Bräentu screamed in pain, his eyes wildly pleading with Cédron to stop.

The young man's heart had hardened, and he felt no compassion for this brutal man, only contempt. The power pulsing from the firestone throbbed brighter and brighter while Bräentu's screams got fainter. Then in a flash of glimmering light, Bräentu's body exploded, the shreds of flesh and bone charring even as they floated back to the ground, leaving only a few scattered shards and a sky full of ashes.

Cédron fell to his knees, his Árk'äezhi depleted and the firestone cooling in his grasp. He stared at Räesha's face and gently reached up to close her eyes. Rováen stepped up to him and placed a hand on the boy's shoulder, giving it a squeeze. Cédron looked up to see tears in his uncle's eyes and felt the shame of his inability to save Räesha well up in his body.

"I couldn't save her," he choked. "I'm so sorry."

Rováen nodded. "You did what you could, as we all did," the old man sighed deeply and his shoulders sagged. "Now, give me that stone."

Cédron hung his head and handed his uncle the firestone. He wasn't sure if Rováen took it for safekeeping or to get it away from his dangerous hands, but it didn't matter now. He looked across the bank to where Anéton and Tóran were still fighting with the remaining guards. Both were taking a serious beating and it looked as if they, too, would join Räesha at Orwena's table.

"Help them." Cédron's strangled cry stirred Rováen to action.

Whistling for Yongäen, Rováen herded the raptor back into the thick of the remaining combatants, directing it with whistles and gestures taught to all Shäeli who worked with the beasts, to capture the two guards with its talons. Yongäen jumped skyward, plucking the Council Guard from their battles and lifting them high into the air. The two warriors twisted and fought the vice of the talons, each prying against the bird's claws with their knives.

The raptor shrieked in pain as their blades struck home, releasing the two to fall headlong into the swift, flowing river. Rováen watched as both silver-haired heads bobbed to the surface before getting caught in the eastward current. Tóran and Anéton staggered over to Rováen and nodded their thanks for the intervention. Both saw Räesha's body and hung their heads, dropping to their knees to honor her sacrifice.

"That's done," Rováen said wiping his hands on his trousers. "Now, what are we going to do about you?" Rováen faced Trilläen with his hands on his hips.

Trilläen smoothed the hair from Räesha's cheek and laid her head carefully on the grass as he stood. Facing the group, he cleared his throat.

"We must give this noble warrior a proper burial."

Cédron stood as Trilläen bent over and picked Räesha's body off the ground. The tall man carried her toward her läenier. The raptor had landed and strutted slowly toward Trilläen. The large beast turned his head in order to see his rider fully. A low rumble emanated from Yongäen's throat, and he danced back a few paces in agitation. Cédron was moved as the enormous bird then knelt and placed his forehead on Räesha's chest in a gesture of grief and farewell.

The keening from deep within his chest would ring in Cédron's mind for the rest of his life.

"We will give her a water burial," Rováen said to Trilläen as he paced along the bank of the river. "We need to find an appropriate spot."

Trilläen nodded. He placed Räesha's body on Yongäen's back and jumped up behind her, holding her close to his chest. Rováen and Cédron climbed up behind him.

"You two stay here," Rováen instructed Tóran and Anéton. "Build a fire and prepare some food. Stay hidden. Algarik is still out there. We'll be back later."

Tóran and Anéton nodded and began clearing an area for a fire. Yongäen ran several steps along the bank of the river, gathering the speed he needed to become airborne with his burden. Cédron's stomach lurched as the great beast's wings spread and he leapt into the air. Higher and higher they flew, following the river towards the mountains and away from the marshes.

Cédron's face became numb from the cold wind of the high mountain elevations biting his skin. He wondered what a water burial entailed. In Dúlnat, the dead were interred in tombs beneath the city or in the old mine shafts. He hoped that, whatever ritual they performed for Räesha, it would be worthy of her sacrifice and her warrior's spirit.

The läenier flew for many long hours while following the river. Rováen and Trilläen continued their search for a proper burial spot late into the afternoon. Lord Shamar hovered along the horizon, dancing with the tops of the trees before Rováen called out and pointed to a spot near some falls. Yongäen slowly began to spiral down toward the ground.

The air warmed as they descended, the feeling returning to Cédron's frozen extremities. The rush and crashing of the nearby falls filled the air as they landed. Cédron and Rováen dismounted first, reaching up to catch Räesha's body as Trilläen carefully lowered her from the raptor's back. The

two carried the Sumäeri the short distance to the large pool
that formed at the base of the waterfall. Gently, they placed
her into the shallow water near its edge.

"She was taken violently from us. She will need
assistance if her spirit is to avoid becoming a Mäuli,"
Trilläen said quietly as he approached the water's edge.

Cédron felt a stab of fear. He had encountered a Mäuli
only once before in his lifetime and had no desire to repeat
the terrifying experience. Mäuli could be harmless, simply
annoying energy, but those who had been strong spirits in
life were dangerously evil as Mäuli. Räesha's spirit had the
potential to be devastating.

The three Shäeli gathered around the edge of the pool
where Räesha's body lay. The spray from the falls above
misted their bodies and tickled their faces, but they showed
no signs of discomfort, only respect for the fallen warrior.
The beads of water caught the first of Orwena's scarlet
beams as she lifted in the heavens, bathing the scene in her
radiance.

"I will see to the läenier." Trilläen cleared his throat and
walked away with slumped shoulders.

Rováen watched him go, wondering if the childhood
friendship between the two Sumäeri had blossomed into
more during the years of his absence. Frowning slightly,
Rováen walked over to Cédron and began rummaging in his
pouch.

"It is time." Rováen pulled out the firestone and handed it
to Cédron. "Hold it up to catch Orwena's light."

Rováen began singing the words of power. Cédron
watched in fascination as the stone in his hands took on the
glow of the moon daughter. Rováen stepped into the shallow
pool and stood at Räesha's head, bidding Cédron stand at her
feet, thus defining the area and preventing the spirit from
escaping should it become Mäuli.

Cédron was unsure of his role in this ceremony, but he
could feel the stone drawing power from the water of the

falls and from himself. He closed his eyes and cleared his mind, breathing deeply as he'd been taught. Opening his mind, he was surprised and ecstatic to feel Räesha's living energy surrounding him.

Cédron felt her gentle caress and love suffusing through his body, causing his hair to stand on end and bumps on his skin to rise. He joined Rováen in his song of gratitude and joy for the life the warrior had lived, and of their desire for her to return to Lady Muralia. Not knowing the words, Cédron hummed the melody that the pulsing energy inspired in him, creating a perfect counter harmony to his uncle's song.

The shapeless spirit rose from the body in the pool and hesitated. Her unfinished business held her spirit to the physical realm and caused it to waver in frustration. Cédron could sense strongly her disappointment and anger at the failure of her mission.

The energy rising from the body in the water coalesced and took Räesha's form in front of him. Her eyes begged him to listen. Inside his mind, he heard her desperate plea for him to gather the elemental stones and present himself to Auräevya. She and her family had already perished on this quest. He couldn't refuse her.

Cédron broke into a cold sweat. Sheer terror washed through his body at the thought of attempting to wield the Sceptre of Kulari and of facing the immortal demon Laylur. He thought of the many failures he'd had with just the firestone: burning the watchtower and killing Bräentu. He realized that it wasn't only that he couldn't control the innate magic he had, but that he was afraid to try again and cause even greater damage. *How many people will suffer before I master my abilities? Besides, you told me that Auräevya would reject me if I used my power to kill. I can't present myself to her now!*

The spirit felt Cédron's fear and rejection. The ephemeral being hovering over the pool slowly altered, her beauty ravaged by despair as she became monstrous before their eyes. Her face elongated, along with her teeth and nails, and a spectral wail tore through their heads as the Mäuli was formed.

Rovä̈en leaned over Rä̈esha's body, grasping Cédron's hands and covering them with his own. Their combined energy caused the stone's light to explode with the splendor of a star.

Cédron felt his uncle's energy guide the stone's magic and send it coursing through his veins. Confidence surged through him with powerful control, preventing his magic from losing focus. He could feel Rovä̈en encouraging him to accept the spirit's challenge and assuring him that he was capable of this task.

Cédron's body tingled with the current of focused magic, and he could no longer feel the ground. Opening his eyes, he could see the Mäuli straining at the prison the firestone had created over the body, and he reached out to it with his mind.

"Do not despair cousin," Cédron said to the spirit, his confidence buoyed to a foolish level by the energy of his uncle's Árk'äezhi and the firestone's magic. "I will finish the task you and your sister were given by Lady Muralia. Be at peace."

The Mäuli shrieked one final time and slowly deflated into her true form. Rovä̈en assisted Cédron in guiding the Árk'äezhi spirit form back into the water where it would be purified and she would be reunited with their source energy. Rä̈esha's body began to glow with the red iridescence of the firestone as Rovä̈en and Cédron focused their powers on releasing it to the deity of their world. The water began to roil and bubble with their power.

Cédron could feel his uncle's intention directing the individual particles of the body into releasing their hold from each other and returning to the source. Their joy for complete liberation of form was palpable. Cédron understood, for the first time, the concept that his own body was a mass of energy that could change form or be released. He remembered trying to grasp that concept when he was learning to become invisible by channeling his own Árk'äezhi through the bloodstone. Although he'd achieved a good measure of success, he now realized how powerful the concept could be.

Orwena's light shone down on the pool from her place in the skies as if to say farewell to her fallen warrior. The waters calmed as the powerful surges from the firestone subsided. Cédron was surprised at how strong and alive he felt. He expected to be exhausted from the drain on his energy for the water burial, but the residual feeling was almost giddy. Trilläen returned and knelt at the water's edge, gasping.

"Mistress!" he cried and prostrated himself on the ground, his fingers just touching the pool, causing tiny ripples.

Cédron looked over at the prone form of the Sumäeri warrior and looked around for the cause of his supplication. R300äen's face was skyward and filled with awe. The pool reflected the moon Orwena and bathed it in her celestial light. Staring at the reflection, Cédron was shocked to see a luminescent face staring back at him.

"Long have we awaited your birth, Child of Muralia," the image in the reflection greeted him in an airy voice.

Cédron looked around for the source of the voice, but inside, he knew it came from the water. Looking into the pool, he marveled at the beautiful woman rising from the reflection of the red moon.

"I am Orwena, daughter of Lady Muralia and Lord Shamar," she answered his unspoken question as she hovered, fully formed and ethereal above the pool. "You have been charged with a difficult task, but do not despair. You are not alone in this battle."

Cédron watched in awe as the luminescent form of the warrior goddess reached into the water and pulled forth an ornately carved white staff with a sunburst crown. She held out the staff to Cédron and indicated he should take it. Grasping it in his hands, he was surprised at how light it was, yet he could tell it was extremely strong.

"Your cousin was not ready to leave this battle. She has requested an opportunity to continue her mission and has sacrificed her place with our mother to join you." Orwena smiled at him. "As her patroness, I have the discretion to grant this wish. She will protect and guide you on your journey. You must heed her, for you have already compromised your success this day with your anger. Only through purification of spirit can you gain acceptance by Auräevya and access the Sceptre of Kulari. Do not fail us, or your fate and that of our beloved world will be beyond the horrors of your worst fears."

Orwena's image smiled at the confusion in Cédron's soft green eyes. The deity held her palm towards the staff, lighting it with her glow. Upon closer inspection, Cédron realized that the staff wasn't ornately carved at all. It was made up of Räesha's bones, arranged artfully into a staff that carried her essence.

Orwena held her hand over the staff and it began to glow from its own internal light. Slowly, the bones fused together solidly, yet kept their distinct form. The smooth surface of the staff was white and unblemished, then Cédron noticed the green vines winding their way up the staff. With a final flash of light, the image of Orwena fused the vines with the staff, decorating it with the tattoos the Sumäeri warrior had worn so proudly on her body. She then retreated back into the reflection of her moon in the pool.

"You have the blessings of the warrior goddess Orwena," Trilläen acknowledged, rising to his feet and scrutinizing the boy again.

Dumbfounded, Cédron held forth the staff for his inspection. Trilläen smiled sadly and looked down at the pool. Nothing remained of Räesha's body except the evanescence of her life's energy sparkling in the water. The warrior seemed older and careworn in the moonlight, but his eyes gleamed brightly.

"You have immense power," he said. "Orwena identified you as the Child of Muralia, one who could wield the Sceptre of Kulari. I cannot defy her blessing. And you," the Sumäeri laid a hand on the boy's shoulders, his eyes piercing Cédron's, "cannot ignore her mandate."

Rováen waded out of the pool and grasped the staff with his hand, pulling it to his chest. He caressed the staff gently in his hands, tears running freely down his face. "Räesha, my dear girl," he said softly. "Only once before has such a selfless gift been given."

Cédron stood silently for a moment. *Did he just talk to the staff?* The boy shook his head to clear the impossible thought and turned to face the raptor that had stepped towards him.

Yongäen lowered his head in respect and touched the staff with the top of his beak, crooning softly. Cédron blinked back tears as Trilläen held out his hand.

"I owe you an apology," the tall warrior clasped the boy's arm. "It appears that the Näenji Council has indeed been corrupted as you said, but there is nothing I can do about that." He stared down the river toward where his two men had floated and grimaced. "Those two will report of our failure here. The Council will summon the Sumäeri to war."

Rováen stroked his beard thoughtfully before placing the firestone into the sunburst array of bones at the tip of the staff. Räesha's fingers grasped the stone and held it firmly in place.

"That's amazing!" Cédron gasped. "How did you know to do that?"

Rováen pushed his lips out and scratched his head. "Well," he said, "she put the image in my mind."

Trilläen's face lit up. "Then she lives!"

313

"Yes…and no." Rovaen smiled sadly. "Her Árk'äezhi remains with us in this staff, not unlike the Sceptre of Kulari."

The warrior's face fell, and he nodded. "I understand. I will go now to her remaining sisters and inform them of her sacrifice. We will meet again, Child of Muralia."

Chapter 31 - The Hazzara Army

The tick in Algarik's cheek jumped spastically as the red mage paced around the parapet of the Mage's Guild in Taksábai. He stared out to sea, trying to glean the answers to his questions in the swirling waters as the waves struck the stone walls surrounding the Guild, sending spray into the air. The tiny droplets adhered to his skin and the fabric of his red robes, annoying the mage further.

The master was growing impatient with the mage's delays. Cédron's location continued to elude him, despite having his best agent seeking the boy. Algarik felt as if all the powers of the universe were conspiring against him. Frustrated and angry with his thwarted efforts, he'd returned to Taksábai to fetch his most reliable beast. He would have to make short work of finding Cédron and getting the boy to Thoromberk Fortress for his master. He would then join forces with the army that he would lead into battle against the Shäeli.

As Lord Shamar rose above the edge of the sea, bathing the sky in the deep plum and lavender of the morning, Algarik was struck by the force of energy that radiated across the land. The power of the Árk'äezhi nearly knocked him over the side of the parapet as he grasped firmly onto the stone merlon to keep from slipping past the crenel and into the open water. *That's Cédron's Árk'äezhi. I know it!*

Algarik quickly recovered from the initial wave of energy and raced back along the parapet towards the heavy oaken door that led to the red mage's chambers. Bypassing his room and ignoring the black mages that nodded respectfully to their superior as he hastened past them, Algarik sprinted to the bowels of the Guild's central radient where the main furnace was housed.

Feeling the stone slab that functioned as the door to the furnace room, and noting its warmth, Algarik smiled. The novices were getting lazy in their duties and hadn't dampened the flames the previous evening. Normally, such dereliction to duty would have infuriated the red mage, but today it served his purpose more than adequately.

Gingerly, using just his fingertips, Algarik pulled at the lever that would open the massive slab. Heat blasted through the small opening, scorching his eyes and mouth as he gasped for breath. Stepping inside, the red mage adjusted his hood to shield his eyes and took a moment to become accustomed to the dry heat emitted by the pit of fire burning deep within the bowels of the hold beneath him.

Algarik looked around once to ensure he was alone before closing the door and blocking the lever. He couldn't afford to have one of the novices interrupt him, or he would have to answer some very inconvenient questions. He didn't have time to explain his actions to the white mages, nor was he ready to have his dual mission compromised.

Striding towards the fire pit, Algarik pulled his ruby amulet from the folds of his cloak and held it before him, facing the flames. A light barrier spread out from the stone and shielded the mage from the heat and destruction of the fire as he skirted around the pit. Reaching the far wall, Algarik located the discolored brick housing the latching mechanism for the revolving door that granted him access to the treasure chamber. Pressing the stone into the wall, the mage tapped his foot impatiently as the complex mechanism grated. Slowly, the gears operating in sequence from floor to ceiling forced the heavy stone door sideways, allowing the mage to enter the dark room.

Algarik lifted the cover off the basket of glow rocks suspended in the wall near the door, grabbing two stones and charging them while the stone door grated shut. It snapped into place with a click as the locking mechanism caught in the ceiling, reversing the sequence. After placing the glowing stones back in the open basket, Algarik made his way across the small, dimly lit room.

He navigated his way around the desk filled with writing utensils and glowing jars of liquid. The walls of the room were lined with shelves that housed objects and relics from ages past that nobody knew how to operate. Tiny mechanical twillings lay scattered among gear-driven statues of diclurues and other unrecognizable creatures. The mage surmised that these machines had likely been used as messengers in times past, but how they operated had been lost along with the rest of the knowledge destroyed during the War of Betrayal.

Algarik skirted the low wooden table upon which a glass case that housed a beautifully carved staff rested, and strode over to the floor-to-ceiling shelves of books adjacent to the map that was engraved on the far wall. Reaching inside the folds of his robes around his neck, he pulled out his ruby amulet and placed it into the depression of the compass rose that represented Taksábai on the map. The torus knot fit snugly into place and the ruby set in its center pulsed gently with power.

"*Terbaes!*" Algarik invoked the power of the map.

He watched eagerly as the red line spread from the ruby eastward to where the source of the powerful Árk'äezhi wave had originated. *I've got you!* The mage grinned widely, ignoring the pulling of the scar on his cheek as the red line ended just north of the Zig'orman Marsh on the banks of the Sharäedan River.

Cédron was either near or among the remaining Meq'qan tribes of the Zig'orman Marsh. Algarik knew that he would seek the aquastone from them, and it was likely that he would secure it. The boy's power had grown exponentially in the past few days, and the mage was certain that Cédron would convince the goddess to relinquish her sacred stone to him.

There would still be time to intercept the boy before he reached the Tawali and attempted to gain the rest of the stones, then go to Samshäeli and present himself to Auräevya. Algarik's main concern was that the Shäeli hunting the boy would reach him first and terminate him as the blasphemous abomination they believed him to be. Such a loss could not be tolerated.

Algarik had to reach Cédron first or Laylur would throw Algarik's spirit into the eternal abyss that was his own prison. The mage had known the danger to his soul when he agreed to free the demon, but the promises of power had been worth it. Now the boy was within his grasp, and Algarik would reap the benefits of the demon's promise. He just had to get his agents to the marshes ahead of the Shäeli, and that could prove difficult.

Algarik unhinged the amulet from the map and hung it around his neck. He crossed the dank room to the far wall where a simple slate of polished silver hung at eye level. Grasping a vial of blue liquid from the desk, he poured a few drops into his hand which immediately ignited as they touched the ruby ring that was still turned palm-ward. He swiped the flaming liquid along the top of the polished metal and waited as the sheet became engulfed in blue flames.

"Mairk," he called into the slab.

The shiny silver glowed with an internal luminescence before an image solidified in the depths of the metal's center. The misshapen head and colorful attire of Mairk Lerkinan materialized, bent over a desk strewn with maps. From his vantage point, Algarik could see that his agent was still in his chambers at Thoromberk Fortress and hadn't followed his earlier instructions to mobilize his forces to the Rabe'en

Plains. Anger flared in the mage as he surveyed the disarray of his agent's quarters.

"Mairk," Algarik repeated, his voice tinged with annoyance.

The figure behind the desk stiffened and straightened abruptly, staring at the wall in front of him with thinly-veiled distaste. He removed his spectacles and laid them carefully on the table between the rolls of parchment before ambling over to the identical slab of silver hanging on his own wall.

"Algarik," he said with a cursory bow. "I expected to see you within the walls of Thoromberk Fortress with your nephew before now. How goes your search?"

Algarik pursed his lips at the deflection of the conversation. "I instructed you several days ago to mobilize our army. Why haven't you left Molonark?"

Mairk rolled his eyes. "I contacted Zen Hazad as you commanded. He agreed to your terms and is preparing to receive Laräeith's codex. He suggested that we wait for the new Hazzara warriors to arrive, as they have intercepted a large shipment of racing husan from the Merchant's Guild that was on its way to the track at Taksábai. Perhaps you've heard of the theft? No?"

Algarik decided not to dignify Mairks evasion with a reply. Mairk sighed at Algarik's stony silence and continued. "Well, I decided that it would be wise to mount as many of our men as possible if we are to face the Shäeli within your requested timeline. It wouldn't do to have them exhausted from the march only to be slaughtered by fresh opposing troops in battle, don't you agree?"

Algarik bit back the curses he longed to shout at his agent, but realized that the man's logic did make sense, particularly with the change in circumstances.

"As it happens," Algarik said smoothly, "your insubordination has turned out to be well-timed."

Mairk's eyebrows rose, giving him an even more comical appearance. "Oh, how so?"

"I've located Cédron just north of the Zig'orman Marsh," Algarik said. "He's with the Meq'qan and will attempt to secure the aquastone from the shrine to Lady Muralia. That gives us time to get down there and retrieve him before the Shäeli organize their Sumäeri. How many husan did Zen Hazad steal?"

"Close to two hundred, according to the reports."

"Excellent." Algarik smiled. "Belay my earlier orders. Contact Zen Hazad and have him put Hazzara on those two hundred mounts. I want them to ride with all haste to the Zig'orman Marsh. They need to engage the Meq'qan and keep any Shäeli that arrive at bay. I'll be there shortly to pick up the boy and bring him back to the fortress."

Mairk nodded. "Two hundred will be much easier to coordinate than ten thousand. Shall we continue with the preparations for the rest?"

"Of course. The first major battle will most likely take place on the Rabe'en Plains. The Shäeli won't let Cédron slip through their fingers without a fight. Get O'zan busy on the rest of his stone army. They will turn the tides of this war for us."

"It would be better if you could speak with him yourself," Mairk said, scratching the top of his head through the knit cap. "He doesn't seem to respond to me or any of the other Hazzara. He just keeps working on his figures as if they were a commission from the Shaultan of Yezmarantha."

Algarik's eyes narrowed dangerously. "They *are* a commission...from the King of Demons. He'd be wise not to forget that!"

Mairk clicked his tongue and shook his head sadly. "It's always difficult resurrecting the dead from their crystal tombs and expecting them to follow instructions. I'm not sure we can count on him to complete the army in time for the war."

Algarik clenched his jaw together, the vein in his temple throbbing. "You just worry about your duties and the consequences of your own insubordination," he seethed. "Let me deal with O'zan."

Algarik terminated the fire scry, but not before noting the pleased grin on Mairk's face. Algarik knew that Mairk loved to bait him, and everyone else, for that matter, and it annoyed Algarik that he let his subordinate succeed. *I'll make an example of that fároc once I'm through with Cédron.*

The red mage took several deep, steadying breaths before contemplating his next maneuver. He knew that Cédron was working on acquiring the aquastone, but the boy still needed to get his hands on the terrastone from the Tawali and the windstone from the Yezman.

In all his recent research, he still hadn't been able to locate the exact hiding place of the windstone, but he was certain that the Yezman still had it in their possession after all these centuries. There would have been stories to the contrary if they didn't. The Askári made no secret of the Garanthian theft of their sacred firestone.

Algarik smiled to himself and walked over to the ornately carved staff resting inside the glass case. He lifted the lid and pulled the staff off of its holder, caressing it gently with his long fingers. *Soon I'll have the firestone from Cédron, then the Rod of Shouman will be active once more! None will be able to stand in my way with the power of lightning at my command. Lord Shamar himself will be forced to treat with me.*

In all his study of the rods and staffs of power, none had the destructive capabilities of the Rod of Shouman. It had taken him decades of searching to find all the pieces. The sacred firestone and silver sheath were the final pieces that would bring the rod to life, and they would soon be in his grasp. *If the boy had any idea of what he was doing...but he doesn't. That Shäeli mentor of his has kept him clueless as to his true heritage and destiny. I won't make the same mistake.*

The red mage reveled in the feeling of power and control that holding the Rod of Shouman gave him. Too long had he lurked in the shadows of others, skulking and hiding his true intentions. Soon he would be able to implement decades of planning and preparation. Even white mage Bín Nétar would be forced acknowledge him as an equal.

Algarik felt the thrill of exultation at the thought of exacting revenge upon Shozin Chezak and his brother Kásuin. Never again would they demean and marginalize him and his abilities. They would cower before him in fear and pain before he would mercifully execute the pair of them. The grin on his face widened as he took his thoughts a step further. *Perhaps it would be even better to have the boy kill them. They would know, then, that all their hopes and efforts for his safety were in vain.*

With a spring in his step, Algarik returned to the low table and replaced the Rod of Shouman in its glass case. He gazed at it one last time, then turned and covered the baskets of glow rocks and pulled the lever that began the series of gears that slid open the door.

The heat of the furnace struck him in the face, causing him to step back and blink. Algarik's eyes watered and he wiped at them several times before they cleared. He secured the opening to the secret chamber and made his way quickly across the walkway towards the main door to the furnace.

Preoccupied with his thoughts as he was, Algarik neglected to check the outside corridor for others. He'd barely closed the door and turned around when he was startled to come face-to-face with white mage Gérand Kiél.

"So, Algarik, you have returned." The wizened mage smiled benignly, his sharp eyes missing nothing. "I wondered who was emitting the energy from this deep inside the radient."

Algarik clenched his hands into fists as the older man peered right through him. "Mage Kiél." He bowed slightly. "I am surprised to see you down here."

322

"Obviously."

"Can I be of service to you?"

The white mage regarded Algarik briefly, studying him as he always did. Algarik clamped down on the urge to squirm beneath the intensity of the older man's gaze.

Gérand Kiél had always made him feel uncomfortable. He was the one mage that never took anything at face value. Kiél always questioned everything, and Algarik was certain that the white mage was aware of his clandestine activities with the Hazzara. Still, Kiél had never let on if he had suspicions, so Algarik had been hesitant to pursue the matter. He'd always tried to make sure he came in contact with the white mage as briefly and infrequently as possible, so as not to arouse the older man's suspicions.

Now as the white mage's surprisingly sharp eyes raked him over, Algarik was sure that Kiél had felt the Árk'äezhi used during the conversation with Mairk. He began to sweat. If the Mage's Guild found out about the Hazzara and his dealings with Laylur, they would cast him out and take his ruby ring. The loss of that talisman would be devastating. Algarik dropped his eyes and bowed again, trying to edge his way around the corridor and back to his chambers.

"How has the search for new recruits been going?" Gérand asked, blocking Algarik's escape.

The red mage ground his teeth and forced a smile. "Reasonably well. I have found one lad with particular talent that I hope to recruit very soon."

Kiél's eyes lit up and a smile played on his lips. "Really? You haven't brought him with you?"

"No. His family objects."

"Ah, it is still the same out there then."

"Indeed. Most still do not trust the Mage's Guild and fear those of us who wield any magic."

"I see." The old man nodded. "So, what brings you to the bowels of the radient?"

Algarik cleared his throat and wiped self-consciously at the beads of sweat inching down his temple. "I...had to recharge my ruby." He held out the ring for inspection.

Gérand Kiél noted the throbbing of power within the depth of the stone and raised his eyebrows. "You are using that much Árk'äezhi in your search?"

"Well, there were unexpected dangers on my most recent travels," Algarik explained. "I encountered a Garanthian patrol and had to defend myself."

Kiél nodded sagely. "That would explain the excess energy."

"Yes," Algarik said. He cleared his throat and adjusted the amulet within the folds of his red robes, buying time while he considered his next words more carefully. "The boy I'm seeking lives near Molonark...we were surrounded by the Garanthian armies and were desperate for a way to escape. I had no choice but to use what was available to me at the time."

"I see," Kiél said. "I've felt several powerful waves of Árk'äezhi in recent days, but I didn't recognize the traces. They weren't yours. They would be this boy then?"

Trapped, Algarik nodded. If Kiél figured out that the boy was his nephew, he would close all avenues to him.

"He is powerful, maybe too-"

"It is my goal to bring him to us here at the Mage's Guild for further training," Algarik interrupted. "If we can guide him, he could be a most valuable addition to our ranks."

Kiél frowned, his brows knitting together tightly. "I want you to bring him to me for an interview before you make any promises. Is that understood?"

Relieved at the shift of the white mage's attention, Algarik relaxed and nodded. "Most certainly Mage Kiél," he said smoothly. "I wouldn't consider anything else."

"Go then," Kiél said, dismissing the red mage. "Fetch this lad and bring him to us here. Use whatever means necessary. I want to meet this young man."

Algarik bowed and swiftly strode up the walkway to the main courtyard of the guild's keep. His body cooled in the fresh air of the courtyard where his husan was being saddled for his departure. As he rode along the radient towards Taksábai proper, he considered what Gérand Kiél had said.

It was clear to the red mage that Kiél had felt Cédron's power, and that meant the old man was probably more sensitive to the Lluric field than Algarik had initially realized. He would have to be more careful. Perhaps the Mage's Guild had outlived its usefulness to his cause. Algarik turned around in his saddle and watched the towers and battlements of the guild retreat behind him.

The Mage's Guild had been his home for so long. They had welcomed and accepted him when everyone else had turned their backs on him. He felt a twinge of regret at the necessity of having to destroy his beloved guild, but he couldn't risk the other mages learning of his plans.

Spurring his heels into the husan's thick hide, he traveled down the road to the starburst-shaped intersection to where it split at the walls surrounding the city of Taksábai. Instead of taking the main road into the city, Algarik turned his mount down along the waterfront.

Lord Shamar's brilliant light reflected off the water, causing the mage to squint and shield his eyes. The stench of dead shellfish and warm seaweed assailed his nostrils as he guided his beast along the rocky shoreline. Picking his way over the large boulders and around the derelict boats that had been abandoned by owners unable to afford repairs, Algarik spied the small skiff he'd hidden.

Mindful of the husan's curved tusks, Algarik dismounted and unloaded the saddlebags. He swatted the beast on its powerful hindquarters, sending it back towards the city. He then made his way over to the skiff and unfurled the plain blue sail. To the casual observer, it would appear that he was one of the Merchant Guild's decadent members out for a day of pleasure sailing. As he tacked out of the makeshift harbor and out into the Bránon Sea, Algarik felt a chill of apprehension in the pit of his stomach.

Years ago, he'd found the cache of warped Aruzzi eggs where Laräeith the Betrayer had hidden them at Thoromberk Fortress. He'd found a breeder in Taksábai whose work had been critical in both hatching and growing the beast into the fearsome mount he'd need to complete his quest. The rinzar was an evil creature that required powerful binding spells to maintain obedience to the mage. He'd left the rinzar chained to a boulder inside the large cave in the cliffs just north of the Mage's Guild. If the beast had managed to free its bonds, it would take him nearly a week to hike to the Zig'orman Marshes.

Algarik cursed his lack of foresight and berated himself for not taking the time to renew the obedience spells on the beast. He hadn't planned on being away from the rinzar so long. He would have to find a way to appease his mount, or it would turn on him.

The wind picked up, creating small whitecaps on the water. Algarik struggled to maneuver his boat in the cresting waves. He didn't dare use his magic to calm the waters now that he knew Gérand Kiél was monitoring his Árk'äezhi. *Blast that interfering old fool!*

Algarik fought the waves and winds, and he slowly made his way up the coastline. It was late afternoon when he spotted the gaping entrance of the cave high above the water line. On the shore to the north, Algarik spied a young woman with her herd of mijáko making their way back home from the grassy plains above the falls. He smiled. His rinzar would appreciate the feast of ungulates, and perhaps the sweet young maiden.

The mage ran the skiff aground and raced up to the cave to face his beast. After taking a few minutes to enchant the fearsome avian with his amulet, he released the rinzar to feed. Algarik watched the slaughter from his vantage point like an indulgent father. The rinzar initially swooped down upon the small herd but was distracted by the screams of the young woman as she defended her livelihood. The mage wasted no time in shooting a fireball straight into the woman's chest, leaving the warm corpse for the carrion beast to relish as a tender repast.

The mage waited patiently for his mount to finish the steaming entrails and delicate soft parts of his meal before whistling. Sated, the foul raptor obediently flew to the mage's side and knelt for him. Once aloft, Algarik urged his mount eastward. *Now it's my turn to hunt.*

CHAPTER 32 - THE MEQ'QAN VILLAGE

A wave of nausea crashed over Zale'en, the ancient priestess of Lady Muralia, as she sat braiding her long hair. The ground shake that often accompanied her queasiness rumbled beneath her feet. They had become more powerful lately, heralded always by the sick feeling in her soul and validating the foreboding dreams and omens that Lady Muralia had been sending her. Her gnarled fingers twisted deftly the graying strands despite the arthritic pain such tension caused. As the shaking ground quieted, along with the illness, the high priestess's thoughts turned to Räesha and her mission. The Sumäeri warrior had told Zale'en that the power making her ill was from the half-demon boy that would be seeking the sacred aquastone, and that the ground shakes were the demon Laylur's minions being loosed into the world.

The priestess wasn't sure if she believed Räesha's words of doom, but she had become hypersensitive to the fluctuations in the field which told her that significant changes were coming to their world. The Seeress from her sister tribe in the Tek'kut Marsh had already informed her of the horrific tragedy of their kinsmen. Zale'en knew that if the Meq'qan were to survive, they would have to at least meet this young harbinger and decide for themselves their best course of action.

Thoughts of this change in their world filled her mind throughout the day and into her evening services to the goddess, distracting her from the ritual. Twice her acolytes had to prompt her to begin a song or prayer as the course of the evening rites continued. Zale'en declined the offer to join her priestesses for a walk in Orwena's light after the rituals were completed, opting instead to continue her ruminations in solitude.

The high priestess was kneeling at the shrine in her hut, composing her mind for meditation when a shriek filled the air, causing the skin on her arms to pimple and her teeth to grate. Zale'en rose from her mat and made her way out of the hut to see what had caused the disturbance. Outside, on the island of mats that kept her hut afloat, the vermillion rays of Orwena's moon gleamed eerily off the wakazan bones that supported her home.

Glancing into the sky, Zale'en was mildly surprised to see the Sumäeri warrior's läenier approaching. Even more surprising was that the beast was ridden by four men, three young and one old, and not the Sumäeri Räesha. The group was dirty and bloody as if they'd recently been in battle. *What is this new mischief?*

Zale'en skirted the low fencing around her island of layered woven mats and made her way to the common area, converging in the center just as Mak'ki, her mate and the community's Caf'iq or chieftain, arrived with his guard. Mak'ki nodded curtly to the priestess then stepped in front of her, facing the landing raptor. Zale'en suppressed the flicker of irritation at Mak'ki chauvinism and stepped up next to him, earning a scowl from the Caf'iq. Zale'en snorted. *Whatever news these strange visitors bring, we will face it as equals.*

Zale'en turned her head at a movement to her right. Four of her young acolytes breezed up behind her, taking their proper places on either side. Smiling slightly, Zale'en folded her hands in front of her and cleared her mind of all preconceived feelings the stranger's arrival stirred within her. She would need to remain open to see clearly what her mother goddess would require of her.

The fairest rider dismounted first, sliding down the side of the enormous raptor's golden wings, then assisted the elderly man. Zale'en raised her eyebrows slightly as the characteristic features of the riders registered in her mind. *Odd, two Shäeli and two Askári. Strange companions in these times.*

The golden-haired boy carried a unique staff. Although Zale'en had never seen its like before, it felt familiar to her. The other two darker young men slid off the läenier and approached behind the Shäeli, all countenances grim. The young Shäeli lad carrying the staff seemed to have a glow about him and Zale'en knew instantly that he was the cause of her recent bouts of illness. The power that radiated off the boy was tremendous. She felt a chill down her spine as she looked into his luminous green eyes.

"Hold," the Caf'iq challenged the visitors, his warriors holding their spears defensively around their chieftain. "What business brings you here?"

The largest warrior stepped forward brandishing his spear at the interlopers, a fierce gleam in his yellow eyes.

"There have been too many strangers come to our lands in recent days," he snarled, "First that Shäeli woman and her beast and now these. Who knows, maybe more are coming." He turned to face his Caf'iq. "I knew we should have killed that Shäeli warrior when she landed."

Zale'en stepped from behind the warrior and placed a hand on his shoulder.

"Peace, Chaq'ta," she said softly but with a note in her voice that broached no argument. "We will hear what they have to say."

Chaq'ta lowered his spear slightly and slowly stepped back, keeping his wary eyes on the group.

The old Shäeli knelt and touched his head to the ground in a gesture of supplication. The other three followed suit, kneeling slowly due to their their injuries. Even the boy with the glowing staff bowed. As one, they rose and offered their palms to Mak'ki and Zale'en.

"We come in peace with tidings," the elderly Shäeli began. "I am Roväen Angäersol, Sumäeri of Samshäeli." He gestured to the golden-haired lad carrying the staff, then the two young men. "This is Cédron Varkáras of Dúlnat, his brother Tóran Varkáras, and Anéton Bessínos."

"What tidings have you that would concern the Meq'qan?" Mak'ki spat, glaring up at the visitors with his watery yellow eyes. "We have no interest in your affairs."

Roväen cast his eyes downward briefly and took a deep breath. Zale'en saw great pain behind his eyes as he cleared his throat.

"My niece Räesha, the Sumäeri who brought your kinsmen to you from Tek'kut Marsh, has fallen in battle. Orwena has granted her wish to continue to fight in the coming war." The old man gestured for Cédron to step forward with the staff. "The warrior goddess has transformed her into this staff of power. She is now called Räeshun."

Zale'en stepped forward, brushing off Mak'ki's prohibiting hand, and gently touched the staff made from the Sumäeri's bones. The Sumäeri tattoos etched along the fused bones glowed faintly in Orwena's light. The significance of such a transformation was not lost on the high priestess. She turned and faced the young Shäeli.

"You," she said huskily. "What is your purpose?"

Cédron swallowed before answering the intimidating woman. "I seek the sacred aquastone of the Meq'qan. The fallen deity Laylur continues to weaken the bonds of his prison with ground shakes that compromise Lady Muralia's hold on him. I intend to use the aquastone to remove the toxin contaminating the ground and strengthen his prison."

Zale'en's eyes narrowed. She could sense more to his story and knew from Räesha's own mouth that there was more to this boy's agenda than what he was revealing.

"What makes you think we will just hand over our sacred aquastone to you? What is your true purpose? And don't try to deceive me again!"

The boy's cheeks flushed and he cast his eyes downward. When he spoke, his voice was barely above a whisper. "I have been charged with acquiring all of the sacred elemental stones. I am to present myself and the stones to Auräevya and ask that she release the Sceptre of Kulari. Only then can I hope to challenge Laylur face to face."

Zale'en blanched. She felt her palms instantly turn clammy and cold. As she stared deeper into the young man's eyes, she saw a darkness lurking there. She realized he'd already been tainted by the power he possessed, and that Auräevya may refuse him. If he was the only one alive with the power to wield the sacred staff, then their world was certainly on the brink of complete chaos and war. Laylur's minions must have breached their prison in the abyss, which would explain the slaughter of their kinsmen and the appearance of this child before her, impure as he was.

"Be gone, impostor!" Mak'ki snarled. "You have no claim to our sacred aquastone. Lady Muralia has given us no sign that we are in danger."

Zale'en raised her hand to silence her spouse and stepped forward. "You may be the one with the ability to wield the staff, but you have been tainted." The high priestess bore into Cédron's eyes with her yellow gaze. The boy shifted uneasily on his feet under her intense scrutiny. "No, you bear too much darkness. Auräevya will not accept you, and neither will Lady Muralia. I cannot allow you to take our sacred stone." She noted their looks of disappointment and surprise. *Could they have had the temerity to simply think I would hand over our most sacred relic to a twisted child and his companions solely based on their story? The audacity!* "That is my final word," she said, nodding her head.

Caf'iq Mak'ki stepped up next to Zale'en and addressed the intruders. "Mount your beast and be gone. We have no use for your lies."

The guard surrounding the Caf'iq hefted their spears. Zale'en's heart skipped a beat and tightened in her chest as the two young Askári drew their weapons. *Surely, they don't believe they can take our aquastone with force!* Nobody moved. The standoff lasted another three heartbeats before the staff in the boy's hands pulsed with a soft blue glow. Zale'en felt the bands around her chest loosen and her breath flow easier. Glancing over at the Meq'qan warriors, she noted that their faces no longer scowled. *By our Lady, that staff channels the power of the goddess! I must pray.*

Zale'en waved her hands across the bristling spears and pushed them aside. "Lady Muralia demands that we honor her tenets of hospitality." She turned to her acolytes. "Give them water for bathing, food and a place to sleep. I will pray to the goddess for guidance this night." She turned to her guests and nodded her head. "Put your weapons away. No one will harm you unless you provoke them. Sleep well, but be ready to leave at first light."

* * *

Levirk Sirkran crouched in the shadows behind the long house in the center of the village. The number of lights flickering beneath the doors of the huts dwindled to just a handful before the Hazzara agent decided it was safe to move closer to the hut where the boy was sleeping. The unfriendly Meq'qan wouldn't pose any opposition to him. They wanted the boy and his companions gone before Lord Shamar rose in the east.

It hadn't been difficult to find the Shäeli boy after his recent display of power with the firestone. The fire snake burned within his forearm, guiding him unerringly towards the source of the elemental flame. He had initially cursed the mage for infecting him with the snake, certain at the time that Algarik had done it more to control him than to find the boy. However, as the snake's hunger for the stone's elemental energy compelled Levirk inexorably towards its fire, the man realized that Algarik had given him a great gift.

Levirk glanced down at the curled reptile that graced his arm. It glowed softly orange-red, content being in proximity of the stone whose essence it craved. He had remained hidden in a tree behind the central fire pit where he'd had an excellent vantage point from which to observe the confrontation between the Meq'qan and their guests. His symbiotic companion was close enough to where the snake could feed off the constant flow of magic emanating from the firestone, leaving his host in relative peace.

Levirk waited in the tree until both Orwena and her sister Azria had graced the night skies with their light before he decided to make his move, inching his way slowly down from the tree and around the back side of the line of huts. Hamra's violet beams illuminated the woven islands between the dried water channels, making his journey an easy one. The Hazzara agent knew that, even as enhanced as he was, it would be foolish to attempt to abduct the boy with his three companions about. He would have to be cleverer than that if he was to succeed where Algarik had twice failed.

Glancing skyward, Levirk watched as a few clouds drifted across Hamra's plum surface, intermittently obscuring her light. It was the darkest part of the night, just before the dawn. The huts were all silent, not a soul stirring within the shadowed area of long, round-roofed buildings. He'd watched carefully to know which of the huts was occupied by the group from Dúlnat.

Levirk slunk over behind Cédron's hut, skirting the illuminated areas where the fire cast its glow, sticking only to the shadows to limit the likelihood of discovery. Levirk crouched in the hidden space beneath the steps that led up to the rough thatched hut. He pulled back his sleeve, fully exposing the coiled fire snake, and willed it to awaken.

The serpent's eyes flared at the summons and it slowly unwound itself from its coils. Levirk set his hand on the bottom of the steps and watched as the snake slithered out of his forearm, down the back of his hand, and onto the wooden steps. Smoke curled up beneath it as the fire snake slithered across the surface, burning the wood beneath its molten scales.

Levirk's lips curled into a wicked grin as the steps burned. The snake wormed its way into the hut, combusting everything it touched. Blowing gently behind the serpent and fanning the blazing line that it left in its wake, Levirk Sirkran knew that if the boy survived the fire, he would be easy prey. He hunched back down beneath the only exit from the hut and waited for the snake to do its job.

Several moments went by before Levirk heard the gurgling scream and the thump on the floor. He tensed, waiting for the stampede as the occupants would try to escape the burning building. Shouts and cries of alarm from inside the hut alerted the neighbors. All around, candles were being lit and glow rocks were being uncovered. *That blasted boy had better get out here soon or...*

Levirk decided not to wait to be discovered. He tore up the stairs and burst into the smoky room. He came face-to-face with Cédron. The lad staggered towards the door, the fire snake's fangs clamped down solidly on his neck. Blood oozed from around the serpent's mouth and trickled in two rivulets into his shirt. He was grasping his pouch and fumbling inside it when he lurched into Levirk. The two fell backwards down the stairs where a small crowd of sleepy villagers had gathered.

"Grab him!" Tóran yelled from the doorway of the hut. "Don't let him get away."

Hands reached out to restrain the agent, but he was as slippery as the snake that released his hold on Cédron and slithered back into the safety of Levirk's arm. He sprang to his feet, knocking several women aside as he backed away. A little girl dragging her rush doll in the dirt as she wiped the sleep from her eyes wandered towards the group from the hut next door. Levirk saw his opportunity and took it. He grabbed the girl and, pulling his knife from his belt, held it to her throat.

"Back away," he hissed, lifting the girl's throat with the knife as he pulled her closer towards him. "Or I'll bless the ground with this child's blood."

CHAPTER 33 - HAZZARA

Nobody moved. All stood frozen, afraid to act and cause the stranger, stabbing the point of his knife into the little girl's throat, to carry out his threat. Rovāen kept his eyes on the Hazzara agent as he herded Tóran and Anéton out of the burning hut. Levirk's black eyes glittered in the firelight, reflecting the gleam of his blade. Rovāen knew instantly that the man had been altered, that evil lurked behind his wicked eyes. He needed to know who sent him and what other dangers may be approaching.

"Ra'lina, no!" Chaq'ta shouted, emerging from the entrance of his hut. "Spill one drop of my daughter's blood and I swear to Hamra that your death will be excruciating and slow."

Rovāen sent out tendrils of his consciousness, rummaging through the agent's brain and siphoning memories and information despite the stranger's best efforts to block it. Rovāen broke through Levirk's barriers, his mind finding the scorching heat of the fire snake that Algarik infected him with. The Shäeli felt the heat searing his inner eye as he waged a mental battle with the flaming reptile.

Rovāen staggered down the burning stairs of the hut and into Cédron's arms. The boy seemed to sense his uncle's condition and offered him support. Rovāen felt Cédron fumbling at his side, then the smooth hardness of the firestone being placed in his hands.

Bolstered by the boy's quick thinking, Rovāen accessed the magic of the firestone and engaged the fire snake directly, shooting a bolt of fire into Levirk's head where it was nestled above the little girl's shoulder. The Hazzara agent was knocked backwards, his hold on the child broken.

Chaq'ta raced to his daughter, enfolding her in his immense arms and patting her smoldering hair with his beefy hands.

"There, I've got you now," he murmured to the sobbing child. "He can't hurt you."

Anéton and Tóran sprang into action as soon as the fire bolt was released, holding the rogue legionnaire down. Tóran sat on his legs while Anéton knelt on his chest and held Levirk's arms above his head.

"Bind his wrists together," Tóran ordered, nodding to Chem'ewa, who had come to the fore of the crowd. "Then shackle his legs so he can't escape."

Chem'ewa raced back into his hut and returned after only moments, carrying a long length of rope. He tied Levirk's wrists securely, the cord cutting into the wrists to prevent him from twisting them loose. The Meq'qan survivor helped Anéton to his feet, then wrapped the other end of the rope to Levirk's ankles.

"I don't think he's in any shape to run," Chem'ewa said, staring at Levirk's frozen face. "But I guess we can't be too careful."

Rováen approached, weakened from his mental battle with the fire snake but prepared to send the creature back to the bowels of fire. He stared into Levirk's eyes. *He's not dead, yet there is no life in his eyes. How is this possible?*

"What did you learn from his mind?" Cédron asked, still holding Rováen's arm.

Rováen knelt down and placed one hand on Levirk's forehead and the other over his heart. He closed his eyes and listened, his mind open for any signs of awareness. Slowly, Levirk's mouth sucked in a ragged breath, as if the body was being forced.

"I see you Shäeli," a voice rasped from Levirk's mouth. "I am coming for you and the boy."

"Who are you?" Cédron shouted. "What do you want?"

Levirk's mouth laughed roughly. The head turned its glassy eyes towards Cédron. "I am coming for you, and I will destroy all who attempt to keep you from me. This village will burn to the ground."

RovÄen saw Cédron's face pale. He recognized the voice but wasn't sure if his nephew did. All his suspicions were validated in this moment. *Algarik is behind this.* Roväen knew that if the red mage got his hands on Cédron, nothing would stop him from warping the boy and manipulating Cédron's powers to his own destructive ends.

Algarik had managed to find them each time they'd escaped. It was only a matter of time before the mage caught up with them. *I have to do something!* Common sense told the old man that the right thing to do, the only guaranteed safe thing to do, was to kill Cédron now and eliminate the danger he threatened by simply existing. Cédron may be able to thwart the mage, but there was no way he would be able to resist Laylur's demonic powers. *Yes, I have to do this now, and get it over with.*

RovÄen looked at Cédron and saw the fear and uncertainty. He also saw trust and love reflected in his green eyes. The old man's resolve wavered. RovÄen looked away before Cédron could see the guilt written on his face. He placed his hands back on Levirk's body to discern whether or not the man lived without the snake inside him.

Life still pulsed inside the body, although it was barely discernable. Somewhere deep within the man's mind, his own personality lingered, weakened and probably dying, yet it was there. RovÄen reached out to the spirit of Levirk, willing him to emerge from the dark recesses he'd retreated into. Levirk grabbed RovÄen's hand and feebly moved it off his chest.

"Don't defile me with your Shäeli magic," he croaked. "Leave me to die in peace."

Tóran recognized the speaker as Levirk and pounced on him. "What have you done to the legion, traitor?" he snarled. "How many are compromised?"

Levirk turned his head to face the young legionnaire, a smile tugging at the corner of his mouth. "The legion is weak. They will never be able to stand against the Hazzara and the Garanthian armies who march upon Askáribai." Levirk coughed and blood mixed with spittle dribbled down his chin. "You will all burn!"

"No!" Tóran shouted. He raised his right fist and slammed it into Levirk's mouth, breaking his jaw.

Blood spurted from the mangled face. Levirk gurgled through it as he cackled, an insane fire burning in his eyes. "Burn!"

"Hazzara?" Anéton asked, looking at Roväen. "Who are the Hazzara?"

The old Shäeli stared at the soldier's clothes, seeking some clue that would answer Tóran's question. He spied the silver chain that glinted beneath the man's shirt and pulled on it. The amulet attached to the silver chain was completely foreign to Roväen. It was a torus knot surrounding a cabochon red tourmaline set in the center. The stone pulsed balefully from within the setting.

Unwilling to touch the evil talisman, Roväen stood up and ordered everyone back from the Hazzara. He held the firestone out in front of him and sent a huge ball of fire into Levirk's body. The agent thrashed and screamed as the fire engulfed him, melting skin and blackening bones until he collapsed in a heap of ash, silent. The amulet exploded from the heat, sending tiny shards of red crystal flying towards the travelers from Dúlnat who surrounded him. Cédron got the bulk of the shards, as if they had been magnetically attracted to him. The explosion lifted him off the tiny woven island of their hut and into the dried channel where waters would flood during the rainy season. Bones cracked audibly as he struck the hard ground with full force.

Tóran and Anéton received a few cuts and scrapes where small shards had grazed their skin. Roväen gave each of them a cursory scan before crouching at Cédron's side. He placed his fingers at the side of the boy's neck and felt a twinge in his chest as a barely discernable pulse fluttered against his fingertips. The debris from the Hazzara's body swirled in the air, filling his nostrils with the caustic scent of scorched flesh and hair. He nearly gagged. He pulled Cédron's head into his lap and used his dwindling Árk'äezhi to heal the unconscious boy. After the flames from the stranger's corpse died down, a soft breeze blew the last of the ash into the sky. The crowd watched aghast as the remains swirled into the wind and dissipated above the treetops.

"We must leave as soon as possible," Roväen said grimly. He stood, lifted Cédron in his arms, and turned to Zale'en and Mak'ki. "Your people are not safe. You need to get them away from here."

The warriors and villagers surrounding them murmured and looked to one another and their leaders for guidance. Roväen saw fear and revulsion etched on nearly every face that stared out at him. Women clasped small children to their breasts to still their crying.

Zale'en smiled sadly. "There is no place else for us to go. Our bones are here. We will remain and face whatever dangers approach." She turned to her four acolytes. "Take them to the mud baths and heal them. We may need their strength."

Cries of fear and outrage erupted from among the villagers.

"Ridiculous, woman!" Caf'iq Mak'ki cried, raising his hands in the air to quiet his people. "This boy's story is outrageous. The demon is safely imprisoned in the abyss. There have been no signs of a breach. It is the Shäeli attempting to steal our aquastone again. That's what this is about."

"I *am* the high priestess of Lady Muralia," she said coolly, her eyes grazing across the sea of yellow stares. "And I have *seen* the deity's will." She turned to Rováen holding Cédron and grasped the staff, lifting Räeshun high in the air. Raising her voice above the din, she addressed her people. "The Sumäeri Räesha has been transformed into Räeshun so that she could continue her duty of aiding this boy in his quest for the Sceptre of Kulari. You know what that means, all of you."

A collective gasp breached the still morning air, followed by wails of despair. Voices rose as the import of Zale'en's words hit home. The Sceptre of Kulari held the spirit Árk'äezhi of a Meq'qan priestess, and the Meq'qan never forgot the sacrifice that girl had made to save their world when faced with Laylur's threat once before. The entire tribe recognized the danger present if the Sceptre of Kulari was required again. Only one refused to acknowledge the danger facing them.

Tóran stepped forward and grasped Mak'ki's forearm gently. "Honored Caf'iq, we are in earnest. The rift in the abyss is widening daily. We have already encountered Laylur's minions on our journey."

"Pah!" Mak'ki spat and stomped over to the high seat made of ornately braided and woven rushes. The old man sat down heavily and looked back at the young legionnaire with his beady eyes. "You have no proof, only stories."

Tóran shook his head and wiped the blood out of his eyes. "The Garanthian armies have been mobilized and have already slaughtered the Meq'qan tribes of the north. Their numbers are swelling with Arkmuln as they make their way south into Askári lands."

Caf'iq Mak'ki looked up at the mention of the Meq'qan who were infested by Laylur's demons. "Arkmuln? Are you sure of this?"

Chem'ewa stepped up. "We have seen the atrocities with our own eyes. We told you that my kinsmen, myself, and our

Seeress were the only survivors of our tribe…except for the scores of Arkmuln that now follow the Garanthian army."

Chaq'ta slammed his spear on the ground. "Lies! The Arkmuln are just stories we tell our children to frighten them into behaving. There are no such creatures!"

Zale'en pursed her lips and glared at the young warrior still clutching his shaking daughter. "Always so hotheaded, Chaq'ta. You speak before thinking." She faced Tóran and Chem'ewa and raised her hand for silence. "I see no duplicity in their eyes," she said, her yellow eyes boring into Chaq'ta's, causing the warrior to lower his to his feet. "The Tek'kut Seeress has also seen the Arkmuln. She shared with me the agony of watching her granddaughter succumb to the demon's spirit. Do not doubt, my people, what is coming for us."

"Then we are lost," Chaq'ta choked, handing his daughter into her mother's arms. "We cannot survive an attack by the entire Garanthian army."

Rováen faced Mak'ki and Zale'en. "It is not the Garanthian army that threatens you. It is the Hazzara, and the Shäeli."

The old Sumäeri shared with the Meq'qan the events of recent weeks. The Garanthian army was moving from Tamóna towards Taksábai, growing ever larger as it gathered Arkmuln from those it conquered. He explained Cédron's mission and the rift between the Shäeli Näenji Council and the Sumäeri warriors.

Rováen wasn't sure of the amount of Sumäeri sympathetic to Cédron's quest, but because the Wushäen and Näenji Council appeared to be compromised, he could assure the Meq'qan that Shäeli warriors would be marching to war to oppose Cédron and any who supported his mission. Their recent conflict with the Council Guard only served to widen the rift in the Shäeli people's loyalties. Zale'en nodded as he spoke, and Rováen knew she was their greatest ally, but she required clarification when he broached the topic of the Hazzara.

"Who are they, and what is their agenda?" she asked, trying to grasp the concept of a secret society dedicated to destroying their beautiful world. "How could anyone be so completely duped into believing that returning Laylur to the world would benefit them?"

Roväen's face darkened. "A secret society of primarily Yez'men. I have my suspicions as to their origins, and I can only guess at what they were promised. They have powerful magic at their disposal. They can tap into the imbalance that Laräeith's Betrayal left in our world. They are strong and dangerous because we don't know who they are, how many they number, or what they are capable of. We do know that we are being hunted-"

"But we don't know for sure by whom," Anéton spoke up. "We just know that he is powerful and that Cédron's Árk'äezhi is like a beacon, attracting him closer each time he uses it." He looked down at Zale'en with a sad expression. "I'm afraid we've put your people in grave danger by being here."

Anéton winced in pain as he spoke, leaning against Tóran. Roväen noticed that the wound in his side had begun oozing again, its bright red stain darkening his tunic. He noted similar injuries on Tóran. He turned to Zale'en. "We will leave as soon as your healers have seen to the boys."

"Enough of this," the high priestess commanded. Turning to her acolytes, she directed them to assist their guests into the healer's huts. "See to their injuries. Give them a purifying draught and mud baths. I will continue my prayers."

Caf'iq Mak'ki stood and crossed his arms. "What are you doing, woman? These are not guests of ours. They should be cast out!"

Zale'en faced her mate, raising herself to her full height and infusing her image with the glamour of Lady Muralia through the chain of moonstones surrounding her neck. "I speak with the voice of our Lady. The Meq'qan do not forget to honor her will. If it is her desire to receive this boy, then it is my job to prepare him."

Mak'ki's eyes narrowed at his wife. "Well then, O wise priestess, what is my job?"

Zale'en raised one eyebrow and sucked in her cheeks, preparing a tart reply when a runner from the north came skidding into the commons.

"Caf'iq Mak'ki!" the young runner huffed, screeching to a halt in front of the chieftain. "Caf'iq Mak'ki ... army ... back ... there." The young man nearly collapsed as Chaq'ta lunged to steady him.

Mak'ki turned his watery eyes to the arrival and placed a hand on the youth's shoulder. "Take a breath. When you're ready, give us your message."

The young man's labored breathing took a few moments to calm, then he stood erect and nodded to Chaq'ta, whose support he no longer needed. "I am Ma'lok from the northern tribes. My brother and I were out hunting. We saw an army. They are garbed in black and are massing along the northern outskirts of the marsh."

"How many?" Chaq'ta asked urgently.

Ma'lok glanced up at his fellow warrior, fear reflected in his eyes. "At least two hundred, all armed and astride husan. They will be here in two days."

Tóran nudged Rováen. "The Hazzara?" he whispered.

Rováen nodded slightly, shifting the boy higher in his arms. "I would presume so."

Zale'en turned to the runner Ma'lok. "How is it that you were able to get here so far ahead of a mounted force?"

Ma'lok grinned sheepishly and scuffed his foot along the woven reed matting. "We slowed them down a bit. We started a stampede of wakazan towards them. Each beast is over fifteen feet long and weighs at least two thousand pounds. The herd of three hundred ploughed through them, causing enough damage and confusion to halt them in their tracks for at least a day. I ran straight here as fast as I could to warn you."

Zale'en nodded her thanks to the young man and patted him on the arm. She turned back to Mak'ki, first glancing at her assembled people, then down at her mate. "Your job is to prepare the men for war, for it will soon be upon us." She turned to her acolytes. "Go now, and I will convene with you later."

The four young women bowed and bade the travelers follow them. Roväen shifted Cédron's weight in his arms, sliding Räeshun into the crook between Cédron's arm and Roväen's shoulder, then nodded for the other two to precede him. The Shäeli knew their time was limited, that Algarik was on his way. He also knew now that another army had joined the fray. *Who are these Hazzara? Who is behind them and what do they want? They must be connected to Algarik in some way, but is he their leader or just someone else's lackey?* The more he thought about it, the further answers seemed to slip away.

ChAPTER 34 - FACINC ThE CODDESS

Cédron floated in a blissful haze of peace. His foggy mind was only barely conscious, rising from the soft depths of restful sleep as a hand shook his shoulder gently. Opening his eyes, he smiled to see Anéton and Tóran hovering over him like worried mothers.

"Is it time?" He yawned and stretched, reveling in the freedom from pain afforded by the healing draught and few hours of sleep.

Tóran nodded handing Cedron one of the meat rolls he'd gotten to break their fast. "The Priestess of our Lady has requested your presence in the temple. Let's go."

The three young men exited the thatched hut perched on the hill next to the hot springs that had cured his body. They hiked over the rocky bank and back down the incline to the village. Cédron marveled at the myriad of little islands that appeared to be made from layering thick woven mats. The sheer scope of work required for each hut's own little island boggled his mind.

He wondered if, after the rains began, the mats floated on water, or if they just stabilized the silt and mud of the swamplands. He'd have to get his architectural questions answered another time. He felt his heart beat a little faster as he followed Tóran and Anéton toward an ornately decorated hut.

This hut had double doors that were framed by enormous, curved tusks that stretched from the ground to the rafters on either side. The enormous teeth were smooth and so tall that Cédron had no idea what sort of animal had owned them. If they were once wakazan, they had been monstrous, dwarfing the beasts of burden found in Askáribai. Running like a banner between the two tusks was a macabre festoon of skulls and bones from deceased tribesmen. The bleached bones gleamed white in the midday light, but the recessed scores of eye sockets spoke to Cédron of the darkness of eternity that no glimmer of illumination could penetrate. He shivered as he walked beneath them and entered the hut that was the temple to Lady Muralia.

Tóran closed the doors behind them, and the young men stood silently at the end of the room. There were no windows in this temple. It took a few moments for their eyes to adjust to the gloom. Tóran nudged Cédron in the arm and nodded towards the end of the room where a priestess was slowly advancing towards them with a lighted candle. It was Zale'en. She wore her floor length grey hair unadorned and it fell loosely about the folds of her pale blue robes. She stood tall and erect, walking gracefully despite the age that lined her face. She stood before Cédron and held out her palm, beginning the ritual with the formal greeting.

"I am Zale'en, High Priestess of our Lady," she said in a voice that reminded Cédron of a breeze blowing through dried leaves.

Tóran stepped behind Cédron, bowing slightly to the priestess. Cédron stepped forward and placed his hand over Zale'en's.

"I am Cédron, son of Kásuin Varkáras of Askáribai and Maräera Angäersol of Samshäeli." Cédron felt little warmth in her bony hands, but her smile put him at ease.

"Come, we must prepare you." She dropped her hand. The old woman beckoned Cédron deeper into the dark recesses of the temple where the candle light had yet to pierce.

Cédron looked at Tóran and Anéton, who shrugged and nodded respectively.

"You may leave us," Zale'en instructed the two legionnaires.

Anéton and Tóran hesitated briefly, concern registering on their faces, but Cédron waved them away. He knew they would station themselves just outside the door and would come in a moment if he called. Cédron followed Zale'en as she turned away from the door. She led him down the center of the hut to an altar made of bones.

The structure was firm and laden with bowls and chalices all made from bony parts of people, wakazan or ur'luqs, the reptilian creatures that haunted the swamps. Zale'en had Cédron kneel in front of the altar. She picked up a bowl that Cédron saw was the top half of a head. It was filled with a blue pigment that the old woman painted on his slender torso with her thumb and forefinger.

The heavy, cloying scent of the candles made his eyes burn and his head pound. He couldn't identify the smell, and he hoped he'd never have to endure it again. The tendrils of smoke entered his nose and settled on his tongue, filling his mouth with a burnt orange flavor.

Cédron tried not to breathe deeply as the yellow-eyed priestess ran her blue-coated fingers over his abdomen and towards his heart. She muttered her prayers while she worked, covering his lower torso and chest with the indigo dye. Two younger priestesses emerged from the shadows and fanned the wet paint with fronds of grasses tied together. Their gentle motions caused the blue dye to dry quickly.

"You are tense," Zale'en murmured in his ear as she fanned the heavy incense from the candles towards him. "You must release the fight within you and embrace yourself, or you will be doomed along with the rest of us."

The smoke filled Cédron's nose and thickened the fog in his head. "I…uh…what fight?" He struggled to clear the citrus tang from his tongue.

"Breathe deep," the high priestess admonished. "Release the shackles of fear and expectation. You must allow yourself to flow with the wave of Árk'äezhi, no matter what form it takes. The goddess will test you. If you try to force the outcome with your own desires, you will perish. You must trust the power, trust the goddess, and trust yourself."

Cédron's head swam. The high priestess's words echoed in his wavering mind, floating just outside his consciousness before evaporating completely. The scent of the candle made him ill as he fought to clear his thoughts. The harder he tried, the further he sank into the waves of nausea.

"Relax!" Zale'en chided again. "Breathe, boy. Let the Árk'äezhi flow freely."

Cédron gritted his teeth against the illness that threatened to overwhelm him. *The only thing that will be flowing freely is my vomit if I don't get out of here!* One of the other priestesses waved her frond behind the candle just as Cédron turned her way. The thick, roiling cloud of incense assailed his nostrils, forcing its way into his head and lungs despite his efforts to expel it. His mind exploded in a flash of brilliant white light. The burnt orange flavor on his tongue mellowed to a light citrus as his extremities tingled until he felt light and buoyant. Falling back, he floated on a beam of soft light that cradled his body like a newborn babe. Breathing deeply, Cédron felt the flow of his own Árk'äezhi coursing through his body, throbbing with each heartbeat. *I am divine…invincible!*

Just as the warmth of his epiphany spread over his entire body, the incense was gone. Fresh air sucked him down into the cold wave he'd been surfing, and he opened his eyes, gasping and coughing. Cédron's knees ached, and he couldn't tell whether he'd been kneeling the entire time or if he'd just landed on them. Glancing around, he noted that the candles had been extinguished and the harsh, caustic smoke burned his eyes. A mat hanging on the wall had been rolled up to allow fresh air in, and Lord Shamar's light made him squint after the gloom of the ritual. *I feel like I've been run down by a flock of kessäeri.* Blinking in the light, he tried to capture the feeling he'd just lost, but it slipped through his fingers like vapor.

"Now you are ready," Zale'en said, cleansing her hands in a bowl of water held by her younger assistant. "I understand your quest, but you must prove your worthiness to bear the sacred aquastone to our deity. Even though the Seeress and I have both been convinced, the goddess will challenge you. You must keep your mind clear and your wits sharp."

"I understand," Cédron whispered through the fog in his head, though nothing was further from the truth.

Cédron's mind was whirling. Perhaps it was the lack of solid sustenance for the past two days. More likely, it was from the feeling of being buffeted about his life without any control. He felt like he was a small piece of wood in a rushing river, cascading down dangerous rapids. He had no oars, no rudder for steering, and the deadly waterfall loomed inexorably before him. That momentary feeling of exhilaration had completely evaporated. His knees felt weak and buckled. The younger priestesses caught him under the arms as he started to collapse.

"Drink this." Zale'en offered him a goblet full of red liquid and chuckled at his hesitation. "It is the juice of the erdberry. It will give you strength."

Cédron exhaled in relief. For a brief moment, he thought she was offering him blood. Given the macabre décor, he didn't feel it was too far-fetched an idea. The liquid burned slightly as it slid down his throat and warmed his belly. It had a tart flavor similar to the berries of his homeland but with a musky undertone that was unfamiliar. He felt his head clearing and his legs strengthen beneath him.

"We will leave for the deity's cave as soon as you are ready," Zale'en said, retrieving the empty goblet and setting it on the small table.

Cédron nodded. "I will collect my things and be right back."

Exiting the temple, Cédron was greeted by Tóran and Anéton's startled expressions as their eyes took in the blue markings covering his torso.

"Part of the ritual." Cédron shrugged, stumbling down the steps.

Anéton chuckled and hit his arm. "You look like you're standing in a raging sea that originates in your privates."

Tóran snorted. "It's a good look for you,"

"Knock it off!" Cédron growled, striding back to the hut that held his gear.

Rovaën was sitting outside the hut as the three young men approached. Räeshun lay across his lap, the firestone in her starburst head glinting in Lord Shamar's early morning light. Cédron felt a twinge of apprehension as he approached his mentor and held his hand out for Räeshun. Rovaën hesitated only briefly, then handed the beautiful staff over to its keeper.

"You must present yourself to Lady Muralia in all humbleness and contrition," Rovaën admonished. "You will need to be cleansed of the killing if she is to relinquish the aquastone to you."

Cédron nodded mutely.

"I'm sure you will do well," Rovaën said softly, standing up and placing his hand on Cédron's shoulder. "Just try to keep your emotions in check and don't give in to fear or anger. They will deceive and poison your mind."

"I-I'll do my best," Cédron mumbled, gripping Räeshun firmly in his hand.

Clad only in his breeches, with bare feet, Cédron swallowed hard and clasped arms with the rest of his group. He nodded to each of them.

"We will help Caf'iq Mak'ki prepare the tribesmen for battle," Tóran said as Cédron released his grip on his brother's arm.

"Don't waste too much time, or you'll miss all the fun!" Anéton grinned.

Cédron's lips twisted slightly, and he promised he'd return as soon as he could. With a final farewell, the young man turned and made his way back to Zale'en's hut. With a small escort of priestesses, he began the march to the foothills where the cave entrance to the goddess's main temple awaited him.

* * *

After walking a couple miles, the marshlands turned into an amber sea of dried, swaying grasses. Chirping and buzzing from insects and their crunching footsteps were the only perceptible sounds once they'd lost sight of the village. Their journey took them into the dry foothills to the sacred cave of Lady Muralia, where the deity's priestesses had buried the Meq'qan for millennia. Nothing lived around the cave this time of year. The knee-high grasses were dry as the bones buried deep within the hills, and they rustled eerily as the group made their way through them.

Zale'en had spoken no words to him during their entire journey, leaving Cédron to his own thoughts. He was surprised at her pace, considering her advanced age and apparent frailness. *She must be made of steel beneath that withered exterior.*

He was grateful that it didn't take them long to reach the cave; he was anxious about leaving his friends behind to face the Hazzara army without him. The priestesses gathered around him with meat rolls of cámbor meat seasoned with cress and a small flask of wine. Cedron knew these delicacies were both offerings of goodwill and potential final meal. With the cave looming over him, Cédron decided that he could have used a little more time to prepare himself for the challenge he was about to undertake. His fingers ached from gripping his staff. *I don't know how I'm supposed to fight the goddess for her aquastone while relaxing and allowing my Árk'äezhi to flow, but maybe Räeshun can help. Thank Our Lady that the high priestess didn't forbid me from bringing her!*

Zale'en turned and stopped in front of the entrance to the cave. Placing her wrinkled hand on Cédron's forehead, she closed her eyes and muttered a word of power. Warmth spread from her hand into the young man's head. She placed her other hand on his chest, sending the power into his heart.

"You have demonstrated the passion necessary to wield the firestone," she said, opening her eyes and holding Cédron's gaze. "Now you must prove to Muralia that you have the strength and courage to acquire her aquastone. You must get through the cave to the sacred pool. The aquastone will be on a pedestal in the center of the pool. Retrieve the stone. Muralia will not make it easy for you, and if you fail, you will die. Now go. Find your destiny."

Cédron turned and faced the deep darkness of the yawning cave entrance. Fear caused his skin to crawl uncomfortably. *This is it, Räeshun. If we don't make it out of here, at least we'll go down together.* Cédron felt the reassuring throb of the staff's Árk'äezhi and saw his cousin's face smiling at him in his mind. Taking a deep, steadying breath, Cédron nodded to Zale'en and stepped into the blackness of the cave.

Cédron stared at the morbid entrance to the goddess's lair and felt the apathy of the thousands of hollow eyes from the skulls sunk into the walls, staring back at him. The entire cavern had been mortared with bones from generations of Meq'qan and their wakazan. It was strange to see the people's remains used for flooring and structural elements, leaving the beasts for the more decorative artwork adorning the passageway. Two enormous wakazan skeletons flanked the entrance with their heads down, horns pointed aggressively. *Not good.*

Cédron gripped Räeshun with the same force as the fear that gripped his heart. *I don't know if I can do this. What if the goddess doesn't accept me?* Räeshun glowed softly in his hands, emitting a feeling of reassurance and encouragement. He saw himself exiting the cave with the same luminous glow he'd felt in the temple. Räeshun was in his hand, with the firestone held in one side of the sunburst crown, and the aquastone held fast in the other.

Buoyed by Räeshun's optimism, he changed his line of thinking. Cédron imagined the desolation that had resulted from Laylur's previous tenure in their world and strengthened his resolve. Muralia had largely recovered from the War of Betrayal and was green and thriving again, despite the loss in the balance of magical energy. He would not let centuries of healing and growth be sacrificed. Swallowing the bile that inched up his throat and threatened to choke him, Cédron closed his eyes and tried to calm his mind.

Stepping forward on his bare feet, Cédron felt the smooth roundness of the skulls buried in the floor. He stepped gingerly, half expecting them to crumble and crunch beneath his weight, but they were strongly cemented into the clay floor. Raised bumps prickled up and down his arms and back as he continued on his journey over the rounded floor and tried not to think about what he was treading on.

The cavern was extremely high, and the light of the few glow rocks hanging from the wall sconces was meager. It didn't reach the ceiling that disappeared into the gloom. Cédron craned his neck and tried unsuccessfully to discern how high it reached. His nostrils flared in the dank and musty air. He felt the cold tendrils of a faint breeze caressing his bare skin. He imagined the spirits of the dead reaching out to him with their clammy fingers, and he shuddered.

Cédron didn't know much about how the Meq'qan worshiped the deity, other than believing that she kept the dead and was aligned with the element of water. He thought of the water burial that he and Rovãen had performed for Räesha and remembered Rovãen telling him that Lady Muralia was the source of all living energy. He had no need to fear her. She was the mother of all.

Yet Räesha's warning echoed in his ears of how Lady Muralia was weakened, allowing a breach in the abyss. If he could wield the Sceptre of Kulari, then he would be able to heal that breach and restore Lady Muralia. *If I can figure out how to wield such great power without destroying everything. At least I can try to get the aquastone and stop the ground shakes. That will slow Laylur down until I can figure out how to wield the Sceptre of Kulari.*

The passageway narrowed considerably and wound tightly, switching direction every few yards. After a while, Cédron became completely disoriented. He wished he had the compass Sahráron had given him to help navigate the catacomb maze, with its walls of dead faces grinning at him in various stages of disintegration. He'd left that behind in the village, along with everything else he carried except Räeshun.

Trying not to stare back at the hollow eyes marking his passage, Cédron gripped Räeshun so tightly that his fingers ached. Every muscle in his body was taut with the strain of reaching out with his mind to sense any force that would try to hinder his progress. Something caught his pants as he walked. Cédron jumped. His heart lurched up to his throat. He clamped his jaws together to keep from screaming out loud.

Looking down, he saw a bony hand protruding from the wall, its desiccated skin turned to leather, its index finger separated from the rest like it was pointing. The index finger had caught the side of his pants. Exhaling loudly, Cédron bent down to extricate his pants from the dried, bony finger. Standing up, Cédron saw that the tunnel reached an end, with passageways running to both the left and right. Looking back at the pointing hand, he decided to follow the sign and go left.

This tunnel was narrower than the rest. It wasn't wide enough for two people to walk abreast. Cédron had almost determined that he'd taken the wrong turn when the tunnel opened into an illuminated cavern. The walls glimmered from the crystals embedded in the stone.

Looking to the center of the cavern, Cédron saw a clear pool. Stalagmites and stalactites grew throughout the cavern, but the aisle to the pool was smooth and clear. Behind the pool, carved into the wall, was an enormous statue of Lady Muralia seated upon a throne. She wore a necklace, dangling earrings, and bracelets of rounded turquoise stones that were the only elements of color in the sable marble. In her hands, extended together in front of her at heart level, she held the sacred water stone. It was a smooth, polished stone, unfaceted but set neatly in the statue's hands. The stone gave off a slight glow that caught in the flat surfaces of the crystalline walls, making them seem to flicker and dance.

The cavern appeared to be empty. Cédron could sense no other living beings. Not even the winged diclurues were this deep within the system of caves. He approached the pool and looked across to the throne where the image of Lady Muralia sat in eternal vigil over the dead. The water was clear, and it was hard to determine how deep it was.

Cédron figured he could swim across, but swimming in a sacred pool felt disrespectful. He didn't want to offend the goddess. He decided that appealing to the deity would be the logical first step. Cédron knelt down at the edge of the pool, facing the marble deity, and bowed his head.

"Lady Muralia, I come to you as a supplicant to ask for the right to use the sacred aquastone in the war against Laylur," he said, keeping his eyes shut in prayer.

Nothing happened. Cédron opened one eye and peeked around quickly before squeezing his eyes together tightly again.

"I am Cédron Varkáras, son of an Askári and Shäeli, grandson to a Tawali and Meq'qan, with the blood of all the races that will allow me to wield the Sceptre of Kulari. I beseech you to allow me the sacred aquastone to complete my quest." Cédron listened, his ears straining for any response from the deity. He heard the slow drip of condensation from the stalactites into the water below. Silence.

Cédron waited. And he waited. *I am an idiot.* The cool dampness of the cavern began to seep into his body, chilling his bones. His legs grew stiff from being folded on the hard floor, but he dared not move. The blood flow through his legs was restricted from the pressure of kneeling on the stone, the tingling numbness causing sharp pains from his hips to ankles. *This isn't working.*

Cédron slowly unfolded his legs and stamped the hard ground, wincing as the shooting pain resulting from the restoration of circulation caused him to stumble. He looked again at the statue of the goddess and decided that he'd have to take matters into his own hands. Obviously, the deity wasn't going to respond to him as a supplicant.

Keeping one eye on the statue and the other one on the water, Cédron slowly placed one foot into the tepid pool. His heart pounded in his ears and he held his breath. Nothing happened.

Exhaling slowly, Cédron put his other foot into the pool and eased himself away from the edge. He held Räeshun out in front of him, facing the statue as a ward should anything attack him from that quarter. With his attention focused on the statue, Cédron didn't immediately notice the change.

The water began swirling slowly, almost imperceptibly, until it felt like a current against Cédron's thighs. Startled, he glanced away from the statue's face and into the middle of the pool, where the water began churning and roiling. *Something is down there!*

His grip on Räeshun tightened as he crouched down and held her out defensively. Cédron tried backing out of the pool, but the current threatened to knock him over. He decided to hold his position, with both legs solidly planted against the bottom. He wasn't sure yet what the goddess had to defend her statue, but he felt more confident with Räeshun in his hands.

Watching with morbid fascination, Cédron nearly forgot to breathe as the heads of three strange creatures broke the water and rocked towards him from the extremely deep center of the pool. The enormous water steeds had blunt, orange snouts with jagged teeth, two spiked horns that protruded from above their eyes and tails covered with spikes that flicked towards Cédron as he tried skirting around them.

Cédron racked his brain to put a name to the awesome creatures, with their slick, dark green hides and ruffled underside that propelled the creatures through the water smoothly. None of the usual water creatures he'd learned about fit this image. Perhaps he should consider mythological creatures. *What would guard a goddess?*

He ran through all of the magical creatures that had once supposedly roamed the land of Muralia before Laräeith's Betrayal had wiped them out. One finally triggered his memories: ser'aq. The ser'aqs were Lady Muralia's water steeds. *What do I know about ser'aqs? How can I get around them to the aquastone?*

Sifting through all the stories he'd ever heard about ser'aqs, which weren't many, Cédron tried to determine how to defeat the fearsome beasts. They didn't seem to be aggressive and weren't attacking, but they were certainly obstructing his path to the aquastone. He'd have to figure out a way past them. He knew that their spikes would gouge him and that their horns would be lethal if they gored him, but other than that, he couldn't remember. Cédron glanced around the cave and grimaced. The walls and floor were too smooth to scale along the edge of the pool. He'd have to swim past the ser'aqs to reach the statue.

Cédron shifted his weight and stepped around to the right of the beasts. As one, the three monsters changed their positions and blocked him. The closest swung its spiky tail towards his unprotected head. Cédron dodged the attack and sidestepped back to his original position. He watched the ser'aqs carefully. They didn't seem to be looking directly at him as they bobbed along the surface of the pool.

Cédron swung Räeshun around with his left hand, monitoring the ser'aq's focus. They didn't respond at all to the movement. Slowly, Cédron stepped to his left. The unavoidable ripples in the water alerted the ser'aqs to his movement and they instantly swung their heads his direction. *Ok, poor eyesight and hearing, but hypersensitivity to water disturbances. Mijáko piles! I'm never going to reach that stone.*

Räesha pulsed gently in his hands and Cédron opened his mind to her images. He saw himself raising Räeshun high, the firestone glowing brilliantly. Water hissed and steamed as the firestone heated the water, causing the ser'aqs to writhe in pain. Cédron shook the image from his head. *I can't do that. I'll kill them, and then Lady Muralia will certainly reject me.*

Räeshun pulsed slightly faster. Cédron knew he was running out of time. The Hazzara army would be nearly upon the Meq'qan. He had to return with the aquastone and continue his quest or there would be no hope for his friends in the coming war. Nodding, Cédron stepped back out of the pool and raised Räeshun above his head.

Closing his eyes, Cédron felt the warmth of his Árk'äezhi flowing from his heart through his body and out of his palms into Räeshun. His hands burned with heat as the firestone ignited in Räeshun's finger bones. The ser'aqs were blinded by the stone's brilliance, their squeals echoing painfully off the walls and reverberating in the water.

Cédron longed to cover his ears but instead just gritted his teeth and willed the water temperature to rise slowly. He desperately wanted to incapacitate the ser'aqs and get to the stone without causing them any lasting damage. Their wails rose in pitch as the steam from their bodies hissed. Cédron watched warily as the ser'aqs writhed and thrashed in the pool. He wasn't convinced that he was doing the right thing, but they did appear to be retreating.

Stepping slowly around to the side of the pool, Cédron inched his way towards the statue and the elusive aquastone. The ser'aqs appeared to have forgotten about him in their distraction with the water temperature. Cédron took his eyes off them for a moment and focused on climbing over the slick floor towards the statue. He had to navigate carefully with one hand while holding Räeshun aloft with the other.

With his concentration fractured into three directions, Cédron wasn't able to maintain the firestone's magic. He was instantly aware when the ser'aqs honed in on his location, and he swung Räeshun wildly around to protect himself. The waving threw him off balance and Cédron slipped off the smooth stone and into the warm water.

The ser'aqs were upon him immediately. He ducked beneath the churning waters, avoiding the spikes of one tail, but was butted in the stomach as another pounded him with the side of its head. The third ser'aq stretched out its head, elongating its neck impossibly and catching Räeshun between the horns on the top of its head. The beast hurled the staff away, opening its mouth and spewing a viscous substance that caused Räeshun to stick to the wall of the cavern.

Cédron was stunned. The beasts had carefully not injured him, but now Räeshun was out of his reach. He looked around for anything else that he could use to fend off the mythical steeds, but there was nothing. All three of the monstrous beasts had their jaws open and their sticky mucus covered him from head to toe before he could duck back under the water.

Every inch of his skin tingled from the bile as the goo spread all over his body. Cédron squeezed his eyes shut and pursed his lips to keep from ingesting the foul-smelling stuff. He tried to bend down and wash it off and realized with a flash of panic that the substance had immobilized him. *Laylur's beast, I can't move!* The thought had barely run its course through his awareness when one of the ser'aqs grasped him in the middle with its huge jaws and carried him back towards the center of the pool.

Cédron's stricken mind raced as the beast submerged with him, still in its maw. Blood thundered through his body, pounding in his brain and causing spots to sparkle beneath his lids. His lungs felt like they were going to explode as the ser'aqs dove with him down into the pool. His ears and nose throbbed painfully from the pressure of the depths, but Cédron had bigger problems to deal with.

The goo had washed away from his face as the ser'aq swam deeper into the network of subterranean caves beneath the pool. He had opened his eyes and spotted a mound of bleached bones near the mouth of a dark cave. The cave yawned widely as if to accept the offering the goddess's steed was bringing it. Cédron began thrashing within the jaws of the ser'aq, trying to loosen the beast's grip on him. The ser'aq clamped down harder, causing the boy to cry out, expelling the last remaining pocket of air inside his body.

Involuntarily, Cédron's body gasped for air that wasn't there. As the water rushed down his throat and into his lungs, despair filled his mind. He knew he was about to die in this cave, far below the goddess's statue. Räeshun was still stuck fast to the wall above and couldn't help him. The priestess wouldn't find his body and would have nothing to tell all those he left behind. His quest was over before it even began, and Laylur would win. Overwhelming sadness filled his heart as the blackness closed in, and he lost consciousness.

* * *

Cédron floated in the interminable darkness, initially not noticing he'd become cognizant. He realized, almost as an afterthought, that he was alive, and that something was touching the outskirts of his awareness. Cédron felt the feathery touch of something trying to reach inside his mind. In his weakened state, Cédron could offer no resistance, and the entity exploded into his brain. The being filled his mind, charging every particle of his body with its powerful presence and energy.

Opening his eyes, Cédron saw lights playing across the ceiling of the cavern he'd been retuned to by the ser'aqs. The statue still sat impassively on the other side of the cave. He turned his head slightly and watched as the water in the pool slowly began to whirl. Luminescent particles within the water shimmered with the agitation. In the center of the pool, something solid was beginning to form. Cédron watched helplessly, deep within his incapacitated body, as a golden head crested the water and a female form lifted slowly from the pool.

With wide eyes, he gasped as the familiar, long, golden hair and liquid amber eyes of his mother appeared before him. Her manifestation complete, Maräera stepped from the pool and gently pulled her son to his feet. She was slightly shorter than he was, and his stomach twisted in a painful knot as he warred in his mind with the image in front of him.

The creature standing before him certainly looked his mother. She appeared as lovely and whole as she'd been in his oldest memories in her garden, not torn and bloodied as she'd been when she'd died in the explosion. Cédron wasn't sure if this was a gift from Lady Muralia or a challenge to defeat. He wanted to throw himself into her arms and tell her how sorry he was for causing the explosion and ground shake that had killed her. He wanted to tell her how much he loved and missed her. He was afraid that if he did, she would disappear or turn into something horrible. So, he did nothing. He stared, slack-jawed and wide-eyed at the solid apparition that continued to smile benignly at him.

"Cédron," the image whispered at him, touching his cheek with her cool hand. "You have grown into a fine young man."

Cédron stepped back out of her reach, stumbling on a small rock behind him. He caught himself before losing his balance, but his eyes never left Maräera's.

"Am I dead?" he asked the apparition of his mother.

Maräera's eyes clouded slightly and she shook her head.

"What are you?" he breathed, grasping at the crystals in the wall behind him.

The woman tilted her head back slightly and laughed. It was like the cascading water of a merry stream, and the sound reverberated off the walls of the cavern and in Cédron's mind. It was a lovely and infectious sound that made Cédron's heart beat faster and his head seem light and giddy. Cédron couldn't help but smile shyly in return.

"I am a part of the life force that was once Maräera, your mother," she said.

"Are you Mäuli?"

A pained look passed quickly over Maräera's face. "No, child, my life wasn't taken from me forcibly. My death was not an intentional part of the plan that changed the courses of both our lives."

"Then how are you here? Only Mäuli spirits remain after the body dies." He looked at her with narrowed eyes, a suspicion growing in his mind.

Maräera turned to face the statue of the goddess, raising her arms in invocation. The features on the statue softened and animated. The head inclined towards Cédron and smiled.

"The energy that was Maräera returned to me, and we remain connected. I am Lady Muralia. My responsibilities to the world do not normally allow me to focus my attention on just one matter, but your quest is essential. You must learn to master your power before Laylur breaks free of the abyss and overruns all life. I thought it best to release the piece of energy that you would recognize and trust to help you gain the knowledge and experience you need to fulfill your quest." The statue smiled slightly at the two beings beneath her.

Cédron fell again to his knees and bowed low, touching the floor with his forehead. "I am not worthy of your attentions, Great Mother."

"By showing my ser'aqs compassion, you have proven the pureness of your heart despite the small stain upon your spirit. If you had tried to boil all the water in the pool, they would have dragged you down to your death, but because you were merciful to them, when they reached cooler water and calmed, I was able to command them to bring you back to me. A weaker man would never have faced them. A more murderous man would have died in their jaws. You are the only one, my child, who can heal the world. You must find a way to bring the peoples of the world together to face Laylur and his demons," the statue said.

Cédron's mind spun with the enormity of the request. How would the people believe him when Lady Muralia had not appeared or spoken to anyone for over a millennium? The deity's sole purpose was to give life and maintain the balance of magical energy on their world, and she had failed. Laräeith, the Shäeli woman, had exploited the deity's trust and inattention, destroying the balance of magical energy with her own dark powers.

Cédron knew the history well. Laräeith's was a cautionary tale of greed, ambition and destruction told to every child born in Muralia. Laräeith had been one of the Wushäen of Auräevya, the tree of life and source of all magic. She had delved deep into the secrets of magic and learned how the deities created life from the source of all energy. She manipulated that knowledge, twisting it into a warped caricature of the pureness of being that it was.

Laräeith and her partner Salzem had stolen an entire flock of potently magical Aruzzi hatchlings. They slaughtered the Lítrol, the mythical caretakers of the young Aruzzi, then the evil woman had infected the younglings with her malignant powers. The resultant monstrosities, called rinzar by the Yezman who'd fought them, were flown into battle with the lesser races. The twisted beasts destroyed their cities and decimated the Mages' Guilds and warriors of each society before throwing the land into an age of magical darkness. Samshäeli had closed its borders to all outsiders, and the lesser peoples had become equally isolated.

Still bowing, he spoke into the stone floor. "I don't know how to unite the peoples. I understand why the Askári and Meq'qan hate the Shäeli."

The deity had been following Cédron's thoughts. "The minds of men are easily swayed and led astray. Do not let yourself become distracted with the falsities that have been created to divide my peoples." The goddess's voice echoed softly throughout the chamber.

Cédron raised his head from the ground and looked at the statue. His thoughts were conflicted. *What falsities are distracting me? The Askári and Meq'qan are right to fear the magical abilities of the Shäeli; they nearly destroyed the world, didn't they?*

Maräera approached her son and knelt down to eye level.

"The malicious destruction by one student of the Shäeli doesn't define the entire race. We Shäeli are the First People, dedicated by Lord Shamar and Lady Muralia to the nurturing of our world. You cannot destroy Laylur through strength of arms, but through the creation of a new covenant. You must understand this or you will not succeed," she pleaded, holding his gaze.

Cédron leaned backwards and sat. Sighing heavily, he shook his head. "But I don't understand. And, my magic is uncontrolled. It's destructive. I've already killed one man out of anger and vengeance. I cannot wield the Sceptre of Kulari yet; I just don't have the skill. I'm more likely to complete Laräeith's work and destroy the world."

Maräera swiveled and sat down next to her son, resting her back on a thick stalagmite. She grasped her son's hand and squeezed gently. "My Lady has charged me with teaching you how to manage your great power so that you can achieve what she cannot."

Cédron looked at the alabaster hand with its fingers entwined in his. He turned his head and looked into the dark golden eyes. "I've missed you, mother."

Maräera's eyes softened. "I've never been far from you, my son." She released his hand and stood. "We must prepare you for what you must face."

She reached down with both hands, grasping Cédron's in her firm grip. She lifted the youth to his feet, and they turned to face the statue. The marble arms of Lady Muralia lowered slightly, bringing the sacred aquastone within reach of Maräera as she walked across the top of the pool. She retrieved the large stone from her deity's cupped hands and brought it back to Cédron.

"Stand in the center of the pool. You must first be purified," she ordered.

Cédron hesitated. The last time he entered the pool, the ser'aqs had nearly killed him. He kept a watchful eye on the deity's face as he gingerly touched the clear water with his big toe. The dust that clung to his feet lifted from his skin and floated off in concentric circles around his ankles. He was becoming clean, but the water would no longer be pure. He started to retreat, but Maräera shook her head firmly, rooting him in place.

"The water will cleanse your body and your mind. Release your thoughts and let the knowledge flow to you."

Maräera held the stone above her head. A shaft of light flooded out of the stone and onto Cédron's forehead. Its brilliance caused him to close his eyes tightly. "Relax and let go," Maräera whispered.

Cédron inhaled deeply, willing his mind to relinquish the protective barriers that years of defending himself from the fear and hatred of others had developed. He had learned to hate and loathe himself as those around him had done, causing him to doubt in his worthiness to even attempt this quest and his ability to fulfill it. The power of the stone infiltrated his mind and filled his body with a sense of well-being and energy that bordered on transcendence. He could feel his skin glowing and his hair crackling with the power. Unlike when he'd assisted Rovään with Räesha's transformation, the power of the stone wasn't flowing through his body, just in his mind. Visions came to him of others in the past using the aquastone.

The visions were more like memories, as he felt them rather than saw them unfolding in front of him. He saw a warrior lying next to a river. Blood was spurting from a deep gash in the warrior's thigh and staining the pebbles beneath him. He saw gnarled old hands that seemed to be his own reach into the water with the stone. He watched, mesmerized as the water around the stone thickened and turned crimson. Willing blood back into the weakened soldier, Cédron watched as the water poured into his wound and restored his health. *Blood is mostly water! I understand!*

With his new understanding of how water flowed through the world much like blood flows through each individual's body, Cédron's eyes flew open. A wide grin spread over his face. "I can heal anything!"

Maräera stood in front of him, the stone lowered. "Yes, you can. Water is the lifeblood of our world, and now you understand that element of your quest." She waded across the pool and placed the stone back in the statue's open hands. "With this knowledge, you must now purify your own body and mind."

Cédron's face flushed from the strength of the blood rushing through his veins. The power of the stone heightened all his senses, and he felt the firing of each nerve as it tasted the water and air touching his skin. Confidence radiated from the boy as he stepped forward and bowed before the statue.

"I am ready." Cédron stood and grasped the stone from the goddess' hands.

The water from the pool roared to life, forming an impenetrable wall and completely encasing him. Cédron's mind exploded. Every cell in his body flooded with the power of the water, until he felt as if he was an intrinsic part of the wall that flowed up from the floor to the vast ceiling of the cavern. His mind was captured in the heartbeat of the world, the rapids of life energy that coursed throughout their land and tied them to their source of creation.

As his body and mind expanded to become part of that living source energy, he felt the overwhelming love and sadness of their creator. Their world and everything living within it was created by and remained a part of their deity Lady Muralia. *The whole world is a living being! It's her!* The understanding overwhelmed the young man's mind. Every bug he'd squished under his boots, every rock he'd thrown into the river, and every flower he'd picked were all living parts of their deity.

Cédron recognized the life cycle of water and how it contributed to the creation of life. He could call it forth from the skies or the ground and manipulate it any way he could conceive. His chest heaved with the effort of containing his excitement at understanding this power. He could create life, heal life and, if he so chose, he could take it.

The blinding blue light of the aquastone darkened and with it came a vision. He saw a woman holding the sacred aquastone. Her face was twisted with power that coursed from her into the field of unhatched eggs spread out before her. A dark figure lurked in the shadows behind the woman. Cédron watched in horror as the power radiated from the stone and into the eggs, causing them to rock violently. The warped, black monstrosities that emerged from the shells made his blood run cold. *This is what Laräeith did to the Aruzzi hatchlings.*

Understanding crashed over him like a frigid waterfall. The immense sorrow of Lady Muralia pervaded his senses and nearly choked him with grief. Laräeith had learned the secret of life, as he had just done, and she'd distorted it. She'd taken the perfection that was the balance of all things and bent it to her will, throwing the world into chaos in her lust for power.

The realization that he now had the same knowledge terrified Cédron. What would prevent him from making a mistake and misusing the power? He remembered how he'd tortured and exploded the Shäeli warrior who'd killed Räesha. Cédron felt a flush of shame at his lack of control. If he couldn't keep his emotions in check or master his abilities, how could Lady Muralia trust him with the knowledge of life? *I can't do this. I'm not the right person to have this much power.*

In his anguished mind, he called out to his creator. "Mother, I am not ready for this!"

"What is the source of your fear?" came the reply in his mind.

Cédron paused. There were so many things that he was afraid of: making a mistake, losing control, destroying those he loved, decimating the world and irreversibly tipping the balance of negative energy, allowing Laylur to overrun their lands.

"What is your intention?" a voice asked softly inside his mind.

Cédron clamped down on his whirling thoughts. The fears that were spinning out of control, bringing visions of destruction and chaos, slowed and settled on one underlying fear: hurting those he loved. *I'm afraid of hurting or killing my loved ones. My mother, Zariun, Lanäe and Räesha have already perished because of me. But that wasn't the question.* Cédron thought briefly. *My intention is to heal the rift in the abyss and restore the balance of magical energy to the world. But-*

"Then your heart is pure," the voice in his head cut off his trail of thought. "You have passed the challenge. You must take the aquastone to its source beneath the Shaláen Falls. Heal the source and trust my servants to guide you on the rest of your journey."

The darkness of his mind receded and was replaced by a feeling of overwhelming peace. Cédron floated in this ebb and flow of harmony, reveling in the gentle strains of music that caressed his senses. His fears dissipated and his body felt the warmth of the deity's blessing.

The markings that Zale'en had painted on his torso glowed blue against his pale skin. Looking down at their heat, Cédron felt the waves of ink burn and absorb into his being through the power of the bright blue stone. Slowly, the churning waters lowered to the ground and calmed into the still, clear pool. Cédron stood in the shallows of the pool, his skin glowing from the power of the sacred stone.

Maräera knelt before her child and touched her forehead on the tops of his feet. "I am proud of you, my son. You have accepted a huge burden, but I know you have the ability to succeed. Promise me that you will always remember that it is your intention and your choices that create who you are, nothing else."

Cédron pulled his mother to her feet and embraced her. Releasing her, he stared into her beautiful face, memorizing every curve and angle. "I am your son and the son of Kásuin Varkáras. That is who I am. For the first time in my life, I can embrace my heritage. Now I can finally do something good with it."

Cédron was surprised to see a fleeting expression of sadness cross her face. She reached up and caressed his cheek, resting her thumb on his chin.

"When the time comes," she said, "I hope that will be enough. You must remain true to who you are and your intention. Know this: you cannot triumph with resistance. You must trust and allow your power to flow. Do not waver."

Cédron stared at her, unable to give voice to the myriad of conflicting emotions racing through his body. He wanted to assure her that he would remain true and succeed in his quest, but the lingering fears kept him silent. He'd already disappointed his parents so many times.

As if sensing his thoughts, Maräera smiled. "Please remind Kásuin of my abiding love."

A shock of inspiration ran through Cédron like a bolt of lightning. "My father still lives? He survived the Garanth attack in Tamóna?"

Maräera gazed off into the distance, her eyes unfocused. "Kásuin's energy has not joined the river of life that flows to the source. He remains in the world of the physical, but I cannot sense him."

Cédron's heart skipped a beat. *My father lives!* He pondered her words for a moment. "You cannot sense him... What does that mean?"

"It means that I cannot sense his presence. He could be unconscious or magically hidden from me." She sighed. "There is much evil at work in the world right now."

"The Garanth! Why have they attacked?" Cédron asked, hoping that his mother's connections could help him understand what was happening to his people.

Maräera closed her eyes. She remained motionless except for the rapid movement of her eyes beneath her delicately-veined lids for several minutes. Cédron held his breath, hoping that she would be able to give him some understanding of what caused the fierce tribes to leave the safety of their homelands.

"Men came while the warriors were hunting and stole the sacred firestone," she began. "They slaughtered their females and their young, leaving the oldsters to recount the tale to the warriors when they returned. The Garanth village that held the firestone was burned; its streets ran red with the blood of innocents. The Garanth vowed to slaughter all the races of men for their crimes."

"Who did this?" Cédron asked. "What men?"

Maräera put her hand upon his brow and closed her eyes. She gave him a vision. He saw the back of a cloaked man standing before a mirror encased in blue flame. Inside the mirror gleamed two bright blue eyes within an amorphous body. The cloaked man bowed to the demon within the frame and turned to leave. As the cloaked figure turned, Cédron noticed the red stone torus knot amulet. He gasped. *The Hazzara!*

The scene changed to a battlefield. Cédron saw the scorched remains of woven huts with wisps of grey smoke still spiraling into the sky from the sodden reeds. The bodies of Meq'qan lay everywhere. Amidst the carnage, demons were gathering the wounded and sitting them against the wall of the only hut left standing. Cédron retched internally as the demons infused their essences into the weakened bodies of the wounded. The eyes of the Meq'qan frosted over, the yellow irises turning milky from the demon's presence.

"Arkmuln," Maräera said, her voice cracking. "The abominations of demon spirits inhabiting human bodies. The bodies' former owners are still trapped inside, unable to control what their bodies do, forced to watch as they carry out the demons' bidding. It is a tormented existence for what shred of the soul remains. Their creation demonstrates the growing power of Laylur and his minions. The breach in his prison grows wider."

Cédron cried out, his body jerking from the horror in his mind. The connection to the visions was lost. He sat with his chest heaving for breath as if he'd been running for his life. "Is that what attacked Tamóna?" he asked his mother. "What happened?"

"Tamóna was destroyed," she said in a faraway voice. "Some survived and fled to Taksábai, but many were killed. The Arkmuln numbers increase with each battle."

Cédron was sick. Tamóna was gone and the horror of the Garanth and Arkmuln were marching towards Taksábai. *The Shaláen Falls and the caravan are directly in their path! How can I get around them to accomplish my task? What if they consume the caravan and kill Shozin and Sahráron...or worse?* "I must go. I have to reach the caravan before the Garanth and those...those Arkmuln..." Cédron shuddered. He couldn't complete the thought.

"I, too, must leave for now. We may meet again when you have retrieved the next stone." With that, Maräera turned and walked back into the pool towards the statue. Her body wavered and disappeared as if it had only been wisps of vapor rising on the water.

Cédron continued to stare at the spot she lingered last for several minutes, hoping against logic that she might return to him. He glanced at the statue, but it remained solid and lifeless. Hardening his resolve against the growing anxiety knotting in his bowels, Cédron turned his back on the statue and pool. He pulled Räeshun from the wall, grimacing as the viscous slime coated his hands. Bowing one last time to Lady Muralia's statue, he turned and made his way back to the living world and his duty.

CHAPTER 35 - URCLEK STRIKE

Anéton watched Cédron's back until his friend and the priestess with her entourage disappeared over the crest of the westward hills and into the glare of the morning light. Shading his eyes, he squinted until the glinting off the stone in Räeshun's prongs was lost behind the mound. Turning to Tóran, the young legionnaire smacked his companion on the back.

"Shall we see what kind of trouble we can get into before Cédron returns?" he asked, a mischievous grin playing about his lips.

Tóran pursed his lips briefly, then smiled. The mirth didn't reach his eyes. "They will be here soon," he said grimly. "We should help with the fortifications."

The two Hármolin legionnaires strode over to Caf'iq Mak'ki's hut and offered their services to the leader of the Meq'qan tribes. Their offer was met with hostile stares and silence.

"We know how to defend our own lands, Askári," Caf'iq Mak'ki stated flatly, his milky eyes narrowed with suspicion at the two foreigners. "You would be wise to take the old man and leave before the battle starts."

Anéton almost laughed out loud at the ancient chieftain's temerity, but Tóran nudged him in the ribs. He bit back his retort and followed Tóran's lead as his companion bowed reverently to Caf'iq Mak'ki and his warriors, then exited the hut. He kept his mouth shut until they had crossed the village to the hut where Rováen was waiting for them, then the curiosity overcame his discretion.

"What was all *that* about?" he asked.

"What?"

"Just simply bowing and walking away," Anéton exploded. "That old monsaki insulted both of us and our people, and you let him!"

Tóran turned and placed a hand on Anéton's shoulder. "Fighting with the Meq'qan on the edge of battle isn't a wise move," he said. "They are frightened, and, honestly, I don't think the Caf'iq really understands what he's up against. It wasn't my place to force the issue."

Anéton chuckled and shook his head. "I've never known you to back down from a challenge or insult like that before." He shrugged. "It just took me by surprise, I guess."

The two legionnaires rolled up the mat doorway into the hut and found Rováen filling his pack with food.

"Are we going somewhere?" Anéton asked.

Rováen turned to face the young men, his eyes shadowed in the gloom of the hut. "Tóran suggested we scout the area, and I agree with him," the old man said, shouldering the pack and handing the other two their gear. "I know the runner said they'd slowed the Hazzara's progress, but I'm not convinced they will all be stopped. Tóran thinks a patrol would likely sneak through and try to hit the flanks of the Meq'qan tribes. We can see if they are launching any kind of strike from the east."

Anéton thought about the soundness of the argument and decided that, other than missing the meal he'd been promised at the end of the day, he really had nothing better to do. It was very likely that the Hazzara would send scouts, if nothing else, to see what the Meq'qan's defenses were like. He grasped his pack from Rováen's outstretched hand and nodded. The three had just left the hut and rolled down the mat over the doorway when Anéton felt a tugging on his shirt. He turned and looked down to find the upturned nose and gap-toothed grin of a little Meq'qan child.

"Well hello, little one." He smiled and knelt down to talk to the girl at eye level when the shock of recognition struck him. "Little Ra'lina, right? How are you doing?"

The girl giggled, covering her mouth with two very grimy hands. She batted her eyelashes at the legionnaire and blushed. "I'm fine, silly. My grandfather has asked me to escort you out of the village."

Anéton watched Tóran and Rováen exchange glances. Rováen shrugged and Tóran looked back at Anéton and nodded. Anéton smiled engagingly at the little girl and took her filthy hand in his own.

"Your grandfather?"

"Yes, Caf'iq Mak'ki."

"Well, in that case, lead on fair one." He bowed, eliciting another hysterical giggle from little Ra'lina.

"My friends want to go with us. Is that ok?" she asked.

Without waiting for an answer, Ra'lina put her right thumb and middle finger in her mouth and gave a piercing whistle. She waved her hand and two young boys that were lurking behind the hut opposite theirs came scrambling from their hiding places. Their freckled noses and half-grown front teeth told Anéton that the escort was the Caf'iq's way of keeping the kids from getting underfoot during battle preparations. *Banished with babysitters…but who's watching who here?*

Little Ra'lina tugged on Anéton's hand, pulling him along with her eastward into the thick of the swamps. Rováen and Tóran followed with the two little boys scampering around them like excited monsaki.

"Where are you taking us?" Rováen asked, bemused at their escort.

One of the little boys stopped up short and winked at the old man. "To the ledge," he said under his breath, glancing around to make sure nobody heard him. "You can see everything from there."

"Excellent," Tóran said. "I want to get the lay of the land and see if there is any Hazzara movement."

"My father said that the black army is coming from the north," one of the little boys piped up, his eyes wide and shining. "But we saw some of them sneaking through the swamps when we were out hunting this morning."

Anéton pulled Ra'lina back with his hand and grabbed her shoulder. "Why didn't you report that to your grandfather?"

The little girl pouted, narrowing her yellow eyes with her grimace. "We did. Grandfather didn't believe us because only the Meq'qan know how to navigate through the swamps. He told us to take our stories to the aunties watching the babies. But you believe us, don't you?" Ra'lina smiled wistfully into Anéton's startled brown eyes.

"S-sure we do." Anéton laughed nervously, shooting his companions a panicked look.

Tóran knelt down and caught Ra'lina's gaze. "Can you take us to where you saw the black soldiers?"

The little girl's face beamed with pleasure at the attention. "Sure! Follow me!"

The three children tore off toward the swamp as fast as their little legs could carry them with the three adults in close pursuit. Anéton marveled at how nimbly the children leapt from clump of solid ground to clump of solid ground without slipping into the dangerous muck of the marshland. They paused after a couple of miles to eat and rest. The young ones, while filled with excitement at the outset of their journey, tired and grew eager to share the smoked cochäera meat that they could smell in the older man's pack.

"How much further is it to the ledge," Anéton asked his young companion who was still stuffing her mouth with the tender meat.

Ra'lina swallowed and wiped her mouth with the back of her hand. She glanced around and nodded.

"Not far," she said pointing to the north. "We will be there before Lord Shamar is high."

The group continued their slog through the marsh. Anéton was wondering how any army could hope to navigate successfully through such treacherous landscape when the first high-pitched cackles of a beast reached his ears. The sound made his skin crawl.

Anéton glanced over at Rováen and saw the old man's visage pale and harden. The legionnaire realized that whatever beast was making that sound, the Shäeli seemed to both recognize and fear it. He felt his guts twist with apprehension. They had faced many dangers in recent weeks, and Anéton had never known Rováen to demonstrate any fear, but as Rováen quickened his pace, Anéton realized they were about to face something horrible.

With his thoughts elsewhere, Anéton nearly ran over Ra'lina and the two boys who had stopped dead in their tracks and crouched down. Only a last-minute swerve and tumble into the tall grasses kept the legionnaire from smashing into the children.

"Hey, what the…?"

"Shhh!" Ra'lina scolded, her finger to her lips. She pulled the tall grass slightly to the side and pointed with her finger. "See, they come."

Anéton scrambled on his knees over to the ledge where the children huddled behind the clumps of grass. His gaze followed Ra'lina's finger to where dark shapes were crashing through the underbrush a hundred meters northeast of their position. Rováen and Tóran crept up alongside and peered out into the afternoon glare.

"Whoever they are, they have some kind of creature with them that is helping them navigate through the swamp," Tóran remarked quietly.

Anéton squinted against Lord Shamar's brilliant light, unable to discern the nature of the beasts. The three creatures pulled on the tethers being held by nearly a dozen Hazzara soldiers. The beasts walked on all fours fairly low to the ground and seemed to have long quills or spikes protruding from their backs. He couldn't tell if they had hooves or claws, but was certain that he wouldn't want to face one alone. Their high-pitched cackling sounded like the laugh of the insane, and it scraped down his spine, causing his skin to pimple and crawl.

"You'd think the Meq'qan would have heard that racket and come to investigate," Anéton said, looking at his companions. "Why are there no warriors along here?"

One of the little boys crawled back from the edge, his cheeks flushed. "My father and the warriors are preparing for battle. They are making the offerings to Lady Muralia and Lord Shamar to ensure their victory. The dancing and singing will go well into the night They won't even hear these things."

"We have to warn them," Tóran said, crawling back from the ledge and getting to his feet. "They will reach the village before we do unless we run." He hitched his pack up tightly on his shoulders and prepared to sprint off when Rováen's hand on his shoulder held him back.

"We cannot fight these beasts," he said quietly. "They are lethal."

A look of irritation swept across Tóran's face and Anéton thought that perhaps the young man was going to strike the elder, but Tóran clenched his fists by his side instead. "What do you mean? We can't just let them ravage the village!"

"Come on!" Ra'lina cried, pulling again at Anéton's hand. The boys grabbed Tóran's pants and pulled at the leather.

Anéton picked up Ra'lina and set her on his hip, then faced Rováen. "What are those things? What do you know about them?"

Rováen looked at Anéton, then at the little girl in his arms, and sighed. His eyes cast downward before returning Anéton's accusing glare. "They are urgleks, the scavengers of Molonark. They have thousands of long quills arrayed across their backs that contain a lethal toxin. Even if we reach the village before they do, we couldn't stop them. They will kill everyone in their path with their painfully slow poison."

Ra'lina gasped, her eyes round moons as she clenched her arms tightly around Anéton's neck. "Mama! Papa!"

"It's too late, little one," Roväen said sadly, stroking her cheek as he pulled a strand of hair behind her ears. He looked up at Tóran and Anéton and shook his head. "We can perhaps take these three with us and save them... That's the best we can hope for."

"No!" Ra'lina slipped out of Anéton's arms and sprinted towards the village, the two little boys falling in directly behind her like a royal escort.

"Mijáko piles!" Roväen cursed and took off after the children with Tóran on his heels rapidly catching up.

Anéton hesitated for a moment, unsure whether to chase the children or try to slow down this new threat. *I know we shouldn't split up, but what good would it do to race headlong into a pack of urgleks and their poison darts?* The young legionnaire racked his brain, trying to come up with a way to protect the villagers and themselves from the lethal urgleks. The more he thought, the fewer ideas came to him.

Anéton decided to catch up with his companions before they lost him altogether, and he continued to create and discard scenarios as he sprinted through the marshland. He knew that their swords would be no use against the shooting darts of the urgleks, so maybe if he could find a bow and arrows or similar launching device, he could do something practical.

As he closed the distance between himself and the children, Anéton could hear the panicked wailing of the villagers as the urgleks pounced upon the unsuspecting inhabitants. He spied a hut just up ahead that was in the process of being built. One of the large wakazan skulls sat just outside where the entrance was planned. With a burst of speed, he sprinted past his friends and the children. Stopping in front of Ra'lina and herding her around to her left, he guided the terrified children into the enclosure of the wakazan's skull.

"Look, you kids need to stay here and stay quiet," he said urgently. "We'll get your families out of the village if we can, but you *must not move!*"

Three sets of wide eyes stared back at the soldier from within the wakazan's enormous eye sockets. They nodded in unison, and Ra'lina accepted the water skin that Rovӓen pulled from around his shoulders. Anéton cast about the area for anything else that he could use and spied a pair of upside-down mashufs, the small two-man boats used to fish in the marshes. He strode over to them and turned them over, knocking several spiked metal falahs onto the ground. Tóran stepped up next to him and pulled out a couple of the five-pronged fishing spears, hefting one in his right hand and nodding appreciatively.

"These may prove effective against those monsters," he said. "Let's see what kind of damage we can cause, shall we?"

Anéton nodded and handed two of the falahs to Rovӓen, claiming the last three for himself. The three men skirted the village commons where the urgleks and their Hazzara masters had recently begun their mayhem.

"The warriors are still performing their ceremony." Rovӓen frowned. "The women and children and the rest are completely unprotected."

Tóran looked at his two companions and Anéton noted a dangerous glint in his dark brown eyes. "Good. Let's show the Meq'qan how the Hármolin Legion handles interlopers."

As one of the beasts loped by, Tóran stood up and lifted the falah above his shoulder to throw it, but Rovӓen held him back. The urglek charged into a group of women a few feet away that were trying to herd their terrified children into the tall grasses. The monster turned on its clawed feet, causing its grotesquely-humped shoulder to curl its back even further as it sprayed its screaming victims with its darts.

The three foreigners watched in horror as the large darts sank into the soft flesh of the babies, unsuccessfully shielded by the slender women and the young children hiding behind them. Two of the smallest ones died instantly from the trauma of the large spikes goring their vital organs. The rest stumbled for several feet before collapsing, the toxin spreading slowly throughout their bodies.

Anéton saw red and leapt up from behind the hut. He raised his falah and hurled it into the chest of the urglek as it inspected its own handiwork. The beast was knocked backwards as the five prongs of the spear lacerated its spiny flesh, crying its high-pitched bark as it died. The Hazzara immediately attacked their position, calling to their companions to bring the other urgleks.

Rováen turned and retreated behind the hut, calling for Anéton and Tóran to follow him. The two glanced at each other briefly, then nodded and followed. Rováen led them in a zigzag pattern through the high grasses and past the now-empty huts. The Hazzara shouting behind them were getting closer, and Anéton thought he would feel the hot breath of the urglek's jaws closing in on him any second.

They raced for the hills where the warriors were performing their rituals, prayers to Orwena for their safe arrival on each pair of lips. Anéton was sick at the carnage they were leaving behind, but without any way to shield themselves, they would suffer the same horrible fate as the villagers. Suddenly an inspiration struck the young legionnaire.

Turning back around, he clambered over the stacks of woven mats that were piled on the western end of the marshes, waiting to be laid down when the rains began. He grabbed one of the smaller mats, pulling it around his shoulders like a cloak, then ducked down behind the piles and waited for the Hazzara to catch up.

Anéton didn't have to wait long. The first three men charged past him without a second glance. The legionnaire stood up and threw the falahs, one after the other, into the backs of the Hazzara agents still chasing Rovåen and Tóran. Both fell instantly, leaving only one for Anéton to fight hand-to-hand. Holding the mat around his back with his left hand, Anéton pulled his sword from the scabbard and screamed his war cry.

"Askáriiii!"

The Hazzara agent stopped up short at the cry at his back and turned to face the furious legionnaire. Anéton swung his blade, limbering up his shoulders and intimidating his foe. The Hazzara agent smiled wickedly and gave a piercing whistle.

In the distance, above the cries from the village, Anéton heard the high cackle-bark of the two remaining urgleks. He knew that he'd have to finish this battle quickly or the urgleks would reach him with their darts. Anéton wasn't sure how well the mat would protect him from the toxin, but it was the only option he'd found in such short order.

The Hazzara pulled a short knife from his sash and brandished it at Anéton. The young legionnaire nearly laughed out loud. He knew he had the reach of the man, so he feinted to his left, feeling out what his opponent planned to do with the small dagger.

The Hazzara danced out of Anéton's reach and pulled out a red tourmaline amulet that lay just beneath his shirt. The blood-red stone glinted balefully in Lord Shamar's light, reflecting ominously in the Hazzara's black eyes. Anéton lunged at the man, thrusting his blade towards his chest, but the Hazzara easily backed away. The black-clad stranger held his dagger in front of him and muttered an unintelligible word. Instantly, the small dagger burst into flames.

"Laylur's beast!" Anéton cried, realizing the man was a magic wielder.

Anéton had just enough time to swing the mat around before the flaming blade sunk deep into the woven reeds, igniting the mat and scorching his hands where he held it. The legionnaire flung the burning mat away from his body and into the oncoming Hazzara. The mage caught the mat and incinerated it with his amulet, grinning at Anéton through the cascading ash that billowed in the air. Anéton coughed as the acrid flakes stung his eyes and throat, squinting to keep his opponent in his vision.

The Hazzara stepped sideways and grasped his amulet with both hands. Fear prickled the follicles of every hair on Anéton's body as he waited for the magical attack for which he had absolutely no defense. He turned and ran, darting to the left and right as the magic wielder charged his stone. Anéton spied another of the tall stacks of woven mats that would be used during the rainy season to fortify the village huts. He made for the protection of the stack when the heat of the Hazzara's fire swept past him and struck the mats. The dried grasses exploded, knocking the legionnaire back and cutting off his escape. Anéton sank to his knees and placed his sword across them. *I cannot give in to fear. I need to face it.*

Anéton closed his eyes and took a deep breath through his nose. The ashes flayed his tender nasal passages, but he ignored the pain. Anéton knew he was going to die by magic, the kind that was painful and slow. He'd never cared about dying in battle as a legionnaire and bringing honor to his squad, but now that he was faced with his own demise, he didn't want to be cowardly. He inhaled again and opened his eyes.

The Hazzara agent was standing just a few feet in front of him, his amulet raised above his head. The stone began to glow with the power being added to it by the Hazzara, and Anéton swallowed against the tightness in his throat. He thought briefly of his sisters and hoped they'd survive without him to look out for them.

"Time to die, you Askári scum," the Hazzara hissed.

Anéton closed his eyes again and wondered if Lady Muralia was as lovely as all the murals in Dúlnat depicted. He'd know soon enough. He held his breath and waited for the final blow, but it never came. Anéton heard a slight whistling, then a deep thud. He barely opened one eyelid and peeked out.

The Hazzara agent lay on his back in the grass in front of him, a Meq'qan spear sticking out of his chest. Relief washed over the young soldier, nearly causing him to faint. Behind him, in the deeper grasses, the Meq'qan warriors were running towards the village while Ta'riqk accompanied Rováen and Tóran to his position.

"True aim." Tóran nodded to Ta'riqk appreciatively. "And not too soon either, by the looks of things."

Rováen hastened over to Anéton and gave him his hand. Anéton grasped it and shakily pulled himself to his feet. "Thanks."

War cries filled the air as the Meq'qan warriors spilled over the hillsides and into the village, full of power and passion from their ceremony to the deities. Anéton heard the clash of weapons and the screams of the fallen. He looked wide-eyed at his companions.

"Did you tell them about the urgleks?" he gasped. "They're not going in against them unprotected, are they?"

Ta'riqk smiled grimly and placed a hand on Anéton's shoulder. "Our bone shields protect us from the darts." His eyes darkened. "But not from the pain of losing our families."

Anéton hung his head. He was sure he'd witnessed the demise of several families already. The urglek's toxin was lethal and painful. He shook his head in rueful appreciation for the tactic. The Hazzara must have had scouts inform them that the men were away performing their ceremony.

Sending in the urgleks to slaughter the women and children would sufficiently enrage the warriors and compromise their effectiveness on the battlefield. *Laylur's beast, that was brilliant. Twisted and horrific, but brilliant.*

"Come." Rovä̈en pulled Anéton along behind the other two men. "We need to help with the villagers so the warriors can face the main Hazzara army. They are in formation just north of the marshes."

Anéton trudged silently next to Rovä̈en, listening to Ta'riqk and Tóran discuss military strategy and how best to engage an army of magic-wielders. To his surprise, Ta'riqk didn't seem particularly afraid of the Hazzara and their abilities. The two walked faster, their heads closer together as they fed off each other's ideas.

Anéton was startled from his thoughts as Ta'riqk laughed out loud. *Certainly, war is no laughing matter. I wonder what they've come up with.*

"You two go on and help in the village," Tóran said. "Ta'riqk and I have a plan."

"Be careful." Rovä̈en nodded to them, waving them off as they sprinted deep into the marshland.

Anéton watched them go, then turned back towards the village to the gigantic wakazan skull. Three small bodies were still huddled together inside. Anéton lifted the heavy skull while Rovä̈en assisted the children out and counseled them about what they were about to see.

Sufficiently warned that their families could already be lost, and that bravery was now their duty, the children held hands as they followed the two men. Anéton felt the first tendrils of apprehension squeeze his chest as the cloying scent of death wafted into his nostrils.

"I'm going to be sick."

ChAPTER 36 - INVOKING ThE AQUASTONE

Cédron exited Lady Muralia's cave and blinked in the afternoon light. Lord Shamar had shifted in his trajectory over the plains to the west and bathed the hills surrounding the cave with his warm benevolence. The priestess Zale'en raked his body over with her yellow reptilian eyes, her gaze lingering on the tattoos that had replaced the paint she'd decorated him with.

The blue swirls etched into his abdomen like waves cresting on the shore overlapped the sharper red etchings around his heart where the firestone markings lay. He straightened his shoulders, self-conscious of the alterations his body had undergone at the hands of the goddess, and strode as confidently as he could towards the river where he could wash the ser'aq slime from Räeshun.

"The goddess has given you her blessing," Zale'en declared as he walked past her. "I am pleased."

Cédron raised Räeshun into the light, the rays glinting through the aquastone's curve where the phalanx bones held it in the starburst crown opposite the firestone. Even covered in goo, Räeshun glowed like a small sun, spilling her radiance onto her holder. Cédron's pale skin glimmered softly in the light, making the dark blue and crimson markings that covered his chest and torso seem alive as they writhed across his skin.

"The goddess has granted me knowledge." Cédron nodded to the priestess as they continued together towards the river with the acolytes. "I understand now what is expected of me."

The small group continued towards the river in silence, each respecting the others' thoughts. Cédron wondered if the high priestess had any idea of the knowledge the goddess had imparted to him. He suspected that she did, for she seemed to regard him with some deference. He noticed that she remained a half step back behind him as they walked over the hill toward the water.

When they reached the river, Cédron knelt at the bank and submerged Räeshun. The slime from the ser'aqs clung fast to the bone staff and adhered to his skin. Cédron scooped up some of the pebbles and sandy bottom to scrub away the viscous substance, careful not to rub too hard and damage the tattoo etchings on Räeshun's surface.

"We are only a few miles' walk from the village," Zale'en began, kneeling down at the water's edge next to Cédron. "Still, we shouldn't tarry here long. War is upon my people."

Cédron considered her words and tried to discern the meaning behind them. *She doesn't expect me to fight, does she? She is a priestess of the goddess. She must understand that I cannot.* He polished Räeshun's surface with his clean hands and swished off the last of the grit from the carving along the shaft. Standing, he looked east towards the village and shaded his eyes against Lord Shamar's light.

"I cannot stand with your tribesmen," he sighed, turning to face the priestess. "My work is to heal this land, not to harm it."

Zale'en chuckled quietly, touching the marks on his skin with her gnarled finger. "War is not just killing," she said, tracing the lines of the aquastone's tattoo. "It is equally about healing." She dropped her hand and beckoned to him as she and her followers began walking eastward. "Come, we have much to do."

* * *

Cédron and Zale'en strode into the village well before Lord Shamar's rays were extinguished from the sky. A sense of foreboding loomed over them like a storm, pregnant with the tempest barely restrained. Throughout the hike back to the village, Cédron had processed the understanding he'd received from Lady Muralia and was buoyed by her confidence in his ability to achieve his quest.

The glow from the two sacred stones continued to add power and substance to his own Árk'äezhi as their energy flowed down Räeshun and into his hand. The confidence he'd begun with washed away in the dead silence of the village that greeted the travelers.

"Something is wrong," he whispered to Zale'en, who was also treading warily between the huts.

She nodded, walking as if the ground beneath her feet were an illusion that would transform into something dangerous. Her eyes darted from hut to hut and everywhere in between, seeking an answer to their unspoken question. Cédron stepped silently in her footprints. *Where were the villagers?*

Cédron continued next to the priestess, holding Räeshun slightly in front of him. If the Hazzara had already attacked, there would be bodies, burning huts and chaos rather than this interminable silence. Zale'en veered off to the right and headed toward the temple near the commons. The acolytes followed behind her, whispering amongst themselves.

As they approached, faint wailing could be heard from inside the long straw building. Zale'en paused slightly before opening the large, double wooden doors and entering her demesnes. Cédron followed closely behind her. Just like the last time he'd been in this building, the gloomy interior was lit only with candles. Their light wasn't bright, but it was enough to illuminate the tragedy that greeted them.

Priestesses and the young acolytes moved between rows of cots; the temple had become an infirmary. Women, young children and babies lay on the cots, pale with an odd sheen to their complexions. Looking past the dozen or so convalescents, Cédron spied the bodies. Higher level priestesses were wrapping the tiny corpses of the infants and children in some sort of white linen, their silent tears staining the pristine fabric of the wraps.

One of the priestesses looked up at the light coming from the doorway and hurried to Zale'en.

"We were attacked by urgleks," the bony, middle-aged woman said in a hoarse whisper. "The little ones died from the darts." She glanced towards where the tiny bodies were displayed. "But the others linger, succumbing slowly to the beasts' toxin."

Zale'en nodded, taking her priestess's hand. "Vak'ki, have you administered charcoal and red wine?"

The angular woman nodded. The crevices of Vak'ki's face seemed harsher in the shadows of the flickering light. "We tried, but they cannot swallow." She brushed a strand of dark hair out of her eyes and tucked it behind her ear. "I just don't know what else to do." Her lower lip wavered as the tears brimming around her eyes coursed down her sunken cheeks.

Zale'en made her way slowly towards the rows of cots. Cédron followed her, the glow from the blue and red stones on Räeshun illuminating the mats on the floor as he walked. Dozens of bodies lay on the cots in various states of decline. Scores of women were soaked in a clammy sweat that gave their skin a greenish tint. The rows of children, ranging from toddlers through young adolescence, had already nearly succumbed to the poison. Their skin was dry and ashen, and their breathing shallow. Cédron could tell they had only a few hours left to live.

"Where are the men? The warriors and my companions?" Cédron asked Vak'ki as she dipped a cloth in a basin of cool, fragrant water and placed it over a tiny girl's forehead.

The priestess watched the little girl's face for a moment before answering. Her eyes were tormented as they met Cédron's and her voice shook.

"They were in the hills, performing the sacred rites to Lady Muralia and Lord Shamar in preparation for war." She sighed wearily. "Several black-clad warriors snuck around the swamp and attacked us with their urgleks while the men were away. We didn't have a chance."

Vak'ki sunk to her knees with one hand wrapped around a little boy and her head on the cot of the little girl next to him. The sob that she'd held back burst forth uncontrollably.

Cédron awkwardly placed his hand on the distraught woman's shoulder and patted gently. He looked up at Zale'en for guidance, but the woman smiled sadly.

"These are Vak'ki's grandchildren," the priestess said in an undertone. She jerked her chin to the cot above the girl's. "There lies their mother, Vak'ki's oldest daughter."

Cédron felt a twinge in his stomach. He knew how it felt to lose someone dear. He desperately missed his mother Maräera, even more so after his brief encounter with her spirit in the cave. The air in the room thickened from the burning candles, making it difficult to breathe. His heart felt as if it would burst. He couldn't just let these children and their mothers die, not if he had the means and the knowledge to save them.

The idea of using the aquastone to cleanse their bodies of the toxin eased the tightness in his chest slightly. The more he thought about it, the better he felt. Cédron realized that Räeshun was throbbing gently in his hand, encouraging his train of thought. He pulled her up to eye level and stared at the stones resting in the starburst at the top. He felt, rather than heard, her advocate for using his powers.

Cédron opened his mouth to tell Zale'en that he could save the victims of the urglek attack when a darker realization struck him. *If I do this, then I will bring everyone that is hunting me down into this village. I can't put them all at risk like that.*

Zale'en cleared her throat, the sound startling him out of his reverie. "What will you do, Child of Muralia?" she asked, her yellow eyes piercing his in the candlelight.

Cédron stared slack-jawed at the priestess and knew instinctively that she had heard his thoughts. His insides tightened again in the face of her judgment.

"I can't decide," he said. "If I use my Árk'äezhi, I will bring my enemies straight to you."

Zale'en's face softened. Compassion filled her eyes and she nodded. "True. Your plight is a difficult one, but let me offer you this." She smiled slightly. "Your enemies are already upon us. Our warriors are engaging them as we speak above the Rabe'en Plains."

A warm feeling of contentment and righteousness sifted down Cédron's body from his mind to his feet. He knew that Zale'en was correct, and that nothing else out there seeking him could endanger the Meq'qan more than those they already faced. His mind made up, Cédron nodded to the high priestess.

"I must find my uncle," he said. "He will be able to help me access the Árk'äezhi I'll need for this."

* * *

Roväen directed those older Meq'qan not facing the Hazzara to the north to assist the priestesses with moving the victims' cots into a triangle. Cédron stood at the center of the triangle, holding Räeshun. He had been both pleased and concerned to learn that Cédron had not only acquired the aquastone from the goddess, but that he bore the marks of alignment with the stone already. The old Sumäeri warrior had half expected the deity to strike the boy down for having used his powers destructively when he killed the Council Guard, but she hadn't. The very fact that she seemed to favor Cédron complicated his own task tremendously.

Rovaën was helping a toothless old warrior, who rambled on about battles he'd fought in his own prime, move one of the heavier women into the triangle when he heard running steps approach. The doors to the temple flew open and a young man charged into the gloom of the makeshift infirmary.

"Rovaën," Anéton called, bending over to catch his breath. "Tóran sent me to have you evacuate the people. The Hazzara are getting through the Meq'qan's defenses and will overrun the village."

Rovaën frowned and set down the heavy cot, waving the old warrior away. "How is that possible?" he asked. "The Meq'qan outnumber the Hazzara five to one!"

"They are not engaging the warriors on the battlefield." Anéton shrugged and shook his head. "They are sneaky; they have scattered themselves throughout the trees and laid down in the grasses. They strike swiftly then retreat. It's not a tactic I've ever seen before, and we just don't know how to fight them."

Rovaën looked into the young legionnaire's eyes and saw fear. He gripped Anéton's shoulders and shook them slightly. "You need to tell Tóran and the warriors to hold on. Cédron has returned with the aquastone and is going to try and heal the poisoned villagers."

Anéton's face lit up. "He's back! He survived facing the goddess?"

Rovaën frowned and nodded slowly. Cédron's powers were growing, and Rovaën wasn't sure if he was keeping up with the demands such force made of the body and the mind. The young man was reaching a critical stage in his development. Despite his seemingly unlimited power, Rovaën didn't believe that Cédron understood the enormous burden that was placed upon him by wielding the sacred stones. In his deepest heart, and despite his abiding love for the boy, Rováen still wasn't convinced Cédron could be trusted to assemble the Sceptre of Kulari and use it only to heal their unbalanced world.

Rováen could tell Cédron still needed to feel validated and accepted. It wouldn't take much for him to resent the demands of the deities and lash out, destroying everything they had worked so hard to achieve. Rováen shook his head to clear it. *That decision is still before me. I don't have to make it yet.*

"He returned just a little bit ago." The old man sighed. "We're going to need more time. Healing this many people is going to take a lot of energy, and they'll be weak. We won't be able to move them right away."

Anéton nodded. "Well, the healing will be welcome news indeed for the warriors whose families have been afflicted."

The legionnaire placed his hands on his hips and surveyed the area, noting the scores of cots placed in the triangle with Cédron in the center. Anéton watched Cédron wiping the forehead of one little girl who moaned in pain, and he spied the tattoos stretching from Cédron's belly to his chest.

"Are those Lady Muralia's markings?" he asked.

Rováen looked over to where Cédron was bending over. "In a manner of speaking. He has received the goddess's blessing and aligned with the aquastone already," he said, nodding towards the boy.

"Wow! He's become pretty powerful already, hasn't he?"

Rováen pursed his lips and didn't answer. He looked towards his nephew and the staff that was his niece. "He will be guided so that he doesn't overstep his abilities, if that's what you're implying."

Anéton's eyes widened. "No, I was just saying…"

Rováen smiled weakly. "Never mind. Just see if you can buy us more time."

"Right." Anéton nodded and turned back the way he came.

Roväen walked over to the doorway for a breath of fresh air. He watched bemused as Anéton sprinted through the village, dodging the overturned mashufs and the larger tarradas which would normally be used to haul fish. None would be fishing or hunting today. Any men who survived the Hazzara attack would have to patch their damaged vessels before heading out into the waters of the swamp again.

Roväen turned back from the doors after pulling them shut, and he strode over to the cots. He stood at the end of the triangle of cots, stared out at the priestesses scattered throughout the room, and asked them for their attention.

"As you can see," Roväen nodded to the center of the triangle where his nephew stood holding Räeshun, "Cédron has received Lady Muralia's blessing and the aquastone. He is going to attempt to cleanse the poisoned blood of these victims."

Cédron frowned slightly. "I don't know if I have enough Árk'äezhi for all of them. Should I...?"

Roväen held up a hand, interrupting any further questions. "I will channel my Árk'äezhi to you," he said. "Between the two of us, we should manage to get the toxin from their bodies. When they are healed, they will still be very weak and will require your assistance. Be ready."

Cédron's jaw snapped shut audibly. He gave a curt nod and placed Räeshun's base on the ground in front of him. Roväen stepped over the cots and into the central space next to the boy. Cédron placed his hands on Räeshun, and the two Shäeli closed their eyes and began to concentrate.

Roväen could feel the warmth of his Árk'äezhi and Cédron's as it flowed into Räeshun's bones. The staff was a natural conductor for Árk'äezhi and easily poured their energy into the firestone. Roväen felt rather than saw the firestone's increasing glow as the rock bathed the room in its crimson glow. The old Shäeli recognized the regeneration spell as Cédron's intention coursed through Räeshun and into the stone. It was one of fire magic's more complex spells, but Cédron seemed to have it well under his control.

The old Shäeli opened his eyes and watched the Árk'äezhi pour into the bodies surrounding him as they absorbed the light. The greenish tinge of their clammy skin gently transformed into a rosy glow, then paled into normal complexions as the firestone sped up their metabolism. Breathing slowed from panting to deep breaths in all but the youngest child to his left. Roväen increased his focus and felt the pulse of his Árk'äezhi draining his own body as he pumped it into the staff. Cédron directed his energies into the tiny girl and forced the toxin to evacuate.

The priestesses surrounding the triangle murmured under their breaths at the miracle being performed in front of them. Roväen saw Vak'ki kneeling down next to her granddaughter, holding the little girl's hand with tears dripping onto the coverlet. He looked over at Cédron and nodded. The boy closed his eyes again and switched his intentions.

The vermillion cast of the firestone faded as the azure aquastone flared into action. Now that the toxin had metabolized through the bodies, the aquastone's properties would speed the cleansing of the blood and restore strength to the victims. Roväen felt the first wave of Árk'äezhi wash over the bodies as the aquastone's power blanketed them with its light. He was caught up in the weightless feeling of the Árk'äezhi's power when suddenly he felt as if he was falling.

Roväen's eyes snapped open and he shot a look at Cédron. The boy's face was gaunt. His cheeks had hollowed in the past few seconds. *He's depleted all his Árk'äezhi!* Roväen felt his knees buckle as he poured all his reserve strength into Räeshun so Cédron could complete his spell, but he knew almost immediately that it wouldn't be enough.

Rovaen watched in horror as Cédron gripped Räeshun's smooth surface with both hands, his face a grimace of concentration. The aquastone began to glow brightly again, infused with new Árk'äezhi. Cédron's face filled out rapidly, taking on an ethereal glow as the energy poured through the staff and into the boy's hungry body.

Rovaen looked around, trying to determine where the surplus Árk'äezhi was coming from. He saw one priestess sink slowly to her knees, her face pale. Her companions reached for her, but their hands trembled, their own strength leached from their bodies as the glow from the aquastone in Räeshun's bony fingers throbbed powerfully. *Cédron is siphoning their Árk'äezhi without even touching them!*

A coldness formed in the pit of Rovaen's stomach. It spread its icy fingers throughout his body as the realization of what was happening in front of him registered in his brain. *Cédron has figured out how to manipulate the life force itself! He could be as dangerous as Laräeith with such power!*

Tendrils of panic spread around his chest, squeezing and constricting his breath. He knew what he had to do, but it broke his heart. Maräera trusted him to protect her only son from such knowledge, and he'd failed. The Shäeli Näenji Council had been right in fearing such a child. He had forsaken his primary oath for too long, and now the Meq'qan would suffer the consequences. Rovaen gasped for breath, but couldn't seem to get his lungs to function properly. *This is too much for him. I can't let him loose with this much power. I have to destroy him before he kills everyone in this room in his ignorance.*

Rovaen bowed his head. He sent a prayer to Lady Muralia and his beloved Maräera, asking forgiveness for what he was about to do. He opened his eyes and grasped tightly onto Räeshun's smooth surface below Cédron's hands. Focusing on the pulsing blue light of the aquastone, Rovaen forced his exhausted body upright and reached for the stone.

The fingers of Räeshun swam before his eyes, and he couldn't get a solid fix on the aquastone. The boy's power continued to drain his Árk'äezhi. Rováen looked at Cédron, but the lad's attention was fixed on the healing children. His muscles screamed as the old man batted at the starburst crown feebly before the spots clouding his eyes overcame his vision. Anguished with his failure, Rováen cried out in despair, collapsing at Cédron's feet.

ChAPTER 37 - BATTLE Of The
MARSh

Anéton jogged through the village and into the Rabe'en Plains, trying to get the image of Cédron to make sense in his head. He had barely recognized his friend, so full of light and with eerie tattoos covering his torso and chest. The insecure boy he'd met in Dúlnat less than a fortnight ago was gone, replaced by this ethereal and confident mage with his glowing staff.

Anéton's feet squelched in the lingering mud of the marshes as he ran, the marsh greedily holding on to moisture in the Suntide heat. Clouds of flying insects billowed around him as he made his way through the grasses, clogging his nose and throat and causing him to gasp for air as he raced back to the front lines of the battle.

His shadow was longer in front of him than it had been on his journey to the village, and he knew in his heart that the Meq'qan would have only this one day to defeat their enemies. The foreign warriors reveled in the darkness; with dusk would come the deadliest attacks from the Hazzara.

The strange, black-clad fighters didn't engage the Meq'qan as normal armies would. Anéton suspected the Hazzara were used to fighting in the dark. They seemed more comfortable in the shadows of the trees or in the hollows of the grasses, avoiding the open plains and the bulk of the Meq'qan tribes. The Hazzara's sneak attacks and strike-dodge-strike tactics were taking a toll on the weary tribesmen.

Anéton inhaled the scent of decaying reptiles and bugs stuck in the marsh as he skirted one of the deeper areas of the swamp. The fetid stench turned his stomach and reminded him of what lay ahead. Bodies began to litter his path as he picked his way through the tallest of the grasses to the edge of the plains where Lord Shamar's late afternoon light shone on the waving wheat that bore the scars of the day's conflict.

Blood spilled from Meq'qan warriors trying to defend their land coated the chaffs of wheat like frost in Dormantide. The cloying smell of dried blood and dead flesh assailed Anéton's nostrils and reminded him why he'd hated his father for forcing him into the Hármolin Legion. *There is no honor in this sort of death.*

Anéton grimaced at the twisted form stretched alongside his path, the man's mouth sagging and his eyes staring fixedly at nothing. With his senses heightened for any sign of attack, Anéton made his way to the hill overlooking where Tóran stood with the bulk of the Meq'qan warriors.

The Meq'qan force was nearly two-thousand strong, and still they were being routed by less than a quarter of their numbers. Large groups of hundreds of Meq'qan bunched together, their backs to the center and all facing outward into the plains or the sparse trees that rimmed the marshes, seeking their enemies to no avail.

The Hazzara had foiled every one of the Meq'qan's attempts to engage them on the plains with their guerilla warfare of shooting darts from behind trees and striking with small, quick rushes, then retreating. Anéton spied Tóran by the glimmer of his sword in contrast to the spears and bows of the Meq'qan. Hunching down, he sprinted as fast as he could down the small hill and into the relative safety of the cluster of tribesmen.

"Tóran!" he shouted over the heads of the front line of warriors.

"Here," came Tóran's reply as the legionnaire stepped from behind the phalanx of bone shields. "Have they begun the evacuation?"

Anéton shook his head. "No, Cédron is going to try and heal those poisoned by the urglek, so Rováen asked if we could give them a little more time."

Tóran gritted his teeth and nodded. "Do you hear, my friends?" he called to the warriors surrounding him. "My brother will heal your families!"

Anéton looked around at the hope lighting the eyes of several of the men. He was surprised to find a few smiles on the usually stoic warriors' faces. Their exultant cries rang out in the deepening shadows of the plains as word of Cédron's healing spread. With renewed purpose, the Meq'qan formed up their circular ranks and edged closer to the trees, all eyes watching for the unseen attacks that had been picking off their numbers steadily since the battle had begun.

Anéton pulled out his sword and stepped behind the front line of shields to stand next to Tóran. "Do you think we can route them?"

Tóran grinned. "We've got a pocket of them surrounded in here." He nodded toward a copse of trees. "I don't know how many there are, but they won't stand a chance."

Anéton ducked as the Meq'qan to his right called for the archers to launch their attack. Scores of bows twanged from behind the ranks of shields, and the hum of scores of arrows filled the air. Muffled screams could be heard from deep within the copse as the arrows found their marks. Heartened by the sound, the Meq'qan from each group surrounding the trees broke ranks and charged into the grove, thrusting their spears at anything that moved. Anéton surged forward with them, swinging his sword at the darting black forms dodging away in front of him. He could hear Tóran off to his left, grunting and crowing as his sword struck enemy after enemy in an endless barrage of thrusts and counter-thrusts.

402

Anéton watched in awe as Tóran's sword moved like lightning, cutting down opponents faster than any three Meq'qan around him. *It's no wonder he won the Warrior's Challenge. He's certainly in his element.* As the day wore on, the searing heat caused his sword to weigh heavily in his hand.

Anéton turned at a rustle in the grasses behind him. The young soldier stepped back as the hooded Hazzara approached him. The man's white teeth were the only feature visible beneath the blackness of his cloak. The Hazzara swung his long, curved blade around in the air, a move Anéton recognized as one used to intimidate and hating himself because it was effective. He raised his own blade, preparing to engage the taller man, when a dart sunk deep into the bicep of his sword arm. Instantly, his hand went numb, and he dropped his sword. The Hazzara's grin widened as he advanced.

Anéton froze. He refused to believe his time was up. The approaching Hazzara's eyes became visible as glittering points of light within the folds of the cowl. Fumbling with his sash, Anéton pulled out the only weapon he had at his disposal and threw it with all his might. The four-inch throwing knives were good for little else besides target practice unless they struck a vital organ. Yet they'd saved him once already on this cursed venture and the soldier was glad to have salvaged them from the Garanth. Years of practice had honed Anéton's skill, and it paid off.

The narrow blade sank into the left eye socket of the dark-clad figure, knocking him backward and throwing the hood away from his head. Dodging the whizzing darts that now randomly hummed through the air at the Meq'qan, Anéton leaned down and pulled the blade from his victim. His stomach roiled at the gore he had to wipe on his trousers before returning the blade to his sash, but it was worth it. This blade had saved his life again, and he wasn't about to leave it behind because he was a little squeamish.

Tóran sprang over the Hazzara's body and hunched next to his fellow legionnaire. "Are you ok?"

Anéton smiled wanly. "They haven't killed me yet."

Tóran raked his body up and down with his eyes, stopping at intervals that Anéton realized were bloody spots in his clothing. Anéton shrugged and flexed his hands. His right hand remained numb. Anéton turned his right shoulder to where Tóran could see it, and he gritted his teeth as Tóran pulled the dart from his arm.

"Is it poison?"

"Probably. Can you move your arm?"

Anéton rotated his shoulder and made a fist with his right hand. A tingling sensation caused his entire arm to itch, but it reminded Anéton of when he slept too long on one side.

"I think it will be ok," he said, patting at the puncture with his cloak to stop the bleeding.

"You'd better get back to the village before you lose too much blood," Tóran advised.

Anéton wavered for a moment, unwilling to give up the fight just yet. Then he saw the unrelenting order in Tóran's eyes. Lowering his gaze, Anéton nodded.

"If your men can cover me to that rise over there…"

A thousand piercing shrieks filled the evening sky, causing both legionnaires to cower down and cover their ears. As they looked up, a dark cloud of wings blotted out the pale orange and gold of Lord Shamar's rays in the sky.

* * *

Cédron's face pulsed with the pounding of Árk'äezhi thundering through his veins, causing his cheeks to flush and his hair to tingle. Exhilaration like he'd never felt before elated him as he surveyed the room full of healthy women and children that he'd healed. *I've done it! I've actually done it!*

He sent a silent prayer of gratitude to Lady Muralia for the knowledge that allowed him to save the urglek victims. Looking around the room, it appeared that the victims were now comforting the priestesses, who were all being assisted to their feet by those who had been ill. Confused, Cédron whirled around, seeking Rovaën, and gasped as he spied his uncle's prone form at his feet.

"What happened to him?" he asked the closest priestess.

The woman's haunted eyes shied away from Cédron, her head shaking slightly. One of the mothers got up from the cot and strode over to the weakened priestess, offering her an arm of support and assisting the holy woman to the back of the hut where she poured water into a cup and helped her drink. Zale'en approached Cédron slowly, her eyes reflecting the fear and mistrust of her companions. She waved away the children who began hugging her about the knees, her eyes never leaving Cédron's.

"You have overstepped the trust that the goddess gave you," she admonished, a gnarled finger waving towards Cédron's chest. "You used the aquastone to siphon the Árk'äezhi of everyone in the room *without our permission.* That is an abuse of power that we cannot tolerate, even if you do have the goddess' blessing."

Cédron stared at Zale'en, the euphoria draining from his body. *All that power...I took it by force?* Understanding flooded his mind and Cédron turned and raced from the building. He barely made it out the door and down the steps before he retched, doubling over in agony from the force of his spasms. *How could I do that? I didn't realize...* He looked at Räeshun, the glow of the sacred stones mocking him in Lord Shamar's afternoon light.

Conflicting emotions raged through his weary mind. Exhilaration from his accomplishment warred with disgust at the means he'd employed to achieve it. It didn't matter that he'd taken the priestesses Árk'äezhi unwittingly. The sheer fact that he was capable of such magic terrified him.

The thought led directly to the realization that the Shäeli Council Guard may have had a valid point in insisting upon his annihilation as a dangerous abomination. He understood their fear now and found himself to agreeing with it. Wearily, he sat back on his haunches, laying Räeshun across his knees. He hung his head and closed his eyes. Images of him becoming the monster that everyone seemed to fear filled his mind. He clamped down on his thoughts, willing them to disperse, when a shadow crossed over his head, followed by another and another.

Cédron opened his eyes and looked up. The skies seemed to be filled with orange and golden feathers as wing after wing of läeniers hovered in the air above the village. Cédron's heart jumped into his throat as he realized the Sumäeri had followed his outpouring of magic and had arrived to exterminate him and probably the Meq'qan as well. His clammy hands slipped as he grasped Räeshun and heaved himself to his feet. With his chest pounding in fear, he stepped forward to meet his fate.

Three of the läeniers landed in the commons in front of the temple. Each bore two riders who dismounted and immediately walked towards Cédron. The young Shäeli was mildly surprised to see three young women in the group of Sumäeri warriors. Räeshun flared in his hands, scorching his palms and causing him to cry out in pain and surprise. The young women stopped dead in their tracks, their eyes fixed on the pulsing staff.

"So, it is true," the one on the right with dark blue eyes whispered.

Cédron recognized one of the men as Trilläen Villinäes, the captain of the contingent of Council Guard sent to assassinate him. The other two were unfamiliar and hung back behind the women. Trilläen glanced at the woman who had spoken and nodded his head sadly.

"Räesha," Trilläen said, his voice cracking.

The young women on the left were identical and walked up to Cédron as if dazed. Familiar aquamarine eyes filled with tears. They tore at Cédron's heart as together the twins reached for Räeshun. Compelled by the yearning in their faces, Cédron relinquished his staff to the women, his eyes studying their faces as they caressed the bones with trembling fingers. Räeshun glowed pure white from deep within her bones, almost humming from the expenditure of energy.

"She lives?" One woman gasped, staring at Cédron in awe.

Cédron opened his mouth to answer but was struck dumb. He closed his mouth. As much as he would like to answer these young warriors, he just couldn't find the right words to portray the his wide range of emotions.

The boy realized that these women had to be his cousins, Räesha's sisters. The other girl probably was as well. How could he tell them that Räesha had sacrificed herself and her eternal peace with Lady Muralia for him? Not after what he had just done with his powers. He was unfit to wield the Sceptre of Kulari and unworthy of Räesha's ... *Räeshun's* ... gift.

Trilläen stepped up next to the woman and reached out to touch Räeshun. "She was unwilling to give up her quest for something as trivial as death." He smiled sadly.

The dark-eyed woman looked at Cédron. "I am Läerei Angäersol," she said and pointed to the twins holding Räeshun. "These are my sisters, Läenshi and Säeshi."

Cédron bowed awkwardly. "I am Cédron Varkáras...uh, at your service."

Läerei placed her hands on her hips, her sapphire eyes taking in every detail of him. Cédron shifted his balance from one foot to the other, uncomfortable under her intense scrutiny. He didn't know what else to say, so held his tongue. She would make her own decisions about him regardless of what he told her, that much he realized in the first seconds of meeting the tough Sumäeri.

"Where is Uncle Roväen?" she asked suddenly, her eyes sweeping the Meq'qan village.

"I'm here," a weak voice called from behind them in the temple.

Cédron whirled around and looked up at the top of the stairs. Roväen leaned heavily on the tusk frame of the doorway to the temple. His cheeks were sunken and his eyes hollow, but a smile flirted on the old man's lips as he made his way slowly down the stairs and into the waiting arms of Läerei.

"I'm so pleased to see you," Roväen said, his voice gaining strength as he held the young woman close. He released her and turned to the twins, opening his arms wide. "And you two...my, how you've grown!"

Läenshi released her hold on Räeshun, returning the staff to Cédron before enfolding herself in her uncle's embrace. Cédron felt a twinge in the pit of his stomach at the family reunion. He wished that such love and acceptance could be his in this lifetime. His mouth twisted at the bitter irony of his situation. He was finally able to meet his mother's family, only to be destroyed by his own abuse of the unwelcome power Räeshun had sacrificed herself to help him acquire.

Cédron straightened his shoulders and held Räeshun at his side. *How will she fare during this conflict? I don't think she'll let me die with my quest unfulfilled, but I can't imagine her letting me wield the stones against her sisters, either.* Cédron nonchalantly brought Räeshun across his body and held her with both hands as defensively as he could without appearing to do so. Whatever they decided, he would be ready.

"So, this boy is the cause of all the chaos?" Läerei asked, walking back over to Cédron with Roväen and her sisters.

Trilläen stepped up next to Cédron and faced his fellow warrior. "He is," he said quietly. "Although the Näenji Council has condemned him, your sister felt compelled to assist him in his quest. Lady Muralia and Orwena have given him their blessings."

Läenshi and Säeshi stared wide-eyed at Rováen.

"Is this true?"

"He's just a slip of a boy."

Cédron's cheeks flushed, and his ears burned. He knew he wasn't anything special to look at, but certainly they must have felt his power to have tracked him down so easily.

"He is more powerful than he appears," Rováen said, staring at his nephew as if for the first time.

Cédron caught his uncle's tone and glanced at him. For the first time in his life, Cédron saw fear behind his uncle's eyes. Something else registered in Rováen's expression. A cold certainty glinted with a razor's edge. In that moment, Cédron realized that he'd lost his oldest ally after his misuse of the sacred stones.

The weight of such a crushing loss crippled him and he looked away. The pain was too much to bear. Vertigo swelled up inside him and he felt as though the whole world was tilting on its side. Cédron planted Räeshun's butt in the ground and held on tightly, barely able to keep from toppling over into the dirt. The faces swam in front of him, and the wispy clouds in the skies seemed to spin by. Making his decision, Cédron released his grip on Räeshun. The bone staff clattered to the ground.

Cédron began moving toward the trio of läeniers watching him from the commons where they'd landed. He staggered slightly and Trilläen grabbed his arm in support.

"Where are you going?" he asked through clenched teeth.

Cédron's head lolled to one side as he tried to focus on the man holding his arm. "I'm going with you to Samshäeli, of course. I will face your Näenji Council."

Trilläen's grip on his arm tightened, causing Cédron to wince. "What about Räesha's sacrifice?" he asked savagely. "You can't throw that away!"

Cédron sighed and looked towards his uncle and cousins, who stood staring at him from the steps of the temple. He turned his head back to Trilläen. "Without their support I can't succeed, so what's the point in trying?"

Läerei took a step towards Cédron, eyeing him warily. "Who said you didn't have our support?"

"He did." Cédron pointed at his Uncle Roväen, his shoulders slumped in defeat. "He said it with his eyes."

Läerei turned around to face Roväen. The old man released his hold on the twins' arms and shook his head. "He's become too powerful...too dangerous."

Cédron released the breath he'd been holding. He swallowed against the knot that clogged his throat at his beloved uncle's confirmation of betrayal. *I am truly alone now.* Cédron turned back to Trilläen and shrugged his shoulders.

"Will you kill me now or take me back to your council?"

Trilläen looked at Cédron, then back at Roväen. "I...well, uh..."

Roväen staggered over to where Cédron and Trilläen stood waiting. Cédron couldn't bear to look at him. *I've ruined everything. Laylur will rise and destroy the land, and it's all my fault.* The hollowness in his soul was so deep that tears were trivial. There was no emotion left, only the emptiness and certainty of his failure to his family, his deities and his world.

"Blessing or no," Roväen croaked, grasping Räeshun from the ground and leaning heavily on her for support. "The boy has abused the enormous power he's been given. The fact that he's done it unwittingly doesn't spare him his fate. It only makes it harder on those of us who must carry it out."

Trilläen grasped Cédron by the shoulders and shook him slightly. "What have you done, boy? What is he talking about?"

Cédron opened his mouth to answer, but his throat constricted. No air could pass through and his voice remained silent. He shook his head.

"The goddess has given him the sacred knowledge of life," High Priestess Zale'en answered from the top of the stairs where she'd emerged from the temple. Cédron winced as he saw her ravaged features and the anger burning in her eyes. "He has healed our women and children, but he took the Árk'äezhi of my priestesses by force in order to do it. He may have good intentions, but his undisciplined mind makes him more dangerous than Laräeith." She pointed her arthritic finger at Captain Villinäes. "You must strip him of his power now. Taking him to Samshäeli is too dangerous!"

The harsh truth of Zale'en's words filled Cédron with a numbed peace. He could not fight the rightness of her accusations and judgment. Raising his head, he saw the color drain from Trilläen's face as the warrior nodded to the priestess. Cédron watched as Trilläen looked to Roväen and felt the ground give way beneath his weakened knees as his uncle nodded.

Trilläen pulled a twisted length of wicker from the pouch at his side. "Säeshi, if you would assist me please." He nodded to the twin standing behind Roväen.

"No!" The young Sumäeri gasped at her captain, horror filling her aqua eyes. "I can't…"

"You must!" Trilläen snarled. "Now and quickly, before it's too late."

Cédron gulped for air that continued to elude him. The constriction of his throat and chest bound him tighter as images of his torture and death filled his mind. He didn't know what sort of death awaited him at the hands of his cousin and the Sumäeri captain. Trilläen yanked Cédron'shands out in front of him and twisted the length of wicker around his wrists, binding them tightly together. The Sumäeri then pulled another length of the wicker and wrapped it around Cédron's neck.

The läeniers had landed and the riders walked towards the small group. Cédron noted confusion in their expressions, but none stepped forward to challenge the captain or stay Cédron's execution. As one, the Sumäeri riders began to hum a single note. The throbbing of their voices caused the Árk'äezhi in Cédron's heart to flare. Säeshi grasped his wrists and held them firmly as the wicker bindings flared to life and absorbed his energy. Cédron gasped and gaped at his cousin who was enhancing the properties of the bindings. Tears filled her eyes, but she held on with grim determination. *She is draining my life energy! Oh mother, I'm so sorry to have failed you.*

Cédron's vision was filled with a blinding white light as the bindings around his neck and wrists glowed with the transference of power. He sank to the ground and prayed with his final thought that he would be reunited with his mother.

* * *

Tears flowed unchecked down Rovȧen's face as he watched the life drain from Cédron's body. His beloved nephew had been so close to mastering the power of the stones and saving their world. Rovȧen believed it was his own failure that had caused this horrific turn of events. He remembered Elder Räelin's plea for him to watch over Maräera and protect their world against any offspring she and the Varkáras man might have. He thought of the first time he'd laid eyes on the boy, still wrapped in his swaddling, and how his heart had filled with love for the tiny child with soft green eyes that had held such innocence.

Maräera's face swam before him in the glow of the wicker. Her trust in him to protect Cédron had been misplaced. If only he'd taken Cédron from Dúlnat and trained him among the Shäeli when his powers had first manifested, the boy wouldn't have been exposed to so much Askári prejudice or Algarik's influence. *Maräera, how can you ever forgive me? Because of my own foolishness, I have doomed your son and our world. The ground shakes will continue until Laylur and all of his minions are free. There will be no dawn, only the eternal nightmare of the demon's wrath.*

The radiant light that surrounded Cédron filled the village with its peaceful glow. Rováen stepped back as the children emerged from the temple and filed down the steps towards the Sumäeri. Holding hands, they formed a ring around the dying boy. Ring after ring formed as more children, and then their mothers, exited the temple and showed their gratitude for the one who'd given them their lives back and then willingly sacrificed his own. Scores of Meq'qan victims began their own chant, offering prayers of peace to the inert boy on the ground, the light from the wicker fading as the last of his life energy was absorbed and returned to Lady Muralia through the wicker bands.

"It is done," Trilläen said and pulled Säeshi back from the boy's lifeless body.

Rováen's heart felt as if it would burst, and he gripped Räeshun to hold back the anguished sobs that threatened to burst from his lips. The staff warmed in his hands, rising to a searing heat that scorched his skin. He cried out in pain and tried to release the staff, but it held fast to his flesh as if it had melded to it. Before anyone could make another move, the firestone in Räeshun's starburst began to glow. Even in Lord Shamar's light, the crimson beam emanating from the stone bathed the entire group in its glow.

Deep within the center of the beam, a figure materialized. Ephemeral as she was, everyone recognized Räesha's essence at once. The sisters cried out as the specter hovered above the staff. Beads of cold sweat broke out along Roväen's hairline as he felt Räesha's admonition.

"My dear family," Räesha's spirit sighed in the still air. "Our greatest need is upon us and this boy was our only hope." She drifted over to Cédron's body and stood between him and the Sumäeri who had gathered in a loose semi-circle behind the Meq'qan. "Our people have forgotten their vows to Lord Shamar and Lady Muralia. We have abandoned our charge to guide this world in exchange for self-serving isolationism. That is why the deities have abandoned us."

Läerei stepped forward, her face a mask of torment. "What can we do, sister? This boy was the reason our parents and sister were killed. He was the cause behind the war that already rages across the lands."

Räesha's image smiled and floated towards her sisters. She reached out one translucent hand and seemed to caress each girl's cheek in turn. "Lady Muralia has conspired to create this boy, this perfect blending of all races, in order to restore balance. He will need your guidance and support. He is the gift…"

Roväen's jaw was slack as he watched his niece appeal to her sisters and fellow Sumäeri on Cédron's behalf. As her image wavered, he felt the sharp pain of impending loss. "Please don't leave us again," he cried, reaching towards Räesha's ghost.

Räesha turned and faced him, her sisters still visible through the image of her body in the vermillion light. "Do not despair, dear uncle. You are strong enough for this task, even though you doubt. You must believe in yourself and the boy despite what anyone else thinks or says to you."

"But, I…" Roväen stammered.

"I will always be with him to guide and support him, but you must trust me, and you must trust him," Räesha breathed in his ear. "He has the blessings of the deities. Bring me to him."

She stepped over to Cédron's prone form and placed one gossamer hand on his shoulder. As Rovaën laid Räeshun across the boy's chest, bringing his hands over the staff to hold it in place, Räesha's spirit smiled. The old Sumaëri watched silently as her image began to fade back into the etched bone. The glow from the stones flared brilliantly, blue and red mixing to plum as if all three moon daughters shared the sky in the same moment. The bands surrounding Cédron's neck and wrists gleamed with the radiance of the sacred stones, casting Hamra's violet hues across his body.

Rovaën realized in that moment that the deity would relinquish her claim on the boy's life at the behest of her celestial sisters and mother. The sacred stones' representations of Azria's cerulean and Orwena's vermillion rays filled the swampland with the grace of the deities. Waves of power radiated out from Räeshun and lifted Cédron on a gentle cushion of air. His golden hair swirled in the breeze, and his tattoos began to glow. Rovaën had to wipe the moisture from his eyes and blink before he realized that the cushion surrounding the boy was Lady Muralia herself. With Cédron's lifeless body draped across her lap, the mother of the world kissed his brow and raised him to his feet. Shock and recognition flooded Rovaën's brain as Maräera's face smiled at him.

"I have taken this form so that you recognize me," the goddess's voice echoed in Rovaën's mind. *"Remember your promise to protect and guide this boy. Do not forsake it again."*

Rovaën swallowed and nodded wordlessly. In a single moment, the goddess dissolved back into the light of the sacred stones and the gems went dark. Cédron sank to his knees and his eyelids fluttered open. Rovaën and Trilläen both lunged to catch the lad before he fell forward.

"What happened to me?" he asked, grasping the front of Rovaën's shirt as he tried to pull himself up.

The old man stared into Cédron's soft green eyes, still luminous from the residue of the deity's intervention. "Lady Muralia has decreed that you fulfill your destiny."

Cédron held Räeshun reverently in his hands. He glanced around at the sea of Shäeli faces all staring at him and tried to gauge reactions. Some stared at him with fear, while others displayed expressions of awe. Räesha's sisters each approached him and offered their palms up in the formal greeting, introducing themselves in turn. Trilläen held back, watching the boy intently.

Cédron shuffled his feet and Roväen recognized the discomfort he felt at such scrutiny. The old man stepped up next to the boy and placed a hand on his shoulder.

"What will you do?" the boy asked, looking first at Roväen's hand, then raising his eyes to his uncle's face.

Roväen glanced at his nieces and at the staff Cédron held in his hands. "You have been given a great burden, one that you may not even understand the full weight of yet." He closed his eyes and swallowed. "It is the will of Lady Muralia and Lord Shamar that you wield the Sceptre of Kulari. It is not my place to question their judgment."

Roväen opened his eyes and Cédron nodded. Roväen saw the fear and resignation in the boy's face. It wasn't what he'd hoped for, but it was a start. Cédron knew what he had to do, even though it terrified him. At least the boy wouldn't be alone, not anymore. Roväen wasn't sure what Cédron's plan would be, but he knew they couldn't stay with the Meq'qan any longer. Time was running out for Muralia, and their reborn guardian would have to come up with a plan of action. Fast.

CHAPTER 38 - TÓRANS DECISION

The shrieking in the air above the field of battle caused Tóran's teeth to vibrate. He gritted them fiercely as he stood erect to face this new enemy. Scores of winged läeniers filled the air with their armed Sumäeri companions astride their feathered backs.

Tóran inhaled sharply, the majesty of the great beasts filling his chest with both awe and dread. *We won't stand a chance against both forces...and if they're here, that means they've already dealt with Cédron.* Tóran swayed on his feet as the realization of the Sumäeri's presence registered. *My brother is dead!*

"What is this devilry?" Anéton growled next to him. He sheathed his sword, then raised his hand to shade his eyes as he, too, looked into the skies at the wings hovering above them.

"Archers!" Tóran called savagely, glaring at the soft underbellies of the raptors. "Prepare to fire!"

One of the lead läeniers quickly angled itself upright and back-winged as it lowered itself to the ground. The Sumäeri warriors that sat astride the great beast leapt off and raced quickly to the legionnaire, their arms waving over their heads.

"Hold your fire!"

"We come as allies!"

Tóran held up a hand to the archers and pursed his lips, drumming his fingers on his wide sword belt as he waited for the two Sumäeri to reach him. *This had better not be a ruse.* He looked at Anéton, who shrugged. Tóran recognized one of the two Sumäeri as the Council Guard who had come to execute Cédron and he fingered the pommel of his sword in preparation.

"Speak quickly," he ordered the two Shäeli, nodding at the Meq'qan warriors surrounding him to stay on their guard.

"Trilläen Villinäes." The familiar one held out his hand palm up to Tóran, then to Anéton, and nodded to the man next to him. "This is Timäer Gäen, leader of the läenier wings. We are here to help you against the Hazzara."

Tóran placed his hand over Trilläen's and then offered it to Timäer, watching the two warily for any signs of duplicity.

"What have you done with Cédron?" he asked, holding his breath.

Trilläen grinned and clapped the legionnaire on the shoulder. "We've sworn our support for him and his quest." He waved at the wings hovering above them in the sky. "We understand you could use some help against these slippery southerners."

Timäer looked up and whistled a series of blasts from between his fingers, and the wings broke off into several smaller groups. The wings began flying search patterns across the thickly vegetated areas bordering the plains and marshes, seeking out the elusive Hazzara fighters.

"We will help you locate the Hazzara and try to herd them to where they are more vulnerable," Timäer said, then turned and jogged back toward his beast.

Tóran released the breath and smiled in relief. "We are most grateful." He clasped Trilläen's arm.

"Outstanding!" Anéton grinned. "Any chance one of your birds could give me a lift back to the village?"

Trilläen smiled and nodded, whistling to one of the läeniers at the end of his wing's triangle formation. "Just tell him where to go and he'll get you there."

Anéton nodded his thanks and clasped Tóran's arm. "Fight well."

At the sight of the accord between the legionnaire and the Sumäeri, a cheer went up from the surrounding Meq'qan. Heartened by the addition of the formidable Sumäeri läenier riders, the tribesmen returned to their pursuit of the Hazzara with a renewed determination. However, the Hazzara hadn't been idle during the brief respite in the fighting.

The black-clad fighters had taken advantage of the läenier distraction and hunkered down into deeper pockets of brush and trees. Tóran was horrified to see large spears being shot towards the fierce raptors with the power of a bow, and he realized the Hazzara were not about to give up their positions easily. The Hazzara spears tore through the downy undersides of the läeniers, killing three of the beasts in the first few minutes.

Appalled at the viciousness of the attack, Tóran marshaled his warriors and snarled his orders. "Route them all! Leave no survivors!"

As one, the scores of Meq'qan warriors clashed their spears on their bone shields and roared their war cries as they swarmed into the thick brush and sparse trees to flush out the Hazzara. From deep within the tall grasses, loud whooshing sounds could be heard. Tóran looked around, confused, until two warriors on his left were suddenly skewered by a long spear, pinning one to the other and knocking them to the ground.

The Hazzara were using some sort of launching device to add power to their throws with disastrous results. Two more läeniers fell from similar high-velocity spears. Tóran looked around, frantically trying to locate the Hazzara shooters, but to no avail. The spears seemed to be coming from everywhere at once.

Tóran was sick at the loss of so many läeniers and their Sumäeri riders just minutes into their newly-formed alliance. He looked around again to decipher any pattern to the

Hazzara spears and felt completely helpless against their clever tactics. *There has to be a better way! I can't just let them slaughter the läeniers. And what happened to my other plans? Something must have happened to those warriors.*

Off to his right, a clump of grass rustled as if someone was sneaking around within it. Tóran raised his sword and charged into the grass, swinging his sword in a deadly arch. As the grasses fell before the blade, the dark head of a young boy materialized. Tóran wrenched his arm to avoid beheading the youth who'd suddenly jumped up from his hiding place.

"Laylur's beast!" he cried. "What are you doing here? You should be back at the village! Are you trying to get yourself killed?"

The young boy stared at Tóran with wide eyes and opened then shut his mouth repeatedly as he tried to think of something to say.

"Well," Tóran shouted. "What is it, boy?"

"I...I just wanted to help my father," the youth gasped quickly, shying away from the raised sword.

Tóran dropped his sword down and swore an oath. "This is a battle zone, not a picnic."

The boy's eyes filled with tears. "I know. My father isn't a warrior either. He's a herder. I just want to help him so that he can come home to our family."

Tóran recognized the anguish in the boy's face. Many of the Meq'qan fighting alongside him this day weren't warriors. Most of them were herders and farmers, but they felt compelled to protect and defend their land and their villages. After the decimation of the Meq'qan tribes of the Tek'kut Marshes, there were few who felt safe staying behind. Tóran reached down and placed his hand on the boy's shoulder.

"I don't know where your father is," he said. "But I'm sure he'd prefer you safe at home."

The boy dashed the tears from his eyes and glared at Tóran, his mouth set in a determined line. "I'm not going anywhere. I'm going to help my father and my tribe."

Anger flared inside Tóran's chest. He didn't want to be responsible for the death of this young boy as well as his father. Still, he couldn't just summarily dismiss him. The boy had heart and wanted to prove himself. And then it struck him – the solution to all his problems.

Holding the boy fast on the shoulder, he whistled at Trilläen astride the läenier in the wing just above him. Tóran pulled the youth along with him over to where the läenier landed and kept his hand on the boy's shoulder to prevent him from running from the fearsome raptor.

"Change of plans," he yelled at Trilläen, who was just dismounting the beast. "Have your wings fall back toward the village. I'll meet you there with my men in an hour."

Tóran turned to the young boy and knelt down so he could look the boy square in the eyes. "Ok, you want to help us? Here's what you're going to do."

* * *

The withdrawal from the plains above the Meq'qan village took longer than Tóran had anticipated. The tribesmen refused to leave any wounded or dead behind, despite the fact that the Hazzara were getting more accurate with their spears as they pulled their brethren from the battlefield. More were killed or wounded as they tried to salvage what they could of their ranks from the field bathed in blood and gore.

The Sumäeri would wait until after the Meq'qan were safely away before attempting to recover the bodies of their fallen läeniers and riders. There would be a small window of time in which they could attempt to secure the bodies before Tóran's revised plan would come to fruition.

Lord Shamar sank lower in the sky, flirting with the edge of the horizon. His yellow light became a burnished gold as dusk approached. The whining of swamp gnats was the only audible sound as Tóran waited on the northeastern perimeter of the village with Captain Villinäes and the leaders of the other läenier wings.

Thus far, the Hazzara hadn't followed them back into the marshes and to the village, but they could be regrouping and changing course while the next part of Tóran's plan was being put into action. If the Hazzara marched on the village before his plan was executed, Tóran could perhaps salvage some of his goals if they could hold off the Hazzara in the surrounding swamps. But even if he did, there was no guarantee that he wouldn't lose most of the Meq'qan in the process. Tóran began pacing nervously, hoping the boy hadn't dallied too long in following his orders.

If the Hazzara lived to fight in the darkness of night when they were more comfortable, the entire Meq'qan population could be annihilated before dawn. His plan would only work if the Hazzara remained hunkered down in the tall grasses and thickets where they'd hidden themselves earlier. Tóran had learned enough of the Hazzara and their tactics to assume with some confidence that they would remain hidden until dark when their ability to see would give them the advantage over the Meq'qan.

Peering into the deepening gloom of the marshes, Tóran sent a silent prayer to Orwena for the success of the upcoming battle. He sighed silently and sent another prayer to Lady Muralia to watch over Cédron and his companions as they sought the next sacred stone for the Sceptre of Kulari. Zale'en had confided Cédron's quest to him when he returned to the village, but Tóran had been too late to wish his brother well on his journey.

The young legionnaire wasn't sure he understood his brother's quest or knew how he felt about Cédron's new abilities, but Cédron had convinced the Sumäeri to pledge their allegiance to him, forsaking their own Covenant. Tóran realized that had to mean something significant. The young Varkáras just hoped his brother was safe and in good company. He was glad he didn't have to watch out for Cédron in the thick of battle. His little brother had always proven to be somewhat inept with a blade, and Tóran was relieved that Cédron was leaving the fighting behind. It comforted him to know that both Rováen and Anéton had gone with him to keep him safe.

Tóran was so lost in his thoughts that he didn't immediately notice the change in the sounds around him. The dull rumble in the back of his mind continued to increase just outside his awareness until the rocks around his feet began to vibrate and jump. Tóran snapped his head around toward the south end of the village where the sound was emanating from. Trilläen Villinäes and Timäer Gäen grinned from ear to ear. Trilläen slapped Tóran on the back, nodding his appreciation of his tactics.

Tóran ran to the top of the stairs of the nearest hut and scanned the southwestern horizon. Beyond the cluster of huts, a massive cloud of dust was being stirred up as the thundering of thousands of wakazan hooves stampeded towards the village. As the combined herds charged closer, Tóran could see the various boys controlling the direction of the beasts with long whips that lashed inward to the center of the herd from the backs of wakazan on the outside edge. The boys raced their beasts, guiding the herds around the western edge of the village, and set them barreling straight into the clusters of tall grasses and thickets where the Hazzara army had been hiding.

Spears began flying from behind the few trees that the enemy had been using for cover. The boys whistled and called to the wakazan, who dropped their heads and charged forward, waving their tusks to either side. Most of the spears glanced harmlessly off the wakazan's thick skulls, but a few sunk into a shoulder or thick leg, cutting into the thick hide and causing superficial injuries. The grazing injuries caused by the spears served only to inflame the wakazan bulls' fury. They snorted and howled as they stomped through the marshland borders and into the plains, skewering the two-legged creatures that fled before their wrath.

Tóran felt the tension in his shoulders and neck loosen slightly as the screams of the dying Hazzara rose over the stomping and pounding of the wakazan. He allowed a grim smile for the justice served by the young boys of the Meq'qan tribes. Tóran turned to Trilläen and opened his mouth to speak when he felt a hand on his shoulder. He whirled around and came face to face with High Priestess Zale'en.

"You have been fortunate, Askári," she said, the smile on her face not quite reaching her troubled eyes. "But risking the lives of our children was most unwise. Such a choice makes me question your ability to make sound decisions."

Tóran's stomach knotted as he stared into the steely, yellow eyes of the priestess. He knew that sending the boys to stampede the herds had been a huge risk that could have ended tragically, but it had been better than the only other alternative that had presented itself at the time. Tóran smiled wanly at the old woman and held his arm out for her to take as he led her back down the stairs of the hut.

"I agree, Priestess Zale'en," he said softly, looking off toward where the boys were turning the herds back around and rounding them up. "But it seemed safer than allowing them to engage the Hazzara on their own, which is what most of them were trying to do."

Zale'en's eyes flew open and she covered a gasp with her palm. "They wouldn't dare!"

"They would and they did." Tóran sighed. "Fortunately, I came across one of them myself before they got too far behind the lines."

They walked in silence for a few moments as Tóran escorted the blue-clad woman towards the temple. The

Meq'qan warriors who had been waiting in the safety of the village for the stampede to do its work now ran past them as they headed to their next task. Some were on their way to help the boys restrain the herds and corral them for the night. Others had been dispatched to secure the bodies of the wounded and dead. Although the battle was over, there was still much work to be done before Tóran could take the Meq'qan warriors over the Ronhádi Range to meet the Garanthian tribes that had wiped out their kinsmen of the Tek'kut Marsh.

Tóran looked out beyond the village into the deepening twilight where the first of the boys, still atop the enormous wakazan, was riding into the village. The youth was grinning from ear to ear, his chest out and his chin high, astride his mighty bull. The legionnaire pointed at the boy, drawing Zale'en's attention.

"Your boys are as proud and mighty as their fathers," he said, watching the line of bulls being led in a celebratory procession through the middle of the village. "They have earned their place among the men around the fires tonight."

Zale'en's reptilian eyes gleamed in the fading light as she watched the boys slide off the backs of the bulls and corral them. The warriors lifted the half-dozen youths onto their shoulders and carried them to a place of honor around the bonfire that was being constructed in the center of the village square. Zale'en walked over to the bottom steps of the temple and turned around to face Tóran.

"They may have earned their place around the fire," she said, pointing one rheumatic finger at Tóran's nose. "But you will not take them into Askáribai to fight the Garanthian tribes. Their place is here, among their people, where they have a chance to grow up and become men."

Tóran nodded. He unwrapped her hand from his arm and held the bony fingers gently. "In this, we are in agreement."

The legionnaire knelt at her feet and placed his forehead against her palm. Zale'en gave him her blessing and turned to make her way up the stairs and into her temple where the priestesses had been busy preparing the bodies of their dead for the rituals that would keep her occupied all night. Tóran watched her go, impressed with the internal steel that kept the priestess ramrod straight and determined in the face of so much tragedy. He turned as the sound of footsteps approached him from behind.

"Will you join us for a brief council before we leave?" Trilläen Villinäes asked as he approached from the eastern side of the village where the läenier wings had waited out the stampede.

Tóran glanced over at the bonfire now raging in the village square and smiled as the children began dancing in a circle around the flames, their bodies casting silhouettes against the flickering orange light. He was pleased with what they had accomplished together in battle against the Hazzara, but Tóran knew that a larger, more formidable force waited for them in Askáribai. He could only hope that the Sumäeri and their läeniers would agree to join them. The Meq'qan would follow him regardless of what the Sumäeri chose, but Tóran hoped to strengthen the bonds of this newly forged alliance.

"It would be an honor." He smiled at Trilläen. "We have much to discuss."

ChAPTER 39 - ATTACK fROM ABOVE

The warmth of the day had already begun to fade. The dried grasses of the marshlands still gave off their sweet scent as the three figures stomped through them towards the hills. The swarms of insects chirped their chorus of farewell to the travelers, interrupted only by the startled flight of the family of the larger marshland twillings nesting nearby.

Cédron wondered again what their marshlands would look like during the rainy season when all the huts would be individual islands with small, one or two-man mashufs navigating between them. He scanned the yellow landscape and imagined it lush and green as it would be in Autumntide after the rains hit. He would return, if possible, to see the Meq'qan marvels.

Cédron was slightly more confident that the Meq'qan would survive the battle now raging on the plains northeast of the village. With the recent addition of the Sumäeri and their wings of läenier riders, victory was at least a plausible outcome. Anéton had returned to the village just as the Sumäeri left to join the battle, and he'd informed everyone of Tóran's strategy of using the herd beasts to flush out their enemies. Cédron had misgivings about leaving his brother behind to fight the battle, but he knew that nothing made Tóran happier than wielding his sword. Once the Hazzara were destroyed, Cédron assumed that Tóran would take what Meq'qan warriors he could and travel west to Askáribai to face the Garanthian army moving south from Tamóna. The

Meq'qan tribesmen would want vengeance for the slaughter of their Tek'kut kinsmen.

Shaking his head, Cédron grimaced. His breath caught in his throat. The scope of the coming war and destruction caused him to hyperventilate. *How can Lady Muralia put her faith in me? I'm just one person against so much evil and chaos.*

The staff in his hands pulsed gently and he glanced down. Räeshun's etchings shimmered in the afternoon light, reminding him of her promise and her support. Cédron took a deep breath and let it out slowly, calming his thoughts. *Thank you.*

His cousins had easily convinced the Sumäeri warriors and läenier riders to rally to Räesha's cause after the specter had appealed to them. Although Cédron knew they still harbored some doubts, they refused to act against their eldest sister's request and the directive from Lady Muralia herself.

The Sumäeri would be disavowed by the Shäeli Näenji Council, making them fugitives from their own people. But with the evidence that the Council and Wushäen were both compromised by Laylur's minions, they felt there was no other choice. All now had a vested interest in the success of Cédron's quest and would be waiting to guide him once he acquired all the sacred stones.

Cédron brought his attention back to the terrain over which he was hiking. The marshlands were receding as Rovaen led the trio up a slight incline that crested well above the grasses.

"Let's rest here a bit," Rovaen said, unslinging his pack and rummaging through it. He passed meat rolls to the lads and sad down upon a large rock. "We have a long way to go yet, and we won't have much chance to rest once we leave the marsh."

The two young men nodded and ate their meat rolls and dried fruit with little interest.

"I miss the fresh shadfish of Dulnat," Anéton sighed, wiping the crumbs of his meat roll from the front of his jerkin. "It's been dried fruit and jerked mijáko for weeks."

Cedron grinned and nodded but didn't comment. The group packed up their meager supplies and followed Roväen to the crest of the hill. Below in the dell, Cédron saw a läenier picking at the carcass of an ur'luq. The fierce jaws and spiked hide were no match for the raptor's speed and ability to attack from above. The läenier's beak and claws were bloodied from its kill, but it left its prey readily enough at Roväen's whistle.

Bile rose in Cédron's throat at the thought of the raw meat being ripped from the bones and swallowed whole. He averted his eyes from the feasting raptor and focused on the twillings that flew over the marshes a good distance away. At first, he wasn't sure if it was the same beast that Räesha had ridden, but there was no mistaking the broad wingspan and the fierce eyes as the beast stomped the grass restlessly with its sharp talons.

"Is that Yongäen?" Cédron asked once he'd caught his breath.

Roväen looked at his nephew, his eyes sparkling strangely in the afternoon light. "It is. He has been tracking us since we left the Meq'qan village."

Anéton stepped up to the other side of Roväen. "Why? Wouldn't he return to Samshäeli?"

Roväen's eyes hardened. "He didn't get far before he felt a presence in the skies behind him. We are being tracked by something that this beast fears, and that is why he's come to help us."

Cédron scratched his head. "How do you know all that?"

Roväen walked slowly up to Yongäen and stroked its feathered head. "I felt his presence after the other läeniers left. He can send me images and feelings. I saw a large shadow in the skies and felt his terror."

Cédron held Räeshun out to the raptor and felt her pulsing in recognition. He saw an image of Cédron using Räeshun to scratch Yongäen above his eyes. Cédron reached up with the staff and copied the image. The fierce raptor closed his eyes and crooned softly at the touch.

"Amazing!" Anéton said, watching from a few feet away.

"Come," Roväen said. "We need to get out of these marshes before dark. It wasn't just the Sumäeri that were attracted here when you healed the villagers."

Roväen stepped up beside Cédron and, with a quick gesture, instructed Yongäen to kneel. Cédron climbed up onto the beast's back and reached down to assist Roväen and Anéton up behind him. Once the three were mounted and secured with the riding straps Roväen had rigged for Räesha's initial flight with the Meq'qan, Yongäen squatted down, bunching his powerful legs, and leapt into the sky. His broad wings beat the heavy, stifling air of the valley as he rose to cleaner elevations.

Cédron was afraid they wouldn't clear the trees as they loomed closer and the ascent remained low. He held his breath, willing the beast to climb faster and higher. Steadily Yongäen's wings beat the air and forced him higher and higher. Cédron watched the tips of the trees scrape beneath the läenier's underside as they banked over the trees and finally left the clearing. He exhaled loudly.

"That was close!" Cédron yelled back to his companions.

Yongäen leveled out and flew in a lazy zigzag pattern as he approached the Ronhádi Mountains. The steep peaks before them rose to purple heights in the late-afternoon heat. Cédron reveled in the cool air after the sticky heat of the marshlands and shook out his hair in the wind. His leather trousers had stuck to his legs in the humidity and were finally drying out. *What I wouldn't give for a swim in a cold river.*

Cédron spied a small rivulet draining what little remained of the ice melt from the high twin peaks of Zóhai and Zohári rising in front of him. They made for the pass between the two mighty spires, planning to rest there before heading north to the Shaláen Falls and the source of water Árk'äezhi. They landed in a small clearing surrounded by tall evergreen trees and built a small fire. Sleep came quickly to his companions, but Cedron lay staring at the stars and watching the slow progression of the moon daughters.

The events of the past weeks swirled like a kaleidoscope in his mind. The explosion that had taken X'ariun and his mother, the flight from Dulnat with both the Sumäeri and his uncle pursuing him and, most prominently, his aligning with the two powerful sacred stones flashed behind his eyes. He knew his power had grown, along with his knowledge of how to wield the stones, but facing the ancient demon was beyond anything the young man could imagine surviving. Although he knew he only had to stop Laylur from escaping his prison at this point, insecurities warred with logic as he tried to put a plan in place. Cédron wasn't sure how he was going to find the source or what he would do to purify it when he arrived, but he had faith that Räeshun would continue to guide his actions. He settled into that small bit of comfort and slept.

Morning arrived immediately after he closed his eyes. The travelers quickly broke camp and, after a hurried breakfast, climbed back aboard Yongäen's back and continued their journey. Cedron marveled at the raptor's stamina as he bore them higher through the pass. The young man realized the power of the healing stones must have had the same effect on the läenier as it had on him. Yongäen's wounds from the arrow were healed with no trace of the puncture or the resulting infection. Cedron settled into the rhythm of the wings and tried to clear his mind.

The mighty läenier beat the air with his wings, the constant pattern of sound and motion lulling his passengers into somnolence. The morning drifted into the afternoon, and a short break for food and water before they began the final leg of their journey through the pass. Lord Shamar angled across the skies, lengthening the shadows of the trees out leagues before them as they continued on their quest. Zóhai and Zohári rose imposingly ahead of them. The raptor flew lower as he angled into the pass that cut through the great mountains. Cédron felt the pleasant warmth of the lower altitude as they winged their way through the valley. Wisps of clouds obscured the afternoon light, darkening the narrow defile of the pass as it closed behind them and the broad expanse of the Dagán Valley spread out below.

The lights of Taksábai, the capital city of Askáribai, glowed in the gathering dusk to the south, but Cédron knew they'd have to avoid the pleasures of the city until after his quest was fulfilled. Angling north, Yongäen snapped his jaws at a diclurue that flitted across his path. The tiny beast squawked and dove out of harm's way, continuing its search for insects. The boy grinned and shook his head at the narrow escape. As the city retreated behind them, Cédron felt the hair prickling on the back of his neck. Glancing up, he was filled with dread as an enormous black form dove towards them. A terrifying screech rent the air.

"Duck!" Cédron screamed as the larger beast swooped past, its talons brushing the air just out of reach.

The dark mass flapped its long wings, causing a hurricane of wind to whip at them. Yongäen turned his head and shrieked a challenge in return, pounding his wings faster to try and catch the unidentifiable beast.

"Laylur's beast! What was that thing?" Anéton cried.

"Not sure," Rováen yelled back. "Regardless, it wasn't friendly."

Cédron groaned and despair washed over him like the waves of the tide. He felt the cold helplessness drag him under and threaten to drown him. He'd been on the run since Räesha had arrived in Dúlnat. The constant travel and fear of always looking over his shoulder had taken a toll on the young man. Facing the goddess and his own mortality had stripped Cédron of what remaining reserves he'd had.

All that was left was fear and Cédron was tired of running away. Anger began to swell in his chest, evaporating the blanketing waters of despair and warming him clear down to his toes. As the anger flared, so did Räeshun. Cédron realized that he wasn't completely helpless. Sensing his thoughts, Räeshun pulsed brightly in his grasp.

Cédron turned and spotted their attacker. *That thing is closer than I thought!* Cédron could see the wicked, curved talons reaching towards him. They were just inches from Anéton's shoulders. Cédron screamed his defiance and raised Räeshun above his head. The heat from his anger flowed from his hand into the staff and out through the firestone.

A blinding, crimson light struck the black shadow closing in on them, highlighting the fearsome jaws and sharp teeth of the monster before it was hit. The shriek of pain emanating from the beast sent shivers down Cédron's spine. His whole body tingled from the release of power, making all of his hairs stand on end from the dual sensations.

"Yeehaa! You got it!" Anéton crowed from behind him.

Cédron's eyes had been blinded by the light and took a moment to adjust after the brilliance faded. He could see, through the orange cast against the treeline, the spiraling form beneath them as their wounded attacker spun out of the skies. Cédron's euphoria was short-lived, however, as the drain on his body caused him to slump against Roväen. He slipped Räeshun into the shoulder straps holding his pack so he wouldn't drop her from his sudden weakness.

"Whatever that was, you've wounded it," Roväen yelled as the wind of their flight ripped the words from his mouth.

Yongäen screeched and dove after the monster ahead of them. Cédron could sense the malevolent beast rather than see it. He tried to get Yongäen to flee and not pursue their attacker, but the fierce raptor was a warrior. Running from danger or a challenge was not what he was bred for.

"What was that thing?" Anéton called, the wind ripping his words and scattering them behind.

"I'm still not sure," Cédron heard Roväen answer. "But it's bigger than we are and more dangerous. I don't think we can outrun it, even though it's wounded."

Ice trickled through Cédron's body as the fear washed over him. He'd lost sight of their attacker and Yongäen could no longer sense its presence in front of them. The beast had outmaneuvered them in just a few brief seconds.

Cédron opened his mind to try and locate the fiend. The evil that struck his mind was intense. If not for the riding straps, the blow would have knocked him from his mount. Cédron sat reeling in the saddle behind Yongäen's neck, trying to put up the protective barriers he had so foolishly removed.

A terrifying shriek rent the air as the monstrous beast launched itself at them from below. This time, the wicked talons of the attacker kicked back after it flew over and caught Yongäen in the neck. The war bird screamed in agony and folded his wings, dropping from the skies and away from the beast that hunted them.

Cédron could feel Yongäen's blood spraying back on him as they descended. He heard the assailant's cry of triumph and felt it circle around. Cédron bent down over the läenier's neck and willed the beast to heal. He felt Räeshun's energy flowing through his hand and into the deep wound that continued to seep.

Cédron kept his eyes closed, focusing on healing the raptor. He tried not to think about landing, for he could see nothing. He felt Roväen's hands tighten around his waist as they continued their downward spiral towards the ground.

The läenier tried opening his wings to slow his progress. The ground loomed up quickly. Yongäen's legs stretched out as he angled towards the bank at the edge of the Shaláen

Falls, but the beast's legs buckled as he landed. The riding straps snapped under the strain of the impact, throwing the riders from the raptor's back. Yongäen crashed hard into the ground, his bones snapping as he rolled to a stop and remained still. Cédron crawled shakily to his feet, staggering slightly as he made his way over to where his companions lay. Anéton rolled over and groaned.

"Good thing I had my blankets in here," he grunted, getting to his feet. He rotated his shoulders gingerly and nodded to Cédron, indicating that he was unharmed.

"Where's Roväen," Cédron asked. He spied a dark form lying still on the grass a few feet away. "Uncle Roväen," he cried, running over to the prone form. "Can you hear me? Are you hurt?"

Anéton knelt on the opposite side and began probing his neck. "There's a pulse, but..."

Roväen groaned and batted Anéton's hand away. "Get off me! I'm fine."

Relief washed over Cédron. He grabbed Räeshun to heal his uncle. Feeling for broken bones along Roväen's side, Cedron closed his eyes and began to reach deep into himself when a dark shadow and blast of chill air swept over the small group.

ChAPTER 40 - ALÇARIK'S BETRAYAL

In the deepening oranges of the sunset sky, Cédron watched as the enormous winged beast landed. Cédron and Anéton were on their feet instantly. Anéton whipped out his knives to throw at the unknown interloper, and Cédron held Räeshun in front of him like a shield. Sensing the danger, Rováen rose as quickly as he could, standing behind Cédron, ready to add what strength he had to Räeshun's shaft. The fresh blood on the creature's beak and golden feathers caught between his talons identified him as their attacker. Cédron swallowed his grief at the loss of the noble Yongäen.

"A rinzar!" Rováen inhaled sharply. "The spawn of Laräeith's warped Aruzzi. ...But it's enormous! The Aruzzi aren't half that size."

"Is that what's been hunting us?" Anéton gasped.

Rováen nodded. "Without a doubt. It has slaughtered Yongäen."

The tang in Cédron's mouth turned sour. The great beast that landed near them was the most vile, misshapen creature he had ever seen. The winged monster was obviously created from some sort of carrion beast, with a thick, feathered neck that angled strangely. It's head was an enormous, grotesquely-formed skull with a long snout. A forked tongue darted between rows of wicked, sharp teeth. One yellow eye gleamed balefully at the group from the side of the monster's head, behind which sat a tiny figure cloaked in black. The figure sat astride the leviathan raptor with his face hidden in the shadow of the hooded cloak.

"I'm tired of chasing you all over Muralia," the mysterious figured snapped. "Give me the boy now, and I will make your deaths merciful and quick."

Anéton and Cédron looked at each other and shrugged. They each started to approach the bird, but Rováen's quick hands on their shoulders held them back.

"Wait, we don't know what he wants," the old Shäeli warned.

"Sure, we do," Anéton said. "He wants Cédron, but he didn't specify that. I figured we'd just give him a couple choices for "boy" and see if we can distract him." He covertly pulled his jerkin aside to display his brace of throwing knives.

Rováen nodded imperceptibly and Anéton turned back around, tossing two of the blades from his unseen hand. The first landed deep in the shoulder of the rinzar. The second was supposed to be centered on the face inside the cowl, but the figure shifted his weight forward, causing the blade to skim over his forehead and knock his hood back off his head.

Cédron gasped as the face of his Uncle Algarik was exposed by the errant blade. A tiny trickle of blood made slow progress from the shallow nick above his forehead. The rinzar screamed in pain and stepped back, unfolding his wings for balance. The right shoulder didn't open as smoothly and obviously caused the beast discomfort. The rinzar swung around, knocking Anéton sprawling with its left wing as it tried to dislodge the small blade from its shoulder.

Rováen moved from behind Cédron and grabbed onto Räeshun. The staff whipped the dirt and rocks from the ground into a whirlwind, engulfing the mage and his mount. Algarik launched bolts of red flame from his ruby ring. They struck Rováen squarely in the chest and lifted him in the air before depositing the old man near the edge of the falls. Cédron panicked and rushed to his uncle's side. The roar of the falls thundered in Cédron's ears, diffusing the mage's laughter.

Rováen gasped for air. Cédron turned his back on Algarik. With Räeshun, he tried to heal Rováen's collapsed chest, letting the wind storm die down in his preoccupation with his mentor's injuries.

"Get on up here boy," Algarik called. "We have a long and very overdue journey to make."

Cédron was frozen in place, his hands locked onto Räeshun in a tight grip as he tried to come to terms with what his uncle's presence meant. If Algarik was the person tracking them, then he was responsible for the deaths of all those Meq'qan, in addition to causing the explosion at the Festival of Narsham-Vu and killing Yongäen.

Molten fire began to burn in Cédron's stomach. This man had killed and maimed, all in an effort to manipulate Cédron into going with him. Cédron had nearly lost his hope of healing the world because of Algarik's ambition to use him for his own purposes. If it wasn't for Räeshun, he'd still be in Hamra's embrace.

The wind storm returned with the young man's fury, this time ignited with the fire of his grief and anger. Cédron had lost nearly everyone he loved and held dear to him because of Algarik's scheming, and now the red mage would pay for it. The ground began to tremble beneath Cédron's feet as his power coursed through him. The water of the river rushing over the falls began to boil and churn with the heat of his wrath.

The only focused thought Cédron had was to destroy Algarik and his ferocious rinzar. Cedron launched the fiery vortex towards his uncle and his beast, engulfing them with its destructive force. The rinzar shrieked and thrashed wildly. Algarik disappeared from view as the swirling fire raged around its prey. Cedron's anger cooled slightly as the rinzar's struggles ceased. The beast and its foul rider couldn't last much longer. Cedron pressed his lips together and nodded once, turning away to find Rováen.

The explosion knocked him forward. Cedron sprang to his feet and spun around. The remnants of his power sparkled in the air as tiny dust motes of fire, disappearing in the breeze. Cedron's jaw dropped as the red mage became visible through the swirling bits of magic. Algarik had a strange amulet around his neck, similar to the one that Rováen had found on the Hazzara agent in the marshes. It had a cabochon ruby in the center of an intricate looping of knots. The ruby was glowing faintly, causing a pale aura of its light to surround the mage and his beast.

"Your feeble attempts to overpower me are futile boy," the red mage taunted from atop his mount. "And my patience has ended. Get up here before I kill you."

"Go ahead!" Cédron screamed, his anger superseding caution. "You've already killed everyone else I love. I don't care anymore."

Algarik maneuvered the rinzar through the windstorm closer to his target and waved his sphene wand to send the cyclone away from him. The ground ceased to shake as Cédron's anger deflated into grief, allowing the rinzar more stable footing.

"You should care, boy," Algarik said as he brought his beast right up to Cédron. "Each time you cause your own ground shake, you contribute to my master's power. He has poisoned most of the ground now, softening and molding it to his purpose. He will be free soon, thanks to you."

The rinzar turned its head to stare at Cédron with its wicked, yellow eye, and the boy nearly gagged from the carrion beast's fetid breath. He stepped back, both to find fresh air and to clear his head. He couldn't allow Algarik to get away with his crimes, but he wasn't sure yet how he could defeat the powerful mage without compromising himself and contributing to Laylur's bid for freedom.

"How have I helped your master?" Cédron asked.

"Every time your anger causes a ground shake, you strengthen the dark Árk'äezhi flowing beneath the surface, weakening Lady Muralia's prison over my master. You and I share a bond, one that has terrified your father and Rovaën since your birth," the mage explained. "The power that we have between us can restore this world, but the Shäeli don't want to relinquish their status as the first people."

Algarik had Cédron's attention. "What I assume your father and Rovaën have neglected to mention to you is that we, the Varkáras line, are direct descendants of Laräeith, the greatest mage to ever walk this land. That knowledge has been a jealously guarded family secret for generations. I only found out myself inadvertently when my own powers manifested." Algarik chuckled humorlessly and shook his head slightly. "You should have seen your grandfather when he realized..." The mage's expression sobered. "And you have even greater potential than I ever did. Your Shäeli blood connects you to the land and the deities, giving you access to their power and the ability, through Laräeith's blood, to wield it. Did you know that your esteemed heritage nearly cost you your life before you were even born?"

Cédron stared at the red mage. The little color he had in his pale cheeks drained away as Algarik's words registered in his numbed brain. *I'm a direct descendant of Laräeith the Betrayer! No wonder everyone wants me dead. They were afraid I had inherited her appetite for power and would destroy the land. But legend said that Laräeith was a Shäeli. How could we both be descended from that ancient evil?*

"Laräeith was a Shäeli. How do we share her blood?" the boy asked, suspicious of his uncle's story.

Algarik laughed hoarsely. "That is the mythology the Askári have created to live with their shame." He sneered. "Laräeith was a great Askári mage, and her lover Salzem Varkáras was Yezman. That Shäeli you love so much was

440

sworn to kill you if you ever showed any initiative of your own."

Cédron recoiled against that thought, his breathing shallow. A frigid wave of understanding crashed over Cédron. There was the truth to the question he had been asking. This was why he was considered an abomination by his mother's people. He understood the edge of the sword he balanced on. To have the blood of all the races and access to Lady Muralia's flow of Árk'äezhi made him a dangerous threat, but to be a direct descendant of Laräeith the Betrayer made him a destructive force that couldn't be trusted.

"Yes! Everything you have ever been told has been a lie, boy," Algarik countered. "You have an unbelievable amount of power and ability, and I offer you the chance to learn how to access it and wield it. Remember how easy it was for you to siphon the Árk'äezhi of everyone around you, and how effortlessly you can access the properties of whatever you hold. You have a phenomenal gift that my master and I can help you refine. You can choose what you want to do with it. I won't stop you from being who you are and fulfilling your destiny."

Cédron felt the stirring of doubt in his heart as it pounded heavily in his chest. *Maybe they're right. Someone like me with even more power than Laräeith is too great a danger for our world. But I don't want to die...not yet. What if...?* Cédron took a deep breath and closed his eyes. A year ago, Algarik's promise would have been a tempting one. Images filled his mind of standing next to Algarik and feeling the powerful surge of energy coursing through his veins. He knew that he had the capability to force the world to bow at his feet, but was that what he really wanted?

Cédron saw Jorrél and Pánar before him, the terrified looks on their faces bringing him a sense of satisfaction at the retribution. He reveled in the moment, but the feeling soured in his heart as he realized gaining respect through fear rather than through honest sentiment was hollow and without honor. That was what Algarik wanted, not him. *But why does it feel so good to be powerful? I would have no end of followers and those who would give their lives to do my bidding.*

Doubt infected his mind and clouded his reason. He looked down at his beloved uncle and saw the pain etched in the folds of the old man's face. Cédron glanced over at Anéton's prone body, where he had been thrown by the rinzar, and tried to reconcile who his friends were and who had betrayed his trust. At least Anéton had never lied to him. Anéton accepted him for who he was and wasn't afraid of him or what he could do. Confusion filled his mind as Cédron tried to decide what to do next. He thought perhaps Räeshun could help him, and he closed his eyes, sending a silent request to the spirit inside the staff. Räeshun pulsed gently, calming the boy's spirit with her warmth. She showed him images of Rováen teaching Cédron how to focus his intentions and helping him heal the Meq'qan children. She showed Rováen laughing with Cédron and Anéton and conveyed the true feelings of love and friendship, despite the old Shäeli's mandate. Maräera's face appeared behind his eyes along with the knowledge she'd given him when she appeared in Muralia's cave. *Promise me you will always remember that it is your intention and your choices that create who you are; nothing else.*

The warmth radiated from the Sumäeri warrior's bones into Cédron as he held her tightly in his grip. His mother's words now made sense to him. *She tried to tell me this earlier. Being Laräeith's descendant doesn't define who I am. Her intentions were to destroy and dominate the world. Mine are to restore it. That's why I was spared!* His pulse slowed as Räeshun's offerings flowed through his hands and sharpened his mind.

"Now boy," Algarik said sharply, "get up here. We have a meeting that is long overdue."

Cédron turned and faced the red mage. A grim determination filled the boy as he realized how his Uncle Algarik was trying to manipulate him. He understood that Algarik simply wanted him for his power. All his promises of heritage and destiny rang hollow. Cédron also understood that Algarik knew what Räesha's quest had been, and that Algarik was afraid. *I have the power to stop him and to destroy the demons he's released into the world with Laräeith's magic.* In that moment, Cédron knew what he had to do.

Focusing his mind and reaching deep within himself, Cédron called forth the Árk'äezhi he had buried deep inside. He felt Räeshun's caress as she guided him deeper, where the raw energy connected to the source could be found. The staff began to pulse, and Cédron himself began to glow in the light of the aquastone and firestone held in Räeshun's fingers.

Cédron swept the staff in an arc from the falls toward where Algarik sat mounted on the rinzar. A writhing wave of water rose from the sacred source at the bottom of the falls and crashed over the mage and bird. Cédron then swung the staff in a circle and the wave became a whirlpool of liquid on the land, completely engulfing its quarry.

Algarik saw the wave coming and increased the energy output to his defenses. The ruby at his chest pulsed bright, encircling the mage and his beast in its red glow. The two sat suspended within the whirlpool while the mage gathered his power.

With a sudden explosion, fire erupted from the center of the whirlpool, causing the water to blow out in every direction. Steam from the heated water obscured Cédron's vision for a few moments, so he crouched over Rováen's body defensively while waiting for Algarik's next move.

"Foolish boy!" Algarik screamed from his perch. "I've offered you the world and you cast it aside as though it means nothing. Do you not realize who my master is? How great our power is?"

The red mage raised his amulet above his head. The ruby at its center glowed blood red deep within its facets. The ground beneath the rinzar began to shiver, the trembling increasing as the ruby burned brighter. Cédron felt the ground beneath his feet waver, and he fell to his knees next to Rováen. Räeshun flared in his hands, showing him an image of the land roiling and bubbling with molten soil and rock. Bleak and barren, the world became a nightmare in his mind as the ruby's power throbbed. A shadow rose from the ground, enormous and powerful. Cold from the depths of the land rose and chilled the marrow in Cédron's bones. *Laylur!*

"That's right!" Algarik's high-pitched laugh grated down Cédron's spine. "My master has nearly freed his bonds. The balance of power is in our favor, and there is nothing you can do to stop him now!"

The ground tremors increased. Boils erupted around him as the ground undulated and shifted. Rováen's body started to slide towards a sinkhole opening up beneath him. Cédron slammed Räeshun's end into the ground and willed the roiling surface to solidify. The stones in Räeshun's starburst glowed with the effort to purify and heal the ground of Laylur's toxin. For a moment, Rováen's body stabilized as the sinkhole solidified. Concentrating all his effort on thwarting the progress of the toxin, Cédron grasped the staff with both hands and focused his Árk'äezhi.

The glow of the sacred firestone and aquastone filled his mind as their light melded into a soft plum. The boy willed the land to heal, picturing Lady Muralia in warrior fashion like her daughter Orwena. Together they pushed back the demon's shadow and his minions, who were crawling up from the abyss. The image in his mind twisted and Cédron watched in horror as the demons' bodies liquefied and splashed the goddess, coating her in their dark, viscous ichor. She raised her arms towards the heavens, her

444

soundless scream tearing through Cédron's mind as she succumbed to the ooze. Lord Shamar and the Moon Daughters hovered in the skies above, helpless to assist.

Gasping against the tightness in his chest, Cédron wrenched his eyes open. The glow from the stones in Räeshun had dimmed as slimy tendrils of ooze wove up her smooth base from the ground. Cédron tried to pull her from their grasp, but the staff was stuck fast. He roared and pulled with all his might.

"You cannot defeat Laylur, boy." Algarik laughed from his high perch. "You should have joined me willingly when you had the chance. Now I must destroy you, along with the rest of this pathetic world."

Algarik pulled Laräeith's Codex from the folds of his cloak. The mage caressed the withered leather inlaid with a torus knot identical to the one that held the firestone dangling from the mage's neck. He twisted the ruby on his finger so the stone rested in the palm of his hand, then pressed it into the depression at the center of the book's knot. The ribbons of the torus knot turned in sequence, beginning the unlocking mechanism that released the clasp along the side.

"*Maiya am badaiya!*" Algarik cried, and the surface of the tome shimmered and shifted.

The elongated and delicate script of his ancestress raced across the smooth surface of the page, etching the spell he sought with fiery letters. He held the Codex out in front of him with one hand and his amulet in the other. Solidifying the connection to the book, the mage began reading from the book the words of power that would bring about the end of the world.

CHAPTER 41 - REDEMPTION

Cédron gritted his teeth and flattened his hands against the ground. Using all the force he could muster, Cédron willed the rocks in the ground to sharpen and launch themselves at the mage. Anger fueled by the terror of losing his friends, his family and the only world he'd ever known filled the young man with immense power. The shards lifted out of the loamy turf and shot straight towards Algarik's head and torso. The ground trembled and shook from the expenditure of force, causing Cédron to stumble slightly.

Algarik grinned and waved his ruby ring in an arc over his head. The rock shards struck the red aura and disintegrated on impact. "Not bad." He grinned. "But I suggest you work up a little more power if you want to try something like that again."

Cédron saw red. His uncle was taunting him. The boy wanted nothing more desperately than to turn the mage's grin into an expression of terror. This was the man responsible for the death of his mother, Räesha and her family, and the attacks on the Garanth and Meq'qan tribes. Thousands of people had suffered and died from Algarik's lust for power. Cédron couldn't think of a death horrible and painful enough for the mage to give him satisfaction. There could be no peace, no rest in his heart until Algarik had suffered for his crimes.

Casting all reason aside, Cédron heaved mightily on Räeshun and pulled her free. He raised the glowing staff above his head and turned the firestone towards the mage. As the crimson light of the firestone connected to the beam between the mage's amulet and the codex, a shiver of power solidified the triangle and reinforced Algarik's spell of destruction. Searing pain radiated down Cédron's hands and arms, slamming into his body and turning the blood coursing through his veins to flaming acid. With a cry of anguish, the boy fell to his knees. Flesh blistered and oozed as the angry haze of red obscuring Cédron's vision deepened to a painful crimson.

"Excellent," Algarik crooned. "I couldn't have done it better myself. Now just stay there for a moment while I take care of a few more incantations."

Reeling from pain and disorientation, Cédron tried to get a fix on the mage's location and shoot a fireball at him from Räeshun's powerful firestone. Cédron's anger and hatred for his uncle burned hotter than the molten bowels of the Ronhádi Range. White heat seared Cédron's hands against Räeshun's bones and shot out at the mage's chest.

Turning as the Árk'äezhi lashed out from the crown on top of the staff, Algarik absorbed the full thrust of Cédron's energy into the center stone of his torus knot. The stone glowed white before returning to its original baleful red.

"That's it, boy." The mage grinned. "Just let your hate and anger fuel your power. Just a little bit more…"

Cédron ground his teeth and roared, slamming the butt of Räeshun into the soft ground. *That blast should have obliterated him! How is he absorbing that much Árk'äezhi and not feeling the effects? What am I missing?* The boy closed his eyes and inhaled deeply as the mage droned on, reciting from the book in his hands. Cédron knew that he'd accessed the firestone's Árk'äezhi and opened his awareness to the collective consciousness of the deities. That was the gift Lady Muralia had given him in the cave: the knowledge that his intentional shaping of his thoughts was what gave him his power. *But I intended to obliterate him and nothing happened! Algarik must pay for what he's done, and I'm the one to exact the toll.*

Gripping Räeshun tightly with both hands, Cédron reached deep inside his mind to the source of his own Árk'äezhi. He could feel it throbbing in sync with his heartbeat. Dark thoughts invaded his mind as the boy imagined one agonizingly painful torture after another in his attempt to find the perfect method of avenging the deaths of those Algarik had left scattered in his path towards world domination. The more gruesome the punishment, the more Cédron's chest filled with power. The boy realized he was far more powerful than his Uncle Algarik could ever be, with more magic at his fingertips than the other could even fathom.

Cédron saw himself ripping the mage's still-beating heart from his chest and forcing his uncle to smash it with a boulder himself. He envisioned Jorrél and Pánar groveling at his feet, their ears, noses and tongues sliced off in retribution for their abuse of him at the Warrior's Challenge. Cédron grinned. His cheeks throbbed with the thrill of dominance. His heart beat faster and he panted shallow breaths as his excitement grew. Tóran and his father knelt and bowed at his feet, offering fealty to him. Even Uncle Rováen and Shozin Chezak deferred to him as he walked by... *wait, this isn't right!*

"Perfect," Algarik murmured as he closed the latch on the codex and shoved it into the folds of his cloak. "The spell is complete and you will be the greatest gift I could offer my master."

Interrupted from his imaginings, Cédron opened his eyes and gasped. The ground he was standing on had turned to a dark, sticky ooze. Tendrils of the thick substance were winding their way up Räeshun's smooth bones and had wrapped Cédron clear to his waist. The boy tried to free himself and his staff, but they were held fast in the sludge. Icy fear prickled his skin and beaded along his forehead.

"What are you doing to me?" he screamed at Algarik.

The red mage turned to face his nephew, the scar on his left cheek twisting his face as he grinned. "What I should have done from the beginning. I'm using your own Árk'äezhi to hasten the toxins throughout the lands' waterways and destroying Lady Muralia's wards on the abyss. Laylur will be free in moments, all thanks to you!"

Cédron's guts twisted and he retched. *All I've gone through should have prepared me for this. I have the power to destroy him!* Cédron gripped Räeshun, pulling her from the ooze and spun her around in his hands. Perhaps using the aquastone against the mage's firestone would produce better results. Cédron captured all the anger, frustration and hatred he felt for Algarik and let it fester in his mind for a few moments, building up his power. As he swirled the knot of outrage and contempt for the mage within his mind, the crud wound its way further up the staff and his torso, constricting his breath as it reached his shoulders.

Hands reached up from below the oozing slime and grasped at his trousers, slipping on Räeshun's smooth exterior. Cédron cried out in horror and tried to back away, but he couldn't move. The boy's heart pounded in his chest and the blood raging with power roared in his ears with every panicked beat. Focusing every fiber of his being through the agony of loss and betrayal he'd suffered at Algarik's hands, Cédron blasted his Árk'äezhi through the aquastone in Räeshun's starburst. The power flared brilliantly, illuminating the hill top with blue shards of light.

The force of his anger shot into Algarik's chest and swirled beneath the crawling waves of black ooze inching up the boy's body. With each image of death and destruction, Cédron's power grew. He saw Zariun's scorched hair and staring eyes and his mother's pale and bloodied arm reaching from under the collapsed pavilion after the explosion at the festival of Narsham-Vu. The throbbing in the staff blossomed and caused the pool of goo to bubble. His breathing became shallower as he panted with the effort to drown the mage in his ocean of angry righteousness. He could feel the ooze dispersing and filling the sacred pool at the bottom of the falls behind him, spreading sickness and disease throughout the land.

"Yesss boy," a frigid voice hissed, echoing in the still air. "Your anger is powerful. Let it feed on your pain and suffering."

Cédron felt his anger cool to glacial fear as the voice reverberated in his head. Ice formed in the marrow of his bones as he saw the jeweled eyes of the great demon Laylur staring unblinking at him from the depths of the pool formed from the goo at his feet. As the demon absorbed all of the Árk'äezhi flowing from his body through the staff, Cédron fell to his knees, burying himself to his shoulders in the black pool. *He's so powerful! I never stood a chance against him!*

The realization of how the demon had maneuvered Algarik against the boy and shaped his feelings to this point swept through Cédron's mind faster than twilling's wings. Together the demon and his agent had stripped the boy of his home, his family and his confidence in his abilities, leaving only a shell of anger and hatred that fueled the toxins softening the bindings of the abyss. *It's over. There is only one thing left to do.* Cédron closed his eyes and let go, sinking completely into the mire.

Chapter 42 - Understanding

Warmth radiated through his body. Cédron floated on a cushion of air that caressed his cheek as gently as his mother had done when he was a boy. Every inch of his skin tingled slightly, reminding him of the pool the Meq'qan had thrown him in after healing his wounds. *Death is so easy. I had no idea. I wonder if everyone realized, if they would resist it so?*

"You're not dead," Räesha's voice sounded in his head, her tone filled with mirth. *You've finally quit resisting me, and now I can guide you."*

"But I wasn't resisting you," Cédron thought to his cousin's essence. *"I was fighting Algarik and Laylur."*

Räesha laughed, a rippling sound that soothed the boy's confusion. *"Your Árk'äezhi was resisting, and all that did was increase Laylur's strength. When you quit fighting, he lost the power of your Árk'äezhi. Are you ready to get to work?"*

"Sure. What do I need to do?" Cédron thought towards his cousin's spirit.

Cédron could feel her essence surrounding him, bathing him in her serene peace. Her lovely, deep blue eyes danced as she grinned at him. He knew that his body floated lifelessly in the noxious pool, freed from its mundane requirements for air.

"We are both spirits now?" he asked, wondering how he could possibly affect the outcome of the world's future from his current perspective. *"Won't we rejoin Lady Muralia's energy?"*

Räesha shook her head. *"You have a job to do, as do I. We are so much more than just our physical bodies. Now that you have released your mind from the shackles of mortality, you can expand your awareness. Your Árk'äezhi is part of the ever-flowing life-blood of Lady Muralia. Your body is only a temporary vessel to hold the focus of your awareness, just as the sacred stones are vessels for your energy."*

Cédron considered her words and compared it to the effervescent feeling of his energy sparkling around him. He still thought he was himself. He was still aware of his own conscious thought. He could feel the shape of his body as he focused his mind on it, and he felt the smoothness of Räeshun's bone staff in his hand.

"So, my Árk'äezhi goes where I focus it?" He reasoned in his mind. The image of Maräera came to him as her last words echoed through his thoughts. *"She said that it was my intentions that shaped who I am, nothing else."*

Räesha put her hands on her hips and nodded. *"And together, it is our intention to stop Laylur from freeing himself from the abyss."*

Cédron felt a stab of fear and uncertainty. *"How are we going to accomplish that?"*

Räesha's image wavered and dimmed in front of him. *"Relax and trust that we can do this. Your fear resists the flow of Árk'äezhi and blocks me from helping you. Now,"* she said, holding the sacred firestone in her hands and reached towards him, *"focus your Árk'äezhi through the firestone like you did with the Meq'qan children. Burn the toxin from the ground and the tributaries that flow from the sacred pools."*

Cédron relaxed. He pictured the demonic poison heating and boiling as it coursed through the waterways of their world. Steam rose in his mind as he focused his intention through the firestone and caused the lethal essence to evaporate. Screams like the raking of metal pierced his mind, and he shivered. The demons were sizzling in their own juices. He felt their pain and allowed it to wash over him and through his mind, not distracting from his purpose.

Räesha pulled the firestone from his grasp and replaced it with the aquastone. With her hands over his, they held the sacred stone together. *"We must cleanse the land, returning the waters to their original purity."*

Cédron reached out with his mind, spreading his consciousness as far as he could conceive. Lady Muralia had shown him in the cave, where he'd first acquired the stone, how water was the bringer of all life. It was what flowed through everything and everyone. Árk'äezhi was no different. It flowed through the world just like the blood that circulated in his veins. Cédron realized the underground tributaries and streams that flowed throughout the land and into the major rivers to the seas were exactly like the arteries and veins that brought blood to his limbs, just on a much larger scale.

"It's all one being!" He gasped. *"Everything in the world is connected, a part of the whole that is Lady Muralia. Even Laylur and his minions imprisoned in the abyss are an integral part."*

Räesha glanced over at him, her short, golden hair obscuring one eye as it fell over her forehead. She tossed her head back and winked. *"Yes, but Laräeith shifted the balance when she altered the Aruzzi eggs. It's time for us to shift it back. See our world healthy and thriving, the waters clear and clean, and the rohiti fish brilliant with their rainbow colors and as prolific as they were before the Great Betrayal."*

Cédron filled his heart and mind with thoughts of the unending circulation of life's energy. He realized that nobody really died. Their bodies decayed and returned to the ground or water. The spirit energy that returned to Lady Muralia lived on, adding to the joyous harmony of life. Cédron's heart swelled. As he reached out with his mind, he felt the gentle touch of his mother's essence. Embracing her, he sought further, welcoming the exuberant energy of Zariun. Joyful laughter filled his mind and he shifted his awareness to Räesha's family, who surrounded their daughter and added their support and power to the aquastone.

"No, you can't do this to me!" Laylur's scream filled the air, causing the ground to shake and rumble. "I've served my sentence! It's my time to rule!"

Algarik plunged into the ooze for Cédron and the glowing staff. "I'll stop this, Master!"

The mage grasped Räeshun below Cédron's hand and was blasted backwards as his negatively charged energy connected with the polarized bone. The boy felt the ripple in his Árk'äezhi as Algarik's resistance mounted. For the mage, it was as if he were shoveling sand against the tide. Cédron grinned at his own metaphor. *There is no stopping this now. His power over me disappeared with my fear.*

The mage pulled himself to his feet and lunged again for Cédron, but the glow surrounding the pool coalesced into an opaque barrier. For all his magic, the mage couldn't penetrate the aura. Cursing, he pulled the ebony imp from beneath the folds of his cloak. Flinging the vile creature towards the boy, he covered the imp in a shroud of energy from his ring.

"Pull the staff from the boy's hands," he commanded his imp as it hurtled towards the glow.

A bolt of red light speared the imp on its diminutive backside, deflecting its trajectory back. Its high-pitched shriek grated in the back of Cédron's mind, but the boy quickly turned his attention back to the task at hand. Aiming Räeshun at Algarik, he shot a bolt of energy straight into the mage's chest. The amulet shattered, taking with it the bulk of the mage's power.

"Master!" Algarik screamed. "No! This boy cannot defeat you; I won't let him!"

"It is over for now," Laylur hissed. "Go. Gather my armies. They will be the scourge that destroys the lands and all her peoples."

The demon's jeweled eyes dimmed and disappeared back beneath the clearing water of the pool that had formed around Cédron's body. Cédron felt the great demon's fury as the rifts in his prison solidified, locking away the greatest threat to their land and exposing his freed minions to the cleansing.

The goddess' words to him in the cave finally made sense. Cédron focused his intention through the aquastone, invoking the sacred stone's properties. He envisioned the abyss that held the negative energy of the world, deep in the bowels of their planet. The ground that separated the core and its inhabitants was deep and solid, filled with the vibrant life of every stone, root and blade of grass. As he turned his attention to the rohiti, the source and enhancers of water Árk'äezhi, he saw their colorful gleaming scales as schools of the large fish darted and wriggled through the pool and into the waterways.

In his expanded awareness, Cédron touched the essence of the divine. He felt his Árk'äezhi contract and retreat, leaving him reeling from the sudden sense of separation and loss.

"What is happening to me?" Cédron thought frantically to Räesha, whose family shimmered and dissolved as he reached towards them.

Räesha turned and embraced Cédron, filling him with the calm sense of purpose born of the warrior. *"We have fulfilled the first part of our task. Laylur has again been imprisoned in the abyss and we have restored enough of the balance to keep him there a little longer. Rest. You have earned it. We will continue our journey together shortly. You must dim your awareness as you return to your physical body. It is not time yet for you to join us."*

"But wait, I want to know..." Cédron continued the downward spiral away from the brilliant light and into the tunnel of darkness.

Cédron initially noticed the squeeze, like being forced into boots that were too small for his feet, but it was his entire body that was too small. His skin tingled as if every part of him had been struck by Lord Shamar's lightning. Cédron felt the water on his back and the still air on his face. Opening his eyes, he was relieved to find Räeshun held firmly in his grip. Planting the butt of the staff onto the bottom of the shallow pool, Cédron used her strength to pull himself upright.

As he staggered from the water, Cédron noticed that his skin still gleamed with power. The fire and water tattoos on his torso burned with the intensity of his Árk'äezhi and reminded him that he still had far to go before his quest would be fulfilled. Looking around, he was surprised to find no trace of the red mage or his imp. With Räeshun rooted on the solid ground, the boy bent his head to the aquastone in her starburst and sent a prayer of thanks and gratitude to her for her guidance and companionship. The etchings along the staff pulsed once in acknowledgement. As he finished his prayer, a darkness spread out over him.

Opening his eyes, Cédron saw figures racing up the slight slope with weapons drawn and arrows whizzing past him. The rinzar, hovering just over his head with Algarik again perched astride its broad neck, screeched in pain and anger as a couple of the arrows found their mark in the monster's backside. The fearsome beast turned and charged its attackers. Cédron crouched down and raced over to Rovänen's body, protecting him from further harm from either Algarik or this new threat.

"Over here! They're over here!" Cédron heard a voice shout.

"Bring a healer," came the call from another voice.

"Kill that mage!" a third, deeper voice resounded in the clearing air.

Cédron looked up to see the familiar faces of the guards from the Varkáras Caravan swarming past him and charging toward Algarik. Some managed to hold the rinzar and mage at bay with their weapons, and someone was trying to put Rováen onto a stretcher. A blast of fire from the mage's ring knocked back his assailants. The rinzar turned and beat its powerful wings, flying away from the stinging arrows.

Several of the men circled Cedron and Rováen, reaching for the elder's legs and shoulders to pick him up.

"Don't move him. He's got broken ribs and probably some internal damage," Cédron warned.

"We need to get him to the healer," the deep voice argued, and Cédron was both pleased and shocked to be staring into the black eyes and dark, smiling face of Shozin Chezak.

"Shozin! Where did you come from?" Cédron cried.

"The caravan is camped in the Dagán Valley not far from here. We saw the lights on the hill and came to investigate," the Caravan Master explained as he waved over a couple men to take Rováen to the healer.

"Gently with him lads," Shozin cautioned. "He has internal injuries and broken ribs."

The two men shifted the old Shäeli gently onto the litter and took off with him down the hill. Cédron turned towards where Anéton lay and saw his friend being helped up by the men who had led the charge against the mage.

Shozin pulled the boy into a firm embrace, pinning his arms to his sides and rendering any defenses useless. "You've done it, boy! You've saved us all." The enormous man held Cédron at arm's length, scrutinizing him. "Are you injured at all?"

Cédron's head spun. He was so relieved to see everyone unhurt that he laughed aloud. "I'm fine." He smiled, returning the caravan master's embrace, then hugging

Sahráron who had come up the hill behind them. "Räeshun and I were able to purify the water and cleanse the toxin. Laylur hasn't been stopped, but he's been slowed down."

"Räeshun?" Shozin clasped Cédron's forearm and nodded his approval. "Let's get you down to camp and see about something to eat. Then maybe we can clean you up a bit before telling your story?"

* * *

Orwena's crimson light illuminated the evening sky as the travelers celebrated their victory around the fires of the Varkáras Caravan. Titicale ale flowed freely as stories were exchanged and friends reunited. The knowledge that the war had only just begun was shoved down deep behind the desperate smiles and hugs between friends that lingered in unfulfilled longing. Cédron sat in between Shozin and Sahráron, with the remaining members of Zariun's acrobatic troupe scattered around the bonfire, their eyes bright against their dark skin. He rose and toasted Zariun's memory, a single tear glistening on his cheek in the fire's light. Half-hearted cheers rang out, followed by subdued reflection into the ale by the small troupe.

Rováen walked over to Cédron and gripped his shoulder. "Your loyalty to your friends does you credit," he said, nodding to Shozin and Sahráron. "It's one of the reasons we follow you on this crazy journey." The Shäeli turned back to the boy and caressed Räeshun with a sad smile. "You've done well, dear one. Soon you will be able to go to your rest and leave the trials of this world behind."

Räeshun's bones glowed deep plum as the red firestone and blue aquastone flared in her starburst head. From the depths of the light, Cédron could see Räesha's figure emerging as she'd done in the marsh. Her ethereal hand reached out and touched Rováen gently on the face, caressing his skin.

"We have won a battle today, and that is cause for hope and celebration." She turned to face Cédron. *"You have mastered two of the sacred stones and much of the darkness that resides in your heart, but the war is coming. You have healed the land and strengthened Lady Muralia's hold on the great demon, but his minions are still free in the world and have set into motion events that we cannot prevent."* She turned to his companions and smiled. *"Your love of this boy has given him the strength he needed to reach this point. More sacrifice and pain will be required of you and others before this quest is complete. Help Cédron find the other sacred stones and bring him to my people for training. There can be no further doubt."* Räesha turned her attention to Roväen. *"Your vows to the Näenji Council are void; you have a higher authority to answer to now."*

Roväen nodded wordlessly and wrapped his arm around Cédron's shoulders. "I won't doubt you again. The destruction of the world would have been on my head if I'd followed through with my mandate, but the deities have made their wishes clear." He turned Cédron to face him and gripped both shoulders in his hands. Shaking the boy slightly in his fervor, he made his promise. "Maräera placed her trust in me, a trust I nearly broke. I will not make that mistake again. I pledge my life to you in support of this quest."

Shozin and Sahráron knelt at the boy's feet and echoed Roväen's pledge. Cédron's cheeks flushed. He wasn't comfortable with the three people he'd spent his lifetime looking up to kneeling before him.

"Please get up," he said, his voice cracking. "It's awkward enough having these burning tattoos that make me look like a freak. If you start treating me differently, the Askári will just have more reason to hate me."

"No, Cédron." Sahráron stood and laid a gentle hand on the arm that held Räeshun. "You and your staff will become a symbol of hope for our future. The horrors of this war are already upon us. We will have to embrace many things that have previously been distasteful, or even forbidden, in the name of cooperation and survival."

"Yeah, I don't know," Anéton called from the other side of the bonfire, where he and the other men who'd chased Algarik were returning. "Your powers and Räeshun are pretty impressive, but I still think you're a freak."

The legionnaire sauntered across the clearing and clasped Cédron's arm, a wide grin spread across his blood-smeared face. Cédron noticed that his shirt was torn and he had several lacerations across his chest and shoulders that were seeping blood, but nothing too serious.

"Algarik escaped," Cédron said, glancing out towards the cascading falls.

Anéton's grin faded slightly. "For now, but I'm sure we haven't seen the end of him. Do you think you'll have a chance at defeating him next time he shows up?"

Cédron caught the slight twitch in Roväen's mouth and winked. "I think we still have a few tricks that might surprise him." He lifted Räeshun. Orwena's rays captured the light of the sacred stones, flaring brilliantly against the young man's skin and causing his golden hair to glimmer as if aflame. The power of his Árk'äezhi swirled around him like a storm. Linking arms with Roväen and Anéton, Cédron waved Räeshun in a slow circle, causing the air to lift them to the top of the cliff.

"The freak, the deserter, and the outcast," Anéton said, smirking. They landed above the falls. Below them stretched the Dágon Valley and, in the distance, the city of Taksabai with its untold thousands of inhabitants. "Do you think the Askári will help us?" Anéton asked.

"Perhaps, if they can see past their prejudices. Our power lies not in how we've been defined, but in how we define ourselves." Cédron's eyes shone with the energy coursing through him. "In our unity, we gain strength. Let's show the Askári, and the world, what we can accomplish together."

460

ABOUT THE AUTHOR

Mikko Azul is a graduate of The Evergreen State College and served in the United States Marine Corps. She lives in the Pacific Northwest with her three children who share her love of adventure. When not SCUBA diving the waters around Puget Sound, they can be found hiking in the Olympic National Forest. You can follow her at www.mikkoazul.com, on Facebook at www.facebook.com/mikkoazul, on Twitter at @AzulMikko, and on Instagram at @mikkoazul.

ϿANY ϿϿANKS

Although authors work largely in a vacuum, there are none who succeed in publishing their work without the enormous influence and assistance of many. From my cousin Kathy who gave me my first fantasy novel and planted the seed, through my family who have provided inspiration and nurtured my growth, and finally, to the professional team who have brought this body of work to fruition.

I want to acknowledge the San Francisco Writer's Conference where I received my first award for my debut novel. Feedback from professionals in the industry filled that early void and inspired me to keep moving forward. The connections made at that conference led me to a stint at The Writer's Guild of America West, where working with the extremely talented and brutally honest screenwriters Ashley Edward Miller (Thor) and Phil Beauman (Scary Movie 1, 2 & 3) propelled my writing to the next level.

A heartfelt thanks to my editing team of Madeleine Hannah, Brionna Poppitz and Ryan Swan, who tirelessly examined every single sentence, word and character; honing and refining my grammar, structure and punctuation. They kept my writing honest, forced me to be consistent, and reminded me that even the most avid fantasy reader can suspend their belief only so far.

I offer the deepest gratitude and admiration to my publisher, Benjamin Gorman of Not A Pipe Publishing. Sacrificing family, freedom and sleep, but never integrity, Ben has been at once taskmaster and cheerleader, adversary and advocate. Ben undertook the heroic task of pruning my story and dodging my thorns to realize the full blossom of my story's potential. I am proud and humbled to be a part of this organization that values exceptional writing, dedication to craft, and the importance of recognizing the contributions of women writers! Thank you, Ben, for accepting the Shamsie Challenge and only publishing women authors in 2018!